Philip Friedman is a practising attorney and lives in New York City. He is the author of four previous novels, including *Rage*, which was also a film starring George C. Scott and Martin Sheen, and *Termination Order*, which the *New York Times Book Review* called 'one of the best spy stories of the year'. His two most recent novels, *Inadmissible Evidence* and *Reasonable Doubt* are both available from Headline Feature.

Praise for *Inadmissible Evidence*:

'Fascinating . . . every bit the nail-biter you'd expect from the author of *Reasonable Doubt*'
New York Times

'Monumental . . . hypnotically interesting' *LA Times*

'Unusually convincing' *Publishers Weekly*

and for *Reasonable Doubt*:

'A quite splendid courtoom drama, with the shade of Perry Mason surely applauding and a humdinger of a postscript . . . The pleasant burden of proof is yours. Read it' *Sunday Times*

'Reads more like a true-crime story than a made-up one' *New York Times*

Wall of Silence

Philip Friedman

Originally published in the USA as *Act of Love, Act of War*

First published in Great Britain in 1994
by HEADLINE BOOK PUBLISHING

A HEADLINE FEATURE paperback

10 9 8 7 6 5 4 3 2

ISBN 0 7472 4545 2

Typeset by Keyboard Services, Luton

Printed and bound in Great Britain by
Cox & Wyman Ltd, Reading, Berkshire

HEADLINE BOOK PUBLISHING
A Division of Hodder Headline PLC
338 Euston Road
London NW1 3BH

**To Dorothy,
the Best, the Brightest,
and the Bravest**

Author's Note

In the early afternoon of November 22, 1963, I was playing pool with a friend in our eating club at Princeton University. I wasn't much of a pool player, and it wasn't a serious game. Chances are we were playing eight-ball, though it might have been straight pool.

One of our clubmates burst into the room from downstairs, seemingly quite agitated. As it happened, he had also been at elementary school with me: childhood rivals, we had been out of touch with each other from the age of eleven and though we belonged now to the same club, we had not grown close. With a smirk that may have come from nervousness he informed the room that President Kennedy had been shot in Dallas, Texas.

I had no great reason to trust him (our childhood conflicts had been bad enough to bring us to blows), but this kind of prank was not his style. I feared he might be telling the truth. The three others in the room were even less willing than I to credit such a report, but my pool opponent was curious enough to interrupt our game to learn if there was anything to it. He returned with the same news.

At that, the lot of us bolted down the stairs and into the club's television room. Chet Huntley and David Brinkley were on the air, an anomaly at midday, retelling in awed tones what little they knew. The reports were conflicting and for a long time – hours, perhaps – it was uncertain whether the President was alive or dead. Not everyone in the room stayed to find out. A few even said good riddance.

That's one of the surprises, these thirty years of myth-making later: on the day of his death John Kennedy was widely and often deeply disliked. There was considerable grumbling when the university decided to cancel the football game scheduled for that last weekend before the Thanksgiving holiday. It was to have been the Ivy League season closer: something important, after all.

Almost fifteen years passed from that day until I wrote this book, fifteen years in which the United States endured two more horrifying political assassinations – one that killed John Kennedy's younger brother Robert – and a wrenchingly divisive war. In the turmoil of those years the president who succeeded John Kennedy decided not to seek a second full term of office, and the next president created a crisis over his abuses of power that threatened his formal impeachment and ultimately drove him from office.

Those were also years in which the idea that a lone, demented gunman had shot John Kennedy dead – and by that act had started the country on its road to grief and confusion – failed utterly to convince a vast number of Americans, and legions of others the world over.

Then, in the aftermath of the Watergate scandal, there was a rash of Congressional investigations – into the conduct of American intelligence agencies, at home and abroad, and ultimately into the John Kennedy assassination itself, as well as the others that had followed. By that time, the serious scholars of the first Kennedy assassination had been hard at work for more than a decade; the volume of literature on the subject was enormous.

As it happened, I had been young enough (and callow enough) at the accession of John Kennedy to find him almost unequivocally inspiring. I thought his (as I saw it) compassionate but hard-headed patriotism was just the ticket, for me and for the country. I was impressed equally by his creation of the Peace Corps and of the Army Special Forces. I rued the disastrous invasion of Cuba with which he had begun his administration, attributing it more to the mistakes of his predecessor's planners than to any fault of his own. I was frightened during the Cuban Missile Crisis but ultimately proud that he had faced down Khrushchev and Castro. I was thrilled by his call for the country to put a man on the moon and I was transported by the great March on Washington for civil rights, the most dramatic domestic event of his presidency and the high point of that last innocent summer of 1963.

True to my Kennedy-inspired zeal I was willing, a year and more after his death, to consider that I might want to work for the CIA, as a way to serve my country without participating directly in the growing conflict in Southeast Asia. I made myself available for the Agency's recruiting process. Not far into it, I reconsidered and withdrew. But my fascination with the craft of intelligence remained, and as the years passed it was fed by the fact that I found myself friendly with several men who proved to be former intelligence agents.

I read voraciously on the subject, and when the Congress investigated the intelligence community and the various assassination plots the US had been involved in around the world, I followed the proceedings closely. By that time I had also read several books on the assassination of John Kennedy and had been fascinated by the myriad unexplained facts and concealed coincidences surrounding the assassination – information that had been uncovered not by cranks but by men and women of obvious intelligence and sincerity.

The more I learned, the clearer it became to me that seemingly vital information related to the assassination had been covered up. Why had so many obvious and pivotal questions gone not just unanswered but *unasked* by the official organs of investigation? The CIA and the FBI had deprived each other of crucial information immediately before the assassination and, especially, afterwards. Why? Members of the Kennedy administration still serving under Lyndon Johnson, people who should presumably have had the best reasons to uncover the truth, had instead buried it in obscurity and cajoled or threatened others so they would do the same.

What, I wondered, would it have felt like to be a person who saw that cover-up happening all around him but did not know why? In that question I knew I had the material for a book.

First I needed a character whose position would have given him firsthand or, at worst, secondhand knowledge of the most striking anomalies associated with the assassination and its aftermath, someone probably in government service who was confronted with the fact that important information was being hidden from the public and, possibly, from the investigators themselves.

What would a man (or woman) do, given such knowledge?

As it happened, both a man and a woman seemed right for telling this story, and thus were born in my mind Harry Jensen and Jill Lazar, of whose perilous quest (and offbeat love story) you are about to read.

Once I had them in mind, I realized I had set myself a tricky task. These fictional characters, with their fictional motivations, were going to be dealing with a lot of reported fact that was, in its way, a lot stranger than any fiction I would add. How was I to make that mixture work and at the same time keep the fiction from tangling up the facts?

I decided that I would draw a clear and simple line: everyone who appeared on stage, as it were, would be fictional, as would be all the incidents that directly involved them. On the other hand, everything those characters remembered experiencing at the time of the assassination, and everything they learned about the assassination and discussed about it in the course of the book, would be real, at least in the sense of having been reported as fact either during the run-up to the assassination or in its aftermath.

I made only two exceptions. The journalist Stewart Alsop appears briefly in conversation with Harry Jensen. Alsop was no longer alive at the time I wrote the book, and the words I gave him to say were either words he actually wrote or was quoted as saying, or sentiments consistent with his actual words. And Bobby Kennedy (also dead at the time I wrote) has a walk-on to introduce Jensen to a fictional friend of the family.

In directing Harry Jensen's path through the labyrinth of assassination and post-assassination intrigue, I was as inclusive of reported fact as I could be, but I still had to leave out a great deal that is odd and intriguing and, perhaps, important. To be exhaustive would have meant, ultimately, being exhausting. Because I was most interested in the cover-up and the failures to communicate vital information, and because I was advancing what I considered a somewhat novel theory, I concentrated on the parts of the overall assassination story that were related to those issues.

Rereading the book now, I am pleased to find, over and above the quite startling real-life political intrigue, a love story and an adventure story and also a glimpse into a time at once very like today and very different from it. Some of the differences – the newness of all-digit direct-dialing by telephone, the relative absence of multi-lane interstate roadways – would perhaps be apparent mostly to readers in the United States. Other differences, including the copious quantities of gin consumed by the main characters, may strike a more general period note. Because somehow, in what seems to me like not very many years, this book has become not just an adventure and a love story, but a historical novel, too.

Philip Friedman
December 1993

Es una mala noticia.

**Fidel Castro, on hearing the news
that John F. Kennedy had been shot**

Chapter One

It was after eleven when Harry Jensen pulled up the circular drive of the eighteenth-century Arlington mansion where he planned to welcome the New Year. The hostess was relaxed and rosily drunk; she greeted him with a warmer kiss than was necessary for mere sociability.

'Harry, love, I'm so glad you're here. Now all the women will have something to do.'

'Florence, you're the best thing that ever happened to my ego.'

She kissed him again. 'As long as it keeps you coming back. Now go join the party and try not to break too many hearts.'

He started toward the living room, but she caught his arm. 'Just one thing, love. Don't let George Hammond get you off in a corner. George is a dear, no matter what some silly people are saying, but he *has* developed an ability to monopolize the unwary, and if it happened to you, so many people would be disappointed.' She paused. 'And he did ask me specifically if you were going to be here.'

'I'll be careful,' Jensen promised.

She hesitated, as if she were about to say more, but instead pressed his arm and then said, 'You *are* a love. All right. I'll let you run along now.'

1

Jensen eased into the crowd in the living room. Like the other parties he had been to that night, the gathering had a muted tone. There was not as much laughter and animation as there had been the year before and the year before that, when New Year's Eve had been a time to anticipate the glories of Washington's vigorous new era.

The embassy party where he had started the evening had been particularly gloomy and strained. The Kennedy people, still dazed by an abrupt awakening from their dream, stood in tight groups, drawn together to close out the Texas new-comers, who were too boisterous by half – partly because their native manners were broader than those of the Ivy Leaguers they were replacing, but mostly because they felt tense and out of place, unworthy of their freshly minted preeminence, uneasy in the presence of so many Harvard degrees and so much Establishment polish.

Jenson looked for the bar, found it, and began to thread his way in that direction. Florence had a bigger crowd than usual; there were a lot of faces he did not recognize. He wondered about the unspoken part of her greeting. He was convinced there had been something on her mind besides George Hammond.

He stopped and said hello to Florence's husband, a retired admiral from an old Virginia family who still did occasional work for the Office of Naval Intelligence. They had first met at a national security briefing, and Jensen had let himself be drawn into the admiral's social circle as an eligible man for friends of the admiral's lady. Florence had made it clear from the beginning that she preferred to keep him for herself, but that was not a game Jensen was interested in playing.

When the admiral moved on, Jensen traded a few words of small talk with a fellow member of the President's National

Security Advisory Staff, and then he joined the circle of people around McGeorge Bundy, head of the NSAS. They were speculating about the stability of the new regime in Saigon. It was a kind of gossiping, not really shop talk but more an outlet for the frustrations of the real work they did. Here, in a mixed group, nothing of importance could be revealed; the men who were privy to the real information had to lie and equivocate and obfuscate, and in doing that they could feel superior to the others, who knew less and could tell the truth.

He moved on toward the bar. They had run out of something, and there was a crush of people in front of it. Jensen caught fragments of conversation, mostly in English but some of it in French, both languages spoken with a variety of accents – New York, Paris, Boston, but not Texas. This was the old crowd. He doubted there was a Texan in the house.

Among the voices, he heard one that was familiar, a voice he'd heard only rarely in the past three years.

He felt a sharp, electric tingle in his spine, and his breath caught for an instant. He looked around, found her, two people away. He could see the side of her face: smooth, pale skin unclouded by makeup, like a college girl's; her neck; her blonde hair neatly gathered and held close to her head. He was wondering what to do, when she turned in his direction.

He made himself smile. 'Hello, Jill.'

'Hello,' she said. 'Hello, Harry.'

It seemed to him that she hesitated a moment, and then she turned and said something to the man standing next to her. Jensen recognized him vaguely – someone from the FBI. He glanced at Jensen, nodded, then pressed Jill's arm and whispered in her ear as she moved away from him to join Jensen.

'It's been a while,' she said when they were standing together.

'It has. And I didn't expect it to be ending today.' He was annoyed. He knew now what had been bothering Florence.

'Believe me, Harry, I didn't know, either. I thought our hostess was going to die when she saw who Ralph had with him.'

'How is it that you're here?'

'My . . . date is with the Bureau. He's been working with the admiral on something, and one day the admiral said, "Why don't you come out for New Year's?" He didn't ask who Ralph was going to bring.'

'Ralph? The tall one with the steel-gray crew cut? Very distinguished. And brighter looking than your run-of-the-mill FBI man.'

She bridled. 'Let's not, Harry. Please. Hasn't it been long enough for us to be civil to each other?'

He caught himself about to snap back at her. 'I guess I'm just in a lousy mood about New Year's. I'm not feeling very celebratory.'

Her expression clouded. 'No. Neither am I.'

There was a moment of awkward silence.

'Didn't I hear you were out of the country for a while?' she asked.

'They sent me to Honduras after the coup down there. Debriefing, sorting things out, the usual NSAS nonsense. I was there when—' He stopped, thinking of how to say it. He still hadn't come up with a phrase that didn't sound wrong somehow. He skipped it: There was only one thing he could be talking about. 'I got pulled out of Honduras and sent to Mexico City to keep track of what was happening there. I was the nearest White House body with the right kind of training.

4

But I've been back in town for a couple of weeks now ... I'm surprised you know about it.'

'We've still got *some* friends in common. And I ask about you – I like to hear how you're doing, from time to time.'

He supposed there was an appropriate thing for him to say, but he could not think of it. He was having trouble shedding his feeling of awkwardness with her. To cover it, he said, 'How's the PR business these days?'

'I can't complain, really. Until ... recently ... I've been having a ball. And it's getting to feel more and more like lobbying and less like PR. That's the best part.' She looked around, a mock conspirator. 'Don't tell anybody I said that. When I first broached the subject with Dave, he read me the riot act. Washington, it seems, is not ready for a woman lobbyist. So, whatever I actually do, we still have to call it public relations.'

'If I know you, you'll get the title, too, before long.'

The congestion around the bar had eased. 'Drink?' he suggested, somehow compelled to maintain contact with her.

She hesitated. Her eyes searched his for a moment. 'Thanks,' she said. 'I'd love a drink.'

'Still Dubonnet?'

'Well ... usually ... but today I think I'd like a martini.'

He ordered two, and while he waited for them he reflected on how tense Jill seemed. Her voice was strained, her chatter a bit too fast and brittle. But he realized that he might be imagining it. In the nearly three years since their marriage had come apart, he hadn't seen her more than a half-dozen times. His memory of a softer, lower-key Jill might not be accurate, or she might have changed, or her tension, like his own, might just be a combination of the forced gaiety of the evening and the shock of their unforeseen meeting.

And yet, collecting their drinks and a pair of scallop-edged cocktail napkins, he found that he was convinced something else was bothering her, and that it was important.

He moved toward her, carrying the drinks gingerly, avoiding the careless elbows of the crowd around the bar. She had moved off and was standing by herself, absorbed in thought. He didn't know if it was the light or the fact that she was preoccupied and not maintaining her public face, but he saw clearly how drawn she looked, how very tired.

She glanced up as he reached her, and her face was smoothed by a smile that would have looked easy and natural to him if not for what he had just seen.

She took her drink. 'Happy New Year,' she said.

It seemed to him there was no life in her voice. The contrast to her earlier brightness was striking.

Again, he felt awkward. 'Look, maybe I'm out of line. I'm not trying to pry. But, damn it, you look so unhappy. Is something wrong?'

Her eyes blinked rapidly, but she grimaced and put her hand to her forehead and held back the tears. 'Things aren't so hot, you're right about that, but I'll get over it.'

'If there's any way I can help . . .' It was an automatic phrase, yet it echoed in him; he sensed he might actually mean it.

A small, sad smile. 'I wish it was as easy as that. I really appreciate the offer. It means a lot. But . . . there really isn't anything. There's nothing you can do. And' – she shook her head – 'it's not something I can talk to you about. I really can't . . . But thank you.'

'Anytime,' Jensen said. 'Harry Jensen, the big fixer. You must remember how good I used to be at making you feel better.'

She moved her hand toward him, stopped. 'Don't, Harry. It

6

was a nice gesture. Don't turn it to dirt.'

A solidly built man in a three-piece suit was making his way toward the bar. He saw Jensen, nodded, and detoured over to join them.

'I'd like to talk to you, Harry, when you get a chance.'

'Sure, George.' Jensen was grateful for the interruption, but he remembered the promise he'd made to Florence. 'It's getting toward midnight, though. Why don't we wait until a little later, after the festivities have calmed down a bit?'

'Fine. I'll see you later, then.' With another nod to Jill, he continued on his way to the bar.

Jill said, 'That was George Hammond, wasn't it?'

'Mmmhmm.'

'Is he as strange now as they say? Talking a lot about World War Two and getting drunk and repeating the same stories everywhere he goes?'

'I suppose he does have a tendency to repeat himself these days. But I don't know if I'd call him strange.'

The crystal chandelier that hung in the center of the ornate eighteenth-century room blinked on and off. Conversation trickled to a halt.

'Everybody!' Florence called from the side of the room. 'It's five minutes to midnight.'

The tall FBI man appeared at Jill's side.

'Jill?'

'Oh,' she said. 'I'm sorry.' She took his hand, looked from him to Jensen and back again. 'Ralph Norris ... Harry Jensen. Harry's—'

'I know who Harry is. And he's monopolized you long enough. Let's go watch the show.' He pulled her toward the other side of the room, where two men were setting up a large portable television on a Queen Anne lowboy. Over his

7

shoulder, Norris said, 'Happy New Year, Harry.'

Jensen watched them go, fighting down the desire to go after them, to shout something nasty at Norris. Instead, he turned away and snagged a glass of champagne from a passing waiter before turning back toward the television set. He was sourly amused by his reaction to Norris – jealous, after all these years.

The television crackled and hissed, and a picture took shape: Times Square, jammed with people. The music of Guy Lombardo's orchestra struggled from the television's speaker. The picture shifted to show the glowing white ball atop the Times building.

'All right, everybody. Get ready,' Florence said.

People began to move toward the television, getting between it and Jensen. Fleetingly, he was reminded of a crowded conference room in Mexico City, a little more than a month before.

He had been finishing lunch when the phone rang, and he had answered automatically, still paying attention to his sandwich.

'Jensen.'

'Oswald's dead.'

Touhy had hung up before the words had registered fully on Jensen. When they did, he slammed the receiver back into its cradle and bolted out the door, up the stairs, and down the corridor to Touhy's office. It was empty. So were the two neighboring offices.

'Conference room three,' a secretary said, and pointed the way for him.

It was a large room, but it was full of people. And it was quiet. Almost the only sound was the tinny voice of a TV commentator, speaking in agitated and hurried Spanish.

Jensen could make out very little of it. The television set was at the other end of the room from him; he could just see the screen through a blue haze of cigarette, cigar, and pipe smoke.

Abruptly, everyone seemed to lean forward at once. A voice whispered, 'There.' Another: 'That's him.'

Everything on the television screen seemed to stop for an instant. Even the Mexican commentator's voice, which had built to a peak of excitement, fell silent. Then, almost immediately, action swirled on the screen again, and the commentator's voice returned, more excited than before. The tension in the room dissipated; people began to talk, to turn away from the screen.

'What do you think of that?' Touhy asked.

Jensen turned. The CIA man was standing next to him.

'I still don't know what happened.'

'You just saw a man killed on live television. Or it was live, originally. That was a tape replay, just now.'

'What?'

'That's right. Lee Harvey Oswald was just murdered in the basement of the Dallas police headquarters. While surrounded by members of the Dallas police force. I told you they were a bunch of clowns.'

'I don't believe it. Somebody just walked in and killed him?'

'That's right.'

'The whole world's gone crazy.'

Jensen looked again toward the television set. He could hear the frantic voice of the Mexican commentator, but his view of the screen was blocked now by a shifting wall of heads and shoulders.

'Who did it? Who was he?'

'Man name of Jack Ruby. A local nightclub owner, if I get it right.'

'So now we'll never know what really happened.'

'Well, I don't know if I'd exactly say that,' Touhy demurred.

One of Florence's friends came to stand next to Jensen. They smiled at each other, and he put his arm around her. They had met at one of Florence's garden parties that summer, had a brief affair, and drifted apart. Now they were friends. Or perhaps, Jensen thought, just acquaintances.

On the television screen, the ball started down its tower. The crowd in Times Square surged with happy energy. As the ball came to rest in New York, somebody not far from Jensen popped a champagne cork.

The woman was in Jensen's arms, and they were kissing. He became aware of people around him shouting 'Happy New Year!' He broke free and said, 'Happy New Year,' and they joined the others in singing along with the people on television.

> *Should auld acquaintance be forgot*
> *And never brought to mind?*

Their voices rang hollowly under the sculptured ceiling.

> *Should auld acquaintance be forgot*
> *And days of auld lang syne?*

Abruptly they all faltered – a collective quiver in the stiff upper lip they were trying to maintain. When they resumed, it was more soberly, and they lagged behind Guy Lombardo and the revelers in New York.

By the time they were finished, several people in the room were crying.

For a while there was almost no conversation, and what little there was, was subdued and reflective. The mask of New Year's revelry had been pulled away; now, in the first hour of 1964, it was the tragedy of 1963 that reigned. A lot of champagne was consumed, much of it in solitary drinking. And then, toward one o'clock, some of the guests began to urge the others out of their gloom.

Jensen was standing in a small group; they were talking about whether a single human being could affect the world in any permanent way. George Hammond came up and joined them. Stocky and balding, with nondescript features, Hammond looked almost comically ordinary next to Jensen, whose dark good looks and tall, athletic slimness helped make him a favorite of Washington's hostesses.

'Happy New Year, George,' Jensen said.

'Happy New Year, Harry.'

They separated themselves from the others.

'How's it going?'

'Haven't you heard?' Hammond asked.

'No.' Jensen was shading the truth. He had an idea of what Hammond was about to tell him, but he wanted to hear it in Hammond's own words. 'Something major happening?'

'I've quit. We've agreed to call it early retirement, but the truth is I walked out.'

'I'm sorry to hear it, George. It can't have been easy for you.'

'No. No, it wasn't easy. Necessary, but not easy. If you don't mind my bending your ear, I'd like to talk to you about it.'

'Sure.'

11

In spite of Florence's warning, Jensen was eager to hear Hammond's story. He had first met the veteran spy shortly after coming back to Washington with the horde of bright young men who followed the Kennedys to the capital. Hammond was in his mid-fifties, some twenty years older than Jensen, and full of experience, and Jensen had always found him intriguing. Now he wanted to know what could have prompted Hammond to leave the CIA after having been with it since the beginning.

'Let me fill my glass,' Hammond suggested, 'and then we'll find someplace we can sit and talk.'

They tried the library, but it was too crowded, and so was the dining room. They ended up on a couch against one wall of the living room. Their privacy was limited, but they could see the others in the room; Hammond wanted to keep track of the people who might be within earshot.

'No war stories today,' Hammond said. He smiled ruefully. 'They don't seem to be as popular as they used to be. I guess the OSS is getting to be old hat.'

'You tell some pretty interesting stories.'

'But I'm beginning to repeat myself a little too often . . . I know I'm not supposed to notice how people avoid me, but I don't get that drunk. Besides, nobody makes much of a secret about thinking I'm an old bore.'

'It's never been a town that placed much value on consideration.'

'Or tact. Or, for that matter, friendship. With a few notable exceptions.' Hammond lifted his glass to Jensen.

'You know, George,' Jensen said, 'the weird thing is that I can't see the Agency functioning without you. You're more than just one of the founding fathers. It seems to me you're one of the pillars that holds the place up.'

Hammond smiled. 'I don't think any of my colleagues have ever seen me as a pillar. More like a rickety bannister, maybe. But what the hell – I don't mind. I've got a job to do, and I do it. I'm not bad at it, and I've had a lot of luck over the years. It hasn't been a bad life.'

'I always had the impression you loved it.'

Hammond spread his hands. 'You could say that, I suppose.'

'Then why—'

'Because I've had it, Harry. Up to my ears. It's not the same place I went to work for, all those years ago. Something's gone sour. And it's going to get worse.'

Jensen was fascinated. He had never heard Hammond speak so directly about anything more recent than ten years in the past.

For several moments Hammond was silent, staring at his hands. Jensen had the impression he was trying to find a way to begin talking about the things that were so clearly on his mind.

'You know there have been plans to assassinate Castro,' Hammond said without looking up.

'Yes . . .' Jensen replied tentatively.

'How much do you know?'

'Very little. Just what I've pieced together from hints and rumors I've picked up.'

'Well, that's what they've had me on for the past eight months or so. I missed the early stages: The first was before the Bay of Pigs, and then they started it up again and ran it right through the missile crisis.'

'I thought they stopped trying for him right after the crisis, when they were backing off on the whole Cuba issue.'

13

'No, they're still at it, even now . . . They're a bunch of idiots if you ask me. They've done every kind of dumb, irresponsible thing you can think of. Understand, I don't have anything against our using covert action to destabilize foreign governments. I've been doing it myself, off and on, ever since the War. We were all very good at it, too. I have some very fond memories of those operations: Egypt, Iran, Guatemala. They were efficient and well planned; they did the job they were supposed to, and they were relatively clean – no bad side effects for the country or the Agency. That's the worst part of all this Cuba nonsense. Even if they had been able to take Castro out, they would have compromised themselves doing it. They got involved with the Mafia, for God's sake. What the hell can they have expected to come of that? Can you imagine it – the Mafia holding information it could use to blackmail the CIA? And through the CIA, the administration. Crazy. Just crazy. It's been like that from the beginning, handled so stupidly that it was almost sure to do more harm than good.

'And now it seems as if everybody at the top of the Agency, on the operational side, has forgotten what we're in business for. The country doesn't matter anymore. Only the Agency matters. They're playing a different kind of game now, and I don't know where it's going to end. It's like having a private little government, making its own policy, waging its own wars, even making alliances, based on its own ideas of what's good for the country. It scares me, Harry. It really scares me. And there's nothing I can do about it. I've tried to talk to them, but they won't listen. And I can't go public with it. I don't exactly have the temperament to blow the whistle on them.'

'Then what are you going to do?'

'Basically, I'm getting out and I'm going to try to turn my

back on it. All I can hope is that it doesn't get so bad, so soon, that I feel I have to do something about it myself.'

He put his head in his hands for a moment. His whole body sagged. When he looked up again, he said, 'You know, Harry, maybe you'd better get me a drink. Not champagne. Vodka, if you can, or bourbon. And get yourself one, too. You're going to need it when you hear the rest.'

Jensen stood up. 'Sure, George.' He put a hand on the older man's shoulder. 'I'll be right back.'

Hammond drank some vodka, and then he looked carefully around the room. Jensen looked, too. He didn't see anyone within eavesdropping distance.

Hammond said, 'There's a whole separate section now that just deals with Cuba. SAS – the Special Affairs Staff. It's got a full structure all its own, right down to its own private counterintelligence section. Operationally, Des FitzGerald is carrying the ball. You know Des?'

'I've met him. I wouldn't say I know him.'

'Well, he was a good man once upon a time, but he's come up with some very strange notions lately. I think it comes from having a whole area of operations all to himself, with no real direction. He and his people have suggested everything from spraying the sugar fields with a chemical that would make the harvesters sick, to putting poisonous powder inside a scuba-diving suit that was going to be a gift to Castro.'

'Poison powder inside a wetsuit? That's got to be a joke.'

'Not a bit. There's a whole history of that kind of thing, and some of it's even stupider – LSD and botulinus toxin in his cigars, thallium-salt depilatory in his shoes to make his beard fall off. Those things, the silliest ones, were done before the Special Affairs Staff was created. Now it's a lot more serious.

Besides poisoning the sugar workers, Des has some other irons in the fire – his own things he hasn't been telling everybody about. There was one agent, a man they called "Lash." He's been around for a while, off and on. Before the missile crisis we used him to get intelligence from close to Castro, but then he dropped out of sight. He was a physician. I think he may have been Castro's personal doctor for a while. And he was a hero of the revolution. Cubela. Major Rolando Cubela Secades. Well, a few months ago, someone decided to look him up again. Once the contact was made, Cubela started to drop broad hints that if anybody wanted Castro taken out of the picture, he was the boy to do it for us. But he wanted to be sure whatever operations he was involved in had approval at the highest levels.'

Hammond drank the last of his vodka. 'Ultimately Des decided to go and talk to the man himself. I thought he was crazy, and I told him so, more than once: He was too visible to get personally involved in that kind of thing. But he was the boss, so he didn't have to pay any attention to me. He went and saw Cubela, and by one report I heard he not only told Cubela he could have all the guns he wanted but that he – Des – was a personal representative of Bobby Kennedy.'

'Did Bobby know FitzGerald was saying that?'

'Not for a minute. It's always been policy to restrict knowledge of something like an assassination. I'm not sure even McCone knew that assassination plans were being actively considered. And that's what made it so dumb of Des to use Bobby's name. Those people are supposed to stay insulated from operations like that, even when they know about them. You certainly don't bring their names into things they don't know about at all.'

Hammond broke off and looked around the room again.

What he saw didn't seem to please him. He stood up. 'Want another drink?' he asked Jensen.

'No, I'm all right.'

'I'll be right back, then.'

While Hammond was getting himself more vodka, Jensen tried to fit what the CIA man had told him into the things he had learned about Castro and the Cubans while he was in Mexico City. His thoughts were interrupted almost at once by his hostess.

'Harry.' Reproachfully. 'You promised.' Florence sat down next to him on the couch. She leaned softly against his arm and twirled a lock of his dark hair around a forefinger. 'You're not being sociable.'

Her breath was warm on his neck and ear, dense with alcohol. He twisted around to face her. 'We won't be much longer.'

Her hand lingered on his neck. 'You'd better not. All my friends are pining away from loneliness.'

Jensen caught a glimpse of Ralph Norris among the shifting crowd not far away. Jill was not with him. Jensen wondered if Norris could have somehow overheard any of what Hammond had been saying.

Florence turned in that direction and guessed whom he was looking at.

'Oh!' she breathed. 'Isn't it just awful? I'm sorry, Harry. I truly did not know.'

'I don't doubt it, Florence. Even at your most socially suicidal, you'd be more careful than that about mixing your guests.'

'Me?' she asked with mock amazement. 'Socially suicidal?' She leaned against him and kissed him briefly on the lips. 'Don't be ridiculous.'

17

* * *

Hammond let her get most of the way across the room before he came back and sat down.

'Everything all right?' Hammond seemed tenser than he had been.

'Fine,' Jensen assured him. 'That was just Florence, being daring.'

'I envy you your youth.'

Hammond was silent while a couple walked by the couch.

'Now,' he resumed, 'you might think that was enough of a horror story. But there's one more detail. According to information I received not long ago, our friend Señor Cubela, cryptonym Lash – Am/Lash, if you add the Cuba prefix – is a double agent. There are some who think that right from the beginning he was reporting back to Castro about all of the plots he and the CIA were hatching. And it's my own private opinion that some of the SAS people who were dealing with him knew how unreliable he was, even while they plotted with him against Castro. It makes a very ugly picture: The SAS is behind a lot of covert action in Cuba, and it's toying with plots to kill Castro. In September Castro warns us to lay off. He makes specific reference to assassination attempts, and he says he'll retaliate in kind, that American officials are not safe from whatever they plan against him. In late October Desmond FitzGerald meets with a Cuban who's been promoting an attempt to kill Castro. And he tells this double agent that he's a personal representative of Robert Kennedy. They talk about assassinating Castro. A month later John Kennedy is shot down in Dallas by Lee Harvey Oswald, a man who's not a stranger either to communism or to Cuba. End of story.'

Jensen was numb. There had been plenty of conjecture in

Mexico City about Cuban involvement in the assassination. The ambassador himself had been sure Castro was behind it. But that was all theorizing based on loosely connected incidents and unsupported accusations. This was different. What Hammond was telling him made it look like a simple matter of cause and effect. A warning had been ignored, and so a threat had been carried out. The enormity of it was staggering.

After a moment he asked, 'What's being done about it?'

'Nothing. Absolutely nothing. Only a few people know the details of what I've told you, and they're not going to enlighten anyone else. They're content to have the public be convinced Oswald did it alone, if only to save their own skins. I saw a report that at the very same moment the shooting was going on in Dallas, Am/Lash's case officer was giving him poison he could use on Castro. But nobody's ever going to hear about that. They broke off contact with the man almost immediately, and as far as anybody's concerned it never happened.'

'Can't you—'

'Believe me, Harry, I've tried. I've talked to everybody in the Agency who'll listen to me and whom I think I can talk to safely. But it hasn't done any good. When I started to hit a blank wall with everybody, I think I may have gone a little overboard. I wasn't as careful as I might have been where I aired my grievances, and I'm afraid I must have said the wrong thing in the wrong place once too often. I think somebody may be trying to kill me now.'

'You're talking about . . . our own people.'

'That's right. My colleagues.'

'After twenty years, working together, you really think they'd try to kill you?'

19

'They'd kill Castro – why not me? I'm a lot easier to get rid of than he is, and in some sense I'm more of a threat. And sentiment doesn't count, not even twenty years' worth, when they've really got their backs against the wall. So I don't know how much of a favor I'm doing you, passing all this on. I don't want to make you a target. But somebody else has to know. I can't let this knowledge die with me.'

Jensen shook his head, unwilling to believe what Hammond was telling him. And yet, Hammond knew his job, knew the people . . .

'You're sure about this?'

'Who knows? Maybe I'm imagining the whole thing. Maybe it was an accident when the laundry truck almost hit me. Somehow, I don't think so, but I suppose it could have been.'

Chapter Two

Jensen never made it to the rest of his New Year's parties. He sensed that no matter how many places he looked, he would not find a renewal of hope that night. The realities had caught up with him, carried by Jill and by George Hammond.

He spoke to a few more people, and when he could do it unobtrusively, he said thank you and Happy New Year to the admiral and made his way toward the door.

Florence caught him as he waited in the foyer for his coat. She looked limp and exhausted, smaller than Jensen's image of her, as if she had been shrunken by an unusually draining evening.

'Harry, you're not leaving. We haven't had a chance to be alone.' Pouting: 'I never get to talk to you.'

'I tried, Florence, but I couldn't get past your ring of admirers.'

She laughed tiredly. 'Or away from George Hammond. Or your ex-wife, either, I noticed. I hope that wasn't too bad for you. It was the admiral, you know. I can never be sure who he's invited without telling me.'

'Don't worry about it.'

'You know, Harry, there's something I've never asked you.'

'What's that?'

'Well, I wondered how it felt to you – having the President be your ex-wife's lover. Especially, I mean, since you had to brief him sometimes—'

He stared at her. 'What are you talking about?'

'Oh!' Her hand went to her mouth, but she was too tired to give the gesture any substance. Jensen could see how much fun she was having. 'I thought you must surely know . . .'

He shrugged. 'I knew he had women.'

'Yes, he had quite a line of admirers, didn't he? I thought everyone knew Jill Lazar was one of them.'

The maid came in with Jensen's coat.

They waited for her to leave. As he buttoned his coat, Jensen said, 'I know you're always right about these things, but there's one part of that story I find hard to believe. I can't see Jill as part of any line of adoring women. Not even for him.'

'Perhaps, Harry my love, perhaps.' She was clearly not convinced. 'Anyway, it's very loyal of you to say so.'

He laughed and shook his head, acknowledging defeat. 'Florence, as usual it was a wonderful evening. In spite of everything.' He leaned down and kissed her cheek. 'Happy New Year.'

'It was a pleasure to have you. And a Happy New Year to you, too.'

Jill called him early in the evening on New Year's Day.

'I didn't wake you?'

'Hell, no. I got up ages ago.'

'In the afternoon, I presume.'

'Sure. Though I did open my eyes once before noon.'

22

She laughed. 'You're slipping. I remember a time when you didn't get up until six on New Year's. That's why I waited until six thirty to call.'

'It was very considerate of you.'

There was a long pause. He waited for her to say something.

'That offer you made last night . . . is it still open?'

'To help, you mean?'

'Yes.'

'Well, yes, sure. Sure it is. But I thought—'

'So did I. But I've reconsidered. I don't know how smart this is, but . . . let's not examine it too closely, okay?'

'Sure. Fine . . . Look, you want to come over? I don't guess this is something we can talk about on the phone.'

'No, you're right. It really isn't.'

'You know where to find me?'

'On A Street, isn't it? Northeast? Downstairs from Mary and Andrew.'

'That's right – apartment two. Half an hour?'

'Forty-five minutes.'

He laughed. He had always underestimated how long it took her to get out of the house.

She laughed, too. 'Just like the old days.'

She arrived an hour later, breathless, glowing with the cold.

'I couldn't find my keys, and then it took forever to get a cab.'

He helped her out of a thick, heavy mink that had not been part of her wardrobe in her days as Mrs Harry Jensen. While he hung it up, she wandered into the living room. He found her standing by the fireplace, surveying the room.

'It's very nice. Cozy.'

'Thanks. Can I get you something?'

'Irish coffee?'

'Sure. But there's no whipped cream.'

'Just plain milk is fine.'

He led her down the long hall to the kitchen. She watched in silence as he put up the water and filled the drip pot's basket with coffee and a sprinkling of cinnamon. When they had been married, he might have pressed her to say what was on her mind, but he had grown more patient since then, and he knew she would have to approach this in her own way, in her own time.

They carried their Irish coffee into the living room and sat by the fire, watching the flames. Finally, she looked at him and, in a much stronger tone than he had expected, she asked, 'What are you doing about the assassination?'

The question took him off guard. 'You mean me, or the Staff?'

'The Staff.'

'We're not doing anything. As far as I know, the Warren Commission's taking care of all that.' As he said the words, he thought of George Hammond and of his own experiences in Mexico City. 'We've got plenty to do as it is, briefing Johnson on national security and worrying about those dumb damn generals in Saigon. I'm perfectly happy to leave the assassination for Earl Warren and his people to take care of.'

'They're not taking care of it.' She looked at him intently. 'They're suppressing the truth. They're going to bury it somehow.'

'What truth are you talking about?'

She was suddenly desperate, her confusion and helplessness beyond her control. 'I don't know, Harry. I'm not sure. I only know that whatever the truth is, they're not going to let it come out. They're trumping up some kind of case to show that

Oswald did it all by himself, and they don't care if it's true or not.'

He shook his head. 'That's awfully strong talk.' But he knew enough himself to say the same thing, although he was not ready to share his misgivings with her. 'All I mean is that so far it looks like the Warren Commission is trying to find the truth. Maybe you should tell me why you think there's going to be some kind of frame-up.'

'You know that Dave's been consulting with the White House on passing Johnson's legislative package?'

He shook his head.

'No,' she acknowledged. 'Of course not. Why should you? It's only a small contract. Anyway, the point is, he's right in there, and he hears things.'

'And tells you.'

'Yes.' She looked at the fire for a moment. 'Right after the assassination Nick Katzenbach told Bill Moyers that the public had to be convinced that Oswald did it and that it wasn't a good idea to encourage speculation about his motives. It was important for that kind of speculation to be cut off if possible.'

Jensen was surprised. He tried to make sense of what she had said in terms of the Washington power structure. Katzenbach was deputy attorney general, and the Justice Department could be presumed to have a residual interest in the assassination investigation, even though it was officially the Warren Commission's responsibility. But Moyers, as one of the people with privileged access to Lyndon Johnson, was in one sense even higher in the pecking order than Katzenbach. So why should Katzenbach be trying to ram through what sounded like a preformed theory of the crime? And why, even if Oswald was the killer, try to stifle speculation about his motives? Unless those motives were potentially very troublesome ... Jensen thought of George Hammond, running into a blank wall at the CIA. For the same reason Katzenbach was trying to build one at Justice?

'And that's not all,' Jill said, breaking his silent chain of inquiry. 'Katzenbach has been a very busy man. Besides his message to Moyers he wrote a letter to each member of the Warren Commission. He told them he thought it would be a good idea, now that they have the FBI report, for the commission to make a preliminary public statement saying the FBI's investigation showed Oswald to be the lone assassin.'

'Why the hell would he do that?' Jensen asked, this time unable to keep his reaction to himself. 'The way I hear it, that's not even what the report says. They said they couldn't find any evidence there'd been others. That's a long way from concluding Oswald did it on his own. All right, maybe they want to avoid a nationwide witch hunt, but why lie about it?'

'I don't know, Harry. It doesn't make any sense to me either. I thought everybody would want to find out the truth. I really did. It seems pretty important, don't you think?' Her voice broke, she put her hand over her eyes and bit her lip.

'I'm sorry,' she said, looking at him again. 'I just ... Damn it! It's not just that he's deputy attorney general. His boss is Bobby Kennedy, for God's sake! How can he be trying to hold back the investigation of Jack's murder?'

For what seemed to him a long time, she sat there, unable to go on. He waited.

She said, 'Harry, I don't want to impose, but is there something I can eat?'

There was some cold ham in the refrigerator, and a block of white cheddar cheese. He made her a sandwich on French bread, with French mustard, and he put a handful of olives on the side of the plate.

When they were sitting at the table by the living room's bay window, she said, 'See? There's one bad habit I haven't broken. I still have to eat when I get really nervous. Either that or I stop eating entirely.'

She took a bite of the sandwich.

'I'm sorry,' she said. 'I know how difficult I'm being. It's all so crazy. It's been so hard.' She started to cry.

'Oh, shit,' she said. She dropped the sandwich on her plate. It landed askew, spilling pieces of cheese and ham on to the plate and the table. She pulled a large handkerchief from her purse and sniffled into it.

'Oh, Harry, I'm at the end of my rope. I really am. I haven't slept a whole night in weeks. I thought I was strong, but I just can't take it.'

'What is it, Jill? Tell me what it is.'

'It's Jack,' she said, not looking at him. 'Was Jack . . . I guess you must know all that – all about my sordid affair with the President. That's how they talk about it, isn't it?'

'Yes, I heard about it. Last night, in fact. Even *ex*-husbands are the last to know.' It was harder for him to talk about it than he expected. He sat there, unable, for the moment, to say anything more, unwilling to trust his voice.

'I know,' she said. 'You don't believe it, about our being in love. I can tell by your expression. What was it you called me that summer? An unfeeling automaton? Emotionally empty? Something equally soft and caring, as I remember it. And now I'm all teary about the country's number-one fantasy prince. But it's true. There I was, perfectly happy paying attention to my job, and I was invited to a party at the White House. It was the first time I'd seen him since I went back to being Jill Lazar. When he turned on the charm, it made me think of how you

27

and I used to laugh about what a smoothie he was with the ladies. But then, boom, before I knew it, something happened, and we were in love. Sure, I knew about all the others, the cute little office workers and the party girls and the glamorous ladies and the campaign aides. But it was different for us. It wasn't easy, but there was so much happiness in it, in that one year of stolen moments. And then they had to go and kill him.' Her tears were gone now, replaced by the coldness Jensen had seen growing in her in the last months of their marriage. 'And goddamnit, whoever they are, they're not going to get away with it.' The moment of anger passed; again, her face crumpled, but she held back the tears.

'You know how he said I could tell it was different for him? Because he told me about the others. He never did that with anybody else, that's what he said. But with me it was real love, and he didn't want to have any secrets from me. Looking back on it now, it seems crazy, listening to those stories about him and his women. I don't know how I could have put up with it. But at the time it made perfect sense to me. I was so in love with him. We had so much joy. Real joy. That's what made the difference, really. You can't fake that.'

She took Jensen's hand. 'We used to be like that, in the beginning, remember? Just flying all the time, and so smug with it you could die.'

'Yeah,' Jensen said. 'I remember.'

Again, his expression gave away more than he intended. She said, 'Those were the only two times in my life I ever felt like that. With you and with Jack. Even if I did get to be an unfeeling bitch with you after a while. But you got pretty impossible, too, if I remember.'

'I suppose I did,' he said, and in spite of her attempt to soothe him, there was bitterness in his voice. 'But we've already talked that one to death, haven't we?'

She reassembled her sandwich but put it down without eating it. 'I hoped you would know why they're doing this, or what it means. Or if not that, then at least you might have seen something or heard something that made you suspicious too.'

'No,' he said, not knowing why he was lying to her. 'Not really.'

'I can't believe they can be doing this, and nobody knows about it.'

'You know how it is in Washington. It's only if it happens in a bedroom or a bar that everybody knows about it.' He smiled. 'Though, after what I've learned the past couple of days, I guess I can't even count on that anymore. Hell, most people don't even know what the guy two desks over from them is doing, and what's more, they probably don't give a damn, either.'

'You're saying you think they can get away with it.'

'I don't know, Jill. I'm not even sure if that's what they're trying. Maybe they're sure it was Oswald and they just want to save everybody the agony of endless speculation.'

'I don't believe it. It looks to me like they're hiding the truth. Maybe they're trying to protect somebody. I couldn't bear it, thinking his real killer got away.'

'I understand.'

'Will you help me find out the truth?'

'Jill, I don't know very much about it. I don't see what help I can be.'

'You know people. You're in a position to find things out if you want to.'

'What about your friend Ralph? He's an FBI man. It's his job.'

'Well . . . Ralph is limited in what he can do. There are so

29

many rules. And he has to worry about Hoover. But look at the people you talk to every day. Bundy and the others. They must know what's going on.'

'Maybe they do,' he said skeptically, 'but I can't just walk up and ask them. If anything *is* going on, they'll just clam up.'

'You could at least try. It's so important.'

'All right.' He reflected without pleasure that when they were married, she didn't think he had any power at all, and now she was counting on his entrée to high places. It made him angry, yet at the same time he responded to it. He wanted to show her how important he was. 'I'll see what I can find out, and I'll let you know.'

Abruptly, she stood up, stood there a moment awkwardly.

'I guess I'd better go home.'

He closed his eyes briefly, nodded. 'Sure.'

When she had her coat on, she said, 'I know this can't be easy for you. It's just that ... it's all so confusing. I hope I didn't hurt you too much, saying what I did. But I have to know. Can you understand that?'

'I understand.'

She leaned toward him. For a moment he felt the soft warmth of her lips on his.

'I appreciate it, Harry. I really do.'

He watched her leave in a kind of daze, and then he cleaned up their plates automatically, not really paying attention to what he was doing, replaying her visit in his mind. By the time he was finished in the kitchen, he was furious with himself. He could not believe how easily she had manipulated him, and he could not understand why he had let it happen.

He took the Irish whiskey bottle and a glass of ice into the living room and sat by the fire. By his second drink his reaction to Jill had faded. He put another log on the fire and freshened his drink. There was a report he was working on – a backgrounder for Bundy and Johnson on the tension in Panama. He picked it up to reread his first draft. As he sat down with it, he thought briefly of George Hammond and wondered how many people were going to put him on the trail of John Kennedy's murderer. It wasn't as if he were Earl Warren.

Jill called again the following week.

'Have you done anything about . . . what we talked about? I was wondering. It's been more than a week.'

'Has it?' Jensen heard the annoyance in his voice.

'All right, Harry. It was a simple question. You said you'd do something—'

'And I will.'

'—and it's very important to me.'

'Okay, Jill.'

'If we leave it alone too long, it'll be too late to do anything about it.'

'I said okay. I've been working very hard.'

'Are we back to that? Hiding behind your work?'

'For God's sake, Jill, I thought we'd had all that out once and for all. Things are heating up in Panama. The fuss right now may be about whose flag flies the highest, but the stakes could turn out to be very big. Johnson wants us to tell him what his options are and what effects they might have, and the problem is there's a lot of pressure at NSAS. There's been a lot of talk lately about our having taken over from the State Department as the prime advisory body on foreign policy, and that's making a lot of people at Foggy Bottom very unhappy. So we're on the spot. Lyndon doesn't much care for all us Kennedy types, to begin with. There's a chance he's going to fire half of us or even disband NSAS entirely. We don't know what to expect. So we're trying to be indispensable.'

'It's all right, Harry. If you don't want to help, just say so. I'll understand. Honestly.'

'You didn't hear a word I said.'

'Of course I did. And I don't expect you to drop everything for me. But you said on New Year's, if there was any way you could help—'

'Yes, and I meant it. I'll do what I can.'

'But you don't have to take it as an obligation. I don't want to get into that old business where you tell me you'd be happy to do ... whatever ... and then you don't do it, and you tell me it's because work doesn't leave you time to breathe. We both know better than that.'

He felt another surge of anger, but he caught himself. 'Look, this is no good. It's beginning to sound like one of our old fights. We've got to cut it out. I promise I'll do what I can as soon as I have some time. And I'll call you.' But when he hung up, he was not sure he would do anything.

That night he dreamed about her – a helter-skelter mélange of fantasies and distorted memories.

They were together in a large hall. Ranks of business-suited men sat on benches like church pews. At a signal from someone unseen, they all stood up. Jensen stood with them. He looked down at Jill, sitting between him and the man standing to his left. She smiled up at him. She was naked. The others in the room began to speak in unison, in a solemn cadence: They would faithfully uphold the law and obey the canons of ethics. He put his hand on one of her breasts. It felt cool and silky; the nipple was a small hardness against his palm. She had perfect breasts – full but not too large, smooth skinned, with uniform pink aureoles and flawless nipples. He bent to kiss her. While the others were being sworn in as lawyers, they made love on the hard, wooden bench.

They were in a park, picnicking. Jill wore a full-skirted yellow dress that spread around her on the grass; she looked like a spring flower. He put his hand on her thigh under her skirt. She reached down and pulled his hand higher, up between her legs where he could feel the hot wetness through the cloth of her panties. Then she laughed and jumped up. He ran after her, both of them laughing, until she threw herself down on a broad blue blanket with another man. Jensen stopped. The man turned. It was John Kennedy.

They were in a small apartment. Dim. Reminiscent of their first apartment. The walls were covered with bookcases: the law school library. It was time for dinner, or it would be soon, but there was nothing to eat. He followed her down a long corridor, unfamiliar at first, then becoming something from the Executive Office Building: the corridor outside Bundy's office. As they walked, they fought, shouting at each other – outrageous accusations of blame for the absent dinner. The corridor led them to the Capitol rotunda, where John Kennedy lay in state, his coffin surrounded by a dozen cigar-smoking replicas of Fidel Castro in the uniform of the US Special Forces. They pointed their submachine guns at Jill and at Jensen. They fired the guns. He could see flame blossoming from the muzzles, but there was no sound, no bullets.

He was climbing a ladder, but someone was hanging from his belt, behind him. He could barely pull himself from one rung to the next, and it was very important for him to get to the top. He tried to look back over his shoulder to see who was clinging to him, but he saw nothing. He felt the strain on his belt, the pressure of the belt across his waist, the knuckles

33

pressing into the small of his back. He was at least three stories off the ground. The ladder was a hundred feet long or more; it was propped against the facade of the Executive Office Building. He braced himself against the extra weight, tensed his arms, and took another step up the ladder. The rung broke, and he fell.

He was not happy when he woke up. He had not dreamed of Jill in months, and it bothered him that it was starting again.

Later, as he was brewing coffee for himself, one of their last fights came back to him; the memory was so vivid that it brought with it a full measure of the anger he had felt then. He picked up his still-empty coffee mug and hurled it across the room. It shattered against the far wall, leaving a smear of blue glaze on the white paint.

There was a reception at the Mexican embassy that Friday night, and as the National Security Advisory Staff's expert on Central American affairs Jensen had to put in an appearance. It had been more than a month since he had been in a room whose undertones rang so thickly with Spanish, and the rich accents of Latin America took his thoughts back to a restaurant in Mexico City whose bar was perpetually crowded with politicians and businessmen. It was a place the embassy staff frequented when they were feeling affluent. Touhy and he had gone there on his third night monitoring the Mexico City end of the assassination investigation, in a futile attempt to relax. They had spent the whole night talking about the killing and its reverberations south of the border.

They had a booth in one of the alcoves off the restaurant's main room. The flickering glow of the candle on their table emphasized the angry red blotches of burst capillaries in Touhy's nose and right cheek.

'Seems like when our friend Oswald was down here in September, he stopped in at the Soviet embassy,' Touhy said.

'Really?'

'That's what it looks like. They just arrested a receptionist or something from the embassy and took her in for questioning.'

'The Mexicans arrested somebody on the *Soviet* embassy staff?'

'She's Mexican. Name of Sylvia Duran.'

'And she saw Oswald when he was at the embassy?'

'That's what we figure. I don't know the details.'

Jensen sipped at his beer. 'Where'd you hear about it?'

'Sources.'

'But your sources can't tell you any more than that?'

'It's those assholes in Langley. When we wired them that Duran was going to be arrested, damn if they didn't call up and tell us to stop it. So I told them if we try to stop it, we're just going to get the Mexicans' backs up. But no, they get on their goddamn high horse and say go ahead and talk to your people and tell them it's important to us for them to leave her alone.'

'But why?'

Touhy shook his head. 'Shit, who knows?'

He broke off as their waiter approached carrying a fresh pair of Dos Equis beers and a plate piled high with *quesedillas*.

Over coffee Touhy said, 'There's one more piece of news. The best, so I saved it for last. We had a walk-in today, a Nicaraguan gentleman. Quite a fucking walk-in it was, too. The gentleman informed us that he had seen Mr Oswald on his recent trip to Mexico. At the Cuban consulate, if you please. It seems he was talking to a Cuban – a red-headed Negro, for shit's sake. How's that for detail?'

Touhy stirred his coffee. 'And you know what they were talking about, this redhead and our friend Mr Oswald? They

35

were talking about assassination. And at the end of the conversation the redhead gave Oswald a lot of money. Now, what do you think about that?'

'How reliable is it?'

'Hard to say. A guy like this Nicaraguan, his name's Alvarado, you can never tell how straight he's being. God knows what axes he's got to grind. But we have something else, too, from a source we think we can count on. Not a hundred percent confirmation of Alvarado's story, but you could call it corroborating information.'

'But it's still nothing conclusive?'

'Hell, no, it's not conclusive. But it looks pretty damn grim, wouldn't you say?'

'Yeah. I'll admit it's strong stuff. Though this business with the redhead seems a touch public as a way to buy an assassination.'

'I hadn't thought about it that way, but you're right.' Touhy swallowed the last of his coffee. 'What makes you so careful, all of a sudden?'

'I don't want to go jumping to any conclusions. Yesterday, when the ambassador gave me his whole theory about Castro being behind it all, I went crazy with it. I was sure he was right, and I had visions of our bombing Cuba to dust in retaliation. So it seemed to me it would be a good idea if I calmed down a little and tried to keep my head.'

But maybe I'm being too calm, Jensen told himself, coming back to the present. What was it they said – if you can keep your head while all around you are losing theirs, maybe you don't understand the situation.

He thought about Touhy and Hammond and Jill, and about all that he had seen and sensed in Mexico City, and he realized he had begun to doubt seriously that the truth of the Kennedy assassination would be found and exposed, unless some kind of pressure was applied from the outside.

He made his way through the cocktail party crowd and found a phone. It took him a moment to remember the number – it had once been his own, but he hadn't used it in years. He caught Jill on her way out. They made a date for lunch the next week.

After he hung up, he wondered if he had done the right thing. Hearing her voice had reminded him how susceptible he still seemed to be to her instinct for manipulation.

The following Wednesday Jensen got to the restaurant five minutes late for his date with Jill. She wasn't there yet. He asked for a gin and tonic – he wanted something he could nurse for a relatively long time, in case she was as late as he expected her to be.

Half an hour later he was considering ordering another one, when there was a small commotion at the entrance, and Jill came striding toward his table, the maître d' following in the wake of her swirling mink coat. Her cheeks and nose were pink with winter, and she was slightly out of breath.

'Sorry I'm late.'

She took off her coat and her matching mink pillbox hat and handed them to the maître d'. She was wearing a deep-red dress and a red and blue scarf. A few wisps of hair trailed along the sides of her neck. She brushed at them with one hand.

'A double gimlet, please, Billy, on the rocks,' she told the maître d' as, arms full of coat, he tried to hold her chair for her.

'And I'll have a martini,' Jensen said.

'Yes, sir.'

While they waited for their drinks, Jensen looked at her. Her healthy flush and the bustle of her arrival had fooled him at first into thinking she was in a good mood. He saw now that she wasn't. She looked vacant and upset.

He started to ask what was wrong, but she shook her head and held up a hand to silence him.

When their drinks arrived, she took a long swallow of hers, and then she closed her eyes and drew several long breaths. She opened her eyes and sipped at her drink. When she put it down, it was more than half gone.

'I really am sorry to be so late. I know how you hate waiting like this.'

'Trouble at work?'

'Yes. But nothing I want to talk about.' She pushed her glass around on the plate in front of her.

'Harry,' she said, studying the glass and the plate, 'have you seen George Hammond since New Year's?'

He felt suspicion well up in him like something tangible, and with it came an automatic evasion. 'Why do you ask?'

She hesitated. Took a breath. 'He's dead.' Staring at the glass. 'I just heard it. Just as I was leaving the office. That's what ... why I was so upset.' She looked up. 'I know how much you thought of him.'

He sat there, not moving, not speaking. She touched his hand comfortingly.

'Maybe I shouldn't have—'

'No,' he said. 'No. I want to know about it. How did he die?'

She shook her head. 'I don't know exactly. I heard he was run over by a truck. A laundry truck, I think.'

Jensen took only a moment to react. He threw some money on the table, pulled Jill out of her chair, and hurried her to the front of the restaurant.

'Miss Lazar isn't feeling well, Billy. Could you get our coats, please? In a hurry.'

Jensen snatched the coats from the bewildered maître d', wrapped the mink around Jill's shoulders, and got them outside and into a cab.

'Mayflower Hotel,' he snapped at the driver. 'Don't stop to pick up anyone else.'

It was a short ride and a silent one. At the hotel Jensen shoved a five-dollar bill at the cabby and climbed out of the cab. He leaned back in to pull Jill after him.

She was staring at him. He recognized her expression – she was about to dig her heels in and demand an explanation. He tensed. But she changed her mind, gave a tiny nod of acquiescence, and got out of the cab.

He hurried into the lobby, not even looking back, sure now that she was behind him. Walking toward the reservations desk, he composed himself.

The clerk looked up from sorting the morning's reservation cards.

'Yes, sir, may I help you?'

'You have a reservation for Clark, from New York. A room for two. For one night.'

'Certainly, sir. I'll check that for you.'

Jensen felt Jill standing next to him at the counter. He did not turn to look at her.

The clerk came back, a worried look arranged on his face. 'I'm sorry, sir. I can't seem to find it.'

'I don't understand. My travel agent assured me—'

An understanding smile. 'These confusions do happen. It's probably a mix-up in transmitting the request. Perhaps we can find something for you.'

'I'd appreciate it.' Jensen slid a ten-dollar bill across the counter. The clerk took it.

'I'm sure we have a room that will be satisfactory. A double bed?' There was only the hint of a smirk in his tone.

'Yes. That's fine.'

The clerk searched in the pigeonholes on the wall behind his counter and pulled out a key. 'Here we go. Eight twenty-two. It's very pleasant.'

Jensen gave the bellhop a dollar for opening the closet doors and turning on the faucets in the bathroom. He locked the door behind the departing bellhop, threw the security bolt, and slid the door chain into place.

'Well,' Jill said. 'I certainly am flattered.' She looked around the room; her glance lingered on the double bed. 'I don't know when anybody has swept me off my feet quite so impetuously. Especially at lunch.'

Jensen looked at the bed, at the room, at Jill. He smiled. 'I guess that's what it looks like.'

'The desk clerk was certainly convinced.'

He started to explain, realized that he didn't know how to begin.

'Well . . .' she said after a moment. 'Are you going to tell me why we're here? I gather it's not for sex, and I can't believe it's for food. I understand they have wonderful room service, but that seems a little far-fetched, considering the drama—'

'Do you want to sit down?'

She glanced around the room again: There was one easy chair and the bed.

'I'll stand.'

'Okay. I'm sorry about the drama. It was the only way' – he stopped – 'I'm getting this backward. You wanted to know

40

why we're here. It's because of what you said about George.'

She shook her head; she did not understand. 'That he was in an accident?'

'I don't think it was an accident.'

'You don't . . .' Her eyes went wide. She sat down on the edge of the bed. 'Harry—'

'I'm not sure. But there's a good chance of it. I wanted to get us out of there, somewhere we could talk about it in private and not be overheard. Or recorded.'

She stared at him. 'In Washington? You're looking for a private place to talk in Washington? And you picked the Mayflower Hotel?'

He looked around the room. Suddenly, even the nineteenth-century prints on the walls seemed sinister.

He took her hand and led her into the bathroom. He turned the shower on and pulled the shower curtain so they wouldn't be splashed.

'What makes you think George was murdered?' She spoke only loud enough for him to hear her over the noise of running water.

'Because of the things he told me about the assassination of John Kennedy.'

She reached out for Jensen, clutched his hand. Her skin was cold; her grip rigid and frightened.

'What is it, Harry? What did he say?'

He told her. And he added some of what he had learned in Mexico City.

It was more than a minute after he finished before she spoke.

'And that's why George is dead? Castro?'

'He was worried that someone was going to kill him. He said they'd already tried. With a laundry truck.'

41

'My God, Harry, we've got to do something.'

He put his hands on her shoulders. 'First, we have to calm down. There's too much happening here for us to go off half-cocked. Remember, you said yourself that somebody high in the administration – at least at Katzenbach's level – is holding back the truth about the assassination.'

'Yes. That's why—'

'And George said that the Agency was going to cover up its provocations of Castro. It was the Agency he was most afraid of. They were the ones he talked about killing him.'

'The people he worked with? How could they—'

'If they feel threatened enough, if they can convince themselves it's in the national interest, who knows what they're capable of?'

She digested that. 'Then what are we going to do?'

'We're going to be careful. Very careful. George wasn't, and now he's dead. What worries me the most is that the wrong people saw him talking to me, and whoever killed him knows about it.'

'Do you think anyone overheard you?'

'There were a lot of people at that party. We tried to be discreet, but we were talking right out in full view of everybody. I don't know. I could be next on the list.'

Saying it out loud made it seem a lot more immediate and frightening. Jensen suddenly felt claustrophobic.

'It's like a steam bath in here. Let's get outside.'

He reached over to turn off the shower. He thought he could get his hand past the water, but in his haste he misjudged it and soaked his sleeve.

They rode to the lobby in silence. Jensen dropped the room key at the desk and got a knowing look from the clerk.

They walked down Connecticut Avenue toward Lafayette Park. It seemed to Jensen that the winter wind was blowing directly up his sleeve, turning it to ice.

'I've got to get more information,' he said.

'How?'

'Mexico City. It was in a state of advanced confusion when I left there in November. I want to know how some of those things turned out, and if they learned anything else.'

'Wouldn't you know it if they had?'

'No. Not with the lid on the way it is.'

'And you think they'll tell you what you want to know if you go down there?'

'They're used to talking to me. Security-consciousness tends to be habitual. They're going to be a lot more relaxed with me than they would be with somebody else. After all, I already know a lot. And besides, Dick Touhy owes me some favors.'

'When will you go?'

'As soon as I can. Tomorrow.'

They stopped in front of the US Chamber of Commerce Building. Across the street from them in the park the statue of Von Steuben wore a pigeon on each shoulder.

She took Jensen's hand. 'Take care of yourself.'

He crossed the street and walked past Von Steuben, cutting diagonally across the park on the way back to his office. Ahead of him was an equestrian Stonewall Jackson and beyond that the Marquis de Lafayette. He was not happy to find himself in the company of so many heroes.

He stood for several minutes looking out his office window, holding his wet sleeve over the radiator, thinking about how he would broach the idea of the Mexico City trip to Hapgood.

The sleeve warmed up slightly; tepid, it only felt soggier. He took his jacket off and hung it on the back of the door.

He sat down at his desk and dialed Hapgood's number.

Hapgood was out of the office for the afternoon. Jensen left a message asking him to call back first thing in the morning.

He spent the afternoon going through recent dispatches and reports on Central America. There was nothing of any particular interest or importance, except the steadily worsening situation in Panama, and even that seemed to have been brought at least temporarily under control.

It was just as well there was nothing major for him to deal with, because he was having trouble concentrating. He kept thinking of George Hammond, making mental pictures of his crossing the street and being struck down by a laundry truck.

Hapgood called him at ten thirty the next morning.

'If you have a minute, I'd like to see you,' Jensen said.

'I was just going to suggest the same thing.'

Hapgood was not alone when Jensen got to his office. The Panama desk officer from the State Department was sitting on the small couch under Hapgood's portrait of JFK, which bore a small black rosette in one corner.

'Come on in, Harry.' Hapgood looked and sounded grim. 'We've got some work to do this morning, for a change.'

'What's up?'

'The flag, I'm afraid,' the man from the State Department said.

'Ours or theirs?'

'Ours,' Hapgood said sourly. He waved Jensen to a chair.

'I thought that was settled. No flags at all, isn't that how they left it?'

'Yep,' Hapgood affirmed. 'But the word we have now is

that the kids at Balboa High aren't happy about the compromise. They're planning to raise the American flag today.' He looked at his watch. 'Right about now. They may even have done it already.'

'That's awfully dumb,' Jensen commented.

'They think it's patriotic.'

'Wonderful. And what's this patriotism likely to lead to? Suppose you get a mob of Panamanians marching on the school – to take the flag down, to put up a Panamanian flag, whatever? You can't let them do that. So you get a face-off between angry Panamanians and American soldiers backed up by some hot-headed high school kids. That kind of thing could go anywhere. All you need is a little rock throwing and name calling. And if there's shooting—'

'The soldiers are better trained than that,' Hapgood objected.

'Maybe. But Panamanians have guns, too.'

'You think there's going to be shooting, then?'

'I hope not. If there is, watch out. Because if I've been reading the reports right, you could get Yankee-go-home riots all over the Zone.'

'Yeah. That's about how we see it, too. I was kind of hoping you'd come up with a cheerier prediction, and maybe we could relax a little.' Hapgood sighed and pushed his chair back from the desk so that he could put his feet up. For most of the next minute he stared at the ceiling.

'Well, I guess I'd better call Mac,' he said finally. 'We've got to get some briefings together on this one, before it blows up on us.' He picked up the phone and dialed Bundy's extension.

Jensen stared gloomily at the portrait of Kennedy and hoped the situation in Panama would cool off quickly. Until it did there was no question of his taking a trip to Mexico City.

45

They moved the meeting to Bundy's office, and then Jensen went back to his own office to prepare a briefing memo for the President. He had his lunch sent in.

He was still working on the memo when the phone rang.

'Jensen.'

'You bastard.' It was Hapgood. 'Get your ass in here. And bring your crystal ball.'

'What happened?'

'Just what you said. They got a big, angry crowd at the high school, and the troops were there, nervous but controlled, and then some sniper started taking potshots at them.'

'Shit,' Jensen breathed. 'They shot back, I suppose.'

'You suppose right. Instant chaos. So get your ass in here. We've got more work to do.'

As the day progressed, the rioting spread through the Canal Zone. Jensen and the rest of the National Security Advisory Staff's Western Hemisphere section were in their offices all night preparing analyses and suggesting responses as Panama broke off diplomatic relations with the United States and protested US aggression to the UN Security Council and the Organization of American States.

On the afternoon of the tenth, Hapgood came into the conference room where Jensen and the others were drafting alternative responses to the actions they expected from the UN Security Council and the Council of the OAS, both of which were meeting in emergency session to discuss Panama's charges against the United States.

'Good news, everybody,' Hapgood said.

Gradually, work in the room stopped. Policy debates and arguments over syntax were suspended.

'It looks like Panama's buying the peace mission,' Hapgood

went on. 'They've called off the UN special session and agreed to let the Inter-American Peace Committee handle it. It's not much, but it is progress of a sort.'

An hour and a half after Hapgood's announcement Jensen left his office to go home for some sleep. He had been working for more than thirty hours without a break.

Jensen's fatigue and his day and a half under the Executive Office Building's artificial light made even the attenuated sunshine of a winter afternoon dazzling. He hailed a cab and rode in a corner with his eyes closed, drifting toward sleep. Halfway home he realized he had no food in the house. He had the cabby let him off on Wisconsin Avenue. He went to a delicatessen and a grocery store, moving in a kind of daze, fumbling for his change at the grocery store checkout counter. He was not entirely sure what he had bought.

As he walked home, his mind was again on Mexico City: If the Panama crisis didn't heat up again, he might still get down to Mexico within the next few days.

At the corner of Seventeenth Street he turned to cross Wisconsin Avenue. He stopped automatically, subliminally aware of the flow of traffic along the avenue. He looked up: The light was against him. He waited until the cars had stopped roaring by, glanced vaguely up the block, and stepped off the curb. Heard an automobile engine, accelerating, improbably loud.

Someone screamed.

Jensen looked up at a white shape looming toward him. Reflex threw him backward, away from it. He tripped, went down on his back, scattering groceries.

The white bulk roared by. He felt the cold breath of its passing, smelled a stink of exhaust and burnt rubber.

He wanted to avoid the gathering crowd. He stood up.

Swayed. Everything went gray, and then black. He fell to one knee.

He tried it again, more slowly, and this time he made it. He picked up some of his groceries. The eggs were beyond hope, and so was a tire-flattened pound of good cheese. But the can of coffee was all right, and some of the other canned goods. He had to be careful bending down to pick things up, but a few of the bystanders helped him. He thanked them and shrugged off their questions and their offers of further assistance.

He walked slowly across the street and turned to look at the scene of his near-miss. The crowd had already broken up; another, smaller group had gathered in front of a shop window a short way up the block. He asked someone what they were looking at and learned that the truck had catapulted a can of minestrone through the window of a dress shop.

Later, when the shakes had passed and before he fell asleep, he replayed the scene in his mind. In his memory he saw the words on the side of the truck. They were indistinct, but he thought they said Eagle Laundry.

He stayed out of work the next day, to keep off the street and to plan what he would do next.

Whatever the people behind that truck thought Hammond had told him, he did not think he could convince them he was harmless. The best way he could come up with to protect himself – and at the same time to take some measure of revenge for Hammond's death – was to fill in the holes in what Hammond had told him and what he already knew, and make it all public. Quickly.

When he called his office that morning, he told his secretary to put him in for a week's sick leave. It did not seem dishonest to him that he was going to spend that week in Mexico: After his encounter with the laundry truck he was convinced that staying in Washington was bound to result in a severe worsening of his health.

Chapter Three

It was a sunny day in Mexico City, warmer by far than wintry Washington, but with a nip in the air, a product of the altitude as much as the season.

Jensen lounged across the *Reforma* from the embassy. He was wearing sunglasses and a cream-colored suit that would have looked fine on a Mexican businessman. His first stop after leaving the airport had been at a barbershop on the ground floor of a downtown office building. Now, leaning against a sunny wall and reading the morning paper, there was nothing about him to indicate that he was not a native.

When Touhy came out of the embassy, Jensen folded his paper and fell in step with him, staying across the broad avenue and about a dozen yards behind him. Four blocks from the embassy Jensen watched him push through a heavy wooden door under a neon sign that said La Taverna Encantida. He waited five minutes before he followed.

The restaurant was dim; Jensen folded his sunglasses and put them in his breast pocket.

Touhy was in a booth on the bar side of the partition that divided the room into two unequal parts. Jensen slid on to the bench across the table from him.

'Hello, Harry. I didn't know you were down here.'

'I'm not advertising.'

'Want a drink?

'Sure.'

Touhy waved to the bartender. 'José.'

José was wiping glasses. 'Señor?'

'Harry?'

'Tequila. And a Dos Equis.'

Touhy relayed the order. José continued to wipe glasses for several minutes before he brought their drinks.

'It's kind of casual in here,' Touhy commented. 'But it's relaxing.'

They toasted each other in silence.

'How're things in Washington?'

'Not bad.' Jensen was too keyed up to prolong the pleasantries. 'I want to talk to you about Cuba and the assassination.'

'I figured.'

Jensen took salt, lime, tequila. 'What about the Nicaraguan? Alvarado. What ever happened to him?'

'Right to business, eh, Harry?'

'Why not? That's what I'm here for.'

'Yeah. Well, what the fuck. Alvarado. That was a funny business, I'll tell you that. Just around the time you left, we began to wonder about him. Headquarters still thought there might be Cuban involvement in the shooting, maybe even Soviet involvement. But they didn't like that Nicaraguan. So what they told us to do was to give him to the Mexican police. Their timing was interesting, too. Picture this – we've got this guy who's told us a story about Oswald and the Cubans; we have some corroboration, too, but nothing positive. Now here comes the supervisor the FBI sent down to oversee their investigation and he wants to talk to our Nicaraguan. And all we can tell him is, So sorry, no can do, we've been instructed to turn him over to the police. By and by, of course, the native authorities did their usual exhaustive job interrogating Señor Alvarado, at the end of which time the poor bastard recanted. I'm sorry, folks, he says: It was all a big mistake.'

'What do you think?'

'I think they beat the shit out of him is what I think. And I'm not the only one. On reflection it seemed more likely to us that he'd been telling the truth in the first place and that he was lying now. So we sent a cable telling headquarters how we felt.'

'What did they say?'

'Nothing. No response.'

'That's very peculiar.'

'Yeah. You could say that. But it's consistent. Everything connected with this assassination has been peculiar.'

Jensen drank some beer. He did not want to push too hard.

'Harry,' Touhy said in a different tone of voice. 'Are you still in contact with any of the boys from the campout in Guatemala?'

Carefully: 'No . . . Except for Christmas cards.'

'You know where they are, then?'

'A few of them. Gutierrez. Narvaez. Colon. I think about them now and then. Don't you?'

'Sure.'

Touhy peered over at the bar, then leaned toward Jensen, his arms on the table. 'You know,' he said, 'if Castro was behind the assassination, it would be a real shot in the arm for them.'

'How's that?'

'Well, hell, we'd have to declare war on Cuba in response, wouldn't you say? And even if we didn't *have* to we *could*. That's all those guys need. Shit, if ever there was an act of war, having the President shot has got to be it.'

'And you really think Castro was behind it?'

Touhy sat back and studied Jensen. 'I sure do. And when you hear the rest of what you missed, you will, too. The crappy part of it is that the information's being buried, because somebody's up to something very funny in Washington.' He finished his drink, looked hard at Jensen again. 'I have a proposition for you, Harry.'

'A proposition?' Jensen echoed. 'What kind of proposition?' He was stalling, giving himself time to shift mental gears. This was not what he had expected.

'I want to be sure those guys don't get another royal screwing like they did their last time out. I want them to know what's happening. So I'll tell you everything I know. On one condition – that when you go back to the States, you see Colon or Narvaez and tell them what's up.'

'Isn't that a little dangerous? If somebody's made a policy decision that they shouldn't know—'

'Policy decision! That's a crock, and you know it, Harry. Give or take a few, we're talking about the same bastards who made the policy decisions that killed all those good men on that beach in Cuba. I can't go up there and talk to Colon and Narvaez myself, and it'd be dangerous to bring them down here. Until now I haven't been able to think of anybody I can trust to carry the message. But I trust you, Harry. You were there with us, and you're old-fashioned enough to keep your word. What do you say? Will you do it?'

Jensen considered it: He badly wanted the information Touhy was offering to trade.

'I'll have to be careful,' he said.

'Damn right. Just so they don't get left in the dark. It's enough to get to one of them; he'll pass it on.'

54

'What do you have?'

Touhy hesitated a moment, making sure he wanted to go ahead.

'Okay,' he said. 'I want them to know about the Nicaraguan. Not just Oswald and that redheaded Negro talking at the embassy – the whole story, including what I just told you about the response from Langley and the cops beating Alvarado up, and what we think about it down here.'

'Fine.'

'And Sylvia Duran – you remember, the clerk at the Soviet embassy who maybe saw Oswald when he was there – the one we were supposed to keep the Mexicans from arresting. You remember her?'

'Yeah.'

'Well, when we told headquarters we couldn't keep the Mexicans from arresting her, we got a cable from Karamessines, Helms's deputy, saying that if the Mexicans went ahead with the arrest, it could jeopardize our freedom of action on the question of Cuban responsibility for the assassination. Now, what the blazing hell does that mean? The only way I can read it is that they thought Duran would spill the beans, that she'd link Oswald up with the Cubans, maybe, or the Russians, and once she did – blooey, there goes our flexibility. But then you have to ask, what the fuck do we need flexibility for? I mean, if they did it, then by God we ought to clobber them for it, and no two ways about it.' Touhy took a long pull at his drink, as if for emphasis. 'After that we got a cable that Duran was going to be arrested again. And they were all upset about it again at Langley, so we were told to make it clear to the Mexicans that they had to take full responsibility for the arrest.'

'Full responsibility?'

'Yeah. Sounded sort of like old Pontius Pilate washing his hands: "Whatever comes of this, it's not our fault." Not that they so much as hinted at what it was they thought might happen.'

'Curiouser and curiouser.'

'There's more: There was a big meeting that day at the embassy – the legal attaché, the big-shot FBI type from Washington, our chief of station, and the ambassador. And the FBI was doing a very hardsell job on the idea that Oswald did it all on his own.'

'How did the ambassador take that?'

'Ah, the ambassador. He didn't like it at all. He's still convinced Castro did it. We got a cable from old man Helms, the deputy director for plans himself, that very same day, and you know what he said? "There is the distinct feeling here, in all three agencies – that's CIA, FBI, and State – that the ambassador is pushing this case too hard." Pushing it too hard! The goddamn assassination of the fucking President! And you know what worried him? Again, I quote: "We could create a flap with the Cubans which could have serious repercussions." Indeed it could. Indeed, indeed. It goddamn well ought to have serious repercussions. So how do you like them fucking apples, my boy?'

Jensen shook his head wonderingly. He did not want to let Touhy know how horrified he was. This fit too frighteningly well with everything else he had learned. The wall of silence was going up everywhere.

A sudden burst of Spanish filled the room. A clump of young men in business suits planted themselves along the bar. They seemed to be in the middle of at least a half-dozen conversations. José made his way listlessly from one to the next, taking their orders.

Touhy took a wallet from his inside jacket pocket and put a small pile of pesos on the table. He slid out of the booth and stood up.

'I think we ought to be moving on, Harry, my friend.'

Jensen followed him out to the street. The sky was pink with sunset; it was a surprise – after so long in the dim bar, he had expected it to be night.

'Well, what do you think? Where to?' Touhy wanted to know.

'You have some time free tomorrow?'

'Saturday? Yeah. I can arrange it.'

'Fine. I'd like some time to absorb what you've told me. Let's meet at the university, say, at noon tomorrow. At the big tree by the reflecting pool in front of the library, the one with the mosaic mural.'

'I know it.'

'Noon, then. We can take it from there.'

Touhy was waiting for him when he got there. Jensen thought the CIA man looked very out of place among the students in the plaza – very American.

'I've got a car,' Jensen said.

'Good.'

It was a Hertz car, a big Chevrolet a couple of years old, as out of place on the narrow road Jensen picked as Touhy had been at the university.

Jensen said, 'Dick, I'm worried. What if the chief of the station here or somebody at Langley finds out you're talking like this?'

'Hell, why should they? You're not going to tell them.'

'No.'

'All right. If you keep your mouth shut, nobody can trace it to me, because you're not going to tell Narvaez or Colon exactly what I'm telling you now. They wouldn't understand it if you did. You'll have to generalize for them, make them see the big picture. But you've got to make them believe you, Harry. Because if Castro's behind that assassination, and Washington's sweeping it under the rug, then that's it, boy. Those poor Cuban bastards have had it forever. That's the only thing this can mean. Somebody's decided: Hands off Castro, no matter what. So it's now or never for Narvaez and Colon and your friend Gutierrez and all the others. Once this one goes by, forget it.'

For a while they rode without speaking, each lost in his own thoughts.

Touhy broke the silence. 'You came in on the night of the twenty-second, didn't you? I remember you got to the embassy about eleven or so.'

'That sounds right.'

'Did you happen to notice a Cubana Airlines plane that had been delayed taking off when you were at the airport?'

Jensen moved his mind back through the confusion of that November day.

'There was a hell of a crowd in the terminal, yeah. Something about a delay.'

'Well, Harry, old son, you should have paid closer attention. You may have just missed running into one of the assassins.'

'One of the assassins?'

'Or an accomplice. We got this from the home office in December, and I'm damned if I know how we missed it here. That Cubana plane was held from six o'clock until eleven. At ten thirty a twin-engined plane landed with one passenger. That's why I said you probably just missed him.'

Jensen remembered now the squeal of tires as a light plane bounced to a landing. 'Could be I saw the plane. One came in just after mine did.'

'Yeah. Well, the guy on that plane got right off it and got right on the Cubana plane. Did not go through Customs. Did not show anyone his passport. In fact, he didn't show anybody his face at all. He just climbed into the cockpit, where none of the passengers could see him, and he rode in there all the way to Cuba. And, by an interesting coincidence, while the Cubana plane was waiting for its mysterious passenger, there was a whole passel of Cuban diplomats at the airport, looking nervous and expectant.'

'Has anybody followed this up? Do you know who the mysterious passenger was?'

'No, and no. I even suggested once that maybe we ought to check into it, but I got my wrists slapped. Forbidden territory. All we know is this guy got a top-secret, top-priority trip to Cuba the night of the assassination, right after he flew in from some unidentified place within the range of a twin-engine plane. Like for instance the Texas border.'

'Shit. How can they let that go?'

'There's another one, too. Some guy who cleared the border just after the Mexicans reopened it on the twenty-third. They'd closed it on the afternoon of the twenty-second, after the news of the assassination registered on them. So this guy waits around until they reopen it – we don't know when he got there – and he comes down to Mexico City. He stayed for a couple of days and then he left for Havana late on the twenty-seventh. Cubana Airlines again. But this guy didn't ride in the cockpit. He didn't have to. He was the only passenger. Just him and a crew of nine. We know some more about him, too. A Cuban, basically, but he was an American citizen. He crossed from Texas to Mexico at Nuevo Laredo using a tourist card he picked up in Tampa. So it figures that he was probably in Tampa when Kennedy was there on the eighteenth. And if he crossed into Mexico when the border opened on the twenty-third, it also figures he was in Texas on the twenty-second. And Nuevo Laredo is pretty much a straight shot south from Dallas.

'So we've got a couple of mysterious guys doing some very mysterious traveling from the scene of the crime to Havana, Cuba. And nobody wants to know about it. They're trying awfully goddamned hard, in fact, to pretend none of it ever happened.'

Chapter Four

Hapgood looked across the desk at Jensen for several heartbeats before he said, 'We were worried about you, Harry. We wanted to send you some flowers, sort of a get-well gift, but then it turned out you weren't at home.'

'I was in Mexico,' Jensen said.

'It's not the phony sick leave that bothers me, you know. It's the lack of consideration. We were in the middle of a crisis.'

'The crisis had passed. You were preparing for a second one, maybe, but the first one was over.'

'I suppose that's right. But you could have told me where you were going. You could have asked for those days as personal business.'

'You wouldn't have given them to me.'

Hapgood put a finger in his ear, took it out, and examined the wax on his fingernail.

'No, I wouldn't have given them to you.' He wiped his finger on a tissue. 'What did you want to see me about?'

'My trip to Mexico, among other things. I've heard about some very peculiar incidents over the past month and a half. One at a time, they were disturbing. Added up, I think they may be dangerous.'

'To?'

'To the country, ultimately.'

Hapgood took a yellow legal pad from a pile of them on the table next to him and plucked a colorfully hand-painted pencil from his desk.

'All right.'

Jensen took a moment before he spoke. He had planned his approach to play to one of Hapgood's central concerns, and he didn't want to get it wrong.

'The basic problem may be information flow. Two kinds – factual information is getting delayed and diverted on its way to the policy level, and policy decisions are not getting to the information-gathering and operational levels with the right kind of supporting detail. What's happening now, I think, is that we've got operational people working at cross-purposes to policy because they don't understand it.'

Hapgood was interested. 'You're not just theorizing?'

'No. I have something specific in mind.'

'I'd like to hear about it.'

'It comes out of what I saw in Mexico City in November. The CIA started to bring in information that pointed to a link between Lee Harvey Oswald and Cuba and the assassination. Something a lot more substantial than the Fair Play for Cuba Committee.'

Hapgood stopped writing. He took the color-swirled pencil in both hands and leaned forward slightly, his attention fully focused on Jensen.

'The people up here at Langley were acting as if they didn't want to know what was happening in Mexico, no matter what it was. And the people in Mexico were not very happy about that, because they thought they had important information.'

'Harry . . .'

'Yes?'

'I don't want to hear about it.'

'But—'

'Now you listen to me, and listen carefully. The assassination is none of our business. It is, especially, none of *your* business. Your job is Western Hemisphere analysis and interagency liaison for the National Security Advisory Staff. You're not a member of the Warren Commission. None of us is. You are to leave the assassination alone. Do I make myself absolutely clear?'

'Perfectly.'

'Good. Excellent. Now, why don't you go back to your office and do some work? That Panama crisis you so cavalierly dismissed is far from resolved, and we would appreciate your expert assistance in preparing for future contingencies.'

Jensen stood up.

Hapgood said, 'I'm going to let that sick-leave business ride. Just don't do it again.'

Jensen walked to the door. Hapgood called him back.

'One more thing.' Hapgood's voice was milder. 'I don't like playing the heavy the way I just did. Especially with you. You're a good man – you're one of the best people Mac has on the whole staff, for my money. And I'm pretty sure Mac thinks so, too. You've come as far as you have for a lot better reasons than just going to college with Bobby and Teddy and working hard on the presidential campaign. And that means you're more likely than some of the others to come out in good shape after the election, when Johnson is building his own team. I know how much that means to you. So far you've built yourself a very impressive record. This is no time to ruin it by being stupid. It would be a tragedy if you threw away all those years of hard work just when they were about to add up to something for you.'

Tonelessly: 'Thanks, Hap. I appreciate it.'

'All right. Now get back to work.'

Hapgood's parting shot had a strong effect. By the time Jensen got back to his office, he had almost convinced himself that he was creating a problem where none needed to exist. Jill and Touhy each had more than enough reason to distort and exaggerate the events surrounding the assassination. But there was no reason for him to let them draw him into their schemes and delusions. Hapgood had given him a tantalizing glimpse of the future. He did not want to spoil it for himself.

He worked very hard that day, at peak efficiency. He cut through the mass of paper that had accumulated on his desk while he had been gone, and he drafted four memos on different aspects of the Canal Zone negotiations. By eight o'clock he was exhausted. He decided he had produced enough for Hapgood to chew over for most of the next morning. On his way out he left the rough-draft memos on his secretary's desk with a note about the format she should use when she typed them.

Outside, on Pennsylvania Avenue, he realized that he was even more tired than he had thought, certainly too tired to cook himself dinner. And he had skipped lunch. He hailed a cab and told the cabby to take him to Duke Zeibert's.

He asked for a table in the back, where he wasn't likely to run into anyone he knew. He had a double martini and ordered a sirloin, rare, a baked potato, and a salad. At first, all he wanted to do was relax. He watched the waiters and the captains and the other diners. When he finished his martini, he considered ordering another one, but he asked for a beer instead.

He took a long swallow of beer and put the glass on the table next to the bottle. And his mood changed as if a switch had been thrown in his head.

He felt an aching need to talk to someone he could trust. To separate the conjecture from the facts. To try to make sense out of the whole mess. But there was no one who was not a threat, no one who did not have a personal axe to grind.

Then he remembered that he had promised Jill a report on his trip to Mexico. He would call her in the morning.

Once he had made the decision, he felt better. He ate his dinner; instead of coffee, he had a double cognac. Then he went home to sleep. In his dreams he was pursued by a broad, white shape that constantly seemed about to squash him. Once, when he stood his ground, the shape dissolved and metamorphosed into an eagle, which circled overhead watchfully. It had long steel talons, and behind its curved steel beak was Hapgood's face.

In the morning he called Jill. He got her assistant.

'She's gone for the rest of the week.'

'Is there anywhere I can reach her? It's important.'

'Well, they're at the Homestead, but she did say no one should bother her there unless it was really important.'

'Thanks, Ruthie. I appreciate it.'

He got the Homestead's number from information, called, and left a message for Jill to call him back as soon as she could.

As the morning progressed, Jensen got more and more impatient, and the call assumed a growing significance. By late morning he was sitting next to the phone, unable to do anything but wait for Jill to call. At intervals he got up and paced his office. When the phone rang, he jumped, answered it with a dry mouth and a racing heart. It was not Jill. That happened twice more. Each time his reaction was worse.

It was after lunch when she called.

'I just broke away for a minute, Harry. You're back?'

'Last night. I've got to see you. Even if it's only for a few minutes.'

'You've learned something.'

'I've learned a lot. Too much. When can I see you?'

'Let me look at my schedule.'

There was a rattling of paper in Jensen's receiver. He could hear her reading snatches of her schedule to herself. Her subvocalization had a strangely intimate quality to it.

'Can you come right down?' she asked.

'Now?'

'Well, I think I can sneak some free time before dinner. We have a couple of afternoon meetings, and then I'm supposed to have cocktails with some of the client's people, but maybe I can get away for a little while.'

'Anything is better than nothing. What time?'

'Oh, say six thirty. In the cocktail lounge.'

'Fine. Six thirty, then.'

He put a few papers in his attaché case, locked his desk and file cabinets, and left the office.

'I'm going to be out all afternoon,' he told his secretary. 'If Hapgood calls, tell him I went somewhere I could work in peace. I'll talk to him about those memos tomorrow.'

For the first time in months he was impatient with his lovingly maintained old drophead Jaguar as he went through the ritual of warming it up properly. But it repaid his patience by threading through Washington's afternoon traffic with speed and sureness, taking him quickly out of the city and into Virginia.

* * *

He arrived early. There was nothing for him to do but wait. He went for a walk.

It was a warm day for midwinter, part of what people farther north called the January thaw. There were even a few men out on the golf course. In the waning light of late afternoon Jensen watched them as they bent over their putters.

There was a bench in an arbor by the side of a path. Jensen sat down and enjoyed the cool green of the pines and firs and the sunset colors in the sky. He closed his eyes and tried not to think. A breeze ruffled his hair; it was not cold, but it had a wintry edge. When the wind grew cooler and he could not force himself to stay at peace any longer, he got up and walked slowly along the path toward the main house. He paused when it came into view; the lawn and the stately old building among the trees made a striking vista.

There was the sound of voices. A small group of people came up the path that ran around the side of the building – a half-dozen men clustered around a beautiful woman. Jensen got only a brief glimpse of the woman, but there was something about what he saw that gave him an impression not only of beauty but of a thorough enjoyment of life and people. As they turned to enter the building, the group parted and he had a better view of her, seen almost from behind, with the final light of sunset lingering in her long, pale hair. The tableau lasted a moment, then it dissolved into motion and laughter, and they were all through the door and inside.

Jensen was seized by a sudden restlessness. He wandered the paths around the main house, unable to shake off his vision of the woman's grace.

He looked at his watch. Five fifty-five. He went inside to the men's room, washed, ran a comb through his thick hair. He looked in the mirror at a strong jaw and clear, wide-set brown eyes – a woman had once told him his eyes alternated between being darkly mysterious and comfortingly trustworthy.

He walked slowly to the lounge; the Homestead was a place that by its very atmosphere discouraged hurrying.

A hostess approached him as he stood in the room's entrance letting his eyes adjust to the almost tangible darkness.

'Good evening, sir. Are you a member or a guest?' The lounge was a private club: There was no public drinking in Virginia.

'I'm meeting Miss Lazar.'

'Oh, yes. Are you Mr Jensen?'

'That's right.'

'Would you come with me, please? She's expecting you.'

Most of the room's tables were occupied. Small groups conversed in soft tones.

Toward the back of the room three men were sharing a table with a woman. She saw the hostess and said something to the men, who got up and left, reluctantly it seemed to Jensen, as he and the hostess arrived at the table.

'Here we are,' the hostess said.

Jill stood up to greet him. She wore a simple dress of soft, dark-blue cloth, set off by a many-stranded gold necklace; her hair, which she usually wore up, was combed out now, framing her face, gleaming with candlelight.

Jensen stared at her. She was the beautiful, vital woman he had seen outside.

He forced himself to smile, to say hello, to thank the hostess, as if everything were normal. He ordered a martini and he joined Jill in small talk about his trip to Mexico and the job that had brought her here to the Homestead. The conversation passed in a haze of unreality for him until he lifted his glass to his mouth and found that he had already finished his drink. He put it down, glanced at hers. It, too, was empty.

She said, 'I don't have too much time. Maybe we should take a walk.'

'Good idea.'

Outside they had privacy and – what was more important for Jensen – darkness. If it had not been dark, he thought, he would have been too distracted by her to be coherent about what he had learned from Touhy in Mexico. As it was, he got it out in reasonable order. He did not say anything about Hapgood's threat, though he was tempted to. Much as he still needed an ally, he wanted to know more about her reaction before he trusted her with his suspicions of Hapgood. Besides, he was not entirely sure those suspicions were anything more than his own paranoid imaginings. He said nothing about the Eagle Laundry.

Their way was lit by footlights along the path and occasionally by an old-fashioned streetlight. In these larger, overhead pools of light, he saw her again in the perspective of that earlier, captured moment.

He had known, in an abstract way, that his idea of her had been frozen long ago, and that it had been many years since he had seen her clearly, with the unclouded eyes of a stranger, but he was astonished at how much she had actually changed and how little of it he had recognized before. She held herself with more confidence; even her small motions were graceful, where once they had been awkward with uncontrolled energy. The more he saw, the more he was able to see, and the more accurate seemed his initial, distant impression of her, earlier that day, when she had been not his ex-wife but a beautiful stranger.

When he was finished telling her about Mexico, they walked for a while in silence. Then she stopped and turned to him.

'It's awful,' she said. 'It's so dirty, the way they're handling it. What can they have in mind? What prompts them to act like this?'

'I don't know.' He shook his head. 'I don't know. It doesn't make any sense to me, either.'

'It's even worse than we thought.'

'What do you mean?'

'Well . . . It's not only the CIA. You remember, I told you about those letters that Katzenbach sent, to Bill Moyers and to the Warren Commission?'

'Yes . . .'

'There's more. In the Justice Department. Not Katzenbach, though. J. Edgar Hoover.'

'Hoover!' Jensen said, and then he realized that it shouldn't be a surprise.

'He's up to the same kind of thing, then?' Jensen spoke with his voice even lower and more guarded than it had been when he was talking about Touhy. 'How do you know about it?'

She began to walk again, her head down.

'Ralph . . .' she began.

Jensen felt the night get colder. He put his hands in his jacket pockets.

'Ralph Norris. The one you met on New Year's. He . . . he's been interested in me for a long time, starting back when I was in the middle of my mad affair with Jack, and it was nice to have someone who would take me places and not ask questions and not push me too hard . . .'

Her voice trailed off and she walked again in silence.

'I don't know why I'm bothering you with all this.' She stopped and looked at him.

I don't, either, he thought, with a twinge of unexpected pain.

'The point is he was involved with the FBI's assassination investigation in an administrative way, and some of his friends were part of the operational side of it. At first he didn't want me to bother him about it. He said I was being silly. But after a while, when he saw how upset I was, he gave in a little. Maybe he's just humoring me now, but he's told me some interesting things.'

I wonder how many of us she's got working for her, Jensen thought sourly.

'I think you ought to talk to him.'

'What?'

'It would be much better if you could hear what he has to say yourself, instead of having me try to repeat it. And that way you could ask him questions if there was something you didn't understand or if you needed more information.'

She was right, Jensen saw, but that did not make him enthusiastic about the meeting. He could not see himself making polite conversation with Jill's current lover. It made him think of an old joke that offered alternate definitions of the French phrase *savoir faire*, based on how a husband and his wife's lover reacted to each other. He had to remind himself that he was no longer anyone's husband.

Touhy had hinted that the FBI might be part of an attempt to stifle the investigation. So far, Jensen only had the story from the CIA viewpoint. If he could learn how the FBI had seen it all, he would have a unique perspective on what had happened.

'Harry?'

'What?' He was startled. 'Oh. Sorry . . . I was just putting it all together . . . Sure. Of course I'll talk to your friend Ralph. It's a very good idea.'

'Good. I really think it'll help us if the two of you get together. I'm glad you agree.'

But he was not sure that she sounded glad.

Chapter Five

Following Jill's instructions precisely, he boarded the north-bound train just as it was leaving Union Station. He had no ticket.

The second car from the end – the one specified in his instructions – was grimy and badly maintained, like the rest of the train. Jensen put his suitcase in the overhead rack and sat by a window almost opaque with dirt; he watched a blurred and fragmentary line of buildings slide by.

When the conductor asked for his ticket, he said he wanted to go to New York. The conductor grumbled at him for not having bought the ticket in advance, but he took Jensen's money and he punched a one-way ticket.

Jensen settled back under the stub the conductor left to identify him as a paid, New York-bound passenger. He closed his eyes, but he did not sleep.

Just before Baltimore he got up, walked to the back end of the car, and stepped into the toilet as the train entered the switching yards outside the station.

The tiny, metal-walled room reeked of urine; he was glad he did not have to stay there long. When he heard the clang of the passenger car's doors being opened and the shuffle of people waiting on the platform, he slipped out of the toilet and got off the train, leaving the empty second-hand suitcase to make the rest of the trip alone.

A taxi took him to the Roger Smith Hotel, and from there another taxi took him to Johns Hopkins University. He wandered around the campus for a few minutes and then asked a passing student where he could find the administration building. The student's directions were vague; Jensen had to ask again. By the time he got there, he was running late, but the first student he asked directed him immediately to the student center.

The phone booth he had been told to use when he finished his excursion around the campus was occupied. Jensen fidgeted while he stood outside it, making sure the young girl on the phone was aware of his impatience. His antics did not seem to have any effect on her. She continued her conversation at her own speed, and when she was through she took her time picking up the change she had laid out on the ledge under the phone. Jensen was afraid that she was going to make another call, but she put the change into her purse, stuffed the purse and a small address book into the bag slung from her shoulder, and left the booth. She gave Jensen a brief, contemptuous glance as she walked by him.

He slid quickly into the booth and picked up the receiver, holding the hook down.

The phone rang almost at once. He let go of the hook in a convulsive reaction.

He took a deep breath and said, 'Novocaine.'

'Yellow?' A male voice.

'Blue.'

'Green.'

'Parrot.'

It was the agreed-upon sequence. Jensen had expected it to

74

feel contrived and awkward, but it was actually reassuring.

'Take a bus from the northwest corner of the campus to Druid Hill Park and go four stops more,' the voice on the other end told him. It was a soft voice, but it carried an undertone of asperity, like what he remembered of the few words he had heard Ralph Norris speak. The instructions were delivered with a steady rhythm that made no allowance for any response but total attention and complete recall. 'From the bus stop, walk two blocks south and then three blocks west. Use the left-hand sidewalk. You'll be met by a green car with Virginia plates. Don't leave the student center for ten minutes.'

Jensen went into the cafeteria and got himself a cup of coffee. He felt awkward among the clumps of students burdened with spiral-bound notebooks and heavy texts. He was reminded of Touhy on the university campus in Mexico City. From the way the students here looked at him – and avoided looking at him – Jensen guessed he was at least as out of place as Touhy had been.

After ten minutes he left the student center and crossed the campus to the northwest gate. The sky had darkened; while he was on the bus, it began to rain. He had no umbrella; carrying one would have called too much attention to him on his trip to the train's toilet.

It was still raining when he got off the bus, a cold, unpleasant drizzle that made him wish for snow. He walked the two blocks south, trying to look as if strolling in the winter rain without an umbrella or even a hat was the most natural thing in the world. He paused at the corners, waiting for the light to change and looking both ways before he stepped from the curb. He had become a very cautious pedestrian.

After he turned west he walked more quickly. Cold water

trickled from his hair down his neck and back. He wiped his face and pushed wet strands of hair back from his forehead. He was on a one-way street in a residential district. Small, old houses set close together. The front lawns were tiny; a few were neglected, but most were well kept. Every third house or so there was a cracked stone birdbath on the lawn or a gaudy plaster statue or a shrine to some stone-robed woman – a saint or the Virgin Mary.

At the end of the block a green sedan pulled past him, started to make a left turn, and stopped so that it was diagonal to the intersection, blocking the corner. Jensen could see the license plate just well enough to make out that the car was from Virginia. As he reached the car, its rear door opened. He got in and the car started at once. He was impressed by how smoothly it had been done. To a casual observer the car would barely have seemed to have stopped.

'Good trip?' Norris asked.

'Lousy.'

They said nothing more until Norris had put them on a highway leading out of the city.

'Sorry about all this.'

'It's all right,' Jensen said.

'It's touchy. Nothing against the Bureau, you understand, but the old man's been disciplining agents with a vengeance lately. Seventeen good men got it in the neck over the way the Oswald case was handled.'

Jensen thought of Touhy – 'good men' was what he had called the Cuban exiles who had been at the Bay of Pigs. A lot of rule breaking was being done by intelligence officers in the name of 'good men.'

He said, 'You don't have to convince me that security is important. I'm as glad to be doing it this way as you are.'

They drove for three quarters of an hour, most of it on the highway. Once, after they got off the highway, they took a complicated series of turns that Jensen assumed was designed to throw off anyone who might still be following them. They also confused Jensen thoroughly about where he was. The trip ended with a long, bumpy ride up to a big square stone farmhouse that looked like it had been there since before the Revolution.

The house was surprisingly well appointed – polished wood floors with tasteful rugs; period furniture, mostly reproductions, but some real antiques, Jensen thought. The drapes and wallpaper were new, but they were in the proper period style, and they looked like they had been chosen and installed with care. Jill was waiting for them in the front parlor.

Jensen stopped, trying not to see her the way he had at the Homestead.

'Hello, Harry.'

'Jill.'

She turned from him to greet the man who had come in behind him. Jensen glimpsed them embracing and kissing and walked across the room to stand by the oversize fieldstone fireplace. His clothes were soaked through; the heat of the fire felt good.

'Harry?' It was Jill. 'You want to dry off?'

'Thanks. Is there something I can put on?'

'Upstairs,' Norris said. 'There's a bathroom at the end of the hall. You'll find dry clothes in the bedroom next to it. They'll be big for you, but it's all there are.'

'Fine. I'll be right down.'

'No hurry. Coffee or tea?'

'Coffee.'

On his way upstairs Jensen thought about Norris – gray

77

hair, gray eyes, a gray suit, and a total absence of excess motion; at times he seemed almost immobile. But in spite of the grayness and the stillness, Jensen was instinctively wary of the FBI man: He was like a long fuse, one that would burn slowly and intently and for a long time.

Jensen brought his wet clothes downstairs with him and hung them over the back of a wooden chair in front of the fireplace. Jill came into the room carrying a tray with a coffee service on it. She put it down and sat on the couch across the coffee table from the easy chair Jensen had taken.

'I'm glad you're here,' she said.

'It was an interesting trip. I hope he's got something to say.'

She was about to pour a mug of coffee, but on Jensen's words she stopped, with the pot poised in the air.

'Don't worry, Harry. We're not wasting your precious time.' There was an unmistakable snap of anger in her voice. Norris came in and sat on the couch next to her. He waited to speak until everyone had coffee.

'You all right now?' he asked Jensen.

'I'm fine.'

'Good. Then let's get down to it.'

'All right. We're interested in the assassination. We think there's information that's not coming out. Jill said you could help. She thought we ought to talk about what's being suppressed.'

Norris nodded.

'I'm eager to hear what you have to say,' Jensen told him.

Norris gave his attention to his coffee mug. When he put it down, he patted Jill's knee, and she refilled the mug for him, adding milk and sugar. He smiled and again put his hand on her leg. Jensen wondered if the performance was for his benefit.

'First of all,' Norris said, 'you should know that we were warned about the assassination before it happened. If we had responded properly, we might have averted it.'

'You knew about it? In advance?'

'That's right. We had two separate warnings. They may or may not have been related to each other. One we got from the Miami PD. They had an informant who was talking to a white-supremacist agitator who was down in Florida to do some recruiting. The informant was wired, and he recorded a conversation involving an attempt on President Kennedy: Shooting him in a southern city, from a height, using a high-powered rifle that could be broken down or disguised to get it into a building undetected.'

'That's a precise description of the assassination.'

'Yes, it is.'

'What happened with that tip?'

'Miami picked it up on the seventh of November or so. The Florida AG's office relayed it to us and the Secret Service on the ninth.'

'And then what?'

'The Secret Service had prime responsibility. They were notified in New York and Washington. The Bureau left it up to them. The information I have is that they put some extra people on for Kennedy's trip to Florida on the eighteenth. Then, when nothing happened on that trip, my impression is that they decided it was a bad lead and dropped it.'

'You said a southern city. Dallas is a southern city.'

'Yes. I'd say so.'

'Then why didn't they—'

Norris shook his head. 'I have no idea. And it bothers me.' He broke off for a moment to look at Jill. He put his hand on hers where they rested in her lap and smiled at her. She smiled

79

back, a little stiffly, Jensen thought, and shifted on the couch. Norris took his hand away.

He went on: 'It bothers me largely because of the fact that we had a second warning. On November seventeenth there was a teletype transmission, over the Director's name, to all special agents in charge; the subject of that teletype was a threat to assassinate President Kennedy on his trip to Dallas on November twenty-second and twenty-third. Basically all it said was that the Bureau had received information that there was going to be an attempt in Dallas by a militant revolutionary group, and it asked all receiving offices to check with their informants – criminal, hate group, and racial – for confirmation or contradiction. I happened to see a copy of it when it was sent. I looked for it afterward, but it's not in the files.'

'But it should be.'

'It should.'

'Did anybody do anything about it when it was sent?'

'Not that I know of. That would be surprising enough by itself, but coming after the information from Miami, it's incredible. I've tried to find out if the two pieces of information were ever put together and if the Secret Service was ever told about the tip that was the subject of the teletype on the seventeenth.'

'And . . .'

'I have a lot less information than I'd like. This isn't a good time to be poking around the Bureau about the assassination. I told you, seventeen people have already been burned by it. And the Director's got a bug in his ear about the Warren Commission, too. As far as he's concerned, it's a slap in the face not to have the Bureau doing the investigation. If it came out now that we had this kind of warning *before* the assassination, it would embarrass the Bureau even more. And we can't let that happen. Never. So I can't talk to everybody there I'd like to. I even have to be careful who I'm seen with. That's why we're here.'

'I understand,' Jensen said. The calculus was a simple one: Hoover couldn't live forever, and a man as high in the Bureau as Norris had to be very circumspect, because any misstep he made now could hurt him badly in the shake-out that was inevitable once Hoover was gone.

Jensen settled back in his chair. The coffee and the fire were beginning to warm away the damp chill that had seeped into his body on the ride to the farmhouse.

'There's an agent in the Dallas field office whose name is Jim Hosty,' Norris said, 'and one of the interesting things about him is that his name and phone number and the license number of his car were found in Oswald's notebook when they arrested him. That hasn't come out yet, but I think it's bound to. It should cause a bit of a stir. After all, why should Oswald have an FBI agent's phone number?'

'It's a good question. Why did he?'

'The simplest reason I can think of is that Hosty was in charge of the internal security investigation of Oswald and his wife. That's one of the reasons our faces are so red about this. Oswald's been on our files since he defected in fifty-nine. The case was closed for a while, and it was Hosty who got it reopened. Then he was off it while Oswald was in New Orleans – we have file material on all Oswald's pro-Castro activities there – and he only picked it up again when we traced Oswald back to Dallas at the beginning of November.'

'Then Oswald knew him?'

'He sure did. And when Oswald was arrested, Hosty told a Dallas cop that we already knew about Oswald, that he was on some file of ours listing communist subversives. Not only that – he said Oswald had been in touch with foreign subversive agents within a couple of weeks before the assassination and the Bureau had information he was capable of assassinating the President. I haven't been able to find out what he was talking about, but that's apparently what he said, because Jesse Curry, the police chief down there, repeated it to the press a little later on; then Curry got a cable telling him to retract what he'd said, which he did later that day.'

'The cable was from?'

'The special agent in charge of the Dallas field office.'

'Oh.'

'After Hosty shot his mouth off to the cop, he showed up at Oswald's interrogation. As soon as he saw Hosty, Oswald started to shout and bang the table. He said Hosty had to leave because he had accosted his wife Marina and threatened her and wouldn't leave her alone, even though Oswald had told him to. And that brings us back to the notebook with Hosty's phone number and license number in it. It seems that about the twelfth of November, give or take a few days, Oswald showed up at the Dallas office asking for Hosty. Hosty wasn't there, so Oswald left a note. A note threatening something – maybe to blow up the office – if Hosty didn't leave Marina alone. Hosty didn't do anything about that note until after the assassination, when the special agent in charge discovered it and asked Hosty to write a memo on it. Then, immediately after Ruby killed Oswald, the Dallas office thought it would be the better part of valor to forget the whole incident. So Hosty destroyed the note and the memo. And now, as far as anyone is concerned, none of it ever happened.'

'How did you find out?'

'I put it together, here and there, after Jill first asked me to help her. But every bit of that story is getting buried, and it shouldn't be, because it's full of interesting implications. Like, what was Hosty talking about when he shot off his mouth to that cop? And why did they destroy that note of Oswald's? It could have been just one more attempt to keep the Bureau from being embarrassed, but that seems like a lousy reason to cover over something so important.'

'Christ, yes. Isn't there anything you can do?'

Norris shook his head. 'Things are very touchy right now.'

'But you do think the Dallas office knew enough to suspect Oswald, even without those two warnings you told me about.'

'Oh, yes. They should definitely have been watching him. There was even more information. We had cables from the CIA about his Mexico City trip. That should have been the clincher, as far as our keeping Oswald neutralized. One of the people he saw down there was a Soviet vice-consul named Kostikov. Now, in the first place, American citizens don't get in to see Soviet embassy officials in Mexico City very often. And on top of that, Kostikov is marked down as KGB. Not simple intelligence, either. One of the people I talked to at headquarters told me the best opinion was that Kostikov was from Department V – sabotage and assassination. When Oswald saw him in late September, the CIA let us know about it. On November twenty-second, their cables about it were sitting in somebody's "in" box in Washington, waiting to be read.'

'Still,' Jensen said, 'it could all be coincidence, sloppy procedure . . . just carelessness.'

Norris shrugged. 'Maybe.' He turned to Jill. 'Honey, didn't you say something about checking on dinner?'

She seemed startled. 'It's in the oven. I think it's still got a few minutes.'

Norris continued to look at her; there was a strained quality to his smile.

At first she returned his gaze, then something changed in her face, and she glanced down at her watch.

'Oh. It's later than I thought. I should go in and start the salad.'

Norris got up with her. As she turned toward the kitchen, he put his arm around her and leaned to kiss her. She moved her face so that the kiss landed on her cheek.

When she had left the room, Norris turned abruptly to Jensen.

'I don't know you, Jensen. All I know is that Jill says she trusts you. Even after you ran out on her . . . All right, never mind that. She trusts you. She says you're helping her determine what's behind all this confusion. That's enough for me. I'm sticking my neck way out by telling you the things I have. I don't know what light it sheds for you, but I hope it helps. The one thing I can tell you for sure is that these things are going to be buried. The public will never hear any of it, not as long as Hoover's alive and probably not after he's dead. And he's not going to let anybody breathe a word of it to the Warren Commission, either, not even in secret. If he had his way, nobody would say *anything* to the Warren Commission.'

Norris gave Jensen a drink and went into the kitchen to join Jill. Jensen stood by the fire, staring into the flames. He reflected that the simplest conclusion he could draw from what Norris had told him was that the Bureau had had enough information to prevent the assassination, but that in spite of that they had *allowed* it to happen. Nothing Norris had said indicated that it hadn't been intentional. No wonder Hoover wanted it all hidden behind a wall of silence, just like the others.

Jensen got a sudden mental picture of a political cartoon – the FBI, embodied in the power-obsessed form of J. Edgar Hoover, relaxing at his desk and smoking a cigar, ignoring Lee Harvey Oswald, who was standing behind him at the office window, aiming a rifle out and down at a passing motorcade.

Jensen had no difficulty believing in that image of things, and it made him furious. He welcomed the anger, because it obscured his annoyance at the way Norris was making such a point of being physical with Jill.

He turned away from the fire and began to pace restlessly. When his glass was empty, he found his way to the kitchen.

Watching Norris and Jill from the kitchen door, Jensen thought they looked very domestic together. Norris was stroking a carving knife on a sharpening steel while Jill stood next to him, spooning green beans from a saucepan into a serving bowl. A three-rib roast, richly brown and redolent, rested on a serving platter on top of the stove. On the counter next to it was a plate of baked potatoes and a full salad bowl. Jensen assumed they were all favorites of Norris's. As he remembered Jill's cooking, she liked to play with French and Italian recipes that she considered interesting. While they had been married, they had gone out to eat whenever they got a craving for plain meat and potatoes. Jill had said it was a waste of time and effort to cook such simple food, and restaurants got better meat and had better facilities for preparing it. In their early days they had been once-a-week customers at Duke Zeibert's.

Norris tested the knife, found it sharp enough, and put the sharpening steel in a drawer, then walked over to the roast. On his way by, he kissed the back of Jill's neck.

Turning with the knife and the platter of beef, Norris stopped, surprised to see Jensen standing in the doorway.

'Oh,' he said. 'Need a fresh drink?'

'I'm fine,' Jensen said.

'Good. Dinner's ready. We ought to go into the dining room.'

By tacit agreement dinner was a time for small talk, not business. The meal passed in relative silence. Jensen found there was very little he wanted to say to Norris, and the FBI man's constant attention to Jill made any conversation between himself and Jill seem impossible.

After they had eaten, Jill cleared the table and went into the kitchen. Norris and Jensen lingered at the table over brandy and coffee. Norris smoked a long black cigar while he talked about Jack Ruby.

'We used him several times. In fifty-nine, when he started with us, he was working for the Dallas police as well. One of the things that made him interesting to us as an informant was his long history with organized labor and organized crime. He knew Jimmy Hoffa, for instance. And he had a friend named McWillie who ran the Tropicana casino in Havana. In fact, Ruby took a couple of trips to Cuba in fifty-nine, after the revolution, to see McWillie. The casinos were still open then. And they were still smuggling heroin. Ruby was supposed to be pretty well up on the heroin business; he may not have been directly involved, but he seems to have known the operation and some of the people. And he knew a lot of Mafia big shots.'

'Which big shots?'

'Sam Giancana, probably. And Johnny Roselli. I don't know who else.'

It fit with what was already in the back of Jensen's mind. He would have to check a few old rumors and talk to people with more information, but he was sure there was a connection between Giancana and Roselli and Cuba and the CIA. The two Mafiosi were almost certainly the ones who were involved in the plots to assassinate Castro. And now Norris was adding Jack Ruby to the picture, with connections of his own to Cuba and Roselli and Giancana.

Jensen suddenly had the feeling that whatever road he took next, it was going to circle back in this same direction.

Jill finished in the kitchen, and they all went back into the parlor for a final cup of coffee.

'This whole thing has been a mess from the very beginning,' Norris said. 'But bad as it is, it's not part of my job to worry about it, and normally I'd have let the parts of it I saw go by without doing anything. But Jill was so upset about the assassination . . .'

He paused to put his arm around her and squeeze her shoulder. Then he leaned forward, elbows on his knees, his eyes intent on Jensen's.

'All right. Jill asked me for help, so I gave it. Now, I'd just as soon it ended right here. If you absolutely have to have some follow-up, life or death, okay, I'll see if I can do anything. For Jill's sake. And you'll have to deal with me through her.'

He took Jill's hand, squeezed it.

Jensen stood up. 'Thanks,' he said. 'I appreciate your help.'

Jill drove him to the Towson airport, where he could get a local feeder flight to Washington. They rode in silence at first. Jensen felt unaccountably awkward being alone with her.

'What do you think?' she asked him after they had gone a few miles.

'About?'

'What Ralph was saying.'

'That business about Oswald's talking to the KGB sabotage-and-assassination man in Mexico City – that's intriguing. I suppose it's possible that the Soviets were dealing with Oswald, helping him in some way without knowing precisely who the Cubans were going to have him assassinate.'

'Why without knowing?'

'Because basically I agree with the ambassador in Mexico City. I think the Russians are too smart to get involved with anything like assassinating an American President.'

They fell silent again.

He looked at her. She was intent on her driving; the Maryland countryside streamed past her profile, framed in the car window. His eyes traced the line of her brow, the slightly curved bridge of her nose, the red softness of her lips, her gracefully rounded chin, the strong, clear line of her jaw that ran back to a slim neck.

A woman like that, Jensen thought – beautiful, intelligent, talented – should not have to put up with the kind of childishly possessive demonstration that Norris had inflicted on her.

Chapter Six

Jensen locked the apartment door, hung his coat in the entrance hall closet, and walked down the long hall to the kitchen. He was weary: The long, complex trip to Norris's safe house and the emotional strain of their *conférence à trois* had sapped his energy completely. He flipped on the overhead light and opened the refrigerator. Stopped.

Something was wrong. He closed the refrigerator and turned around slowly, letting his eyes scan the room. He let his uneasiness carry him along, drifting toward the countertop near the sink, feeling the sense of wrongness grow, then wane as he passed the sink. It was like the old finding game of his childhood – he could tell when he was getting hot or getting cold. He ended up standing at the counter staring blankly at the gray French-mustard crock full of wooden cooking spoons and spatulas, the row of spice and condiment jars, the cannisters of flour and sugar and coffee. The spice jars were an idea he had picked up from Jill; they were larger than the usual spice jars, and more fragile. He didn't use them much, but they dressed up the kitchen, and when he cooked they made him feel like he was doing something significant.

He did not know how long he stared blankly at them before the word *cinnamon* popped into his head. He focused sharply on the spice jars. Allspice, basil, bay leaves, cloves, cumin . . . Bay leaves, cloves. No cinnamon. And at the edge of the Formica, where the metal beading ran around it, there was a faint powdering of brown dust. He tore a piece of paper towel from the roll, dampened it, and ran it back and forth in the joint of Formica and stainless-steel edging. It came away with a thin brown line on it. He touched it to his tongue. Cinnamon.

He stood there, looking around the kitchen, panic warring in his mind with perplexity. The cinnamon jar was gone. Broken, presumably, and cleaned up almost perfectly. He brought his foot down on the pedal of the wastebasket, and its silver lid swung up. No broken cinnamon jar; just what looked like his own garbage. Under the sink the paper bags he kept to line the wastebasket seemed undisturbed.

But someone had been there. Someone had broken the cinnamon jar and gone to a lot of trouble to cover up the traces.

It could have been the cleaning lady, he told himself. She had been there two days before, and it was possible that it had happened then and he had not noticed it until now.

That had to be it. He could not make himself accept the notion of someone – he visualized him as thick-bodied and dressed in dark clothes, with skintight black gloves – skulking around the kitchen, looking for secret documents under the ice cube tray and in other standard hiding places, breaking a spice jar, scrubbing cinnamon off the countertop, and carrying the garbage out with him when he left.

Something glistened on the dark-red tile of the floor. He bent and pressed his finger to it. A small shard of glass.

He stood in the living room doorway wondering what had

been disturbed here, what the intruder had handled, gone through, read.

The whole room felt soiled to him. Even if he found nothing out of place here, he would be convinced that his home had been violated. The very air seemed to bear witness, as if it had been bruised by the searcher's moving through it.

He went to the old rolltop desk in the corner of the living room and went through its drawers and pigeonholes. Everything was as he had left it, with very few exceptions. If not for the broken cinnamon jar, he would never have noticed that some of his papers were piled more neatly than he had left them, and some were slightly out of order.

There was no doubt in his mind what the intruder had been after. He sat at the desk, paging through the slim looseleaf notebook that held the notes he had made on the assassination. Almost all of what he had learned so far was there – Mexico City, George Hammond, the second trip to Mexico City. And his tentative conclusions.

He closed the notebook and put it away, wondering what the intruder had made of it, and who he was. Then, alarmed, he opened the drawer and took the notebook out again. He reread carefully the early pages and the last few pages.

When he replaced the book in the drawer, he was very relieved. There was no hint of Jill's involvement, and there was no explicit reference to Touhy in his description of the second trip to Mexico. Whoever had read it might be able to deduce Touhy's identity from the facts listed on the final page, but Jensen was almost certain that no one could identify Jill from what was there, even his notes on Katzenbach and the rest of the things she had told him.

It was bad enough, Jensen thought, that he was haunted by

the Eagle Laundry; he did not want to add anyone more to
their list.

It was not until he got up the next morning that he
considered the possibility that his apartment might have been
searched by someone other than the Eagle Laundry.

It was a bad morning all around. He read the reports
and memoranda that had accumulated in his office 'in' tray,
but the words did not register. He kept seeing fantasy
images of someone searching his apartment. And the white
laundry truck. He was confused about what was happening
to him. If the near-miss with the laundry truck had been
a murder attempt, why hadn't the laundry truck tried again?
Would he be a target again – if it was again – because of
what the searcher had found in his apartment? Before the
break-in he had been able to convince himself, intermit-
tently, that the incident on Wisconsin Avenue had been
an accident. Now he could no longer afford such com-
placency. It was not enough to change the locks on his doors.
For his own protection, if for no other reason, it was time to
share his knowledge of the anomalies surrounding the
assassination.

He pulled his copy of the Federal Directory from the shelf
and found the phone number of Alexander Thomas. Judge
Alexander Thomas of the Eighth Circuit, United States Court
of Appeals.

After law school Jensen had been Alex Thomas's law clerk.
Then, Thomas had still been in the federal district court in Los
Angeles; his appointment to the Court of Appeals had not
come until 1960, as Eisenhower was on his way out. Thomas
had been a fiercely independent and iconoclastic jurist, in
some ways years ahead of his time. But even the law students

who were drawn by his brilliance to apply for a clerkship had been cowed by his reputation as a man who ate law clerks for breakfast. Thomas's reputation was well deserved, but Jensen had done a hard tour in the Marines between college and law school, and he was not intimidated. By the time his year of clerking was over, he and Thomas had come to understand each other and to work together in a way that felt to Jensen very much like friendship.

Jensen was lucky. He got through to the judge on his first try.

'Harry Jensen?' Thomas's voice was thin and high-pitched, but in spite of that he had the knack of making it sound gruff. 'Not the Harry Jensen who used to pretend he was a law clerk?'

'How are you, Judge Thomas?'

'You didn't call me from Washington to ask that.'

'No . . .'

'Well, get on with it, boy. I have a conference to get back to.'

'It's not an easy thing to talk about on the phone.' Jensen took a long breath. He had worked all this out before he made the call. There was a page of notes on his desk, but he was still having trouble getting started.

'You want to ask me a favor,' Thomas prodded.

'No. I . . . Well, yes, I do.'

'Good. That's a first step. It's something ethical, I presume.'

'I need to talk to Earl Warren.'

'Then why did you call me? I would have thought you could tell one judge from another.'

Jensen smiled. Still the same old Alex Thomas.

'I have information about the Kennedy assassination. It's information I'm more or less sure Warren himself is not getting, and it's vital to his investigation. That's why I called you.'

'You were never too coherent, Harry, but I'm afraid this is beyond even your usual obscurity.'

Jensen started to flare up, ignited for the first time in years by the judge's obstinacy. Then he saw that Thomas was right – he had to insist on a specific request from Jensen; the judge was in no position to volunteer aid.

Jensen said, 'I'm not sure I can get through to the Chief Justice directly myself, and the information I have for him is extremely sensitive. Possibly dangerous. A friend of mine who was involved in some of it was killed. I think an attempt was made on my life. And my apartment was searched. I'm afraid to take the risk of being sidetracked to a committee staff member when I try to talk to Mr Warren. This information has to be put directly into the right hands, or it may never get there at all. If you could call the Chief Justice and impress on him the importance of what I have to tell him, you'd be doing me a real favor. And I think you'd be doing the country a favor, too.'

This time Thomas had no quick, acerbic response. After a tense pause, he asked, 'You're convinced of how important this is?'

'Absolutely.'

'All right, Harry. I'll see what I can do for you.'

He called back a half hour later.

'Harry . . . It would be a lot easier, you know, if you would talk to one of the staff people.'

'I can't take the chance.'

'Maybe if you can explain why, I can make the Chief Justice understand. I understand your feelings, about having your apartment searched and the rest, but – secondhand – it sounds very much like a case of paranoia, I'm afraid.'

'You spoke to him, then?'

'Yes. I did as well as I could, with what you'd told me. Now you'll have to give me something new to say, if I'm going to get anywhere calling him back.'

Jensen thought about what to do. He was tempted to fly to California so he could lay it all out for Thomas in person, but it seemed a high price to pay to avoid the possibility that his phone was tapped.

He said, 'I'm worried about talking on the phone. I hate to let any more time pass, but the best answer I can think of is to write you a letter. If there's a way we can keep it from being opened by a secretary . . .'

'Put your letter in a sealed envelope with my name on it. Then put that in another envelope and mail it to my sister in San Mateo.' He gave Jensen the address. 'Do your best to mail it today if you're really worried about security. In case whoever you're worried about tries to intercept it.'

Jensen began to write as soon as he had hung up the phone.

Jensen had a nervous week waiting for a reply from Judge Thomas. He spent all his time either at home or at the office, and when he was out, he was careful about where he went and how he crossed the street. Frequently, he found himself looking over his shoulder.

Once, on his way back to the office after lunch, he thought he spotted someone following him. He had stopped briefly to look in a bookstore window, and he caught a glimpse of a burly, medium-height man in a gray topcoat looking in another window about two stores down. Then, waiting for a light to change a few blocks from the bookstore, Jensen glimpsed him again, toward the back of the clump of people waiting on the corner with him. Across the street Jensen walked faster, threading his way among the bureaucrats and secretaries on their way back to work. Halfway along the block he turned abruptly and ducked into a shop.

A silver-haired woman, made up heavily but skillfully, approached him.

'Yes, sir? Can we help you?'

Jensen looked around. It was a custom-made lingerie shop. The public part of the shop was small – he had an impression of dark-blue carpeting and matching velvet chairs, discreet manikins in complex corsets and many-layered nightgowns. A few bewildered women were staring at him.

'I'm sorry. I must have the wrong place.' Turning toward the door. 'Sorry to bother you.'

'Not at all, sir,' the silver-haired woman said to his back. 'Have a pleasant day.'

Outside, he did not see the burly man in the gray coat. He turned back the way he had come and retraced his steps for two blocks before turning again and heading for the office.

Passing a store window set diagonally to the street, he saw the reflection of someone behind him who had a familiar bulk and stride. He whirled. It was not the same man.

By the time he left the office that day, he was almost sure he had only imagined that the man in the gray coat had been following him.

Judge Thomas called him at home.

'Sorry to take so long, Harry, but it's been a busy week.'

'That's all right. I'm glad to hear from you. Did you get my letter?'

'Yes, I did, and I understand now why you're so concerned.'

'Did you reach the Chief Justice?'

A pause. Then, awkwardly, 'Yes, I did. And I did my best to convey your concern to him. I even read him parts of your letter.'

'And?'

'He was impressed, I think. He certainly seemed to want to know more. But he wouldn't agree to see you personally. He said they had already established staff priorities for receiving this kind of information, and the most he could do by way of making an exception would be to have you go directly to the senior staff attorney responsible for the appropriate part of the investigation.'

'For Christ's sake!' Jensen could not hold back the exclamation. He took a deep breath. 'Excuse me. I'm sure you did what you could, and I'm grateful for it. But I can't do it that way. I've got to speak to the Chief Justice, or if not him then at least the commission's chief counsel.'

'I'm sorry, Harry. He was very definite about maintaining staff procedures. There are a lot of people who would prefer to go straight to the top with their information. He feels he can't afford to set a precedent.'

'It's not a question of starting at the top. I said the first time we talked that I thought my life might be in danger. I still do. I think I'm being followed now, too. It would be suicidal for me to talk to the wrong people at this point. It's not just that a staff member could be stopped from moving the information to where it could do some good. I have to take for granted that both the FBI and the CIA have people planted on the

Commission staff. Whoever is behind the attempt to suppress all this has a lot of clout. They have to be monitoring things very closely if they don't want them to get out of hand. If I spoke to someone on the staff, no matter how high up he was, I'd have no way of knowing what other masters he was serving.'

'I can't fault your reasoning, Harry. I only wish I could do more for you, but I'm afraid this approach is a dead end. If you can't speak to Warren, though, and you can't, then what else will you do?'

'I'm not sure. I wanted to take it through the appropriate channels, but that's obviously not going to work. I'll have to find another way.'

The other way that suggested itself to him was the press, and that brought his mind back to Jill. Feeding things to the press was what she did every day; she would have the right contacts, and she would know who was the best person to approach.

Since the meeting with Norris he had been trying to avoid thinking about her, but she was in his mind continually. Most often he saw her as she had been at the Homestead: beautiful, graceful, cool. And he knew the warmth that lay behind that coolness.

He could remember one day with particular clarity. He had come home unexpectedly late from a meeting of the presidential transition staff subgroup that eventually grew into the National Security Advisory Staff, and she had been livid.

'Damn it, Harry, you could have called,' she said when he came into the kitchen.

'There wasn't time.'

She lifted the cover of an enameled cast-iron dutch oven and slammed it back down, then stalked into the living room. 'Next time you can come home and burn your own stew.'

He followed her. 'We're not arguing about a ruined dinner . . .'

She stopped and faced him. 'No, you're damn right we're not. We're arguing about whether you're going to keep on acting as if you're on the verge of ruling the world and you expect me to sit around the house and wait for you until all hours of the night while you play your silly games.'

'Games! We're talking about the security of the country.'

'You see what I mean?'

'The man was elected President. He needs a staff.'

'Sure he does. But don't you see? Just because you went to college with his brothers, sort of, and worked on the campaign . . . Harry, you're no expert on foreign affairs.'

'Damn it, Jill, I have enough trouble feeling like I belong there—'

'That's just it. You're a good lawyer. You could have a brilliant future.'

He turned away from her and went to stand by the garden door, looking out. 'Make plenty of money, you mean. And have a dull, meaningless career that wouldn't interfere with what you want to do.'

He turned back and found her standing next to him, furious. She swung. He caught her wrist, and when she brought her other hand around in a roundhouse blow, he caught that wrist, too. They stood there, eyes locked, almost immobile, struggling. He held tightly to her wrists as she tried to pull them away. She began to pant with exertion and frustration.

And then everything changed. The way she held her body softened, and her breathing became deeper and slower. Her tongue flicked over her lips. She saw him register the change in her; he relaxed slightly. They clung to each other, panting, grasping, stroking, kissing wildly.

They sank to the floor. Their first, frenzied embraces ebbed. The pace slowed. Their passion was no less intense, but it proceeded as if in slow motion or a dream. They explored each other thoroughly, without any pressure to consummate their pleasure. And when they finally did, it was with effortlessly matched rhythms, and it reverberated in both of them for long, voluptuous minutes.

They disengaged, and she stood up and dressed slowly. He watched her.

'I guess I should be more tactful,' she said. 'Or wait to talk about it until I'm not so mad.'

'I guess.'

'But the problem is, it's the truth. They're paying you off for your work and your loyalty, and I'm not saying it's not a good job, but I don't see any future in it for you. It worries me.'

'I'm impressed with your great confidence in me.'

'Harry, it's not that, and you know it. I think you deserve the best, and I don't want to see you selling your birthright for a bowl of porridge.'

He pulled his pants on savagely, suddenly uncomfortable being naked.

'It couldn't be,' he challenged, 'that you'd rather I was just a lawyer because then you wouldn't have any conflict-of-interest problems to worry about and you could keep your job?'

'Harry, for Christ's sake!' She stalked back into the kitchen.

They ate their warmed-over stew in silence.

Bitter as the memory was, it still had the power to arouse him, even at a distance of three years. Until recently almost all of his memories of her had affected him that way. He had buried most of the bad ones in self-defense, cherishing a few images of their better moments. Now, though, Norris was in his mind, too, massive and gray and silent, watching over each image of Jill with the alert intensity of a Secret Service man guarding a President.

Jensen made himself a double martini and finished half of it before he picked up the telephone.

'Earl Warren won't see me,' he told Jill.

'That's awful. Are you sure?'

'No,' he said, his anxiety and disappointment flashing into anger. 'I made it up to see how you'd react.'

'Well, I think it's lousy. Why won't he see you?'

'It's against the rules. He doesn't want to set a precedent.'

'What are you going to do now?'

Jensen had some more of his martini. 'The next step is up to you. I want to go to the press.'

'Is that wise?'

'Wise?' His temper flared again. 'I don't know if anything's wise. I don't know what else to do. I need your contacts.'

'I think we ought to consider what we're doing before we jump into it.' Her tone was severe, almost scolding.

'Look, Jill, I just finished trying to reach the Chief Justice of the United States through Alex Thomas, who's on the Court of Appeals these days, in case you don't remember, and besides that I damn near lost my job on account of this business. So far all you've done is pump one of your lovers for a little information.'

'Nobody asked you to put your job in danger.' Her voice was crisp and curt in my ear. 'If you can't tell how your own boss is going to react to what you do, don't blame me.'

'Fine. And I won't blame you for the truck that almost ran me down, either.'

There was a silence on the line, and then she said, very evenly, 'When did that happen?'

'Last month. Not long after George Hammond was killed.'

'Why didn't you tell me?'

'I didn't want to worry you . . . That's a laugh, isn't it? All you're worried about is protecting your precious contacts.'

'I'm sorry, Harry. You're right.' Her emotions were carefully contained. He could read nothing in her voice. 'But I didn't know . . .'

'That's not good enough, Jill. If your willingness to use your contacts depends on people trying to kill me—'

'For God's sake, Harry, of course it doesn't.' She cut herself short, and when she resumed, it was in a softer tone. 'Look, I'm sorry. It's been a long day, and you came on kind of sarcastic, so I just lashed out at you automatically. It's those shitty old reflexes at work again. Anyway, I didn't mean to snap at you. Can we start over?'

'Sure. Where do you want to start over from?'

'About four years ago – before we started to hurt each other so much,' she said and then rushed ahead: 'How about talking to Stewart Alsop? He might be able to do something with this.'

'He'd be fine. He's right at the top of my list of possibilities, in fact, right under his brother Joe and Drew Pearson.'

'I think Stewart would be as good as either of the others. He's more solid, in a way. Besides, I know Stewart. I'm sure I could get him to talk to you.'

'How soon can you set it up?'

'I'll call him in the morning and I'll get back to you as soon as I know anything.'

'Good. I'll talk to you tomorrow, then.'

'Okay. And Harry, I don't want to fight with you anymore. Let's try to be nice to each other, all right?'

'Sure. I think we've earned it by now.'

Jill had no trouble arranging a meeting between Jensen and Stewart Alsop. It was agreed that they would meet for lunch at a place of Jensen's choice.

He left his office at eleven thirty and took a cab to National Airport, where he went to the Hertz counter. He refused the first car they gave him and asked for one that had just come in. He watched while they brushed it out and refilled the gas tank. He drove back to the city, on the way interrupting his trip twice to make complete four-direction circuits of highway cloverleafs that lay along his route.

When he picked up Alsop outside the French embassy, he turned around and drove back out to the airport. On the way he stopped at a Howard Johnson's for coffee and sandwiches to go.

They sat in the car in the back of a crowded airport parking lot. The weather was cold, and it was overcast; not long after they parked it began to rain. The car's windows steamed up quickly.

'I understand you have some information for me,' Alsop said. 'Considering what we're going through, I certainly hope it's important.'

'It's important,' Jensen said. He handed Alsop a sandwich and unwrapped his own. While they ate, Jensen told Alsop what he had seen and heard in Mexico City and Washington and Baltimore, and what had happened to him and to George Hammond.

'That's quite a story.'

Bitterly: 'That's what they all say.'

'Now, son, I can understand your frustration, but don't take it out on me. Remember, you're supposed to be asking my help.'

'I am asking your help. I'm asking you to get this information before the American people so it can't be covered up any more.'

'I can understand that, too. Unfortunately, I'm afraid it's not quite that simple.' He sipped some coffee. 'There are several things that have to be considered. First, this is very sensitive material, and it has to be handled carefully. I suspect there are some important preliminary steps you haven't taken yet.'

'Like what?'

Alsop smiled slightly. The expression broadened his nose and deepened the creases that defined his cheeks, but it did not touch his eyes. 'Like – for instance, do you know how much of this information the Warren Commission has already developed?'

'I know that some people are trying their best to keep part of it, at least, from ever reaching the Commission.'

'Perhaps they are. But *you* have the information. Can you be sure the Commission is not as resourceful or even as lucky as you are?' He held up his hand to keep Jensen from answering. 'The possibility certainly exists that they have some or all of this information, you'll have to admit that. So it becomes important to consider what the Commission would do with such information if it indeed had it. And let me make clear that I am not eager to interfere with the work of the Commission by releasing potentially controversial information prematurely.'

He shifted his body, putting a knee up on the bench seat so

that he could face Jensen more directly. 'There's another problem, not unrelated. There's been a vast amount of publicity about this murder and about this murderer. Every manner of crackpot has emerged from hibernation to shower us with nut theories. Some of it is harmless enough – I don't suppose anyone is hurt by pointing out the similarities and parallels between Kennedy's assassination and Abraham Lincoln's. But it isn't quite so harmless when people speculate, for instance, on the fact that Richard Nixon was in Dallas on the morning of the assassination. Poor Mr Nixon certainly had reason to wish John Kennedy dead several times over. But an actual murder theory based on his presence in Dallas on the fateful morning is frivolous at best, and at worst it's absolutely pernicious.

'Please understand me. I don't mean to imply that your story is as tenuous as the idea that Richard Nixon might have been involved in murdering John Kennedy. I merely mean to make the point that what you have told me so far is insufficient basis for me to act on.'

He paused to finish his coffee and put the empty cup into their bag of garbage. He brushed some crumbs from his trousers.

'When my brother and I were doing our column together,' he resumed, 'we had a rule that, as far as possible, we should get our news directly, in person. Get out and see it firsthand and ask the questions yourself, that was our motto. We went all over the world following that rule. The Malayan jungle; Saigon; Versailles; Ohio; various places in Russia. Granted, one can't always get the story totally firsthand. At this point I don't expect to be able to witness the Kennedy assassination myself, for instance. But – especially for that reason – I would want to verify a lot of what you said by firsthand inquiry.'

'Fine. That should be possible,' Jensen told him. 'It'll take some persuading, but I think I can get somebody from the CIA to talk to you.'

'That's good, for a start, but it's nowhere near enough. There's the ambassador in Mexico City to be considered, and the Señorita Duran you mentioned, and Special Agent Hosty, to name just a few. And I would want to find someone else in the FBI who had seen those cables warning of the assassination before they disappeared. Even a cipher clerk would do, as long as I could talk to someone about them. Now, the point I'm making is that to verify your story would involve a tremendous amount of work.'

Jensen nodded unhappily. It was clear where the conversation was heading.

'Let me reiterate, I *am* troubled by what you've told me,' Alsop said. 'The foreign threat to this country has always been a central concern of mine, as I'm sure you know. But you haven't given me information that's specific enough and well enough supported for me to do anything with, even if I were to have it all verified quite carefully. We need something more solid. If you could bring me more conclusive evidence of Cuban involvement or of a government attempt to suppress evidence, then I might be able to help you. Otherwise, and until then, I'm afraid, in all good conscience, there's nothing I can do.'

At first Jill didn't want to meet him at his apartment. Then she called and said she'd changed her mind.

He cooked a simple dinner for them: cheese and French bread, herb omelets, rice, and a good Burgundy to go with it all, then a light salad and what was left of the cheese and bread. Port. Coffee.

'You've become quite the bachelor, haven't you?' she said toward the end of the meal.

'I suppose,' he acknowledged. 'I don't think of it that way.'

'Well, let me tell you, Harry. You've become quite the bachelor.'

There were two white candles on the table. Their fragile orange flames brought out the highlights in her hair and gave it the look of red gold. It fell loosely to her shoulders, framing her face. She wore the same dark-blue dress she'd had on the night they met at the Homestead.

'And what about you?' he asked. 'I've been trying not to notice it, but divorce seems to agree with you. You're more beautiful than ever.'

'You were always good at saying the right thing.'

He smiled. 'In this case it doesn't take much insight. You really are stunning.'

She reached across the table for his hand. 'You've changed, too, you know. You're . . . stronger. More confident. Not so frantic. I like you this way.'

For a moment their eyes held each other's, then she looked away and drew her hand back.

'Maybe we should get down to business,' she said.

'Maybe we should.'

'Alsop won't help?'

'That's how it adds up. He said he would try if I could give him some stronger information first. I don't know what to say about that. I thought I had plenty right now.'

'That's what I would have said.'

'Is there anyone else you know we can go to?'

She thought. 'Nobody at that level. These days I'm much more a lobbyist than a PR lady, so I don't have as much contact with the press as I used to. There are people I could call, but it wouldn't be much better than your going to them cold.'

'That s no good. It's too dangerous.' He shook his head. 'So that's it, then. We're out of contacts.'

'I guess we are. Strong ones, at least.'

'Damn!' Jensen poured second cups of coffee for both of them. 'More port?'

She hesitated. 'Sure. Why not?'

They sat at the table with their coffee and port and nothing to say.

'It's really shitty, isn't it?' she commented after a while.

'Yeah. Shitty is the word for it.'

There was another long silence.

'We can't just let it go,' she said.

'No. But like I said, I don't want to go to anybody cold, and if I go looking for more conclusive evidence, the way Alsop wants me to, it means sticking my neck way out.'

She touched his hand again. 'Did they really try to kill you?'

'I wish I knew. That goddamned truck came so close to me, I could have been killed outright . . . but it may have been an accident.'

'Like the accident that killed George Hammond.'

He picked up his port glass and rolled it back and forth between his palms.

'Someone's been following me lately. And the apartment's been searched.'

'Harry!'

'Yeah. Well . . . It's all part of the game, I guess.'

'What are we going to do?'

'I wish I knew, Jill. I really wish I knew.'

He stood up.

She stood up and moved toward him, and then they were in each other's arms.

'It's a lousy world,' she said into his shoulder.

He could not keep his hands still. They moved over her hair, her shoulders, her back. She pressed herself to him, clung to him for support and comfort.

'Harry, Harry, Harry,' she whispered.

His cheek rubbed her head; she moved, lifted her face.

He kissed her.

They broke free and stepped back, their hands intertwined, staring at each other. Without a word, he released one of her hands, turned, and led her down the hall to the bedroom.

Her eyes were large in the semidarkness. She stood immobile while he unbuttoned the top of her dress and pushed it back from her shoulders. He kissed the hollows over her collarbone and the muscles that ran between her neck and her shoulders. She shivered.

He drew the dress upward; she raised her arms so that he could pull it off. She was still staring at him, big-eyed and mute. Moonlight from the window glistened on her skin, turning it to silvery velvet. He kissed the base of her throat and the place where her breasts swelled together at the top of her brassiere. Her navel. He pushed her half-slip down, and she stepped out of it.

He took off his own clothes, never letting his eyes leave her. Then he pulled her to him, felt her firm softness along the length of his body. Her arms went around him. He could feel the heat at her center. He pulled her to the bed and took off the rest of her clothes.

Their coupling was a combination of sweet tenderness and savagery. As he entered her, he felt a flash of the old anger and frustration: A kind of elemental revenge was combined with his lust.

Her ferocity matched his own. Her body rose to meet him again and again. Her nails raked his back and his buttocks; her teeth sank into the thick cord of muscle beside his neck.

His hands roamed over her skin; it felt impossibly smooth and vibrant. Her smell and her heat filled his consciousness, and in the constant rhythm he lost all sense of time and place. There was nothing in his universe but Jill.

They cried out together, and still they kept pounding at each other, driven by something even more fundamental than their sexuality. Incoherent noises spilled from their mouths.

Finally they were quiet. They lay in each other's arms.

Later, still intertwined, they talked.

'That felt good,' she said. 'Like the old days. The good old days.'

He traced a forefinger along her cheek. 'Better,' he said.

She raised herself on one elbow and looked down into his eyes. 'Harry, what are you going to do? I'm sorry I ever got you into this.'

'You didn't know.' He was silent for a moment. 'Besides, there's more to it now. George Hammond. And not just that. Somebody thinks I'm important enough to kill, and I don't know why. I'm not even sure who. And I've got to find out. However I got into this, it's my fight now. I need to find the truth for my own good.'

'But it's dangerous.'

He looked at her.

'Yes, it's dangerous,' he conceded. 'But it's not going to get any better unless I do something about it.'

'But what?'

'Ah. That's the question. The only place I can think to go

right now is to the Cubans. The people Touhy wanted me to talk to.'

'The anti-Castro people?'

'Yes. The old soldiers.'

'But how can they help? It's Castro you want to know about.'

'They know what's doing in Cuba. They may not have direct information about the assassination, but I think they'll be able to confirm some of the things we already know. Or think we know.'

'That means going to Florida.'

'Eventually. But I think I'll start in New Orleans. There's a fair-sized Cuban community there, too, including my best friend from my Bay of Pigs days. I've got some vacation days coming. Hapgood'll kick a little at the timing, but there's nothing he can do if I insist.'

She moved her leg; he slipped out of her. They both groaned in disappointment. She reached down to touch him, then changed her position on the bed and took him in her mouth. He reached out for her and brought her closer, bent his head toward her.

The second time they were gentler than the first, but no less eager.

Chapter Seven

The bell attached to the top of the door tinkled lightly when Jensen walked into the shop.

Misty daylight suffused the broad, shallow room and glowed in highlights on cut-glass bowls and the richly carved dark wood of antique furniture. The shop was so densely filled that Jensen wondered how the proprietor or the customers could get around well enough for anything to be sold. There was no one there, but he could hear sounds from a back room: occasional short comments in masculine voices, an exclamatory laugh.

His eye fell on a large oval glass bowl. It was a dark ruby color except where an ornate design had been cut into it deeply; there the glass was clear. He picked it up; it was heavier than he had expected.

'You want antiques, *señor*?' a light voice asked from the other end of the room. Jensen looked up and saw a boy of about ten, wearing a white T-shirt and a pair of faded blue shorts that were much too big for him. He had thick, dark hair, dark eyes, and dark skin.

'I'm looking for Ramón Gutierrez. I was told he might be here.' Jensen returned the bowl to the inlaid table it had been resting on.

The boy slipped from the room without a word. It took

Jensen a moment to see where he had gone. The back corner of the room was obstructed by a mass of furniture that centered around a towering mahogany armoire; it was almost impossible for Jensen to make out beyond it the frame of a doorway that seemed to lead into a wood-paneled hall.

The boy reappeared, confirming Jensen's guess that there was a doorway and a hall there.

'Who are you, please, *señor*?' the boy asked him.

'Señor Gutierrez calls me Horacio,' Jensen replied, pronouncing the name without the *H*, in the Spanish manner.

Again the boy disappeared. Almost immediately Jensen heard a loud exclamation from the back room. A new figure appeared in the doorway, a man about six feet tall, bony, with gray hair that framed his dark and deeply lined face. He was wearing a plaid shirt and gray slacks.

'Horacio? Is that you, my friend?' His voice was raspy, and as thin as his body.

'Ramón?' Jensen took a few steps, threading his way through the furniture toward the doorway.

'Welcome, my friend. Welcome.'

Jensen stopped, trapped by a chaise longue, a desk, and a pair of carved lamp tables. He laughed.

'How do I get out of here? I'm surrounded by antiques.'

The tall man laughed in response and spoke in rapid, low-voiced Spanish to the boy, who had come to stand next to him.

'José will guide you out,' he said. 'He is the son of my brother's daughter Carmen. A good boy... And this is Horacio, Josélito, my friend from the days in Guatemala.'

The back room was only half as long as the shop itself, but it was twice as wide. There were several floor lamps, and on the walls there were framed pictures, some of them taken from magazines. There was a strong smell of rich, dark coffee.

The room was dominated by a large, round table. Five men were sitting at it. Two of them had been playing dominoes; the other three, and Gutierrez, Jensen supposed, had been kibbitzing. Now, though, they were all looking at Jensen, waiting for Gutierrez to introduce him.

'This is Horacio,' Gutierrez said, in a tone more sober than the one he had used with the boy. 'He is one of us. He was in Retalhuleu with me – at the training camp for the invasion – and before that, in Miami. You have heard me speak of him and how he stood with us in our difficulties.' He turned to Jensen. 'These are my friends. Old soldiers, like me.'

The others stood up. Jensen walked over and shook hands with them, one at a time. He did not recognize any of them, although from Ramón's introduction he assumed they had all been involved with the Bay of Pigs invasion. They all seemed to be in their forties. Manuel, short and heavy and bald, with a warm grip and smile lines around his eyes. Eloy, not much taller than Manuel but as thin as Ramón Gutierrez. Hector, fit and tightly wound, with dark brown skin and icy blue eyes.

As he introduced himself, Jensen had the sense the men were rearranging themselves for some reason of their own, adjusting the order in which he met them. The fourth man was Eladio, as easygoing as Hector was tense. He pumped Jensen's hand enthusiastically and repeated how pleased he was to meet him.

Jensen turned to the last man. He was looking across the room, seemingly preoccupied. Jensen's impression was of a strong profile, remarkably handsome in a rough way, skin the color and texture of old, oiled leather. The man's hair was jet black over the left side of his head; the rest was pure white.

Jensen held out his hand and said, again, '*Saludo. Me llamo Horacio.*'

The man turned. The half of his face that had been hidden from Jensen was a hideous, puckered burn scar: a stark, gnarled whiteness streaked with red; the eye socket was sunken as if it held nothing, and the right side of the man's mouth was fused and twisted into a permanent sneer. The scar tissue ran from his forehead, under the white hair, the full length of his face and down his neck, where it disappeared under his shirt.

Jensen held out his hand again, fixing his gaze firmly on the man's good left eye. '*Saludo*,' he said again.

'*Saludo*,' the man replied. He did not extend his hand; Jensen saw that his right sleeve was empty, pinned to his side. '*Me llamo Esteban*.' The mobile half of his mouth writhed around the words, forming them with near-perfect clarity.

The dramatic final introduction had been accompanied by an anticipatory stillness in the room. Now the others relaxed back into motion.

'Josélito, bring a chair,' Ramón ordered. 'My friend, you wish coffee? *Uno pastelillo?*'

'Just coffee, thanks, Ramón.'

Jensen sat with them and watched the game of dominoes and drank his coffee. There was very little conversation; the game absorbed everyone's attention.

Jensen had been there an hour when the men stopped playing and put the dominoes away carefully in a well-made wooden case.

Eladio looked at his watch. 'Ai!' he said. 'Maria said be home by seven o'clock. Her sister from Tampa is taking us out.' He stood up. 'Her sister is a pain in the ass. But Maria makes me be nice to her because she takes us fancy places. She married an American doctor.'

116

Within a few minutes the others followed Eladio out. José put their coffee cups on a wooden tray and carried it out of the room.

The bell on the shop door tinkled, and Ramón stood up and went to see who it was.

Jensen heard him greet someone; the second voice was almost too low for him to hear – it seemed soft and rich and vibrant. Then the voices stopped, and two people came toward the back room.

The woman with Ramón was tiny, and she looked even smaller beside the tall Cuban. Jensen guessed her height at no more than five feet, and every part of her was in proportion. She wore a simple red silk dress of Chinese design, embroidered with yellow, and she was holding a light coat over one arm. She was slender – her waist was no wider, Jensen thought, than his own thigh; her breasts were full but not large. She had long hair, black and thick and straight, hanging almost to her waist; it went with the dress. So did her face. It was a perfect oval of gold-brown – her features, delicately sculptured, an ideal blend of Chinese and Latin American. Jensen thought that in her own, unique way, she was one of the most beautiful women he had ever seen.

'This is Horacio,' Ramón said. 'My friend, this is Elena Perez, our hostess here. It is she who owns this shop, and it is her hospitality that brings the old soldiers here to play dominoes and drink coffee and rum and make foolish talk about better days and new revolutions.'

Jensen inclined his head, a token bow.

'I'm happy to meet you. You have a beautiful shop, but it can't compare with the owner.'

Her expression changed only slightly, barely acknowledging the compliment. Jensen wondered whether she had ever met a man who did not comment immediately on her beauty. He said, 'I was just going to ask Ramón to have dinner with me. I'd be pleased if you'd consider joining us.'

'You are very kind.' Her voice was even richer and more melodious than he had expected. 'I would not want to interrupt a reunion of old friends.'

'Not at all,' Jensen said. 'I have had a most pleasant afternoon here. I would be delighted to think I could repay you in even a small way.' Elena had spoken virtually without an accent but with the formality of someone educated in a foreign language. Jensen was amused to find his own words becoming stiffer in response.

'Come, Elena,' Ramón urged. 'We can go to La Victoria China for the soup with the egg, and good pork and noodles.'

Jensen laughed. 'I was thinking of something more like Galatoire's.'

'That is for tourists. While you are here, you should eat something special.'

Elena smiled. 'Ramón is very fond of food cooked in the Chinese way.'

'Fine,' Jensen said. 'I'll go back to my hotel and bathe and change my clothes. Can you pick me up in about an hour?'

'Does Ramón know where you are staying?'

'I'm at the Royal. I'll wait by the porte cochère.' On his way out he shook hands with Gutierrez. '*Hasta la vista, amigo.*'

He turned to say something more to Elena Perez, perhaps to shake her hand, too, but she had moved to the other end of the room.

He took a shower and washed his hair, all the while seeing mental images of Elena Perez. She puzzled him. There was something about her, and her antique shop, and her Cubans

118

playing dominoes that seemed vaguely anomalous to him. It was nothing he could put a name to, and when he tried to examine it closely, he found that the feeling made no sense – there was no reason at all why a beautiful Cuban, even one with some Chinese ancestry, shouldn't run an elegant antique shop in the French Quarter, and there was certainly no reason why, if she did, she shouldn't let her fellow Cubans enjoy themselves in her back room. The exiles were from widely separated backgrounds, but many of them had been very wealthy in the old Cuba, and now, in their enforced separation from a shared homeland, they had common ground with their less fortunate countrymen.

Ramón and Elena arrived in a hansom cab. They were sitting next to each other; he climbed in and took the seat facing them. They rode through the dark city, past the old Vieux Carré houses with their ornate wrought-iron balconies. Streetlights and the light from the windows of the houses gave the promenading tourists and prostitutes – male and female – an air of elegance and gentility that went with the architecture but that Jensen knew would disappear if he got any closer. He much preferred the view from the cab, and he said so.

'Yes,' Elena agreed. 'Our city is much more gracious if seen through colored glass or some other distorting lens. I am afraid the reality is rather rude, even now, when it is alive with the spirit of Mardi Gras.'

'*Putas y homosexuales*,' Ramón said disgustedly. 'Some of our *compañeros* are there. *Vergonzoso*.'

They stopped on a street of small shops; one of them had a false-brick front instead of plate-glass windows. A bright red and yellow sign over the door said, LA VICTORIA CHINA – Comidas Chinas Y Criollas.

119

Inside, it was neat and clean; rows of square tables, about half of them occupied, set simply with white tablecloths. A plump, dark man who was clearly the owner greeted Ramón and Elena warmly, and gravely shook hands with Jensen. He showed them to a table and, unbidden, brought them three bottles of Mexican beer.

Elena raised her glass. 'To your stay in New Orleans,' she said, for the first time looking straight into Jensen's eyes. 'May it be a pleasant one.'

The impact of her gaze was very strong. It took him a moment to raise his glass in return. 'And to the nicest surprise I've had here so far.'

'If it is not too personal,' Elena said, 'can you tell me what it is that brings you to New Orleans?'

Jensen felt a sharp pricking of alarm. Like his earlier discomfort about Elena, it seemed irrational to him: The question was a perfectly natural one.

'I'm here to see Ramón,' he said. 'It's been a long time, eh, *amigo*?'

'*Dos años*. We write Christmas cards.' He drank more beer. To Elena he said, 'Horacio was a good friend. We were only at the training camp a short time, but before that there was much politics, and if not for Horacio, there would have been much trouble.' He glanced at Jensen, then back at Elena again. 'So I think my amigo Horacio is kind to an old friend to say he comes only to see him. He is *tambien importante* to come here from Washington only to see Ramón Gutierrez.'

'Is that right?' Elena asked. 'I am not often entertained by important men from Washington.'

'Ramón is very gracious, but he's overestimating my importance. Basically, I'm here to see him, and a few of the other men I knew. I'd like to catch up on old times. We parted under very unhappy conditions. The Brigade had just been dissolved after the horrors at the Bay of Pigs. We've all had a couple of years to put things together again. I thought it would be good to see how everyone was doing now.'

'Things are not so put together again,' Ramón said. 'We have as many fools as before. Now everyone is a *liberador*. They all go to the bayous with their machine guns and plot a new revolution. They shoot each other. Fidel and Raoul must have a great joke about this.'

'There are a lot of factions, then?'

'*Sí.* Alpha-Sixty-six. *El frente Secundo de Escambray. Los Commandos* L-Sixty-six. Many more. They are crazy people. *Pirates*. They leave here in their motorboats. Bang bang bang. They shoot at Fidel's ships, and they shoot at Russian ships. *Locos.*'

Dinner passed quickly. It was Chinese food, but unlike any Jensen had tasted before. Especially the soup – a huge bowl of steaming chicken broth, crowded with meats and vegetables and, floating in the middle, three egg yolks. There was more: strange noodle dishes and something that looked like shrimp creole but tasted like fire.

'The Batistanos are stronger than ever,' Ramón said midway through the meal. His tone was more serious than it had been. 'More reckless. More dangerous. People come to me and say, "Look at what is happening. Our sons go with them, they fight for these men who are worse than the Castros." And what can I do? Because I was once a man of influence, they think I can help. But here I am no longer an important lawyer. I am not much of a politician. My only power is that there are still people who listen to me. But the Batistanos – if I went to them and said, "Stop this insanity, stop recruiting the sons of your old enemies," they would laugh at me. They know who I am. They know I fought with Castro against their beloved leader. They know how much I hate them, still.'

'I've been worried about this since before the invasion,' Jensen said. 'The trouble is that the farther away you get, the harder it is to see these differences. What matters in Washington is that you're all anti-communist and anti-Castro. That some of you would bring back the same dictatorship the rest of you fought to destroy – not everyone cares about that. I tried to make them see it when I was with you in Guatemala, at the training camp, and I thought I'd succeeded. But now . . . I think they want to treat it as an internal problem, something for you to solve on your own.'

Ramón made a derisive noise. 'So the CIA comes and helps to train our young sons as soldiers, and the FBI raids their training camps and confiscates the weapons. In the end we will eat each other up and Raoul and Fidel will grow fat.'

'Ramón!' Elena chided. 'Horacio is our guest. You must not be so serious.' She looked at Jensen, her eyes sparkling, inviting him to join her.

'Have some more beer, Ramón,' he said. 'You'll feel better.'

Ramón laughed. 'You are both right. I am too gloomy.' He piled fried rice on to his plate.

'Tell us about Washington,' Elena said, her eyes on Jensen again.

For the rest of the meal they gossiped about embassy parties and celebrities and the risqué pleasures of New Orleans. There was a lot of laughter, and for a short while Jensen even forgot why he had made the trip south.

The Cubans had gathered at the round table in the back room

of the antiques store to play poker, but instead they were swapping stories about the Cuban exile communities in New Orleans and Miami and Tampa and Dallas.

'What about this new President?' Eloy asked Jensen. 'He is no friend of Cuba, I think.'

'*Por qué?*' Jensen asked.

'My cousin in Miami says now they cancel raids on Cuba. Big raids. They are ready for months, and then men come from Washington and tell them go home, wait for new orders. Kennedy was better than that.'

'You think that son of a bitch Kennedy was a friend of Cuba?' Hector wanted to know. 'You believe that shit?'

'*Sí.* I believe it. Horacio, *es verdad, no?*'

'He wanted to get Fidel out of power, I know that.'

Hector made his spitting noise. 'Like at La Bahia des Cochinos, eh?' He poured rum into his coffee cup. 'That communist bastard Oswald did us all a favor to kill him.'

'Ai, Hector!' Gutierrez chided. 'Do not say such things. You will make grief for us all. If we give the district attorney another excuse to cause trouble . . .' He let the implication hang in the air.

Jensen was surprised. 'What kind of trouble did you have with the DA?'

'He arrested a man,' Gutierrez said. 'A pilot named Ferrie. There was much talk of a conspiracy. He said Ferrie was the pilot for the getaway from the assassination. This Ferrie *is* a pilot, and he is friendly with people who are close to some of us from Cuba. Ferrie is *homosexual. Grotesco.* He hires out to drop bombs on Cuba for the extremists. Some of us were afraid people might think *we* killed Kennedy because this man Ferrie was involved. A right-wing Cuban plot, you see?'

Jensen saw. It did not matter if the DA's theory was

accurate – it could still do severe damage, especially at a time when the future of the Cuban exile movement was probably being reviewed in Washington.

'Oswald was here in New Orleans before the killing,' Gutierrez went on. 'That is why the question is so dangerous. He said he was for Fidel, but he said also he was for our revolution, to get Fidel out.'

'You ought to talk to Carlos,' Eladio said, smiling. 'He had some fun with that *loco* Oswald.'

'Who's Carlos?' Jensen asked.

'Carlos Bringuier,' Ramón told him. 'One of us. An adventurer. Not so long ago he took fishing boats and put mortars and machine guns on them and went off to shell a hotel in Cuba.'

'Did he do it? Shell the hotel?'

'Oh, *sí, certamente*. Very important, shelling hotels. To make the people rise in protest, you see.'

'What did he do with Oswald?'

Eladio laughed. 'In the summer, last year, this Oswald comes to Carlos in his store, Casa Roca. Carlos is a big man here with the DRE, you know, the students. In the store Carlos is there, and a couple of kids. They have talk about raising money for the cause. This *loco* comes into the store, and Carlos asks him, "Can I help you?"'

'Oswald tells Carlos no, *he* wants to help Carlos – he hears Carlos is a big man in the cause and Oswald wants to train Cubans to fight against Fidel. Blow up bridges. Make trains fall off the track' – he pantomimed a derailment with a sweeping gesture of one flat hand, flipping it over abruptly and following the motion with a dramatic 'Boom!'

He shook his head. 'In the store he says all this. Out loud. And very serious. But Carlos has friends in the FBI. They told him FBI men would try to become members of his group and also of the training camps up on the lake. So he sends Oswald away. The next day Oswald is back. He gives Carlos a Marine Corps book. To show how he knows all these things – blowing up and train crashes. A training manual from the Marines . . . Maybe two, three days later this same Oswald is outside the store. He has a sign, big sign like this, on his chest. It says, *Viva Fidel!*' He looked around the table with an exaggerated expression of disbelief. '*Viva Fidel!*'

'Carlos sees this in the street and he goes running out, with two men from in the store, shouting at this Oswald. Oswald stands there, he says, "Okay, okay, hit me." Carlos keeps yelling. Oswald keeps saying, "Hit me, hit me." Then the *policía* come and take them away for making so damn much noise.'

Elena came into the room with a big pot of coffee and put it in the middle of the table. As she turned to leave, her eyes met Jensen's. He watched her as she left the room, moving with a preternatural grace and lightness.

'There is something about all this that is very troubling to us,' Gutierrez said. 'In the summer Oswald gave out papers about the Fair Play for Cuba Committee. It is a communist, Fidelista thing. On these papers it said Five forty-four Camp Street. But at Five forty-four Camp Street is the Cuban Revolutionary Council. It is very anti-Castro, very right-wing. Also there are offices for a private detective called Bannister who knows the pilot Ferrie, the one arrested by our big DA, Mr Garrison. No one knows what all of this means. But I am afraid of it.'

'Why?' Jensen asked.

'There are too many people who do not like us, who say we hated Kennedy for the Bay of Pigs.'

'*Es verdad*,' Hector said. 'I hate him.'

'And the missiles? Do you forget that?' Ramón challenged. 'Or the raids he has supported?'

He turned to Jensen. '*Sí*, many of us are bitter about the invasion. But we did not kill him, and we do not wish to be tied to this Oswald.'

There was a loud chime, the night bell that signaled someone at the locked front door of the antique shop. Elena came through the back room from her apartment and returned with Esteban. He greeted the men at the table and pulled up a chair. Elena brought a cup and poured coffee for him; he added a generous measure of rum to it.

'*Qué pasa?*' he asked.

'We were telling Horacio about Carlos Bringuier and that *loco* Oswald,' Eladio reported.

'*Verdad?*' Esteban turned his good eye on Jensen. 'You are interested in Oswald?'

Jensen hesitated, momentarily uncertain how to handle the question.

He said, 'Sure I am. Isn't everybody?'

'Not everybody. I am not.'

Jensen kept his eyes on the ravaged face. He had learned from Ramón that Esteban's disfigurement was a badge of honor; his scars came from a series of horrors – torture at the hands of Castro's people and wounds he had received both at the Bay of Pigs and later, when he had been the lone survivor of a CIA-supported infiltration team that had been landed on the island.

'I'm interested because of Oswald's connections to Cuba,' Jensen said.

'So, then, you care about Cuba?' There was a clear challenge in Esteban's tone.

'Yes,' Jensen responded with carefully measured indignation. 'Do you doubt me?'

'I doubt all *gringos*,' Esteban said. 'Until they have proven their beliefs by action. Words are cheap in this place.'

'Horacio has proven himself,' Gutierrez said quietly.

Esteban turned his face toward Jensen again; the good eye bored into Jensen's as if to underline the fact that they were not yet finished with each other. Jensen stared back with what he hoped was a look of calm certainty.

That night he dreamed of Jill – fragments from their marriage and before. He awoke with disconnected parts of the dream still in his mind.

As he showered and shaved, he puzzled over what had triggered the dream. Coming out of the bathroom, his eyes swept over his hotel room, and he stopped. A large chunk of the dream came back to him, a distorted memory of the night they had spent at the airport Sheraton in Los Angeles when Jill had come out to join him. The California hotel room and the one in New Orleans were virtually twins.

Jill had not been happy to be in California, and he had wanted to ease her adjustment; so, instead of going directly to the apartment he had rented for them, they had stayed at the hotel.

As soon as they were in the room, she pulled the drapes across the window, shutting off the view of their balcony and the palm trees and swimming pool in the hotel's inner courtyard.

'God,' she said. 'Everything is so bright.'

'Sunny southern California.' He put her suitcase on the rack at the foot of the bed.

'Give me Washington any day.'

'For God's sake, Jill, give it a chance. I know it's not paradise . . .'

She moved to him, pressed her hips to his, and leaned back a little to look at him.

'You're right. I'm just grouchy from the flight. And I missed you. I forgot how long two weeks can be without you.' She put her head on his chest. 'Take me to bed with you and then buy me dinner, and I'm sure I'll feel much better.'

They stayed in bed for almost three hours. By the time they went downstairs it was dark. He drove them to Beverly Hills for dinner. The freeways still confused him, but he only got lost once.

The Hollywood celebrities at the restaurant diverted Jill for a while, but she became more silent and withdrawn as the meal passed. He tried to draw her out, and when that failed he left her alone.

Back at the hotel she stood for a moment in the middle of the room and then said, 'Damn it!' And again, 'Damn it!'

Standing there, she began to cry.

He put his arms around her. She pushed him away.

'I don't want to be here, Harry. I don't want to.'

She lay down on the rumpled bed and stared at the ceiling. 'I know we talked about it, and I know why it's important for you to be with Judge Thomas. I want you to succeed. I want you to have what you want. And I'll make the best of the time we have to spend here. But somewhere down deep I'm going to hate every minute that seems like time taken out of my life, and I'm going to remember that things were just starting to click for me in Washington when we left. I had more going for me than any other woman in public relations, the few of us there are, and you took me away from it.'

Her second week there she got a job as an assistant media buyer in the west coast office of a New York advertising agency, and she never again complained about being in California. But during those two years they fought more frequently and more fiercely than ever before.

A few days before Mardi Gras Jensen went to see Ramón Gutierrez. They sat in the sun, behind the house; on the lawn between their chairs Ramón put a chest of ice. The brown necks of beer bottles stuck out of the ice at odd angles.

'*Una cerveza?*' he asked Jensen, prying the top off a bottle.

'*Certamente, gracias.*'

Jensen took the cold bottle and waited while Gutierrez uncapped one for himself and took a long drink.

'*Bueno,*' the Cuban said with great satisfaction, and belched. 'What were we talking about?'

'Esteban,' Jensen prompted.

'Ah, *sí*. Esteban. He is' – Gutierrez shrugged – 'a strange man. He is very angry.'

'About the Bay of Pigs?'

'That is what he says, but it is more. What is most strange is this – he is one of us, he believes in the people, but in some ways he is worse than the Batistanos. He trusts no one, and he is a killer.'

'And he thinks I'm going to betray you somehow?'

Gutierrez looked across the lawn to where his three children were working on a small float for the Cuban community's own local Mardi Gras parade.

'I have told him all you did for us. How the Batistanos and their CIA friends kept us out of the executive committee and made false reports to Washington, and how it was you who made the truth known so that there was an order to make us a part of what was happening.' He shook his head. 'But Esteban said the order did no real good because in the end we were kept out of command, and no use was made of our commandos in the Escambray. Esteban said if not for that order, in March, we might have done things on our own. He said the order was only a way to keep us quiet while the Batistanos took over command. A betrayal. And it was your doing.' He turned to look at Jensen. 'A man like Esteban will think what he wants. I cannot make it different.'

'What about you, Ramón? Do you trust me?'

Gutierrez hesitated. 'Esteban is right, in some ways. We were betrayed. We were lied to. But I believe you helped us. I do not think it was all a big plot. You did as well as you could. It was others, above you, who betrayed us. And they betrayed you, as well. So I do trust you. But why do you ask me this now?'

Jensen looked off toward the float. Ramón's three teenagers were covering the side of a papier-mâché hill with the branches of small trees and bushes.

'I'm not here only to visit my old friends,' he said.

Ramón laughed. 'No. I did not think so.'

'I need information about Cuba.'

'Yes? What kind of information?'

Jensen looked at him. 'About the assassination of the President.'

'Ah, *sí*. Of course. That is why you listen so well to stories about Oswald and Carlos and the others.'

'Yes. It's part of my job here.'

Jensen tried not to think of that as a lie. He said, 'Do you think it's possible Fidel was behind it?'

The Cuban's surprise was visible only for an instant. He looked at Jensen appraisingly before he answered.

'Why do you come to me for this? I am here in New Orleans. I do not know about anything in Cuba since 1960.'

'No, of course not. But there are people here in New Orleans who run agents in Cuba, people who get information from close to Castro. I need to talk to them.'

Gutierrez's expression hardened. 'The CIA has agents in Cuba. Some of them are near Fidel. Talk to the CIA.'

Jensen turned the challenge over in his mind, looking for a way to meet it. 'I can't,' he said. 'Remember what you said about my report to Washington and the white paper and how it was ignored? Remember how I fought with some of the CIA people in Guatemala? I have no control over the CIA. I don't even have access to everything they know about things that are important to my work.' That much, he thought, was certainly true. 'You think of me as being powerful in Washington, and in a way I am. But the agency I work for is often the rival of the CIA, at least from the CIA's point of view. So I must learn these things on my own.'

Gutierrez opened another beer and handed it to Jensen. Then he opened one for himself and took a drink.

'So, we are not the only ones who use all our energy fighting our friends until we have none left for our enemies.' He drank again. 'All right,' he said. 'How can I help you?'

'I have to get the best information available about what Fidel and Raoul and some of the others were doing in September and October and November. And perhaps afterward. If I could talk to someone who was in Havana last fall and who's come out since . . .'

Gutierrez said nothing for a minute. 'There are such men,' he conceded finally. 'But I cannot tell you who they are.'

'I must talk to them, Ramón. If Fidel is responsible for that horror in Dallas, we must know it. Can't you see how important it is to you and your friends?'

'*Sí*. I am not blind. An act of war against the United States. It could be the answer to all our prayers. But I cannot expose these men to you. The men who could help you are like a secret weapon for us, because we do not trust the CIA or anyone in Washington to help us except when it is in their own interest. And if they knew what agents we had and who runs them, they could take them away from us or make them useless and we would be without resources of our own. We cannot take such a risk.' Gutierrez reached out and put a hand on Jensen's shoulder. 'Do not be offended. I am not alone in deciding this. There are others, the ones in charge, who do not know you as I do. Whatever I say, they will say no.'

'Suppose you go and talk to these others. Tell them who I am and what I've done, and tell them what I want. I'll meet them anywhere they say. I don't have to know who they are. I don't even have to set eyes on them. Just so long as I can talk to them and be sure they're telling me the truth. And I'll do it on their terms – whatever security they want.'

Gutierrez thought about it.

'*Sí . . . Sí*, I could ask them that. But they will probably say no.'

'If they say no, I'll worry about it then. The important thing is to ask them. And to make them see how much it can mean to them.'

It was two days later, as he watched Ramón's eighteen-year-old son Gilberto help his two sisters maneuver their float into its position in the line of march, that Jensen got his answer.

'It is arranged,' Ramón told him. 'There is one man who has agreed to talk with you. He is an agent here among the Fidelistas and he has run agents in Cuba. He is placing himself in danger to do this, trusting you because of me.'

'I appreciate it, Ramón.'

'He will meet you on Tuesday. Mardi Gras. He will be in costume. I do not know what. We will be told where to go and what to look for on Mardi Gras morning. You will have to go alone. I think there will be two meetings. First you will find a go-between, who will give you more instructions. Then you will meet this man, who may be able to answer your questions.'

'Fine. It sounds fine. Thank you, Ramón.' Jensen put out his hand and shook the Cuban's warmly.

Chapter Eight

On the morning of Mardi Gras Jensen and Ramón stood together on the balcony over Elena Perez's antique shop. Jensen wore the costume Ramón had given him, provided by the men he was going to meet. It was a one-piece lavender suit with a yellow horse tail, surmounted by a yellow-maned lavender papier-mâché horse head that fit over his head and rested on his shoulders.

Jensen looked down at Royal Street through the horse head's eye slits. The street was so dense with people that he could not see the pavement. The crowd milled and shifted like a multicolored river at the confluence of a dozen streams. Its surface was in constant motion; there was a tumult of mechanical noises and music and celebratory voices.

Gutierrez repeated to Jensen the instructions he had been given in a phone call at dawn. Jensen made him go over them a second time, then a third, doing his best to visualize the places he would have to go.

When he thought he had the instructions straight, he reviewed them for Gutierrez, who caught a couple of mistakes. Then, finally satisfied he knew where to go and what to do, Jensen shook Gutierrez's hand, thanked him again, and went downstairs. The horse head restricted his vision enough to make his progress on the stairway slow and precarious.

At street level the sense of a vast crowd that had been the predominant aspect of the view from the balcony was replaced by an almost claustrophobic immediacy: The crowd around him could have been ten people deep or ten thousand, it almost didn't matter. What did matter were the sounds and smells and colors and textures of the short, pudgy Harlequin next to him; and the tall scarecrow; and the woman whose breasts – bare but for pasties over her nipples – brushed his arm; and the gaunt man, wearing only a loincloth and mask, his body painted alternate stripes of red and blue. Bodies pressed against him and against each other with an indiscriminate energy that he was sure would feel sexual if he were in the right mood. As it was, all he wanted to do was get into the flow of the crowd so that he could make his way through it as efficiently as possible.

But he soon discovered that he would have to give himself up to the spirit of the day. His purposefulness had stiffened his body in a way that the others in the crowd seemed to sense; they responded by resisting his progress past them. He saw that the harder he tried to reach his destination, the more trouble he would have, so he relaxed, let himself become part of the crowd around him, let his body respond to the music and the other happy noises. His face was invisible to his neighbors behind the hollow horse head, as theirs were hidden from him by their own masks – communication was mostly a matter of body language and the occasional meeting of eyes.

He had no idea how long it took him to get to Bourbon Street. On the way he danced in the crowded streets with a harem girl and then with a bearded pirate with large bare breasts and the thinnest waist and hips he had ever seen, and with a woman dressed as a London bobby – unless, he thought, it was a man dressed as a woman dressed as a bobby.

That encounter was the most overtly sexual of the three, and there was something about the woman's – man's? – urgency that made him suspicious.

The horse head meant he could not kiss anyone, but it did not prevent embraces, and there were plenty of those. There were also less direct encounters – hands on his arms and chest, breasts and groins rubbed against him. A few times people caressed his genitals. The first time he thought it was a pickpocket; it did not take him long to realize he was wrong.

He wondered, as he made his way through the crowd, if the mood was as free all over the city.

He turned on to Bourbon Street and let the crowd carry him two blocks before he began to edge toward the side of the street. His attention was absorbed for a moment by a black man playing Dixieland music on a cornet, about half a dozen people away. The blare of the horn, pointed in Jensen's direction, was at once pleasant and painful. Backing toward the sidewalk, watching the cornet player, he stumbled. His foot came down hard on something yielding, and he heard a loud, deep-voiced shout.

'Motherfucker,' the voice said, and someone grabbed Jensen's shoulders and spun him around.

He found himself facing a bull-headed man with broad shoulders and chest and an immense pot belly. The man shoved him backward. He collided with a series of people before he could get himself back under control. By that time the crowd had closed around the bull and hidden him from sight. Jensen was preoccupied with getting away from the people he had collided with. He pretended to be drunk and very full of holiday enthusiasm and goodwill until he got past a Harlequin and a skeleton and a fat wolf.

He reached the corner where Ramón had told him he would

meet the intermediary and get further instructions. It was a
major intersection; the currents of moving people were
stronger and more complicated here than any he had
encountered so far. He had been told only to expect a cowboy
with a red mask. But he had already encountered an
abundance of cowboys, of various heights and both sexes. At
first he tried to pursue every cowboy he saw near the corner,
but it was hopeless. Worse, it occurred to him as he bumped
from reveler to reveler in pursuit of a cowboy with a red mask,
if he went after the wrong cowboy, he might well miss the one
he was there to meet.

He concentrated on maintaining a position near the corner,
turning around as he did to keep himself visible from all sides.
There might be a lot of cowboys, but there weren't very many
six-foot-four-inch horses with lavender heads and bright
yellow manes and tails.

He was beginning to wonder if he was in the right place,
when someone grabbed his tail and pulled him backward. He
set his feet, bent sharply forward, and whirled, almost
dislodging his horse head mask but succeeding in yanking
himself free. At first he did not see who had grabbed him. The
people in that direction were all thoroughly absorbed in their
own business. Then he felt a sharp pain in his shin and he bent
his head so he could look down.

He saw a dwarf in a black cowboy suit: The boots were
patent leather, and the tight-fitting pants and shirt seemed to
be leather as well, ornately decorated with curlicue patterns of
metal studs. The outfit was topped off by a black silk bandana
and a ten-gallon hat half as big again as the dwarf's head. His
face was the face of Fidel Castro, painted a glaring red, except
for the beard, which was striped lavender and yellow.

The effect was so outlandishly striking that it was a moment before Jensen noticed that one of the dwarf's black leather gauntlets was wrapped securely around the grip of a western-style revolver, king-size in the tiny hand and pointed steadily at Jensen's stomach.

'Giddyap, old paint,' the dwarf said. His voice was muffled by the red Fidel face.

They were not the right words. Jensen stared with increased alarm at the gun. He bobbed his head vigorously four times, his part of the password routine.

'*La vida es sueno,*' the dwarf told him.

That was better. Jensen shook his head three times.

'Tomorrow is another day.'

Jensen thought he heard a faint Spanish accent in the muffled words. He reached up and undid a strap on his mask; a piece of lavender papier-mâché under the horse's chin swung away.

'How much is that doggie in the window?' he said.

A passing clown saw the dwarf and his gun and laughed and pointed; he tugged at the sleeve of a witch and pointed again. The witch did not seem amused. She screamed.

'Shut up,' the clown said. 'You crazy? It's a joke. Hey, mister, ain't that right? A joke, huh?'

The witch was pulling at him frantically.

'Only a joke,' the dwarf agreed and holstered the gun. He turned and pushed his way into the crowd.

Jensen had trouble following him. The little cowboy made his way through spaces that would not admit a far taller and bulkier lavender horse. After less than a block Jensen was afraid he had lost him, but the dwarf came back after a moment, and then they went through the crowd hand in hand, the dwarf leading and Jensen trailing behind. It was like being pulled along by an enthusiastic child.

139

They made it to the sidewalk and then to a doorway where they could take temporary refuge from the crowd. The dwarf began to tell him where he should go next and what he should do. The instructions were simpler this time, but they were harder to absorb because of the constant noise and pressure of the crowd. They were frequently interrupted by others – masquers and tourists – who stopped in their doorway, also seeking a moment's rest.

Before Jensen was at all confident of what he was to do, the dwarf said a curt *adios* and lost himself in a passing group of revelers.

Jensen's next rendezvous was on Canal Street. It was a lot easier getting there than it had been going from Royal Street to Bourbon Street. Most of the way the crowds were thin; Jensen used as many back streets as he could, stopping frequently to look at the small map of the city he had armed himself with before he started out. Once, it led him into a dead end; he had to retrace his steps for almost a quarter of a mile to find an alternate route.

And Canal Street itself was a shock: The crowds were the densest he had encountered. Most of the people crushed together here were not in costume; they were tourists, bent on ogling the natives and waiting for the big parades to begin. Jensen drew a lot of attention. He was not sure if that was good or bad for his purposes; he assumed the Cubans had anticipated it when they gave him the costume.

The dwarf's instructions called for Jensen to cross Canal Street. It was going to be no mean feat. He looked across the street, over the heads of the tourists and the revelers, reading the big signs on the sides of the buildings so that he could get his bearings. He saw Mayer Israel's and, a few blocks up,

Godchaux's and, beyond that, the Hotel Roosevelt. At the limit of his view he could make out a sign suspended in air over a tall building: Hotel New York. It was about a dozen blocks away, and his destination lay just beyond it. He waded out into the stream of people, but he made no real headway until he plunged into a group that was moving faster than the surrounding stagnant crowd; he let the group carry him along, once more deliberately surrendering his sense of time and place to the rhythms of the people packed around him.

Amid the voices and the music and the laughter there was suddenly the shriek of sirens and a rumble of motors. Forward motion turned into a confused milling.

Jensen was bumped by a shoulder; a paunch pressed into his side.

The sirens grew louder and, with them, the growl of many motorcycles. Drums, cymbals. Happy shouting.

More soft flesh pressed against Jensen; someone went off balance against him, forced him off balance against someone else. He staggered, regained his footing, went several steps in the wrong direction.

A path was opening for the parade, and now the motorcycles were not as loud, their sirens rising and falling with less strident insistence. More drums and cymbals, and then music: 'If Ever I Cease to Love,' the carnival anthem.

Jensen was pushed again, harder than before, and then pushed again. He stumbled, ricocheted off a tourist, staggered clumsily a few steps.

He got his balance and stopped moving entirely. The parade had arrived; there was no question now of making it across the street until it was over. The best he could do would be to get to a spot opposite the Hotel New York and try to cross as soon as the parade had passed. And if he was going to do that, he would be better off closer to the buildings. It meant missing the parade, but he hadn't come to New Orleans for the Mardi Gras parades.

Once he made it to the buildings, he found the next few blocks relatively easy. Then he ran up against a wall of people straining to see the parade – some in costume, most not.

He stopped, stymied.

He felt the pressure of a body at his right side and then another at his left. They moved him toward the building wall at his right. He did not like the way it felt, and he pulled away. Was stopped by a hand on his arm.

He looked to his left and saw an enormous, silver-feathered rooster. On his right was a stocky gaucho wearing a plastic mask of John Kennedy. The gaucho was holding a stag-handled bowie knife with a blade at least a foot long. It made Jensen think of the dwarf and his six-gun. This was not his next rendezvous point, but he thought the rooster and the gaucho might have intercepted him before he got there for some security reason of their own. He decided to go along with them.

They led him back along the building toward an alley. As they approached it, he said, 'Cold for December, isn't it?' His voice was muffled by the horse head, but the gaucho and the rooster had him by the arms, and he couldn't open the flap in its chin. The inane reference to another month's weather was the first part of the identification procedure for this meeting, but it brought no response.

The alley was long and narrow and deserted. Only a dim fraction of the day's light penetrated to its end. Jensen had the sudden conviction that something was wrong.

He willed himself not to stiffen, and for a few steps he

moved docilely along with the rooster and the gaucho. Then, abruptly, he set his feet and twisted, breaking their hold on his arms. Facing the street, he broke for freedom but his feet got tangled in something and he fell heavily. The impact drove the wind from his lungs. He felt the sharp pain of a foot in the ribs.

He was gasping for breath, making a low keening noise. A pair of strong hands gripped him below the armpits; the fingers dug deep into his side and chest. He was lifted to his feet and hustled deeper into the alley, his toes barely touching the ground.

Desperately trying to suck in air, he caught a single, short breath, then another. He was hurled against a brick wall. He worked his feet as he neared the wall, turning himself enough to hit shoulder first; it saved him from hitting the bricks with his head, and it gave him a moment to see where he was and what was happening.

The alley was at its narrowest here, not more than six feet wide. The gaucho stood toward the street, about a dozen feet away, watching him, the bowie knife ready. The towering rooster was closer, within reach, poised to strike. In the false dusk of the alley the silver cloth of the rooster's costume gleamed with dull, sinister highlights. His beak was metal – Jensen abruptly remembered his dream of Hapgood as an eagle – and from the backs of his hands sprung metal hooks that simulated a fighting cock's spurs. The same kind of spurs curved from his boots, just above his heels. He shook his head like a rooster about to crow; his bright red comb – cloth on a wire frame – rippled with arrogance.

He took two quick steps toward Jensen, who ducked and twisted toward the mouth of the alley. A long silver arm shot out; a hand grabbed his shoulder, twisted. Jensen stumbled back, bounced off the wall, and tottered toward the rooster, who sidestepped and swung an openhanded roundhouse against the lavender horse head, caving it in on one side.

Jensen's head rang, and he felt the scrape of shattered papier-mâché against one cheek. Blood trickled down his neck. He put up his hands; they were swept aside, and again his head was battered. His mask went askew, blocking the vision of one eye. Through the other he could see only a sliver of the world, to his left and down – the gray floor of the alley littered with old garbage and broken glass.

Something hit him in the stomach and then his head rang again. He lost consciousness for a moment and when sensation came back, everything was much too clear.

The horse head had been knocked further askew: The flat side of its neck pressed harshly against his nose. He could barely breathe, and with every precious inhalation he smelled his own fear. He reached up to tear off the mask that held him prisoner, and the rooster kicked him in the groin.

He went down on the alley floor, huddled into a ball. He was kicked again, in the side, and again. He pulled desperately at the papier-mâché head that was suffocating him.

The iron hands gripped him and lifted him up and propped him against the wall. He had worked the head around so that he could see a small part of the world. A silver fist flashed toward him, bent so that the curved metal spur would slash him like a scimitar. He tried to block it, but the rooster's other hand caught his chest and pressed him tight against the wall, immobile.

The spur sliced through the horse head just in front of Jensen's face, splitting the mask open. The horse's nose hung loose, and Jensen could breathe again, and see.

The rooster pulled him away from the wall and slammed

him into it. The impact awakened all the pain of the other blows, and it sent his head crashing back against the bricks. There was a flash of agony in Jensen's head; everything went red and then black and then white. He blinked his eyes and shook his head; he was seeing double.

He was aware of the rooster towering over him, very close. A harsh southern voice, devoid of emotion or intelligence, filtered out at him from behind the steel beak.

'Get out of New Orleans. Forget Cuba. Go back and tell the others you were wrong. Get that? Tell them forget the whole thing. You were wrong.'

The rooster drew back, holding him pinned against the wall. Again the spur flashed toward him. This time it cut his face, not the mask. He felt a hot line of blood well up along his cheek, from his left ear to the point of his chin.

'Forget it, understand?' the voice said, and then the rooster began to pummel his body and kick him; there was a rhythm to the blows – one, two, three, four – not hurried, but very steady. Jensen slid down the wall under the constant barrage and he curled up once more on the alley floor and drifted peacefully into oblivion.

It was dark when he woke up. For a long time he couldn't move. He lay there, cold and aching. His head pounded with pain every time his heart beat. His mouth was dry, and one eye wouldn't open. He drifted off again, into a state between sleep and unconsciousness.

He awoke again. It was still dark. He was colder and stiffer, and the aching was worse. But the pounding pain in his head was less severe, or else he could stand it better. He moved his hands, wiggled his fingers. He scraped his hands along the concrete and got them under him. When he tried to push himself upright, the pain in his left hand was enough to make him scream. He blacked out again.

When he came to the third time, something was different, but it was several minutes before he knew what it was – the din of parades and celebration was gone. His hands were still under him; the left felt as if it were the size of a basketball, and every cubic centimeter of it was a separate hammer of pain. He tried to close his mind to the agony, but he couldn't. There were tricks he had heard for doing that; he remembered them imperfectly, and what little he remembered was no help. He levered himself up on his right hand. It took forever.

He was whimpering with pain. It was more than he could stand, and he almost let himself slump down and slide back into soft darkness. But he locked his elbow and hung on. A tiny part of his mind registered the fact that he was actually gritting his teeth, and another tiny part of his mind took courage from the fact that he could perceive what was happening to him.

Maybe you're going to make it after all, he told himself.

After an indeterminate time he was ready for the next stage: to get to his knees. That took even longer, and it set off a horrible throbbing in his head, but he did it, and then he crawled painfully on his knees toward the mouth of the alley.

He stopped often, panting, shivering, sweating. He was grateful for the darkness, because he sensed that his eyes were not working properly, and as long as it was too dark to see he didn't have to think about that part of it.

Midway along the alley he came to a place where there were some boxes piled next to one of the walls. He decided to try to stand up. His first attempt found new places in his body for him to hurt.

Once, as he lunged from supporting himself on a low box to

146

the next higher one, his left hand brushed against something. He screamed and clutched the hand to his chest, sobbing, but that was a mistake, too, so he let go of the hand and let it dangle by his side.

He could not stand on his own; he had to lean against the wall and pull himself along. By the time he reached the mouth of the alley, the first light of false dawn was in the sky.

He had been right about his eyes. He was seeing double, and sometimes triple, and none of the multiple images was clear. He had trouble tracking moving things. But he could tell that there were still people in the street, even at this hour, and he did not want to have to deal with them. He had to avoid good Samaritans. Help meant the police, and that would ruin things for him. Once he was involved with the police, the Cuban agents he needed so badly would never come near him.

He was disoriented and very wobbly on his feet. Three times, along the way, he had encounters with all-night revelers. Each time, he pulled away, feigning drunkenness and being obscenely abusive of the people who tried to help him.

The sun was bright on streets full of confetti and other parade litter, and people were getting ready for Ash Wednesday services when he slumped against the lintel of Elena Perez's antique shop and pressed the night bell.

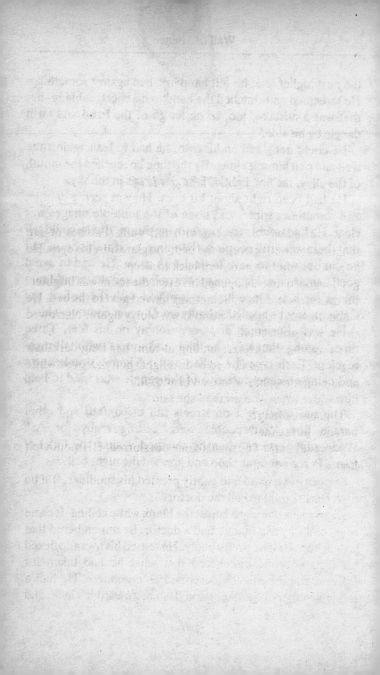

Chapter Nine

He awoke slowly in a room with red walls. Patches of sun shone on the wall opposite the bed; the glare hurt his eyes. He turned away from it and went back to sleep.

The second time he opened his eyes, the room was brighter, but there was less glare. Something moved next to the bed. He rolled his head to the side and saw a blurry figure. Narrowed his eyes, concentrated.

It was Elena. She was smiling at him; her long dark hair framed her face and flowed over a light, puffy-sleeved white blouse. He thought she looked beautiful.

'It's nice to see you awake,' she said.

'Did I sleep long?'

'How do you feel?'

'Not bad. Stiff.' The words came out slurred. His mouth felt clumsy.

She put out a hand and gently pressed his shoulder. 'I'll be right back. I want to call the doctor.'

He lay back and stared up at the blank white ceiling. It came as no real surprise that he had a doctor; he remembered that he had been beat up pretty badly. He tensed his legs and flexed his right arm and discovered that what he had taken for stiffness could better be described as numbness. He had a sudden memory of a steel talon flashing toward his face, and he probed gently with his tongue against his left cheek. There was no sensation there at all; it could have been a block of wood. He fell asleep wondering how badly hurt he was.

'Señor Horacio,' the voice in his dream said. And then said it a second time, and a third. The voice seemed at once patient and insistent. Finally Jensen realized who 'Señor Horacio' was, and he opened his eyes. He saw a double image of a short, brown-skinned man with horn-rimmed glasses, wearing a neat gray suit.

'Aha,' the man said. '*Buenos días. Yo soy Doctor Alvarez.*'

'*Buenos días, Doctor.* How am I?'

Alvarez smiled. 'Ah, that is for *you* to tell *me*, young man. How is your vision?'

'Blurry. Sometimes.' It was still hard for him to talk.

Alvarez nodded. 'You have a concussion. We knew that, of course. The question I must answer now is how severe it is. You have cracked ribs. Your legs were badly bruised. There was, as well, internal bleeding. Your face was very seriously slashed. You cannot leave this bed for several weeks, I think. Your eyesight should be better long before that, and if it is not, we can talk about consulting a specialist. Is that satisfactory?'

'Several weeks?'

'I am being conservative. We shall see how fast you heal.'

'I have to get back to work.'

Alvarez shook his head, as much in dismay as negation. 'It is dangerous even for you to be moved. For many days.'

Jensen looked at Elena.

'I think Doctor Alvarez is right. You should stay here.

150

There are other reasons, too, besides your injuries.'

Jensen was feeling tired again, too tired to argue. 'All right,' he said. 'Talk about it tomorrow.' He fell asleep.

Later that day he woke up again. His vision was still blurred. Marta, Elena's maid and cook, was sitting in a chair by the bed. When she saw that he was awake, she hurried from the room and returned with Elena.

'I have to go back to Washington,' Jensen said. His mouth and tongue were feeling more normal, but his left cheek was still wooden.

'Doctor Alvarez said you can't be moved.'

'Then I've got to call them.' Jensen was not sure why it felt so urgent to him. 'How long is it since . . . Mardi Gras?'

'Four days,' Elena told him. 'You were delirious on Wednesday. You slept for most of Thursday and Friday.' She put her hand on the sheet where it covered his thigh. 'It is Saturday. There is nothing you can do about your work until Monday.'

'I promised my boss I'd be back by Monday.'

'But you are too sick.'

'He doesn't know that. Maybe if Doctor Alvarez wrote to him, or called.'

'In Havana, Doctor Alvarez was a fine physician. Here, he sells insurance. I am not sure how much help he could be with your employers.'

'What about a hospital?' he asked. 'I shouldn't be staying here, anyway. I must be an awful burden for you.'

Again she put her hand on his thigh; he felt the warmth of her palm.

'You are no trouble to me. I'm pleased to help you get well. And it would be dangerous to move you.'

'I don't feel that bad,' Jensen said; to prove it to himself as well as to her, he pushed himself into a semi-sitting position, resting on his elbows. For the first time he realized that his left hand was encased in a large cast: Alvarez had left that out of his inventory. The effort of sitting up set off a violent pounding in his head. He tried not to show it.

'We're only talking about my going as far as a hospital.' That would satisfy Hapgood, for a while. 'I can go in an ambulance. How much damage can they do?'

'That's not the kind of danger I meant,' she said. 'As long as you are here, we can watch over you. No one knows where you are. If you go to a hospital, it will be public knowledge, and there will be no way for us to protect you if the men who beat you come back.'

On Sunday he had his first visitors. He was alone in the red-walled room, sitting propped up against a half-dozen soft pillows that Elena had fluffed up and put in place herself. His first solid meal was a comforting warmth in his stomach.

There was a knock on the door, and Ramón Gutierrez's head poked into the room.

'Horacio?' he ventured.

'*Amigo. Venga aquí.* I'm glad to see you.'

Ramón moved tentatively into the room, as if he were afraid his presence might hurt Jensen or delay his recovery. He stopped next to the bed and looked down at Jensen. 'Whoever did this to you should be shot. Who was it? Tell me and we shall take our revenge.'

'Thanks, Ramón. I appreciate it. But I don't know who it was. It won't do any good for me to send you looking for a gaucho who looks like John Kennedy and a silver rooster. All I can tell you is that the rooster was very big. Maybe seven feet tall. Big enough to lift me off my feet, anyway. With that red comb on top of his head it was hard to tell exactly, and my mind isn't what you'd call clear on the subject.'

He closed his eyes, squeezed them tight to drive away the sudden vivid memory of the rooster.

'*Amigo!* Are you all right?'

Jensen opened his eyes. 'I'm fine.'

'Forgive me, my friend. I am clumsy. In my anger I did not mean to upset you.'

'It's okay.' Jensen shifted on the bed. 'Ramón, I have a favor to ask you.'

'*Sí*. If I can.'

'I want you to call someone and leave a message. My ex-wife.'

'If you wish. What is the message?'

He had not considered that. It would have to be short and unmistakably from him. Jill did not know Ramón, would not recognize his name. Jensen had never talked to her about the Bay of Pigs. On his return from Guatemala he had found the locks changed on their apartment door. She had even packed his clothes and his books and his records while he had been away.

'Tell her . . . her friend in New Orleans . . . No. Her friend from New Year's Eve is staying in New Orleans another little while. Tell her I'll call, myself, to explain in a few days. But don't say my name. Or yours.'

'Her friend from New Year's Eve is staying in New Orleans. He'll call soon. Not many days.'

'Good. That's perfect. And thanks.'

Ramón smiled, shook his head. '*De nada*.'

Night. Jensen woke up, heard the voices of several men in the next room. At first he could not connect the voices with anyone he knew, or even make out all the words.

One voice came through clearly: 'I'm telling you guys, the word's in – take it easy on Fidel.' The accent was American, Mississippi-delta southern or south-western, Jensen thought. 'No more raids. No more assassination plots. We're supposed to collect intelligence, and that's it, except maybe for some resupply missions.'

'I tell you, there are raids,' another voice insisted. 'Big raids, from now until 1965.'

'Kennedy's raids, not Johnson's,' someone else countered.

'Not even Kennedy's,' said a familiar voice. 'Those plans were a lie. They told us lies to keep us quiet while Kennedy sent men to Cuba with messages of peace and understanding. He was our enemy.'

Jensen placed the voice. It was Esteban.

'He was our friend,' another voice said.

'He is better dead,' Esteban shouted. 'I said so before. I say it again. He betrayed us. He deserved to die.'

There was a silence, then something Jensen couldn't make out, then the American: 'Look, fella, I know you've been through a lot. Those are damn impressive scars you got there. But you just watch what you say, and we'll all be a lot happier.'

'I will watch what I say. I say you treat us like dirt. "A problem of disposal," that is what you call us among yourselves. The thousands of Cubans who are armed and ready and waiting to redeem their homeland. We are an embarrassment to you. And I say to you: Go away. We do not want your help. We are not something to be disposed of like garbage. We are men and we are going to free Cuba. And we will kill you if you try to stop us. We will kill you, the way your President was killed.'

Several voices were raised against Esteban's outburst. Then there was a silence, and desultory conversation, and the sounds of people saying good-bye and leaving.

Gutierrez and Elena stood near the bed.

'How do you feel?' she asked Jensen.

'Much better.' He squinted at her. 'I can see clearly now.'

She smiled. 'That's good.'

'As long as I'm looking at you, it's wonderful.' As soon as the words were out, he could feel his face get warm.

'Thank you.'

He kept looking at her. It was true: She did look wonderful – the warm golden skin; the dark eyes; the long jet-black hair; the tiny, flawless body.

Gutierrez coughed.

'Sorry, Ramón. You look wonderful, too.'

They all laughed. Laughing hurt Jensen's ribs, but he thought it was a kind of pain he could learn to enjoy.

'I have something to tell Ramón,' he said, and paused. 'Elena, maybe you shouldn't hear this. All it can do is put you in danger, and I don't want to do that.'

'While you are here in my house, I feel that I am responsible for you. If you can tell Ramón, you can tell me.'

Jensen started to protest, then thought better of it. There was no reason to keep what he was doing a secret from her. If there was danger for her in being associated with him, it was already too late to avert it.

'All right,' he said. 'Ramón, the most important thing is to let your friends know that the meeting they set up for us was compromised somehow. The men who attacked me knew who I was, and they must have known where I was going, because

155

they couldn't have followed me through all that crowd. Someone sent them specifically to intercept me and warn me off. I guess that's why they didn't kill me – they wanted me to deliver a message to you and whoever else was helping me.'

'What message?'

'They told me to go home and forget it all,' Jensen replied. 'And to tell everyone here that I was wrong.'

'That you were wrong?' Elena said.

'I had a theory I was here to check on. Ramón was helping me.'

She looked at Gutierrez and then back at Jensen. 'I don't understand.'

'The details don't matter right now. The point is, they wanted me to convince the people who knew about my theory that I had decided I was wrong. To forget the whole idea.'

Ramón said, 'If they were so eager to say you were wrong, maybe that's because they know you're right.'

Jensen let his head sink back against the pillows. 'That's what I've been thinking.'

For almost a week Marta had been emptying Jensen's bedpan and giving him sponge baths, but when his insistence on getting out of bed finally overcame Doctor Alvarez's objections, it was Elena who was there to help him up and bear part of his weight and steady him on his way to the toilet. He was uneasy about it: He did not see how her small, delicate frame could support someone of his size, especially if something went wrong and he had to depend on her completely. But she was adamant, so he gave in. It was the right thing to do. He was not as strong as he thought.

In the bathroom he could not avoid the mirror. He stood in front of it for minutes, leaning against the sink and staring at the white bandage that covered his left cheek. Once, he put his hand to the bandage, but he stilled the impulse to peel it away from the wound and look at it. On the way back to the bed he concentrated on the progress he was making using his legs, so that he would not think about his face.

'Well,' he said when he was back in bed. 'Thank you. I don't feel quite so helpless now.'

'You did very well. Better than Doctor Alvarez thought you would.'

'What does he know? He's just a doctor. What I need is an insurance salesman.'

She laughed lightly. 'That's good. If you're making jokes, I'm sure you'll be well in no time.'

Her eyes smiled into his.

That night he was awakened by another argument at the big round table in the next room. This time it was in Spanish, distorted by dialect, and he did not understand everything he heard. What he did understand was disturbing and perplexing.

The argument was about Esteban and the Kennedy assassination. Jensen had the clear impression that some of the men who had heard Esteban the night before believed he might know something about the assassination. And they were talking as if one of the extremist exile groups might actually have been responsible for the shooting in Dallas.

There was a story – he couldn't make out all of it, though he strained to hear – about a woman who had been introduced to Lee Harvey Oswald by a couple of rightist exiles who had told her later that Oswald was going to do something important for the cause. Something violent, Jensen thought he heard one of the men say.

It all ran directly counter to his growing conviction that

Castro was behind the assassination. He did not know what to make of it.

Gutierrez fairly bounced into the room.

'Horacio, *felicidades!* I hear you are walking on your own feet again.'

Jensen put aside the newspaper he was reading.

'Sure enough. I made it all the way to the bathroom and back, leaning on a beautiful five-foot-tall woman the whole time. I did so well I'm thinking of entering the Olympics this year.'

'Elena says you were very strong.'

Jensen smiled on the right side of his face.

'That is one special woman, *eh, amigo*?' Gutierrez said. '*Muy guapa.*'

Jensen nodded. 'She's something, all right. What do you know about her? Who is she?'

Gutierrez pulled up a chair and sat down next to the bed. 'That is an interesting question. There are not many people here in New Orleans who knew her in Cuba. She was the daughter of a prosperous Chinese merchant who married a Cuban woman of good family. She was educated in Europe. It is said her father had contempt for many things about Cuba and he did not wish his daughter to think of herself as a Cubana.' He shrugged. 'It is hard to blame him.'

'That's all?'

'*Quién?* . . . Oh. No, there is more. Her father and mother were killed by one of Castro's revolutionary tribunals.'

'Where was she?'

'I think she was still in Europe. She was married to a European. He was a nobleman of some kind.'

'And then?'

'After her mother and father were killed, she came here to the United States. I do not know if she divorced her husband, but I think she must have.'

'Did she come straight here to New Orleans?'

'No. She went to Miami. Her family had friends there. Later she came here and opened this shop.'

'And the back room?'

'One day she called me on the telephone and told me who she was and asked me to come here for tea. She said if there was any way she could help the cause, she would do it. The thing she spoke about was the arguments we are always having with each other.' He made a sour face. 'There are always so many who know every answer to every question.'

'So she suggested using her shop as a place where the factions could meet and iron out their differences?'

'It was not so simple as that. It happened slowly, and even now there are some who do not come here. They think of me as a foolish old man. I am not old; but it does not matter. I am not foolish either. A little at a time, people began to come here. Now it is as you see it. It does not do much good, I am afraid. Elena does not say she is disappointed, but it cannot be what she wanted.'

'Maybe not,' Jensen acknowledged. 'I suppose it's hard to know how much to expect from a thing like this.'

He studied his friend for a long moment. 'Ramón, suppose I told you I had heard a member of one of the militant groups claiming credit for killing John Kennedy.'

The Cuban stared at him. '*Si?*' His voice was tight. 'Suppose you said this . . .'

'All right. Don't suppose. I am saying it. What do you think? Is it possible?'

'Anything is possible, *mi amigo*.' Gutierrez's expression

darkened, and he withdrew into thought.

After a time he said, 'This is a hard question you ask. It is an unpleasant thing for me to think about.' He was silent again, staring down at the floor. When he looked up, there was no expression on his face. 'You are my friend and you have helped me and the cause of Cuban freedom. I feel I must answer you honestly. Yes, this is possible. It gives me pain to say so, but among our young men there are many who are angry and confused. *Quién sabe?* Some of them may be confused enough and angry enough to have become involved in this horrible murder. Understand me, I do not believe this is what happened, but if you ask is it possible, then I have to say yes.'

There was a silence, and then Gutierrez spoke again.

'If it happened that way, it was not a decision that was made by our people. None of the committees who command our groups would have done such a thing. If they did, I would surely know about it. No. It may have been a Cuban, or two Cubans who were somehow involved, but if it was, there can only be one reason – that some agent of Castro came here and pretended to be what he was not and fooled them into helping him.'

Jensen said, 'It would explain a lot of things. Like how I come to have so much evidence that points at Castro and at the same time I think some anticommunists may have been involved.'

'Who? Who is it you think did this?'

Jensen shook his head. 'Not yet, Ramón. I'm sorry, but all I have is some hothead's mouthing off when he was probably full of rum. That's no basis for making accusations. I'm just trying to make sense out of it all myself. When I have something figured out, I'll tell you.'

* * *

Two days later, Elena watched as Jensen pulled and pushed
and levered himself up out of bed. She came quickly to his side
and put her arm around his waist, but he did not lean on her.
He enjoyed the warmth of her body next to his for a moment,
and then he said, 'I want to try it on my own.'

His first step was almost the last. His knee buckled and he
swayed, but she reached out and supported him so that he
could get his balance, and after that, taking one uncertain step
at a time, he hobbled to her bedroom to use the telephone.

'Bravo,' she said, as he sank on to her bed.

'Thanks. I feel like I just went fifteen rounds with Cassius
Clay.'

'You did very well.'

'Yeah. Except there at the beginning when I almost fell on
my ass the first step.'

She laughed, and he smiled without thinking about it and
yelled with the sudden pain in his cheek.

She reached out and touched his face. There was tenderness
in her fingers and in her eyes, tenderness and concern and
connection.

'Are you all right?'

He nodded.

She leaned toward him and kissed his forehead. 'I'll leave
you alone. Call me when you want to go back.'

He watched her leave and then dialed Washington.

Hapgood was not pleased. 'You got mugged! What do you
mean, you got mugged?'

'Just what it sounds like. A couple of guys cornered me and
beat the shit out of me. Cracked ribs and a concussion, and a
six-inch cut on my face. And a broken hand.'

'I never heard such a load of shit.'

'You want me to send you a picture?' Jensen said into the phone.

'No. I want you to get your ass in to work. Do you really have a concussion?'

'That's what the doctor says. That's why I'm staying here.'

'All right, Harry. But get back as soon as you can, huh?'

'Absolutely.'

When he hung up, Jensen knew he was in for trouble in Washington, whenever he got back.

He waited a few minutes before making the next call, calming himself down and collecting his thoughts.

Jill's secretary told him Jill was busy but agreed to give her a note saying he was on the line. He held on, and in a minute he heard Jill's voice.

'Hello, Harry.'

'Hi. How are you?'

'I'm okay. How are you?'

'I'm all right. I'm sorry I didn't call sooner, but things got a little hectic here.'

'I got your message. It was a little scary, and I was worried. Are you sure you're okay?'

'I'm fine, really.' The lie made him uncomfortable, but he was afraid to tell her what had happened. He could not predict what her reaction would be.

'Are you learning anything interesting?'

'Some. Enough to keep me here a little longer.'

'Spoilsport. Can you talk about it?'

'Not really. I'll save it all for when I see you.'

'Okay. But hurry.'

'You bet.'

Chapter Ten

The second Saturday after Mardi Gras Jensen spent two hours out of bed. Doctor Alvarez came by to examine him and pronounced his recovery remarkable. He prescribed a set of exercises to bring back his strength and changed the wrapping around his ribs. He suggested that Jensen might arrange to have his left hand X-rayed at a hospital the next week, and he said that the stitches could probably come out of Jensen's cheek, but he wanted to leave them in for another few days to make sure the wound would not reopen.

Jensen stayed in bed for the rest of the day. From time to time his hand went to the bandage that protected the wound in his cheek. When he caught himself doing it, he resolved to stop. The disfigurement was something he had to live with, at least temporarily, and brooding over it would not help. He tried to read, couldn't, found that he was tired, and took a short nap. It was later than usual when Elena came into his room and announced dinner. It was an occasion of sorts: his first time eating at a real table.

Moving carefully but surely, he swung his legs around and put his feet on the floor. She held out her hand and pulled gently to help him up. But when he was on his feet, she did not let go of his hand. He squeezed hers gently. She squeezed back and looked up at him. Her eyes seemed deeper and more compelling than ever.

She led him into her apartment. It was the only time he had been there except to use her phone. There was a dining room he had never seen before. The table was set with a white linen cloth and napkins; antique china and silver reflected the light of tall white candles.

She held a chair for him, and he lowered himself carefully into it. She kissed his cheek lightly and left the room. He watched her go: Her simple black silk dress fell softly against her and emphasized the elegance of her body.

She served the dinner herself; it was obvious to him that she had cooked the meal, too. It was light, and very French, and superb.

'Elena, that was quite a meal,' he said when they were finished. 'You make me feel like a human being again. Thank you.'

'It was my pleasure.' She smiled slightly, held him with her eyes. 'Do you know what day it is today?'

He shook his head. 'No.'

Her smile widened. She stood up and came around the table, holding out her hand to him. 'Come with me, and I shall tell you.'

Again they walked hand in hand; she led him through the spacious apartment to her bedroom and closed the door behind them. The room was lit by a single tall lamp that beamed its soft light upward to the ceiling, enhancing the rich maroon walls and the deep-pile silver carpet and the large mirrors.

She leaned against him gently. His hand went to her shoulder. The silk was cool and smooth; under it, her body felt at once firm and yielding. She rested her head on his chest for a moment. Then she bent back so that she could look up into his eyes; her body pressed warmly against his thigh.

'It's Leap Year Day,' she said. Her voice, intimately lowered, was even richer and mellower than usual. 'Today, by your custom, women may propose to men.'

Jensen bent his head and kissed her gently. Her lips clung softly to his; she smelled of spices he could not name. After a long time he drew away.

'You're right,' he said. 'That's the custom. And what do you propose?'

'I propose that we spend the next hours together here in my bed.'

He moved his good hand from her shoulder along her spine to the small of her back. She nestled closer to him.

He thought of Jill and could not keep himself from pulling back slightly.

'Horacio? Is something wrong?'

'No . . . Yes.'

He hesitated, unsure of what to do. Elena was the most intriguing woman he could remember, but she was also a complication he did not think he could afford at the moment.

He said, 'It's the nicest February twenty-ninth proposal I've ever had. And you're probably the most appealing woman I've ever met. But I think I used up the last of my sensual energy appreciating that fabulous dinner.'

'Another time, then. I'll take . . . a raincheck, do you say?'

'A raincheck.'

Her hand touched his cheek and moved caressingly over his chest and belly to his groin. She cupped him there gently.

'Kiss me good night.'

As they kissed, her arms went around him, and she pressed herself to his body. It was a long kiss, by turns fierce and tender. It transported him to a strange land of exotic textures and tastes and smells.

She helped him find his way back to his room and kissed him again lightly before she left him alone with the ghost of her body still pressed against his.

Jensen sat on the edge of his bed, alternately lifting one leg and then the other. He had just taken his first solo bath in Elena's bathtub, and he was wearing a new shirt and a pair of jeans that Elena had bought and Marta had altered to fit him; he felt better than he had since Mardi Gras.

There was a knock on the door.

'Come in.'

It was Ramón. 'Horacio. I'm not disturbing you, am I?'

'I'm doing some exercises. I can keep on while we talk.'

The Cuban pulled a chair over and sat facing Jensen.

'I have been thinking about our conversation. About whether anti-Fidelistas may have been involved in the assassination. I have made inquiries, carefully. And I have heard some stories.'

Jensen stopped exercising.

Ramón looked at him, silent, for what seemed like a long time.

'I cannot know if what I have heard has any substance. But I know this – if I have heard it, so have others. For this reason I will tell you what I know, even though it is very troubling. I trust you to have our interests at heart, but I do not want you to hear these things from someone who might ... distort them.'

He paused. Jensen waited.

'There is a woman in Dallas,' Ramón resumed. 'Her name is Odio. Her husband is a man of much importance among the Cubans in Texas. Her parents . . . her parents are in Castro's prisons. Many consider them to be martyrs. And she contributes much money to the cause. Because of these things, many people come to her for help. Schemes against Fidel. Some good ones, many crazy. Or frauds.'

'I can imagine.'

'Last September she had a visit from two men – Latinos. One may have been Cuban. With them was another; they called him Leon Oswald. They had just come from New Orleans, and they said they wanted to introduce this Leon Oswald to the Cuban underground. They wanted money, too, because this Leon Oswald was going to do something important to help the Cuban cause. Something violent. But Señora Odio does not believe in violence, and so she sent them away.'

'And?'

'The next day one of the men called back and asked her what she thought of Leon Oswald. He told her Oswald used to be a marksman in the Marines. She said he should leave her alone, and he called her a coward. He said if the Cubans had any courage they would have assassinated Kennedy after the Bay of Pigs.'

'This was in September?'

'*Sí*.'

'And the man's name was *Leon* Oswald.'

'*Sí*. But there is more. Señora Odio saw this Leon Oswald again. On television. On the twenty-second day of November, in a Dallas police station. They were calling him a different name. Not Leon Oswald. Lee. Lee Harvey Oswald.'

'She was sure it was the same man?'

Ramón nodded. 'That is what I heard. When she saw him, she fainted. And they say she tried to kill herself after that, because she had spoken to people who were planning to kill President Kennedy and she had done nothing about it.'

'Christ,' Jensen said. 'Was there anything more about the two men?'

'They were Latinos. Soldiers of fortune. They are of the extreme right wing, and there may be some connection with the casinos and the gangsters who ran them.'

'That's quite a story.'

Ramón closed his eyes and nodded reluctant affirmation.

'*Sí*. And there is more. Another story to connect Oswald with anti-Fidelistas.'

Again Jensen waited.

'I was at the Tres Cucarachas last night,' Ramón told him. 'At the bar. There was talk about the trial of Jack Ruby. And about Oswald. How he was here in the summer and the things he did. And someone said he had a friend, a Cubano, who had gone with Oswald to Texas to buy guns. There is a gunrunner there, he said, someone who worked for Fidel in the Sierra Maestre. And Oswald wanted to buy rifles from this man. I am not sure who he is; the name was not clear. Oswald asked him for four high-powered rifles. Savages. He offered a thousand dollars each. But the man refused. He said he was no longer selling guns.'

'Four rifles?'

'*Sí*. With telescopic sights.'

'This man who went with Oswald, do you know anything about him?'

'No. Only that he is Cuban, from New Orleans.'

Jensen stood up and walked stiffly around the room.

Holding on to the rail at the foot of the bed, he tried a cautious knee bend. For the first time he got all the way down and back up again without much pain and without using his hold on the bed to pull himself up.

'What do you think of my stories?' Ramón asked.

'To tell you the truth, Ramón, I don't know. They'll give me plenty to think about, though. That's for sure.'

That night he woke up to the voices in the 'club room.' They sounded drunk.

'Eh, Esteban, we figured out who killed Kennedy.' The voice was Eladio's.

'What are you talking about?'

'You know. Bang bang. Shoot the President. We know who Oswald was working for.'

'Shut up. You're drunk.'

'Sure I'm drunk. So are you. Want to know who did it?'

Silence.

'Ricardo Nixon. Eh? How about that?'

'Go home, Eladio. It's late.'

'Can't take the truth, eh?' His tone changed. 'What do you think?' He was asking the others.

There was a ragged chorus of teasing remarks.

'Come on, Esteban. Tell us the truth. He was there in Dallas. What do you say? You know him from the days he was helping us with the training. And you were saying the other night you knew about the assassination. Was it Nixon?'

Jensen did his fifth knee bend, straightened up, then bent and touched his toes.

'Very good,' Ramón said. 'Much improvement.'

'Thanks. But it's not good enough.'

'The young are so impatient.'

Jensen smiled, carefully. 'Thanks again.' He sat on the edge of the bed.

'I have some news,' the Cuban said. 'I have learned the name of Oswald's gunrunner in Texas. It is McKeown. He was very close with Fidel once. There was even talk of his having a job in the new government. It was after the revolution, in 1959. My brother was with Castro on a trip to the United States, and when he returned, we laughed that Fidel would offer a high post in the government to such a man. In those days we still laughed about Fidel. It was before he threw me in jail. Before he killed my brother . . .'

'It is too dangerous,' Elena said. 'Anyone might see you in a hotel downtown. If you are recognized by the wrong person—'

'I can't call from here,' he insisted. 'It was stupid to do it even once. And I have to make this call.'

She stood her ground in silence.

'How about this,' he suggested. 'We could drive out to someplace in the suburbs. Or on Lake Pontchartrain. A restaurant, maybe. We could even have dinner while we were there.'

Grudgingly: 'Well . . . I suppose that would be safe enough.'

It was after nine when he left Elena reading the menu at their table at the lakeside restaurant and went to make his call.

He sat in the phone booth for almost five minutes, steeling himself. He did not want to do anything that would send Jill back to Ralph Norris, but he saw no alternative. The things he had learned recently were far too important for him to let them go by, and Norris was the best source for the information he needed. Still, he could not keep pictures of Norris and Jill

170

together, touching and kissing, from crowding into his mind.

He closed his eyes, took a breath, and picked up the phone to place the call. *Maybe,* he thought, *she won't be home.*

She answered on the fifth ring. She sounded slightly breathless, and she was surprised that it was him.

He had a harder time getting through the preliminaries than he would have liked. Jill, too, seemed stiff and distant. He hurried to get to business, to get it over with.

'I need some information about a woman named Sylvia Odio, who's a Cuban exile in Dallas. She claims some people brought Oswald by to see her before the assassination. I have to know if anybody else has heard that story, and if so, I need to know what they think about it. I'm especially curious about the FBI, with all their informants in the Cuban community. I don't see any way to get the information without asking you to call your friend Norris. Much as I hate to. Believe me, I'd just as soon you never . . . Hell, I'm sorry. That's not what this is about. Just the facts.'

'All right,' she said. 'Let me write some of this down.'

She did, and repeated her notes to him.

'That's fine. And there's something else. A man named McKeown.' He spelled it. 'He was a gunrunner for Castro in the Sierra Maestre days, and then sometime after '60 they had a falling out. He lives in Texas. I want to know if the FBI has anything on him that might be remotely connected with Lee Oswald or with any of the Cuban exile groups, especially the ones on the far right.'

'The exiles? How do they come into this? I thought it was Castro.'

'So did I. But strange things are happening. That's why I want this information as soon as I can get it. I don't want to go off on the wrong track at this point.'

'It's important for you to have this information right away, then?'

'Very.'

'Harry?'

'Yes. What's up?'

'Maybe ... would it help if you could talk to Ralph yourself?'

'I thought he said we should talk through you. He didn't want me to contaminate him.'

'Yes. But ... he's right here, and ... it seems silly for me to have to give a message.'

'Oh. He's right there, is he? How cozy. I hope I'm not interrupting anything.'

'Harry!'

'Well, what the hell, Jill!'

Silence. 'Do you want to talk to him, or not?'

'No, thanks. If it's all the same to you, I'll let you give him the message.'

'Harry, you're being ridiculous.'

'That's helpful.'

Another silence. Tentatively: 'Harry, I'm ... I ... Oh, shit. When will you be back?'

'I don't know. Not right away.'

'I don't understand. What's keeping you?'

'My doctor.'

'What?'

'My doctor. It happens that I got the shit kicked out of me on Mardi Gras.'

'Because of what you're doing?'

'That's right.'

'Harry! My God, why didn't you tell me?'

'I thought you might worry.' He made no attempt to

hold back his bitterness. 'Silly of me, I guess.'

'Oh, for heaven's sake, Harry, can't you stop? Of course I'm worried. Are you all right?'

'I'm getting better.'

'Was it . . . very bad?'

He shifted on the seat of the phone booth. 'Bad enough. I'd rather not talk about it.'

'But . . . All right. I guess I understand.'

'Just get me an answer from Ralph, okay. I'll call back.'

'I'll ask him. But, Harry – please don't misunderstand.'

'Sure.'

He hung up feeling sour and used. His earlier misgivings about driving Jill into Norris's arms seemed ironically naïve.

He had been out on his own for the first time, driving to a small suburban hospital to have his left hand X-rayed. Elena made a special dinner to mark the occasion.

The meal was as excellent and enchanting as the first one she had cooked for him. This time there were three of them: She had invited Ramón to share their celebration.

After Ramón left, Elena and Jensen sat awhile longer. There was brandy and coffee.

'Nice,' he said. 'Very nice.'

'Thank you. I'm glad you enjoyed it. Would you like anything more?'

'No. I'm fine.'

He thought about that: He *was* fine. It was time to stop hanging around behind an antique shop. There were too many things to be learned, and there was the problem of going back and facing Hapgood. He couldn't avoid that forever.

But I can avoid it until tomorrow, he told himself.

He said, 'Maybe I'll have a little more brandy.'

Later they walked slowly through her apartment together; she put her arm around his waist and rested her head on his chest as they moved down the corridor toward his room.

When they got to the door, he turned and held her.

'Good night,' he said. 'It was a beautiful evening.'

She tightened her arms around him. 'Let me tuck you in.'

He undressed in darkness. As he was about to get into bed, she stopped him. She put her arms around him again, careful of the tape that bound his ribs. He felt the texture of silk against his body, smooth and provocative. They kissed, and again he felt transported to a place of rare spices and welcoming softness. His right hand roamed over her back; his left arm came up and circled her shoulders, pressed her to him – the cast was tormentingly clumsy.

She moved against him. Her hands moved up and down his flanks.

'Get into bed,' she said. There was quiet urgency in her voice. She pushed herself away from him.

He was momentarily bewildered, but he moved to the bed and lay down on his back. There was a long, whispering hiss of silk; other quick sounds. He felt a weight on the bed next to him.

Her mouth was on his, her hands moved over his body. He reached out tentatively and touched her nakedness. Pulled her close to him. Too roughly – he winced with a sharp pain in his ribs.

She did not seem to notice. She touched, nibbled, licked, and bit him. His body tingled with desire.

And then her frenzy slowed and she was lying next to him, stroking his chest. They kissed, long and lingeringly. His hand explored her. Her skin was smoother than the silk, smoother than he would have believed. Her spices filled his head.

She caught his hand and held it pressed against her belly, his fingers just touching the top of a strip of black curls.

'Wait,' she said. 'Not too fast. I want to enjoy you.'

Her fingers played in the hair of his groin, caressed him. He thought he would burst. Her head moved. He felt a wetness take hold of him that was at once warm and cool. He closed his eyes and let his hand move out and cup her head as she moved her mouth on him. He stroked her hair: In his mind he saw his fingers sifting through long, pale, golden strands.

His hands stopped.

After a moment Elena sat back and looked at him in the darkness.

'Horacio? What's wrong?'

He gathered her to him. 'Sorry,' he said.

Her fingers touched his lips. 'Not sorry. But what is wrong?'

'Maybe I'm still sick.'

She caressed his face, kissed the corner of his mouth.

'You are not sick. Is it something I did? Did I hurt you?'

'No. You didn't hurt me. It's something else.'

Silence in the darkness.

'You are in love?'

'I don't know. Maybe.' He tried to look into her eyes. 'I don't want to inflict my uncertainties on you.'

'You do not inflict things on me. I am here because I choose to be here. I thought we could give each other pleasure.'

'I would have thought so, too. You are very beautiful. And very . . . provocative.'

'I do not wish to come between you and your love. I wish only for us to enjoy each other. We are friends. We share food and wine without harm to others. That is how I wanted to share you here.'

He touched her face, turned to her, kissed her. 'You're very special.'

She said nothing, but her mouth and her hands and her body were not still until they both shuddered in fulfillment and then subsided and drifted toward a deep, sated sleep.

He awoke once, when she moved herself free of him and got up to go to her own bed.

'Yes, I spoke to Ralph,' Jill said stiffly.

'Good.' Jensen shielded his eyes against the glare in the phone booth. It was hot and stuffy, and he was sweating.

'He said to ask you how your timing was so good.'

'What do you mean?'

'He'd just been going over that file himself. He says the most interesting thing is that there's an odd connection between McKeown and Jack Ruby.'

'Ruby!'

'That's right. Years ago. In 1959, I think he said. Wait a minute and I'll get my notes.'

Jensen wiped his forehead with a handkerchief, opened the glass door of the booth, and berated himself for choosing a phone that was out in the Louisiana sun.

'Harry?'

'I'm here.' He closed the phone booth door.

'April 1959, and May. Ruby visited McKeown and said he was trying to get some people out of prison in Cuba. He offered McKeown money, something like five thousand dollars each, for three people, if McKeown would use his connections with Castro to get them out.'

'Not bad money.'

'He told McKeown it would come from Las Vegas.'

'Really?'

176

'That's what Ralph said.'

'Ruby the mobster strikes again. What did McKeown say?'

'No, I guess. Anyway, Ruby came back to see him in May. He wanted to set up a trade with Castro. He had some Jeeps to trade for the prisoners, and he was offering twenty-five thousand for a letter from McKeown to Castro saying how reliable Ruby was. McKeown says he told Ruby he'd do it, but he wanted five thousand in advance. But Ruby never came back.'

'That's quite a story. But there's no connection with Oswald, is there, besides that he went to McKeown later?'

'Well, yes and no.'

'Go ahead.'

'Ruby went to Cuba, to visit a casino owner he knew – the one Ralph told us about. McWillie. And a few days later Castro deported three prisoners.'

'So maybe Jack did it, after all.'

'Yes. Maybe. But the important part of it is who the prisoners were.'

Jensen wiped his forehead again. 'Who?'

'One of them was a man named Hall. Ralph said he may be the man who brought Oswald to see Mrs Odio, the woman you asked about.'

'And from there Oswald went to McKeown for guns. Closes the circle. Jesus!'

'What do you think it means?'

'I don't know. I wish I did. Maybe we've been on the wrong track all along. Damn.'

There was a pause. 'Harry? How are you?' He could hear concern in her voice, but he could not tell if it was real.

'A lot better. The doctor says I'm still not ready to lead a normal life, but I'm getting damn restless.'

'Take care of yourself, Harry. Please.'

'Yeah. Sure. Say hello to Ralph for me.'

He walked slowly back to the car, where Elena was waiting for him. Suddenly he felt awful.

It was afternoon. Elena's bedroom. The cast was off his hand, replaced by a splint and a bandage. They had celebrated this new bit of progress, and for the first time he'd had enough light to see her clearly as they made love. It did nothing to destroy his nighttime illusions and fantasies.

Afterward she lay beside him, tracing patterns on his body with a fingernail.

'Why are you here in New Orleans?' she asked him.

He stroked her head with his good hand. 'To learn about the Kennedy assassination.' He saw no point in holding it back from her.

'Really? Do you work for the Warren Commission?'

'Oh, God, no. I'm snooping around on my own, that's all.' He stared up at the ceiling. 'I've got some information the Commission doesn't have yet. I took it to Warren, but he wouldn't talk to me. So I'm trying to develop it on my own well enough to shove it down his throat if I have to.'

'You are going through a lot for this.'

'It's important.'

She pushed herself up on her elbows and studied his face. 'Is it important enough for you to be beaten up so badly that you are an invalid for almost a month?'

'That wasn't part of my plan.'

She laughed, deep and throaty. 'I suppose not.'

She put one leg over his and nestled closer to him. He stroked her back.

'Neither were you,' he said.

Chapter Eleven

In the morning he awoke to find her standing next to his bed.

'Good morning,' she said.

'Good morning.' He sat up and swung his feet around on to the floor.

'Getting up?'

He responded by suiting his action to her words. Standing up made him dizzy, but it didn't last.

'Can you get Doctor Alvarez to come and examine me?'

'Don't you feel well?'

'I feel fine. Best I've felt in weeks. I have to get out of here.'

'Horacio! Don't you love me anymore?'

He laughed and reached out and drew her close to him. After he had kissed her thoroughly, he released her.

'I mean I want to be out learning things. I can't stagnate here any longer.'

'It might be dangerous to go out asking questions.'

'Maybe. But I prefer that to going crazy. The Ruby trial will be over soon, and the Warren Commission will finish up, and by then it's going to be too late.'

'You do not think they will find the truth?'

'I don't see how they can, without the information I have. But I'm not even sure that what I know is the truth. That's why I have to get out and learn more.'

179

'But . . . you could not stand to be hurt like that again.'

'No. Probably not.' He went to the closet. 'I'll have to be careful.'

'Where will you go? Who will you talk to?'

He took his jeans off the hook and put them on. 'I've got to get back to Washington. But as soon as I can, I'll go to Tampa. Maybe Miami.'

She regarded him thoughtfully. As always, he felt himself drawn into the depths of her eyes.

'I know many people in Florida. If you must do this, I can help you.'

'You've done enough.'

'Sometimes you are a very silly, willful man, Horacio. You are still weak, whatever your impatience tells you. Perhaps you can do all you want to do alone, without help. But if you can't, and you have trouble, what will you do then, if you are alone? Some of these people do not trust Americans. You have learned that here. It will help you to have a Cubana along. Even a China-Cubana. And I can help you speak to them. Your Spanish is good, but . . .'

He laughed. 'My Spanish is awful.'

'No. It is not awful. It lacks nuances. There are idioms—'

'You're very persuasive. But you have your shop to worry about. It's too much to ask.'

'I can close the shop for a week or two. It is a slow time now, until Easter.'

He bent to kiss her.

'Okay. I won't fight you anymore. You're right, it would be a big help to have you along. But it might be dangerous for you, too.'

'I understand. But as we once agreed, if I am to have danger because of you, it is too late to avoid that now.'

* * *

That night Jensen was awakened by a rough hand on his shoulder. His eyes opened slowly, were filled suddenly with a painfully bright light. Squinting, he could barely make out the shape of someone holding a spotlight; he had the sense that there were other people in the room with him, too, beyond his limited field of vision.

For an instant the light shifted away from his eyes and swung toward a second dark figure next to the bed. Still dazzled, Jensen saw the light glint off the dark blue of a gun barrel. The light held long enough for him to identify the weapon as a submachine gun, and then the glare hit him full in the eyes again.

'Mr Jensen . . .' A harsh male voice from near the door. 'We've been watching you, Mr Jensen. We know what you're up to.'

Jensen felt his body stiffening with growing fear. It was hard for him to breathe. He began to sweat.

'You've been doing a lot of snooping around about the Kennedy assassination. That's not your job, poking around to see if maybe it had something to do with Cuba.'

There was a commotion in the doorway. Noise. Scuffling. A brief cry.

Elena stumbled across the room and fell heavily on to the bed. She landed on his left hand: Needles shot through his palm and knuckles, and fire ran up his arm. He clamped down on a scream.

'That's better,' said the voice from the doorway. 'Now we've got both of the lovebirds where we can see them at the same time. And the lady's nice to look at, too. You're a lucky man, Jensen.'

Elena was naked. She arranged herself on the bed so that

she was no more exposed than necessary. It was a natural movement, with no appearance of covering up; there was nothing provocative about it. A corner of Jensen's mind registered surprise – sexy as she was, she had somehow made herself temporarily neuter.

'All right – enough games,' the man by the door said. 'You want to know why we're here, right? Well, Harry, it's very strange. The way things work out, we're all on the same side in this. We'd like to see Fidel Castro get what's coming to him as much as you would. As much as the pretty lady would, too. And let me tell you, we've got some nice, juicy things that point the finger straight at him.' He paused. 'We've got one problem, though. Nobody's going to believe a word we say. We're not exactly your pillars of the community, you know what I mean? But you – you're different. You're a class act, Jensen. Big shot like you, way up in the government, if you talked, people'd listen. So, what it is, we want to help you out. What d'you say, Jensen? Interested?'

'I don't know what you're talking about.'

'We're not going to have to do this the hard way, are we?'

Another voice said, 'Harry, baby, get smart, will you? If we wanted you dead or damaged, we wouldn't be here. And neither would you. Like the man said, we need your help... And let me tell you, buddy boy, you need our help, too, or else the minute you're back on your feet and asking questions again, you're going to be so much dead meat.'

'All right,' Jensen conceded. 'Tell me what you want.'

'That's more like it,' the second voice said. 'It's just what my friend told you. All you have to do is keep on doing what you're doing. Keep finding evidence that Castro was behind the assassination, and we'll all be happy. We need somebody clean, somebody high in the government, to take off the lid they've slapped on this business. Truth is, we were about to give up and go ahead on our own with it, when we got wind of you digging around, stirring things up. So we've got plenty of leads of our own we can give you. And we can help you get confirmation of some things.'

'Like what?'

'Well, you talked a lot to your friend Hammond. He was a real talkative guy, and that's too bad, because it killed him. He told you some things about American assassination attempts against Castro, right?'

Jensen said nothing. His jaw tightened.

'Harry. You got to loosen up. We know what Hammond told you. And he's dead. You can't hurt him anymore.'

'Why was he killed?'

'Certain people didn't want the connection between us and the CIA on the front pages. There was more involved in that than just Cuba. They were afraid of what would happen once any of it came out. It's one of the things that's been slowing us down.'

'And that's what you want me to walk into?'

'We've got that cooled down some. Other things are more important. Right now all that matters is getting the Castro business out in the open. Which is where you come in.'

'I don't know.'

'You don't have to know. Just do what we tell you. The point is, we've got the straight goods on those assassination attempts. When the time comes, if we need to, we can produce some of the people who were involved. And that gives old Fidel a pretty good motive, right? What's better than revenge? Or maybe he wanted to save his own hide by getting Kennedy before Kennedy got him. And that's only the beginning. We can be more help as you get deeper into it. That's all we want. Just keep doing what you're doing. And while you're at it, we'll keep the blackhats off your back.'

'What blackhats?'

'You telling us you really don't know?' the voice by the door asked.

'That's right. Unless you mean the beating I got.'

'That's part of it.'

'I kind of thought that was you.'

There was rough laughter.

'You've got to be kidding,' the second voice said. 'Why would we do that? We're on your side; we told you. We need you to do our talking for us. Look, you're a smart guy. Why don't you think about it a little? You're out there trying to prove Castro killed Kennedy, right? Never mind Oswald and whoever else was in on it. What it adds up to is – Castro killed Kennedy. Are you with me so far?'

'Go ahead.'

'Okay. If you start talking about it, people are going to listen to you. All kinds of people. High-up people, Joe Average. And that's got to be pretty bad news for our friend with the beard and the cigar. So who's out to stop you from proving it?'

'Castro, if he knows about it—'

'Give the man a kewpie doll. Right on the nose. Castro wants you to dry up and blow away. Who else?'

Jensen had no answer.

'What do you think about General Khanh?' the second voice asked.

'Khanh? The Vietnamese?'

'The very same.'

'I don't see what he has to do with . . . Oh – yes, I guess I do.'

'Yeah. I think you get another kewpie doll,' said the man in the doorway.

'This is more up your alley than ours,' the second voice said. 'We've had some help figuring it out from friends of ours in Washington, but we want to know what you think about it.'

'I hadn't thought about it at all, until now.' Jensen was disgusted with himself. 'But if what you're getting at is that the United States isn't going to fight a war in Vietnam and a war in Cuba at the same time, I'd have to say you're right.'

'Yeah.' It was the voice at the door. 'That's how we had it figured.'

'So you're saying the South Vietnamese want to keep the lid on any Cuban involvement in the assassination because they're afraid if we pay too much attention to Cuba, we'll forget them.'

'Something like that.' The second man, now.

'But what about all the rumors that the Vietnamese were behind the assassination themselves? That they did it in revenge for Kennedy's having the Diem brothers killed?'

'We don't know about that. Maybe they figure nobody's going to believe those stories. They just don't want us going to war with Cuba.'

'All right,' Jensen conceded. 'I'll buy it.'

The second voice shifted, as if its owner were pacing. 'Thing is, once you bring them into it, once you figure it's war there or war in Cuba, there are other people who come into it, too.'

'Like?'

'Like the whole fucking Department of Defense. If those guys with the brass braid figure they have a shot at fighting a war in a middle-sized country halfway around the world, or else they can throw a quick invasion at a little island right by Florida, which the hell way you think they'll jump?'

'Okay. I can see that.' They were right, Jensen saw. Once you made it a question of war in Cuba or war in Vietnam, the implications became very broad. 'Professionally, the military is a lot better off with a war in Vietnam. Even a short war there would be better for them. But I'm not sure that's enough reason for them to try actively to prevent the truth from coming out.'

'Shit,' came the voice from the doorway. 'How could a guy get where you are and still be so wet behind the ears? I wish I had your faith in all those generals. Myself, I think they're the dirtiest bunch in the country. Worse than the politicians.'

'If the stakes are high enough, anybody'll do anything,' the second voice interjected. 'And all we're talking about is whether they'd step on Harry Jensen and a couple of other people in order to hang on to a war that's a lot better for them than anything else that's likely to come along in a hurry. With stakes like those, a murder here and there doesn't seem like a big deal to me.'

'When you put it that way, it doesn't sound like a big deal to me, either,' Jensen acknowledged. 'So I'm up against Castro and the South Vietnamese and the American military.'

'At least. And there are some people in the CIA who still don't want the truth to come out. Figure, if Castro got Kennedy because of what the CIA was trying to do to Castro, it doesn't help their image much. And the oil companies. Don't forget them.'

'The oil companies?'

'Sure. What we hear, they think there's oil off the Vietnamese coast. If that's true, they'd like to get their hands on it. And they've got the clout to get a war going.'

'You have intelligence people inside the oil companies?'

'We're not here to answer questions, Harry,' said the man by the door. 'We just wanted you to know we were interested in you, and what you're up against. And to speed you up a little.'

'All right. You've made your point. One thing before you go. Which one of these enemies of mine had me beat up?'

'That was a couple of local boys did that to you. Very talented, too, for pick-up labor. It was the Vietnamese hired them. Truth is, you're lucky to be alive. Human life doesn't mean much over there. Guys like that, somebody's in their way, they're just as likely to kill him as not.'

Jensen slept fitfully. He had dreams that disturbed him but that in the morning he could remember only in flashes. Elena was in them all, and there were a lot of images from old gangster movies – Edward G. Robinson looking sinister, and Paul Muni in *Scarface*. It was all dark and frightening in an unspecific way. When he awoke, he was tired, and he felt a residue of anxiety, as if he had spent the night running from something, or someone, and he might have to start running again soon.

He got up and did some knee bends and stretching exercises. He was stiff, and his legs still ached, but he was sure he would be able to get around on his own without any real trouble.

He pulled on his jeans and wandered back into Elena's apartment. She was in the kitchen.

'Good morning,' he said. 'Coffee smells good.'

'Would you like a cup?'

'Love it.'

She put it on the heavy wooden table that took up one corner of the open, country-style room.

'We had visitors last night,' she said. It was as much a question as a statement.

'You didn't dream it, if that's what you mean.'

'What was it all about?'

'Just what you heard.' He put milk and sugar in his coffee.

'You think Castro ordered the assassination?'

'Maybe. That's what I'm trying to find out. The information I told you about makes it look that way.'

She went to the stove; her back was to him. She put butter in a skillet and cracked two eggs into it. He could hear them sizzle as they hit.

'And those people last night. Who were they?'

'I don't know exactly who they were. You could say they're in the gambling business.'

'The Mafia?'

'That's what some people call it. But you should know as much about them as I do – they did a lot of their business in Havana. That's why they're so interested in what I'm doing.'

'What will you do now?'

'Go along with them. I don't have much choice. And it's more or less what I want to do.' *Part of it, anyway*, he thought.

'I will come with you, to help.'

He moved his spoon around in his cup. 'I know you wanted to yesterday. But now that we know how strong the opposition is, I thought it would be a good idea for you to reconsider.' He had other reasons, but he kept them to himself.

'Now you need me more.'

'Well, I've got the mob looking after me, so I should be safe. And it would be a lot harder for them to protect two of us than one.'

She slid the eggs on to a plate and brought them to the table for him. She sat down opposite him.

'What will you learn in Florida and Dallas?'

'There are a couple of things I have to follow up. I want to find out if Castro knew what was being done against him by the CIA this fall, and if he had contact with certain people. I'm hoping there are agents in the underground who have the answers. And there are some stories I want to check. Fill in the details.'

'What stories?'

'Well, for one, there was a man in Miami and Tampa in mid-November who came to Texas between the twentieth and the twenty-second, then went to Mexico City on the twenty-third, and flew from there to Havana under peculiar circumstances. I'd like to know more about him. The only place I can start on that is Florida.'

'I could help you there. I have friends who I am sure could find out who he was, if he was a Cuban.'

'Yes. A Cuban-American.'

'You see?' She smiled at her triumph. 'What else will you do?'

'There are other stories to check. I have friends myself, from La Brigada, whom I can talk to. And I have a message to give them from someone they know in the CIA that should gain me their trust.'

She stared thoughtfully at him, then pushed herself back from the table.

'There are people I should call today to tell them we are coming. They can begin to make inquiries while we travel.'

'I don't want you to say too much on the phone.'

She put her hand on his shoulder. 'Let me get my address book. Then we will discuss how much to say.'

He finished his eggs and wondered how he would be able to maintain the illusion of being interested only in Castro as a potential culprit without letting Elena know he was lying, or at least shading the truth. He did not fool himself that it would be easy. She was intelligent and alert; he had to expect she would pick up any slips he made.

He heard her come back into the kitchen. Instead of walking straight over to the table, she stopped at the counter and turned on the radio. Then she came around behind him. He felt her fingers in his hair. She stood there, stroking his head and neck for a moment.

'It has been good to have you here.'

'Even if I had to get beaten up first,' he joked.

Her laugh was low and brief. 'I would not have wanted it that way. But it could not be helped.' She kissed his neck.

He twisted in his chair so that he could face her, kiss her.

She stepped back quickly, out of his reach: She made a motion that drew his eyes to her right hand. It took a moment for him to recognize what she held – an automatic pistol.

'I'm sorry, Harry Jensen, but I cannot let you do those things.'

The gun in her hand was neither large nor small; looking into its muzzle, he thought it was precisely the right size to command his complete respect. It rested in her hand without awkwardness. He was sure she knew how to use it.

'I don't understand.'

She said nothing.

'What I want to do is in your interest, isn't it?' he asked. 'If I expose Castro as being responsible for the assassination, he can't possibly last. With a provocation like that, the United States would blast him out of existence, if Cuba didn't first, to prevent American retaliation.'

190

'That is why I cannot let you do it.'

'But you ... your friends. You could have your country back. End your exile.'

'I have my country,' she said simply. 'It is these people, the ones you call my friends, who would take it from me. And my exile is voluntary.'

With difficulty he lifted his eyes from the gun and looked at her. 'You're an agent for Castro.'

Some of the tension left him. They were both silent as he thought about it.

'I guess it's pretty clever,' he said. 'Take one daughter of the middle class, someone who's been educated not to care too much for the old-style Cuba and who maybe picked up some radical notions in the course of her fancy education. But someone with the right credentials to pass. Like an aristocratic marriage. That wouldn't hurt. Then you set her up as a benefactor to the exiles. What a fantastic listening post your clubroom must have been. Is it wired for sound? Of course; it must be. You have my congratulations, Elena. I never would have guessed.'

Her body had stiffened as he spoke. 'I do not like to have you make fun of me.'

'I'm not making fun of you.' He was smiling. He couldn't help it.

'I will have to kill you. Do you understand that?'

'Will you forget your preconceptions for one minute and listen to me?'

Warily: 'If you try to fool me—'

'No, no. No tricks. Just listen. You want to kill me because I'm trying to prove Castro was behind the assassination. But the truth is, I don't believe that myself any longer. I think it's at least as likely it was one of the exile groups, and the evidence that points to Castro is phony.'

'It is not so easy to confuse me as that.'

He ignored her comment. 'There was a story I heard the other day – that some Latinos, members of the Cuban underground, introduced Oswald to a *prominenta* in the Dallas Cuban community and asked for money so Oswald could do something violent that would help the Cuban cause. And that's just the beginning. I'm telling you this all may be a colossal frame-up to get the US to invade and put the Batistanos and the ultraright and the Mafia back in power.'

'*Verdaderamente?*'

'When you were out of the room now, you know what I was thinking? I was wondering how I was going to investigate those stories in Florida without letting you or the Mafia know that I was working against you.'

He studied her. He could see that he had her attention now.

'While I was lying in bed, I heard arguments in the clubroom. Some of your regulars seem to think it was their friends who killed Kennedy. If you kill me now, you're the crazy one, not me. As long as the Mafia is relying on me to do their investigating, they don't pose such a threat to you. And in the meantime maybe I can help you find evidence that will prove it was your enemies who were to blame.'

She lowered the gun. 'You truly believe what you're saying?'

'Yes.' He could hardly say anything else. In fact, he didn't know what to believe.

'What about your CIA? How could any of the exile groups have done this without their masters knowing it? Surely the CIA would not allow the killing of the American President.'

'It doesn't have to have been an official action. It could have been a few people, acting on their own. And as for the CIA, it's got its factions and its internal conflicts. There are things that go on in one part of it that the other parts never hear about. Both the exiles and the CIA could have been involved. That's what I want to find out about.'

'Would it make any difference to how you feel to know that Lee Harvey Oswald was an American intelligence agent?'

'That's what his mother said.' Jensen hadn't given the charges much credence at the time, but now they took on new power. And Elena, for all her own special interest in the question, was much more credible than Marguerite Oswald.

'Poor Mrs Oswald,' Elena said. 'Do you want more coffee?'

Jensen looked at his cup and at Elena, standing closer to him now, the gun held casually at her side, pointing at the floor. He considered trying to take it from her, but he couldn't imagine what he would do after that.

'Sure. I'd love more coffee. Why don't you join me and tell me some more about Oswald?' He handed her his cup.

While she was refilling his cup and pouring one for herself, he said, 'Maybe you ought to bring over some rum, too. I'm still shaky from having that gun pointed at me.'

She came to the table with coffee and rum on a tray. The pistol was gone; he had not seen what she had done with it.

Rum and coffee was the right combination of soothing and stimulating for him. His plight stopped seeming impossible, at least temporarily, and he felt alert enough to deal with Elena.

The radio's Latin music brightened his mood.

'You do your job well,' he said when his cup was almost empty. 'You even maneuvered it so I would overhear those conversations, didn't you? Putting me in the room next door to the clubroom. You engineered my conversion.'

'Yes, you are right.' She held his eyes with her own. 'I could have put your bed elsewhere. I did hope you would hear . . .

indiscretions that might make you feel as you do. But when I took you in, that was not for any reason but to help you.' She picked up his hand and held it in both of hers. Pressed it to her lips. It made him shiver; he thought it was pleasure, but he wasn't sure.

'Understand one thing,' she said. 'My bed is never part of my work. I did not have to make love with you. It was my choice. I did it because you interested me and you excited me.' She kissed his hand again and released it.

'And now,' she said, 'I will tell you about Lee Harvey Oswald. Once upon a time, there was a young man who read about Karl Marx and who liked what he read. Not long after that the young man enlisted in the United States Marine Corps and served for more than two years. He learned a trade: They sent him to radar school. And he traveled. His unit went to a place in Japan where he could use his radar training – a small island on which there is a large CIA base, where they keep U-2 planes that are sent out over China. And the young man went to Taiwan as well. In order to serve in this unit, he had to have a clearance for secret information. All members of the unit did. But the education in radar and the broadening travel was not enough for him. He taught himself Russian, out of a book.'

'Quite a fellow, our hero,' Jensen commented.

Elena smiled briefly. 'Yes, quite a fellow. So perhaps it will be a surprise to you to learn that after spending a little less than three years in the US Marines, our young man told lies to his superiors about how sick his mother was so that he could get an early discharge. And as soon as he had his discharge and was back in the United States, he took passage on a freighter bound for London. The trip cost as much as half his total earnings while he was in the Marine Corps, but all he had in the bank at the time was two hundred dollars. And he did not seem to the other Marines like someone who saved every penny he earned.'

'You seem to know a lot about this young man.'

She smiled again. 'I cannot tell you who my informants are.'

'But they're reliable.'

Seriously: 'Oh, yes. They are very reliable.'

'And where did our young man go from London?'

'To Helsinki. And he went there in only a few hours, at a time when there were no commercial flights. We will have to guess how he traveled, and where he got the money for that trip.'

'Why would a young fellow want to go to Helsinki, I wonder. London seems much more attractive.' He was playing along with her tone, but what she was saying was intriguing, and troubling.

'Oh, he didn't stay in Helsinki. He went right on to Moscow. He was admitted into Russia without any trouble. And not long after he was there, he stopped in at the American embassy, offered them his passport, and said he was going to become a Russian citizen and tell the Russians everything he knew about American military radar.'

'What did they do?'

'Told him to come back on a regular business day.'

'You're kidding.'

'No.'

'Did he go back?'

'He sent them a letter.'

'And then?'

'He applied for Soviet citizenship, but it was denied and he was sent to Minsk and put to work in an electronics plant. He had an ordinary life there. But in one way he was very lucky.

He met a pretty girl at a dance, and they fell in love and got married. She was in Minsk, living with her uncle, who was an official in the Ministry of State Security, which runs the secret police. When they got married, she moved in with him. Oh, and I almost forgot to say – he had an apartment all to himself, at State expense, which is a luxury of sorts in that part of the Soviet Union.'

'Now, wait a minute,' Jensen said. 'From everything you've said, it sounds to me more like he was a Russian agent than an American. And if he told them about the radar secrets . . . Just how much did he know, do you know that?'

'No. But I understand that when he went to Russia, many American frequencies were changed. And I can also tell you that for years the Russians had been trying to shoot down a U-2 and failing. They were failing because of problems related to how high the U-2 flew. The Russian tracking radar was not good enough. But shortly after our young man arrived, they shot down a U-2. And one of the things the young man had worked on was high-altitude radar for the U-2.'

'So he did tell them.'

'*Quién sabe?* My information is not complete. I do not know if he did or he didn't. I agree that it looks as if he did. And I can tell you one other thing: The Russians denied his application for citizenship and sent him off to Minsk because they thought he was a CIA agent, sent there to become a Russian and then in time, perhaps after very many years, to be reactivated as an agent. They wanted to watch him, and they wanted to keep him out of the way.'

'Not something you'd do with a guy who'd given you a lot of valuable information.'

She shrugged. 'It could be. It is possible he gave them good information merely to prove to them that he was in earnest and that he was trustworthy. His masters in the CIA might not have realized how important the information was. Or they might not have cared.'

Jensen sighed. 'No, you're right. They're capable of it. I can see them now, calculating the difference in value between a U-2 shot down and a sleeper agent put in place in Russia, especially if he had a military job there. But, damn it, I still don't see why this doesn't add up to his being a Soviet agent. He defected, he told them what they wanted to hear, he got a cushy job and a nice apartment, and he married the pretty niece of an MVD man.'

She smiled wickedly and rubbed her hands like a stage witch. 'Aha. You have fallen into my trap. You are right. He sounds like a Russian agent. Now you must listen to the rest of the story: One day he decided he did not like living in Russia. He wrote to the American embassy and asked to be given back his passport and to have a visa for his wife to join him. He also asked for money to make the trip back to the United States. This posed problems for the embassy. He had done many things that made him ineligible. But the State Department decided he had never renounced his citizenship, and they found a way to get his wife past many restrictions to her having a visa, and they encouraged various private organizations to give him money for the trip.'

Jensen was nodding his head. 'I begin to see what you're getting at.'

'Yes. He was helped back into the country. He was never prosecuted. When he asked to renew his passport, it was done without question.'

'And he got a new passport. That's the oddest of all, now that I think about it. They're beyond the pale over at the passport office. These days, it's worth your life to get a passport if you've ever so much as read the *Daily Worker*. Not even that. They're rejecting people for all kinds of reasons. But Oswald got a passport. And it seems to me that there are regulations about not getting a passport if you've tried to transfer your allegiance.'

'So, you see my point. Every evidence indicates he tried to defect and he helped the Russians and gave them military secrets, and yet the American government smooths the way for him to return.'

'Yes. It does seem very odd. Still—'

'Would you be more convinced if I told you that the man in the Mexican visa line ahead of Mr Oswald this past September was an agent of the CIA? And another man, a strange old Briton who claims to be a minister but who is almost certainly an American intelligence agent, sat next to Oswald on the bus to Mexico City, where he was going so he could talk to the Cubans?'

'It might be a coincidence.'

'But you don't quite think so, do you?' She stood up. 'Do you want more coffee?'

'I want to get out and walk. All right with you?'

'That's fine.'

They walked down Royal Street. It was a chilly day for March.

'I don't know,' he said. 'From what you told me, it's hard to get away from the idea that he had something to do with the CIA. Or military intelligence. That's even more likely, it seems to me: He left the Marines early, and he already had a military clearance. The only question I have is – how did they know they could trust him?'

'Perhaps they didn't have to.'

He stopped walking and looked at her.

'Perhaps it was not Lee Harvey Oswald who went to Russia.'

'Who, then?'

'An imposter.'

'What makes you say that?'

'No one who saw him in Russia saw him here. In fact, very few Americans saw him in Russia at all. In Moscow he hid himself in the Hotel Metropole. Except for his visit to the embassy to renounce his citizenship, he saw only a few Americans. There was one person he saw for a long time; she was a newspaper reporter, but it is said she is also an employee of the State Department. There are pictures of him in Russia, but they do not look very much like him. The face is too full, and he seems too short, standing next to his wife. Perhaps all the real Oswald had to do for American intelligence was go into hiding for them.'

'Yes,' he acknowledged, 'they do that kind of thing.' He began to walk again.

For three blocks he said nothing. He watched the people pass in the street and he admired the houses and the ironwork balconies.

'It seems like an awful lot of trouble to go to.'

She did not answer him directly. 'His mother called him, you know, while he was there, and his brother called him, as well. He refused the call from his brother, and he only spoke to his mother for a few minutes. She claims that all he did was grunt. Like, 'mmmhmm,' or 'huh?' Noises like that. She thinks it was not he who spoke with her.'

They turned on to Bourbon Street. It was not recognizable as the street he had been on almost a month before. Still, even without the masquers and the trappings of Mardi Gras, it had a carnival atmosphere. As they walked, they could pick up the strains of Dixieland coming from the clubs that had a matinee or an impromptu jam session under way.

'Do you know who was the Oswalds' closest friend in Texas when he returned?' she asked.

'I remember something about a Mrs Paine.'

'Ah, the neighbor. No, I do not mean her.'

'There was a couple, wasn't there, a White Russian and his wife who helped him and Marina with their marriage when they first started having trouble?'

'That's the one. The Baron George de Morenschildt.'

'Baron? I missed that.'

'Oh, yes. George de Morenschildt is an aristocrat, and he has aristocratic acquaintances. The former Mrs Bouvier, for instance, who is now Mrs Auchincloss: You've heard of her – her daughter's name is Jacqueline Bouvier Kennedy.'

'For God's sake.'

'Yes. The baron has an intriguing history. He prides himself on having been a member of the French underground in World War Two. He did intelligence work for them. But he is not so proud that in the early days of the war he was twice held on suspicion of being a Nazi spy. Now he is a petroleum engineer and he travels a great deal. He has several connections with the CIA. And there is an interesting coincidence. In 1960 and 1961, because of the death of a child, he and his wife made a walking tour of Central America. Do you know where they were in April, at the time of the Bay of Pigs invasion? In Guatemala City. And they made a film of what they saw and gave it to what is called 'an agency of the United States government.'

He absorbed that.

'Let's turn around,' he said after another block. 'I'm getting tired.'

As they turned back on to Royal Street, he said, 'They make kind of an odd couple, don't they? Morenschildt and Oswald?'

'The aristocratic, right-wing former spy and the poor little Marxist who can't quite get anything right? I agree – they make a very odd couple.'

'Unless they have something special in common. Or unless, say, they'd been assigned to each other and George was holding our boy's hand on somebody's instructions.'

'Is it so hard, then, to believe that Mr Oswald was an agent of the CIA?'

'Or the DIA, maybe, or Naval Intelligence. No. It's not hard at all.'

That night Jensen lay awake, trying to make sense of what had happened in the past twenty-four hours.

He realized that without meaning to he had become a kind of triple agent. To the Mafia, he was anti-Castro – and that meant, though they didn't know it, that he was anti-Elena. To Elena, he was pro-Castro and anti-Mafia. And in reality – although reality was getting harder and harder to keep track of – he didn't consider himself an ally of either.

He was walking a fine line, and he had to maintain a precise balance. If he slipped, he would have to worry not only about Elena and the men with submachine guns who had invaded his bedroom but also about the others who were lurking just out of sight – the military, the oil companies, the warring factions of the FBI and the CIA, the Vietnamese.

Thinking about his catalog of enemies brought home to him the enormity of what he was doing. His earlier assessment, he saw now, had been naïve. What was at stake was far more than a yes-or-no decision on a quick invasion of Cuba. The whole ponderous American war machine was being set in motion, and the choice of the direction in which it was turned could toll the death knell for hundreds of thousands and affect the spending of tens of billions of dollars.

He saw himself as a kind of amplifier. Small changes in what he did, what he learned, how much was revealed, could all make a tremendous difference in the way things went. And his hand was being forced.

For now, there was nothing he could do but follow the path outlined by the Mafia and hope that along the way he would pick up the information he was looking for. Because if so many people had reason to influence him or to stop him he badly needed the protection the Mafia offered.

Finally he drifted into sleep. Dreamed:

Pursued by something deadly but unseen, he ran down a long, dim corridor lined with gray doors. As he ran, he tugged at doorknobs, darting from one side of the hall to the other. Frantically looking for . . . he didn't know what. Most of the doors were locked. Some led only to darkness. Behind one – a glaringly bright light and a sense of danger. He slammed it and ran on. The presence that pursued him loomed closer. Another door. A long corridor ending in a blind turn. He took the chance – ran down the corridor, around the corner, headlong into a room full of dark, heavy chairs. Across the room, at another door, beckoning, was a tall, slender, blonde woman. He ran across the room, hurling chairs out of his path, stumbling into them, tripping. They clung to his legs as if they were consciously intent on hindering him. Finally he reached the woman, and together they burst through the door and ran across an open field that turned without warning into a shadowy canyon with high, sheer walls of dark-purple rock.

The sky above them was a sliver of rolling clouds, and all around them on the cliff tops was the presence they were fleeing.

He sat up in bed, wide awake. Jill. He had to get to Jill, had to tell her what was happening now and get her clear. If it wasn't already too late.

He got no more sleep that night.

Chapter Twelve

In the morning he said to Elena, 'I'm going to Washington.'

She put down her coffee cup. 'I'll go with you.'

'With or without a gun?'

'Harry . . .'

'No. There's no point in it. I don't need an interpreter there. At least I don't think I do. While I'm gone, you get things set here, and then we'll go to Florida together.'

'What will you do in Washington?'

'I've got to talk to my boss. And there are some other people I want to look up. I think I can learn some things that will be useful.'

'Won't it be dangerous for you?'

'Yes. But if I can talk to our friends from the other night, they can help me with that.'

'Yes. Of course. Do you know how to reach them?'

'They didn't exactly leave a number, did they? But I think I can get a message to them.'

'How will you do it?'

He finished his coffee and stood up. 'Follow me.'

He walked down the corridor to the red-walled room that he had been sleeping in for almost a month.

Beaming his voice outward, like a public-speaking student, he said, 'Okay, you guys. Listen up. I'm leaving for

Washington tomorrow. I need some false identification and a credit card. Otherwise, you stand a good chance of losing the best ally you've got. I'll be here all day if you want to reach me, and then we're going to Antoine's for dinner. One way or the other, I'm leaving in the morning.'

He smiled at Elena.

She stared at him, alarm stretching the skin taut over her gracefully angled cheekbones.

'Harry. Let's take a walk.' Her voice was so low he could barely hear her.

Outside, in front of the shop, she asked him, 'Do you think there's a microphone in my kitchen?'

'Oh, Jesus, I hope not,' he said. 'I'd hate to think they overheard that little tête-à-tête yesterday morning. But you had the radio on.'

'I hope it was loud enough.'

He spent the day packing and doing short sets of stretching exercises. He called Ramón, and he made an appointment with Doctor Alvarez for an early-evening checkup. He spent some time in front of a mirror fashioning a bandage from gauze and adhesive tape that he could use like a giant white Band-Aid to cover the livid scar that ran from his left ear to his chin.

He and Elena had a leisurely dinner at Antoine's. As they walked out, a short, heavyset man in a powder-blue suit fell into step with them.

'Nobody likes a smart ass, Jensen,' he said gruffly. It was the voice of one of his night visitors: the man by the door.

'Maybe not. But you're here.'

'Yeah.'

A black limousine pulled up next to them.

'Get in. You and the pretty lady.' He opened the rear door for them.

The limousine drove slowly through the night streets.

'What's this about a trip to Washington?'

Jensen told him what he had told Elena.

'All right, look – do it if you have to, but don't go taking forever over it. We've got to get the show on the road. I don't want us to end up sitting around with our thumbs up our asses waiting around for you, all right? Talk to your boss and get your information, and then let's start letting people know about it while it's going to do us some good.'

'Now, wait a minute. We can't go off half-cocked,' Jensen countered. He was worried: He couldn't afford too much time pressure before he had gathered enough information to see which way the truth lay and to decide what he should do about it.

'The United States has never been a country that went to war easily,' he argued. 'You have to bear that in mind. The provocation has always been very severe in the past. Clear acts of war, and dramatic ones. The explosion of the battleship *Maine* in Havana harbor. The attack on Pearl Harbor. And we stayed out of World War One for three years. We went into Korea at a time of national hysteria about communism and the loss of the atomic bomb monopoly, to counter a massive invasion, and even then we had to get the United Nations to act as a kind of front, to give us permission.'

'So okay. So what? Killing Jack Kennedy isn't provocation enough for you? You got to be crazy.'

'Basically you're right. The trouble is, though, if somebody sinks a battleship, that's an obvious act of war, and you can usually see who did it. Or find somebody plausible to blame.

Here it's not so simple. Everybody's already been set up to believe it was this one lone nut. Now, maybe that's not very satisfying, but the assassination was months ago. The trail is cold. The evidence is shaky. You need something strong enough to stir everybody up. And something clear and unassailable. Otherwise you're going to be shouted down as a nut and a troublemaker by all the people who have a different theory of their own or who have a reason not to like yours. Remember, you said it yourself, there are plenty of people who don't want us to pay any attention to Cuba because they'd rather have us go to war somewhere else.'

'Okay. Okay. I get the picture. So go after your evidence and I'll try to convince my friends to be patient. But goddamnit, Jensen, don't take any longer than you absolutely have to. Okay?'

'Do you have the identification and the credit card I asked for?'

The stocky man took a black billfold from his inside jacket pocket and dropped it in Jensen's lap.

'You think we're amateurs or something?'

Jensen went through the billfold. There was a driver's license, a Blue Cross card, a gasoline credit card, and an American Express card, all in the name of Lawrence O. Jones.

'Larry,' the stocky man said. 'We figured you'd answer to that quicker than to Melvin. The *O* stands for Oswald.' He laughed as if he expected Jensen to join in.

'Fine,' Jensen said. 'It'll do.'

'Anything else you'll be needing, *sir*?' He sounded annoyed.

'I'd like a phone number or something. A way to get in touch with you if I need you.'

The stocky man handed him a business card.

'It's an answering service. There's somebody there all the time. You can trust them. Leave a message for Angelo.'

The card said 'A. DiBonato. Carting and Hauling.'

'All right,' Jensen said. 'Why don't you drop us on Bourbon Street, and we'll take a cab home.'

He started early.

He wanted to shake off anyone who might be following him, so that when he arrived in Washington, no one would know he was there. It would give him a chance to see Jill without endangering her and would let him choose his own moment to reveal himself to the people who would surely be waiting for him. Both Elena and his Mafia friends knew where he was headed; he was certain they expected to pick him up there. But that did not mean they would not try to have him followed as well. And there were others, who did not necessarily know where he was going; with a little effort and a little luck, he might be able to give them all the slip. And in the process he might also learn how important they thought it was to keep track of him.

He drove a rented car to the airport and took the first plane he could get, a Delta flight to Houston. He had fifty minutes there before the next plane out. While he waited, he made an advance reservation for a connecting plane. His itinerary was Chicago and then Buffalo.

O'Hare was not as crowded as he had hoped. Under the towering ceilings in the main terminal there were small areas of congestion separated by forbidding expanses of emptiness. Here and there people stood alone or in pairs near piles of luggage, scanning the terminal, presumably in search of some late-arriving traveling companion. Or, Jensen thought, watching for an errant member of the National Security Advisory Staff. He checked the high, black departure board: The plane for Buffalo was due to take off on time.

He turned away from the board and pushed past some people who had gathered behind him. His eyes met the eyes of a square-built Asian in a business suit. They held the contact for a moment, and then the Asian looked sharply away and began talking intently to his companions.

Jensen hurried to the gate where the plane for Buffalo would be boarding. He stood in the waiting area with a growing crowd of Buffalo-bound businessmen and worried about the Asian. It seemed certain to him that the man was Vietnamese, was looking for him or following him.

A few minutes before boarding time he ducked into the men's room. In the soft leather bag he was carrying, he had a toilet kit, two changes of clothes, and a rolled-up, oversize, blue vinyl flight bag. He took off his suit and changed it for his New Orleans jeans and a dark-blue shirt. He recombed his hair to make it look more casual, and he stuffed the leather bag into the flight bag with the clothes and the toilet kit. He slung the flight bag over his shoulder and sauntered out of the men's room and straight out of the terminal. He got a cab to the Loop, and played sightseer there for a half hour before taking another cab to Union Station.

There was a train leaving for the West Coast in two hours. He reserved a double slumber coach to Los Angeles.

He spent most of his waiting time in a stall in the station men's room. The time drew into an eternity as he listened to the strainings and splashings and inhaled the cumulative odors of what seemed like hundreds of men, but he did not want to be out in the open where someone might spot him. He had been badly shaken by his encounter with the Asian at the airport.

Six minutes before departure time he went directly to the train, got on board, and found his compartment. He closed the metal-and-plastic door and sat down. Except for the sealed window next to his seat he was completely isolated from the world.

He felt himself suddenly in the grip of claustrophobic panic: Now that he was here, there was nowhere he could go. He was afraid to open the compartment door, afraid of who might be outside.

He struggled to bring his racing mind under control. He told himself it was ridiculous to imagine sinister people lurking in the corridor. Even if they were, no one could get in unless he wanted them to. He could not be safer. And, one way or the other, he was committed.

The train snorted, hissed, lurched. Lurched again. Jensen sat back and tried to relax. The compartment was not much bigger than the toilet stall he had used in the station. It even had its own toilet bowl, under the narrow vinyl chair opposite him.

For a while Jensen watched the passing lights of nighttime Chicago, then he picked up the news magazine and the paperback thriller he had bought at the station newsstand. The novel's jacket blurb, morbidly anachronistic, suggested that 'if President Kennedy is a fan of British secret agent James Bond, he should switch his allegiance. There isn't a thing the incredible Bond can do that this American agent can't do better.'

He leafed through the news magazine first. It was a stale version of the newspaper that had failed to distract him in the

211

men's room. There was the Ruby jury's quick verdict of guilty, the latest excesses of Beatlemania, a threat by the Congress of Racial Equality to disrupt the opening of the New York World's Fair, a story about the Vietnam trip of Defense Secretary McNamara and General Maxwell Taylor.

Jensen tried to read the piece about Vietnam, to find nuances that might give him a clue to his own predicament, but the article made him too anxious; he couldn't concentrate on it. When he found himself staring blankly at a picture of McNamara and Taylor in steel helmets and flak jackets, braving a threatened assassination attempt, he closed the magazine in disgust and threw it on the seat opposite him.

He started to read the paperback. The smooth, easy prose drew him in and pulled him along until it was too late to turn back – the book was about a former secret agent whose erstwhile colleagues tried to dupe him into assassinating a prominent neighbor. It was an eerie distortion of the situation Jensen found himself in; at first it made him profoundly uncomfortable, but ultimately the fantasy was a relief.

He slept better than he expected to. The seat he was using unfolded in a complicated way and stretched out over the one opposite it to make a narrow berth with a thin, pallet-like mattress that was surprisingly comfortable. When he got up, late the next morning, he was stiff but considerably refreshed.

He left the train in Denver and from there he proceeded in short hops on local feeder airlines to Saint Louis; Springfield, Illinois; Gary, Indiana; and Cleveland. As far as he could tell, no passenger from any one of the flights was on any of the others.

He rented a car in Cleveland, giving his destination on the rental form as New York. He drove out of town, turned in at a Quality Court Motel, had a simple late dinner, and went to sleep, leaving word that he should be called at five in the morning.

The next day, on the drive down to Pennsylvania, he thought again about how best to get in touch with Jill and arrange a meeting without putting her in any more danger than she was in already. He couldn't ignore the possibility that her phone was tapped.

At four thirty in the afternoon he got off the Pennsylvania Turnpike, drove into a small coal town, and found a luncheonette with a phone booth in the back. He ordered coffee and got a couple of dollars' worth of change from the overweight, pasty-skinned girl behind the counter.

He made the call station-to-station. As soon as Jill's secretary was on the line, he started to talk; once he was going, he didn't stop for breath.

'Ruthie, this is an old friend of your boss's. You know who. I'd like to surprise her, so if you'll just tell her there's an old friend on the line and don't say my name or anything, I'd appreciate it. You know I wouldn't ask you to do this if I didn't have a good reason.'

'Um. Yeah . . . Oh. Okay. Sure . . . Wait a minute.'

The line was silent, and then he heard Jill's voice.

'Hello?' There was curiosity in the greeting, and a touch of annoyance. He remembered that she didn't like people who played games on the telephone.

'Hello, darling, this is your old friend.' His mouth was dry; he hoped his voice was recognizable. 'You remember me, and you know what? I've got a new question to pop. Right where I popped the old one. Four o'clock tomorrow. Say yes or no, but nothing else.'

A pause, then: 'All right. I'll be there. Four o'clock.'

He snapped the receiver down on the hook and sat there,

shaking. Then he went out and drank the cold coffee that was waiting for him on the counter.

It was a gray day, damp and chill, but he could feel the Washington spring all around him. The first magnolias were in bloom, and the grass was turning green. It would not be many days before the Tidal Basin was snowy with cherry blossoms and pastel green buds were dusting the oaks and maples.

He parked the car several blocks from where he was going and locked it and began to walk slowly, stopping and turning to look behind him at uneven intervals. Here, in the open, where there were relatively few pedestrians, anyone following him would have no place to conceal himself, but Jensen saw no one who looked suspicious.

He had another reason to walk slowly. He was headed for a spot he had not visited since he and Jill had separated.

When he had suggested the meeting place, he had not thought about it as presenting any problems. It had come to his mind immediately – a place only she would know, that he could identify quickly in a way that would be meaningless to anyone listening to their conversation. But now, as he got closer, he could not avoid the emotions it stirred up in him. He was worried about the effect it might have on both of them to be together again where, seven years before, he had proposed marriage to her.

It had been very old-fashioned and romantic. Early spring, the air heavy with the perfumes of blossoms and moist, rich earth, birds singing heartily. Even the cemetery had seemed full of life. Warm yellow sunlight had filtered through the palest green buds, lighting her skin and shining in her eyes and glowing in her hair: It had been fastened into a high, graceful ponytail that swung languidly when her head moved.

Oh, yes, he told himself, *we were quite a pair, once upon a time. Until we started to carve each other up.*

He was grateful for the overcast. At least it wasn't as sunny as it had been the day he proposed. Rain, he thought, would have been more appropriate to the way things worked out.

He stopped walking for a minute, until the wave of bitterness had washed past him. That part of it was over. Now they had something else. Or nothing else. Whatever it was, or wasn't, it was different from what they'd had seven years ago. It had to be. They were different people.

He wondered, as he passed the familiar gravestones and monuments, where they really stood with each other now. His own emotions confused him. He felt strongly drawn to Jill and jealous of Norris, but he could not deny his involvement with Elena, gun or no. He did not know where that left him.

He came past the first of the trees and entered the small glade.

She was there, sitting on a bench, waiting for him.

He stood looking at her for a moment. Her hair was down, dull gold in the gray afternoon. She wore a light-tan raincoat. Her hands were folded in her lap, and she was looking at the memorial in front of her. She did not turn, but he was sure she knew he was there.

He sat next to her, on her left so that she would not see the bandage that concealed his scar. He said nothing. He did not want to disturb the peace of the moment, and he was not sure he could have spoken if he had wanted to.

His eyes moved to the statue that faced them: a cloaked and hooded bronze figure of no determinable sex, seated on a rock against the background of a six-foot-high slab. Deep shadow obscured the figure's face and its downcast eyes. As always, the statue seemed to blend into its setting, no less a natural being than the trees that surrounded it, and them.

Jill put her hand on his leg; he covered it with his own. For a short but precious time, the tension and anxiety that had dogged him from New Orleans dropped away.

'"The peace of God that surpasseth understanding,"' Jill quoted in a soft voice.

He took his hand from hers and put his arm around her and drew her gently toward him. She rested her head on his shoulder.

'God,' he breathed. 'It's so good to be here. It's so good to be with you.'

She tightened her fingers on his leg. 'Yes.'

She lifted her head, turned more fully toward him. Their lips met softly, barely touched. He inhaled her fragrances and he felt her breath warm in his mouth. Her hand came up to caress his face – her fingers touched the bandage.

'Harry!' She sat back, alarmed.

He leaned toward her and kissed her, cupping her head with his hand. Her lips yielded to his: soft, alive. Then she pulled back.

'What is it, Harry? What happened? Your cheek . . .'

'I told you I got the shit kicked out of me. I've got a scar six inches long; it runs right from my ear to the point of my chin. Kind of like a German dueling scar, only not half so picturesque. At the moment, it's sort of reddish purple. I thought it would be better if I introduced you to it gradually.'

'Oh, Harry.' She put her arms around him. 'What did I get you into?'

He put his hands on her shoulders and pushed her gently away and kissed her forehead and her eyes and the tip of her nose.

'Never mind that. I wasn't careful enough, but I will be from now on. Besides, we've got some allies now. Allies and enemies. The only problem is, I'm not sure which is which at this point.'

He turned away from her and looked at the statue, but the powerful, brooding figure held no answers for him.

'The truth is, I'm no closer to knowing who killed Jack Kennedy than I was when I went down there. In some ways I'm further away. There's been a whole new element introduced. I'm almost certain now that the assassination had something to do with Cuba, but whether it was pro-Castro people or anti-Castro people I can't begin to say. At this point it looks at least as likely to have been the right-wing exiles, with or without help from a faction in the CIA, as it does to have been Castro or someone working for him.'

He turned to her again. 'What I need to find out is how badly I'm being manipulated and lied to by the people who are claiming to help me. There are some things I can check on while I'm in town that will give me a much better idea of how it all really stands. And then we can make some more concrete plans. In the meantime I'm very worried about you. I don't want you exposed any more than you have to be. We can't take any chances. And I don't think it's safe for us to be seen together.'

He touched her hair. He did not want her to think he was pushing her away.

'I've got some errands to run and some people to find, and I want to get ready for tomorrow. It's time for me to go see Hapgood and face the music. Suppose we meet tomorrow in Rock Creek Park? You know the bridge over the creek that's just across from Fort de Russy?'

'Sure I do. I used to go there . . . Never mind. I know where you mean.'

'Good. Let's say five forty-five tomorrow. And don't go there directly. Take a bus and a couple of cabs. Don't act too funny, but make it complicated enough so it's hard for anyone to follow you.'

Chapter Thirteen

'Mr Hapgood wants to see you,' Jensen's secretary told him. 'He said as soon as you came in, whenever it was.'

'Did he?'

'I'd better call him and tell him you're on your way.'

'All right,' Jensen said, 'why don't you do that?'

Hapgood's secretary nodded to him as he came into the outer office. She inclined her head toward the door to Hapgood's sanctum.

Jensen knocked once and went in. Hapgood was standing in front of his desk. He looked as if he had been pacing.

'Hello, Harry,' he said in a tone that implied he had a lot more to say, but he stopped and stared at Jensen. 'You don't look so hot.'

'Well, it's like I told you. I've been sick.'

'That's quite a bandage on your cheek.'

'Yeah. I don't really need it anymore. I keep it on because I don't want to scare anybody.'

'What's under it?'

'A scar.'

'That long?'

Jensen pulled the bandage back.

'Jesus,' Hapgood said.

Jensen smoothed the bandage into place. 'Yeah.'

Hapgood paced for a while. He stopped and looked out the window.

'Jesus, Harry, I had no idea. I mean, when you said you were sick, you know, doctor's note and all, I thought maybe you were . . . well, exaggerating.'

'Lying.' Jensen saw no reason to make it easy for Hapgood.

'Well, all right. Lying. But you'd lied once before, if you remember.'

'So now you know – this time, I wasn't lying. I got cut up pretty badly. Cracked ribs. A broken hand. Internal injuries. My legs bruised so badly I couldn't walk for a week. Does it make any difference?'

'Well . . .'

Hapgood was still looking out the window. Jensen did not think there was anything interesting happening out there.

'Well . . .' Hapgood began again. 'No. I suppose it doesn't make any difference.'

'I didn't think it would. Why don't you get this over with, then. It makes me tired, standing here.'

Hapgood did not turn around. 'It's this crusade of yours, Harry. I told you to drop it. It's nothing to be fooling around with, especially down in New Orleans. We can't afford any more involvement with these Cuban exiles right now. They only see it as encouragement.'

'We used to be happy enough to encourage them.'

'That was in the old days. Things are different now.' He turned to face Jensen. 'Maybe I shouldn't be telling you this, especially now, when . . . well, especially now. But I guess I feel I owe you this much, at least. The whole picture with

Cuba is changing. Jack was putting out the first feelers to Castro about a rapprochement, but all that died with him in Dallas. It's only had one effect that's likely to last – no more help for the exiles. Johnson's a little weak on foreign policy, and McNamara and Rusk have him too busy with Vietnam to pay much attention to Cuba for the time being. So a lot of us think the smart thing is just to let well enough alone until some kind of definite policy gets shaken out over there.'

'That's why you're going to fire me? I assume that's why I'm here, to be fired.'

Hapgood sighed heavily. 'Yes, Harry, that's why you're here. But no, that's not the reason, not really. I thought it might put things in better perspective, that's all. And in a way it's all related. It's this refusal of yours to lay off the assassination. We have a fair idea of what you were up to in New Orleans. That's the basic reason I've got to let you go. You're roiling up waters that some very important people would rather have stay calm. And you started out on the wrong foot with the Johnson people. You ruffled a lot of feathers.'

'That's a shitty way to operate, Hap, and you know it. Those idiots you saddled me with would have strained the patience of Job.'

'Maybe they would have, Harry. I can't say no. But they were Lyndon Johnson's idiots. And you're Jack Kennedy's smartass. You should have been more tactful with them.'

'Sure.'

'Well, that's how it stands. There's all that, and it's not good, and then you disappear for a month, and people start saying, Who does this guy think he is? Even if you *were* sick. Or wounded. In the end they're only going to say, If he'd been where he belonged, he wouldn't have got himself beaten up –

and they'd be right, too – so one way or the other it looks like your fault. I think I understand you, Harry, and I'd like to give you another chance, but my hands are tied. I'm sorry.'

'I'll get my desk cleared out. What about severance and the rest of that?'

'It's all been taken care of. Betty has a check for you. And some forms to fill out. She'll explain it all.'

They stood there, facing each other, for an awkward moment. Hapgood extended his hand. Jensen hesitated, then took it.

'So long, Harry.'

'Good-bye, Hap.'

Norman Cohen had been a physical and social anomaly on the National Security Advisory Staff. He was short, grossly overweight, without polish or grace, and he was propelled by an apparently inexhaustible and omnidirectional energy. He was never still; he talked constantly, his arms waving, pulling papers from a briefcase or making shapes in the air to illustrate a point. His forehead glistened continually with sweat, and he always had at least one cigarette going. But he was a genius, of sorts. He had an encyclopedic knowledge of military and diplomatic history, and he was a brilliant, instinctive strategist and tactician.

His living room was large and bright, and the flat surfaces were covered with books and magazines, every one of which looked as if it had been consulted within the past twenty-four hours.

He was happy to hear from Jensen, one of the few people at NSAS he considered a friend, and he said yes at once when Jensen invited himself over for a drink and a private conversation.

'Sure I quit,' Cohen said, handing Jensen a martini. 'I didn't have much damn choice. They would have canned me anyway, the way I kept telling them they were full of shit.' He swept some magazines off the seat of a broad Victorian armchair and sat down. 'You watch, Harry, there are a lot more guys going to get their tits caught in this wringer. They're not going to be able to go along with it. I don't know how long Harriman can last, not where anybody listens to him. And that's likely to mean Forrestal's going to want to leave. He's more tactful than I am, but he's too smart to be fooled by this nonsense.'

'Is it that bad?'

'Is it that bad, the man says.' He puffed ferociously on a cigarette. 'I'll tell you, Harry, what we've got here is the worst possible thing. What do they teach you at your mother's knee? First thing? No land war in Asia. The primary holy precept of gunboat diplomacy. And that's what we're going to have, Harry. Mark my words. Not right away. Nope. They're going to start in the air and on the water. Already have, in fact, along with some hit-and-run raids into North Vietnam. But all of that's not going to be enough to do the job they want done. They know they need more. And they'll get it, too. They're going to send in the Marines before too long.' He ground the cigarette out.

'You're sure?'

'Of course I'm sure. You think I'd've quit a job like that, happy as a pig in shit, if I wasn't sure?' He poked another cigarette into his mouth, lit it. 'Look, let's not even talk about OPLAN 34. It's not the details that matter, it's the overall grand plan. And the goal at this point is – Win in Vietnam. Has been since the second goddamn day Lyndon B. Johnson was in office. He didn't even let them get Jack into the ground before he started to heat things up over in Vietnam, and the cynical bastard did it in Jack's name, too.'

Cohen jammed his cigarette into an ashtray so hard it broke in half. He fished in his pack for another one, found nothing, crumpled it. He bounded out of his chair and crossed the room to an old rolltop desk.

Jensen waited.

Rummaging in the desk for cigarettes, Cohen said, 'Maybe you remember. Back in November old Lyndon said he was restating Jack's Vietnam policy, so everybody would know where we stood – we had a new President, but things were still the same. And how did he reaffirm the policy of our so-recently-departed President? By issuing National Security Memorandum 273. And you know what? NSAM 273 is an absolute turnaround of Kennedy's policy. Subtle, you understand. Very devious about shifting the fine print, but there it was, a whole new policy. I'm telling you, Harry, it's a bitch. And if you don't believe me, I've got the goddamn document, and you can read it for yourself.' He came back across the room.

'I believe you. Asia's not my area, but if that's what's happening, it scares the hell out of me . . . It's McNamara, isn't it?'

Pounding the cigarette pack on the coffee table, Cohen said, 'Yep. McNamara. Rusk. Bundy. Maxwell Taylor, of course. The whole fucking bunch. I don't know what they think they're proving.' He peeled open the pack.

'Do you really have that memorandum?'

'Sure. You want to see it?' He lit a cigarette.

'Yeah. I think I do.'

Cohen put the cigarette in an ashtray and left the room. He was back in a minute with a looseleaf notebook. He dropped it on the coffee table in front of Jensen.

It had several documents in it, and some pages of typescript that had the look of having been copied out of official documents. Jensen skimmed them all. Then he flipped back and forth, rereading sections.

Cohen leaned over him and snapped the looseleaf rings open.

'Here. It's easier if you look at them laid out next to each other.'

He pulled three of the pages out and arranged them on the coffee table so that Jensen could see them all at once. Some of the words had been underlined in red.

One page was headed: 'Draft Statement by McNamara and Taylor. October 2, 1963.' Its first paragraph got right to the point:

The security of South Vietnam remains *vital to United States security*. For this reason, we adhere to the *overriding objective of denying this country to communism* and of *suppressing the Viet Cong insurgency* as promptly as possible.

Another page was headed: 'JFK Public Statement. October 2, 1963.' Its first paragraph was longer than the one McNamara and Taylor had suggested, and it was considerably milder:

The security of South Vietnam *is a major interest of the United States as other free nations*. We will adhere to *our policy of working with the people and government of South Vietnam to deny this country to communism and to suppress the externally stimulated and supported insurgency of the Viet Cong* as promptly as possible. *Effective performance in this undertaking* is the *central objective* of our policy in South Vietnam.

'You see there how Jack was backing away from what they wanted him to say.' Cohen jabbed a finger at the Kennedy statement. 'He's really putting us in the background there, as opposed to what McNamara was doing. Now look at what the hell Johnson does to it.' He pointed at the third page, 'LBJ. NSAM 273. November 26, 1963. Secret.'

It *remains* the *central objective* of the United States in South Vietnam to assist the people and government of that country *to win* their contest against the *externally directed* and supported communist *conspiracy*. The test of all US decisions and actions in this area should be the effectiveness of their contributions to this purpose.

'Nobody's ever put those two words in the same sentence before – *objective* and *win*. Insidious bastard, isn't he? Amazing. The crazy cowboy's afraid Bobby's going to call him yellow or something. And I'll tell you another thing – the folks in the Pentagon have begun using that stupid document as a peg to hang a commitment on. A full commitment by Johnson.'

Jensen finished his martini. 'It doesn't sound good.'

Cohen shuffled the papers together and put them back into the notebook, snapping the rings shut. 'Understatement of the century, Harry. You want another one of those?'

'No, thanks... Hell, why not? Sure. After all, we're celebrating my freedom. And yours.'

Cohen took Jensen's glass. 'Yeah. We're not the only ones, either. They've canned everybody, here and in Saigon, who had anything really smart to say.' He left the room and came back almost at once with a fresh martini.

'I wasn't the only one who quit, either. Hilsman saw the writing on the wall. Maybe even before I did.'

'He quit?'

'Oh, yeah.' Cohen lit a cigarette. 'So what do you think? You want to hear more of this nonsense, or are you bored yet?'

'There's more?'

'Oh, shit, yes. There's OPLAN 34 and the naval raids and a whole lot of other crap. And the finale of my lecture is the Cohen theory of where it's going from here. That alone is more than worth the price of admission.'

'Sounds like a good program to me. You've got yourself an audience.'

Cohen grinned. 'You'll be sorry.'

Jensen got to Rock Creek Park late. He skirted the zoo and lingered for a few minutes near Pierce Mill before starting north. It was a long walk, and he made it longer by taking a detour west to the equitation field, circling back before he headed for the bridge where Jill was waiting for him. As he had on his way to the cemetery, he stopped at irregular intervals and turned around to see if anyone was following him. He saw only a few people, and they all had the look of being preoccupied with their own business. As he passed the earthworks that were all that was left of old Fort de Russy, part of Washington's defense ring in the Civil War, he began to pay attention to what was ahead of him. With luck, he thought, he would be able to spot anyone who had followed Jill and was now watching her. But there was no one around except a family of sightseers and, standing on the bridge, Jill.

She saw him coming and walked to join him. The sun had broken through the overcast, and she seemed bathed in a coruscating glow.

A fragment of poetry ran through his head: 'She walks in beauty . . .' But that was wrong, because Byron had compared his beautiful woman to the night, and Jill was not of the night but of the day.

It was Elena, he realized, whose beauty was dark – a thing of sorcery and enchantment, but strangely oppressive.

When he reached Jill, he hugged her with a joyful greed. For all the danger he was facing and all the conflicting emotions he felt, the touch of her gave him hope.

They walked slowly north toward the Maryland section of the park, hand in hand.

'What happened at the office today?' she asked him. 'Did you see Hapgood?'

'He fired me.'

'He couldn't.'

Jensen laughed. 'Oh, yes, he could. And did.'

'What are you going to do?'

'For now, not having a job isn't so bad. It makes it easier for me to follow up on my snooping into things that aren't any of my damn business. And there's enough in the bank to keep me alive for a while.'

'But Harry, that job was the key to your career. To be on the White House staff, in national security—'

'Yeah, I suppose. But I'll find a way back.' His voice held a conviction he did not feel.

'I hope so.' She squeezed his hand.

'A bright young lawyer like me? Never fear.' He squeezed back. 'More important – I think I learned something interesting today.'

Eagerly: 'Really?'

'Yes, ma'am. I may know why the connection with Cuba is being buried so thoroughly. I had an idea before why it was happening, based on something I picked up in New Orleans, but what I heard today makes it seem more like a certainty than a theory. As far as I can tell, somebody at the highest levels, as they say – or maybe a lot of people – have decided we can't afford any involvement with Cuba right now because we're too busy gearing up for a big war in Vietnam.'

'What?'

'That's right. In a sense the real war's begun already. We're running raids into North Vietnam. Using American personnel. We have been for six weeks or so, ever since the day after General Khanh booted out Big Minh. Naval operations, too. Just pinpricks so far. Provocations. We're going to harass the hell out of them, and after a while they'll get mad and strike back, and we'll have an excuse to go public with our part of it and step it up.'

'But what does that have to do with the assassination, or with Cuba?'

'It shouldn't have anything to do with it. But figure it this way: We had a good time flexing our muscles at Cuba and Russia about eighteen months ago. We scared a lot of people here at home, sure, but we came out of it all right, full of what big heroes we were. If it turns out now that Cuba was the cause of Jack Kennedy's murder, there's going to be tremendous pressure to go in there and clean the bastards out.'

'That's okay with me.' Anger burned in her eyes.

'Sure it is. But there are two problems with it. First, even if we link the assassination to Cuba, from what I've learned so far it's impossible to tell whether it was Castro or anti-Castroites trying to make it look like Castro. So you might end up in war for the wrong reasons. And that's no good.'

'No. It's not.'

'Now, combine that with the fact that you've got another war you'd rather fight.'

'Vietnam?'

'Precisely.'

'But—'

'You can't have both of them. Not a chance. It's going to take a lot of work and a lot of lying just to get us really involved in Vietnam.'

'Why Vietnam? What can we possibly have at stake there that would justify a major war? The Vietnamese can't even come up with a government they like. They persecute each other. They're corrupt. What's the point?'

'Well, for one thing, there are rumors about oil off the coast. That's a pretty good incentive. It turns out that some guy from Mobil Oil wrote a book last year saying how important the area is strategically. The way these things work, what's likely to be behind that is somebody thinks there's oil over there. Besides, a nice, long war halfway around the world would be good for business without being too threatening to the general public. Cuba, on the other hand, is too close for comfort, and it gives us the Russians to worry about.'

Jill stopped walking. Her hands were clenched at her sides.

'Nobody ever stops lying, do they?' She turned to him. 'What do we do now?'

'I can only see one way out of this. I have to get more information about the assassination. If I can come up with something concrete, then I can go in one direction or the other, and I'll be so visible and so valuable to the people who want to hear what I've got to say that I'll have some protection from the ones who don't want to hear it. But I want you out of this completely. I'll find a way out for myself, but I don't know if I can protect you. And this is too dangerous to play games with.'

Gently she touched the bandage over his scar. 'I'm not worried about myself.'

He put his arms out, and she moved close to him. Their bodies trembled against each other. Then he tightened his arms around her, and they pressed together, as if by sheer physical force they could extinguish all the space between them. It hurt his ribs, and he let her go.

'I'm more convinced than ever that we shouldn't be seen together. But I was thinking – maybe, just for tonight, we can find a place to go where nobody will recognize us.'

Later they lay side by side on a sagging bed in an ancient and out-of-the-way motel bungalow.

'I've got to go to Dallas,' he mused. 'I want to talk to the woman who says she was approached to help Oswald before the assassination. Dallas, and Florida. Maybe I can get a line on the two men who took those mysterious flights to Cuba. Those are my best leads, and the problem is that right now they point in opposite directions. The only thing to do is follow them both and see where they take me.'

'Maybe I can help you when you're in Texas. One of our clients is an oil company. Not one of the majors, but a very big independent. They're based in Houston. The boss man likes me – I do a lot of work for them – and he's got influence all over the state. I'm sure he could get doors opened for you, get you into places nobody'd let you go otherwise. And I know he'd do it if I asked him.'

The idea literally chilled him. He wrapped his arms and legs around her. 'Don't say a word to him. Please, Jill. The oil business is a very tight little world, and if any part of it is in on the squelch that's being put on the assassination, then talking to an oilman like your friend could put you right in the middle of things. Even if it was some help to me, it couldn't possibly be worth the trouble it could get you into.'

'But—'

'No. I'm right, Jill, believe me. You have to promise you won't say a word.'

'All right. I'll be good. Do I get a reward, at least?'

His hand moved on her body.

Chapter Fourteen

The Jaguar started reluctantly. After weeks in the garage, it was badly out of tune. Jensen turned it off and put in new sparkplugs and wiped down the distributor. Then he turned it on again, let it warm up, and synchronized the three carburetors. The engine was still running raggedly. He hoped that giving the car some time on the road would smooth out most of the remaining roughness.

He was glad to be in the car again. He was tired of traveling by train and plane. He needed to feel in control of where he was going, and when, and how, for a change.

He folded down the canvas top and stowed the side curtains. He enjoyed the blast of cold wind in his face as he put the car on the highway to Richmond. He was hoping to make it to Chattanooga or even Birmingham before he quit for the day. If he had to, he thought, he could make it through to New Orleans nonstop, but he didn't see any point in it.

The trip was smooth and easy as far as Richmond. He went more than eighty most of the way, to get a jump on his schedule. He kept a careful watch in the rearview mirror, and as he sped down US 360, he began to weave in and out of the twin lanes of south-bound traffic, slowing down and speeding up, hoping to confuse anyone who was following him. He got off 360 at Burkeville and headed west toward Lynchburg. It gave him the first real chance to leave any pursuit behind. He pressed the Jaguar hard, leaving rubber behind him on the curves. By the time he got on to the divided highway at Appomattox, he was sure there was no one following him.

The route from Appomattox to the Tennessee line was almost all on four-lane highways. He let himself relax and make contact with the rhythms of the car and the flow of traffic. He ate when he stopped for gas, not caring what he had, impatient to be back on the road. By early afternoon he was west of Lynchburg, well into the mountains. The evergreens shading the road made him think of the Homestead, not many miles to the north. As he drove, he daydreamed of making this trip again, with Jill at his side. They could spend a restful week driving up the Shenandoah Valley, or they could get off the road and hike the Appalachian Trail.

They had done some camping when they were first married, and the discomforts of the tiny pup tent and cooking over a wood fire had been a source of pleasure and closeness. Jensen wondered if they could learn to relax like that again.

He was about on schedule when he came to the end of the divided highway at Kingsport, just over the Tennessee line. He filled the tank again and had a quick sandwich. The mountains' sudden night would fall while he was threading his way along the flank of Bays Mountain toward Knoxville, and he did not want to have to find a gas station after dark.

It was just outside of Kingsport that he noticed the car behind him with one headlight out of alignment. Its left beam was adjusted correctly, but the right one dipped too low; it was very dim in Jensen's rearview mirror. The wall-eyed car dropped out of sight for about a dozen miles, and then it appeared again.

234

He considered getting off on to a local road or turning around and heading back toward Kingsport, just to see what would happen, but the pressure to go on was too strong for that. There would be plenty of opportunity on the winding mountain road to leave the American car behind.

He increased his speed, but the mismatched headlights stayed with him. When he pressed the Jaguar, he could feel the roughness that still hadn't been worked out of the engine.

The car behind him made no secret now of the fact that it was following him. He dropped the Jaguar into gear and floored the gas pedal. The car shot ahead. He upshifted and pushed his speed to almost a hundred ten. The uneven headlights dropped back, but then the American car accelerated and began to close the gap.

The road twisted sharply along the top of a ridge. Even with his high beams on, he knew he was outrunning his headlights: He could not stop within the amount of road that he could see.

The car behind him lost some ground on the worst curves, but as soon as the road straightened, it was back on his tail. He could not speed up any more – he was risking his life as it was.

Coming around a sharp curve, he saw a pair of tail-lights ahead of him. He hit the brakes and downshifted, taking twenty miles an hour off his speed. Braked and shifted again, slowing to forty. His headlights showed him an old pickup truck, bouncing calmly southward down the center of the road.

His pursuer crowded in close behind him. They rode that way for more than half an hour: a Jaguar sandwich, Jensen thought.

The road continued along the ridge, but it seemed to be sloping downward, dropping below a much higher ridge on his left. There was no moon, and the mountain wall to the east was a blackness darker than the sky. It was cold now, and he wished he had the top up.

The pickup truck was gone. Jensen never saw the road or dirt track it went off on to. Its brake lights glowed briefly, it turned off to the right, and it disappeared. With a clear road ahead of him, Jensen flicked on his high beams again, downshifted, and rammed the gas pedal to the floorboard.

He gave the car everything he had, and it responded, but it was still coughing and stumbling coming out of hard corners.

He looked in his rearview mirror; the uneven headlights were there. His eyes held the rearview mirror too long; when they returned to the road ahead, there was a curve ahead of him and he was going too fast for it.

His right foot hit the brake hard while his left was playing the clutch and his right hand was guiding the shift lever through its gate. He was down to forty-five in second gear when he went into the curve. The tires protested and the car slipped sideways. He worked the gas pedal and the steering wheel gently to keep the car from sliding off the mountain.

The car behind him nudged his rear bumper. It was barely perceptible: At first he thought it was his imagination.

It happened a second time, more strongly.

Jensen looked in the rearview mirror. The American car was so close he could no longer see its headlights; instead, there was the cockpit glow of its instrument panel and the light of its headlights reflected back on to it by the white Jaguar's tail. It was a new car, one of the small but powerful Pontiacs with the borrowed Italian designation GTO.

Jensen was coming out of the curve. He hit the gas and held the car in gear until the tachometer needle swung well into the engine-speed danger zone.

Behind him the GTO reached the straight and accelerated.

Its driver seemed to be pushing it through the turns in a power slide, breaking rear-wheel traction with the gas pedal. Jensen wondered whether he dared try that strategy himself on the dark, unknown country road.

Ten miles further down the road they were on a long, sweeping curve. Dark shapes of trees loomed on both sides of them. The curve would have to bend back the other way, but Jensen had no idea when the change would come or how sharp it would be. He began to hold back.

The GTO's driver closed the ten-yard gap Jensen had opened between the cars and slammed into the left side of the Jaguar's rear bumper.

The sports car jumped to the right. Jensen stifled an impulse to hit the brakes; he concentrated on steering. He overcorrected and the car fishtailed slightly. The GTO hit him again, the impact timed to increase the sweep of the Jaguar's fishtailing.

Jensen's grip tightened on the wheel. He felt a sudden, sharp pain in his left hand. He grit his teeth and fed the car more gas. The tires took hold and the Jaguar catapulted down the road. Jensen kept his eyes on the place where his headlight beams were overwhelmed by the darkness. He was going too fast, but now he had no choice.

The curve swung back, sharply, but Jensen did not let up. He kept his foot on the gas as long as he dared, stabbed the brake pedal and jerked the steering wheel sharply against the direction of the curve and then back again so the front wheels were pointing straight ahead. Again, his left hand shrieked with pain.

The Jaguar was in an intentional skid on all four wheels. If he had misjudged it, the car would take him off the curve, off the mountain entirely. And he was finished if the GTO caught up with him before he was out of the four-wheel drift. But a drift was the fastest way through the curve, and he was betting that however souped up the American car was, this was one trick it would not be able to duplicate. He said a silent prayer that the man behind him was neither a stock-car racer nor a bootlegger.

Jensen's hand throbbed. He looked in the rearview mirror. The GTO was at a slight angle to him, setting itself up for another attack.

Maybe he is a bootlegger, Jensen thought wildly.

He watched the American car center itself on him and move closer. Everything seemed to be happening very slowly.

Jensen looked off the road into the darkness to his right, in the direction he would take if the GTO hit him. He could not tell what was out there. It could be a slope full of trees or a sheer cliff.

He pulled his attention back to the Jaguar and the road ahead. He could feel the car approaching the point of regaining adhesion.

Maybe, he thought. *Maybe.*

The Jaguar started to take hold.

It bogged down, faltered, coughed. All in a split second. Wrong gear.

Jensen rushed the downshift. There was a loud grinding from the gearbox.

He flicked the lever back into second gear and tried again, double-clutching more precisely this time. The lever went home smoothly, and his foot came down on the gas.

The GTO hit him, but he was accelerating away from it, and it was off target. It caught his rear bumper on the right side and glanced off.

Jensen's eyes alternated between the road in front of him and the rearview mirror, but he was too busy controlling the Jaguar, fighting its wild fishtailing, to keep following the GTO's fate.

Over the roar of the Jaguar's engine he heard the shrill impact of steel on rock. There was a flash in the mirror and the sound of an explosion. He caught a glimpse of the glare of a fire off the road and below it; then the glow was hidden from him by the mountain.

When he could, he pulled over, lurched from the car, and threw up. He leaned on the car, catching his breath. Slowly, favoring his left hand, he raised the canvas top and fastened it in place over the cockpit.

He got into the car and sat there, shivering with tension.

He turned the car around and headed back northward. He had to get off the road from Washington to New Orleans, where he was obviously expected. And he had to get rid of the Jaguar. Driving it now was like wearing a big come-and-get-me sign.

He pushed the car well into the night, back up to Kingsport, and from there west through the Cumberland Gap. The roads were narrow and dark, and there was little traffic.

He drove slowly at first, aware of a constant anxiety that kept him from going faster. As the miles passed, he began to relax and he speeded up.

In Kentucky he headed almost due northwest. Small towns flashed by, some of them no more than a few frame houses, a church, and a store with a gas pump by the side of the road.

There had been no car behind him for hours; the energy that had pushed him so far began to give way to fatigue. He was not aware of making any specific choice of a destination, but as the night drew on it became clear to him that he was headed for Louisville.

It was three in the morning when he entered the suburbs on the interstate highway he had hit just south of Frankfort. When he passed the first 'Road Ends. Construction' signs, he pulled off the road and looked at a map. He took the expressway that skirted the city and led to the airport and Churchill Downs.

He got off at the airport, put the car in a lot, and fell asleep sitting behind the wheel.

He was awakened by someone's knocking on the windshield. He opened his eyes and saw a uniform. Sluggish and tired as he was, it jolted him. He opened the car door and poked his head out.

'You all right, buddy?'

His questioner was about twenty, in the uniform of an airport parking-lot attendant.

'Oh. Yeah. I'm all right.'

'You can't sleep here, you know. This ain't no hotel.'

Jensen looked around. Judging by the sun, it was midmorning. The lot was nearly full. People were hefting suitcases into and out of car trunks.

'Sorry,' he told the attendant. 'I must've been tireder than I thought.'

He turned the key and pressed the starter button. The engine caught.

The gas gauge registered empty. The attendant told him where he could find a gas station.

He took a room in a cheap hotel and slept until noon. When he awoke, he showered and shaved and then he organized the

240

things he had thrown into an overnight bag on a quick stop at his apartment. Most important was the money belt that held his severance pay. It had taken some convincing to get his bank to cash the check immediately – it was a government check, but it was relatively large. He had persisted. He had not wanted to leave behind any record of how much cash he was carrying or the fact that he could do without the Mafia's credit cards.

He strapped on the money belt and put on his fresh suit. He rolled his jeans and shirt into a neat bundle with the toilet kit as a core and fastened it with a belt. The rest of his clothes he packed into the overnight bag.

He checked out of the hotel, got some change from the cashier, and sat in a phone booth in the hotel lobby talking to people at Louisville's foreign car dealerships and used-car lots.

By four o'clock he had another fistful of cash to add to his money belt. He had sold the car for a respectable price, not as much as it was worth, certainly not as much as he had wanted, but more than he had feared he would have to settle for on a quick sale. Parting with the car had been even more painful than he had expected.

He dropped the overnight bag at the Salvation Army, bought a cheap gym bag to carry the jeans and toilet kit, and got a cab to the bus station.

Chapter Fifteen

He made the trip to Florida in easy stages, moving from one small southern city to another. Having shaken off his pursuers, he did not want to show up too soon anywhere they might be expecting him. With time and boredom, they were likely to get sloppy.

Along the way he put himself through a concentrated program of workouts and exercises, trying to get into better physical shape. He got up early at whatever fleabag he happened to be staying in and ran through the back streets and along country roads, going farther each day. When he got back to his room, he did calisthenics. Then, at night, in the next city, he ran again and did more calisthenics. He did not shave; his beard grew in quickly. At first it made him look dirty and dissolute, and it called attention to his scar, but he was relieved to see that when the beard was longer it would obscure the scar almost completely.

On his sixth day on the road he called Elena and told her to meet him in Tampa the following Thursday. On the eighth day he called Jill's office. Her secretary answered.

Jensen said, 'Tell Miss Lazar I'll call back this afternoon, at two minutes after six.'

He hung up without waiting for an answer and walked

across the bus station to where the last passengers were getting on the express bus to Jacksonville.

The bus pulled into Jacksonville twenty minutes late, but he still had more than three hours before he had to call Jill. To pass the time, he went to the movies and saw *Tom Jones*. He found himself identifying with the poor, benighted Tom: thwarted at every turn, frustrated in love while being offered a plenitude of sex, in danger of being executed for no crime of his own. Unlike Tom, Jensen had no expectation of being saved by the truth.

He called Washington at four minutes after six. Jill picked up on the first ring.

Jensen began to speak at once. 'Hi. It's me. I'm all right, but I'm going to be out of touch for a while. Things are even more dangerous now. Just go about your business and do nothing – nothing! – about our mutual problem. Got that?'

'Yes, I've got it, but—'

'Just do as I say. I'll call again.'

He hung up, took a moment to calm down, and went to rent a car for the trip to Tampa. He used the Mafia's credit card. Now that he'd spoken to Jill, there was no reason for Lawrence O. Jones not to reappear, and he saw no point in spending his own money if he did not have to.

'I do not know you with a beard like that,' Narvaez said. 'You look like Fidel, eh?' His grin showed a broad gap of missing teeth. He was a former captain in Brigade 2506; he was in his mid-twenties, but his light-brown face was as slack-skinned and wrinkled as a sixty-year-old's. 'Is a good joke on you: You smoke a cigar, you look like Fidel, only too tall.'

He put his head back under the hood of the truck he was

working on and tinkered with something Jensen could not see.

'You hear the bad news?' The words came up out of the truck's engine compartment, barely intelligible.

'What bad news?'

'Ricardo.' Narvaez straightened up and put a wrench on the fender. He wiped his hands on a greasy cloth and started toward the back of the garage. Jensen followed him.

'*Ricardo es muerto.*' He sat on a high stool at the workbench that ran along the garage's back wall. There was a partly disassembled generator in front of him.

Jensen waited for his first reaction to pass before he joined the Cuban. Touhy was dead. Killed by whom? The same people who had killed George Hammond? The Eagle Laundry? The people who had been behind that GTO in Tennessee? He could not know which it had been.

'How did he die?' he asked Narvaez.

'In a bar. There was a fight. Big fight. One man had a knife.' Narvaez drew the screwdriver he was holding across the front of his neck and made a throat-slitting noise. '*Mucha sangre.*'

'I didn't know. I'm sorry to hear it.'

'*Sí.* Sorry . . . I, too. He was *un hombre formidable.*'

There it is again, Jensen thought. *Regret for the loss of a good man.*

He leaned against the wooden workbench and watched Narvaez repairing the generator.

'There is a man I need to know about,' Jensen said.

Narvaez kept working.

'I need to know something about this man's movements and if anything points to his being an agent for Castro. I don't want to know anything else. Nothing that will compromise him if he's one of yours.'

'Who is the man?'

'I know very little about him. He's a Cuban-American. He was here last fall, and he left sometime around the middle of November.'

Narvaez stopped working.

'Is this about that bastard Kennedy?'

'Yes.'

Narvaez slipped the generator into its housing. It caught on something and stopped halfway in.

'This man, the Cuban-American, he was the killer of Kennedy?'

'I don't know. It is possible he was involved.'

'I must know more.'

'He got a tourist card from the Mexican consulate here sometime in the middle of the month. I need the tourist-card lists for the week of the eighteenth, and maybe the week of the eleventh, too. He may have used his real name or an alias you'd recognize.'

Narvaez freed the obstruction that was blocking the generator and slid it the rest of the way into its housing.

'I do not know if I can help you, but I have a friend who has a *chica* at the Mexican consulate. He will want money.'

'How much?'

'Fifty dollars. A hundred.'

'Fine.'

The next day, for seventy-five dollars, Jensen got a sheaf of lists of names stolen from the Mexican consulate. They covered the whole month of November.

He met Elena, as they had planned, in an old hotel in downtown Tampa. Their reunion was brief; he had an appointment with Narvaez to go over the visa lists.

He and Narvaez sat in a back booth of an Irish bar across

town from the Cuban section. Narvaez read the lists and saw no name he thought might be the man Jensen was looking for.

Narvaez left the bar first. Jensen gave him five minutes to get clear of the neighborhood, then he dropped a pair of dollar bills on the table and went outside. Unaccountably he felt uneasy. He put his hand in the pocket of his work pants and rubbed the smooth wood and brass handle of the folding hunting knife he had bought on his way to Florida.

It was still not quite dark, and there was moderate pedestrian traffic. Jensen began to relax. And then he felt someone walking next to him. He expected the man to pass, but he didn't.

Jensen turned. It was Angelo.

'Hello, Harry. We missed you.'

Jensen said nothing.

'It wasn't nice, you know,' Angelo went on. 'We're supposed to be friends. Where'd you go?'

'No place important.'

'Harry. That's no way to talk to your friends.'

Jensen stopped walking. His hand was still on the knife. Angelo stopped next to him.

'You want to go someplace where we can sit down?'

'No.' Jensen started walking again. 'I feel safer out here in public.'

'Worried?' Angelo seemed amused.

'Look, Angelo, I was on my way back to New Orleans a couple of weeks ago and somebody tried damn hard to run me off the side of a mountain.'

This time, Angelo stopped walking. 'You're shitting me.'

'No.'

'Oh, *Jesus María*. That's why you disappeared.'

'Under the circumstances I thought it was the thing to do.'

Angelo shook his head. 'You were right.'

The two men resumed their walk.

'Maybe it was the Cubans,' Angelo ventured.

'I don't know. I don't think so.' Not unless Elena was playing a more devious game than he thought.

'Nah. I guess not.' Angelo stared at the sidewalk as they walked. 'More likely it was the CIA.'

'Why them?'

Angelo stopped again.

'I'll tell you, Harry. It looks like we've got some trouble, too.'

'What kind of trouble?'

'You heard about that CIA guy in Mexico? I forget his name.'

'Touhy. Yeah, I heard.'

'Right.' Angelo's eyes locked on Jensen's. 'Harry, I'm going to tell you some things now, because of what's happening with us. But if you ever breathe a word of any of this stuff, it's going to be one dead Harry Jensen, with a canary stuck in his mouth. Understand?'

'You make it very clear.'

'Good. The car's around the corner. Let's get in. I can't talk about this on the street.'

Jensen shrugged. 'All right.'

The chauffeur drove them over the bridge to Saint Petersburg and then across the mouth of Tampa Bay to the coastal highway. Jensen watched the city and the bay without interest.

For almost ten minutes, as the car passed palm trees and roadside attractions on the way to Sarasota, Angelo said nothing. Then he broke his silence.

'We want back into Havana. We had a lot of good stuff

going there. The casinos. Broads.' He paused, took a breath. 'And there was something else, too.'

'Heroin.'

'Yeah. So we had all that going, and that's a big investment, you know. We sank a lot of money into that place. And there was a lot of cash coming out that we lost. Maybe a hundred million a year just from the casino skim.'

'Okay, so you have reason to go back. But you said there's trouble.'

'There sure is. It's the horse. The European stuff used to come into Cuba. Mostly it started in Turkey and came through the refineries in France. But now they got someplace new to get it from.'

'Where?'

'Way the other side of the world. Little countries. I can't even remember the names.'

'Vietnam.'

'Yeah. That's one. There are a couple more.'

'Laos. Cambodia.'

'Right. Right. That sounds like it. Okay. They're growing poppies over there all the time and they've got places for doing the refining. A lot of people say that's the future for us, over there.'

'Not Havana.'

'Yeah. Not Havana. The Asian stuff is cheaper, and it's a lot easier to move it around. You've got all that jungle and mountains with trails the natives know how to use, and nobody knows where the borders are anyway. And the fighting helps. Nobody's going to notice a little smuggling in the middle of a war.'

'So some of your ... colleagues would rather deal with Southeast Asia than worry about getting back into Havana.'

'Yeah. And some of our CIA connections, too. Not the ones who were in on the Bay of Pigs and some other little things in Cuba with us. There's a different bunch of them over there in Japland. And they're having a ball. From what my friends say, those guys have their own private war going on over there. They've got their own airline and a private air force, too. And they've got a bunch of slant-eye generals eating out of their hands. These generals, they do whatever they want with the troops – order them to collect the stuff from the poppies, do the deliveries, stand guard. Everything.'

'Sounds good,' Jensen prompted. 'Why don't you join them?'

'You kidding me? Havana was the way, man. You had the casinos to wash the money through, and the broads, like I said before. Besides, it's all set up. The routes are all solid. All we need is to get Havana back. Who wants to mess around in any jungles?'

'I see what you mean. But in the meantime your friends and the CIA are in business together in Vietnam and Laos and Cambodia.'

'That's it.'

Jensen wished he were talking to the other of his New Orleans visitors. Angelo was a fine message carrier, but he was no intelligence analyst.

'And they want the country to stay involved over there. Not in Cuba. That's why you've got trouble.'

'Yeah. Yeah. Right.' Angelo did not hide how impressed he was by Jensen's reasoning ability. 'They say they've got the gold pot at the end of the rainbow and we should lay off Cuba. And man, there's a lot of money in this, more than anything else. These guys, anybody gets in their way, he's dead.'

'Like Touhy.'

'I was thinking of you, getting run off the road, like you said. The CIA guy, I don't know. Maybe. Mostly, my friends don't mess with knocking off CIA guys.'

'But your friends' friends – their CIA friends – might.'

'Yeah. It's like we take care of our own, and they do, too. So the thing is, what I'm supposed to tell you – no more fucking around. You wrap up what you're doing here in a day or two, and then we're putting the show on the road, ready or not. We want you to start talking where people can hear you. Once you do, we have friends who can help spread the word.'

'All right. But I'll need a couple of days in Dallas, too.'

'All they told me was a couple of days here.'

'It could make things a lot easier for all of us.'

'Well, okay. I'll see what they say.'

'Good. Now take me back to Tampa and I'll get back to work.'

Elena was lying naked in the bed next to him. Her breasts stood high and round, as if gravity did not affect them; her nipples, dark against her golden skin, were still erect; a fine sheen of sweat glistened on her body.

'I have learned nothing,' she said. 'It is as if everyone has become suddenly mute. No one will speak to me.'

'You're talking about the exiles now, not your own people.'

'Yes.'

'Do you think they suspect who you really are?'

A frown crossed her face. 'I have been very careful. I think it is more general than that. The community seems to have closed in on itself. There is anger in the air, and suspicion.' She turned on to her side to face him. 'What are you going to do about the Mafia?'

'I'm trying to hold them off until we've been to Dallas. I

have the feeling that between Sylvia Odio's story and Jack Ruby's connections with the mob and the Teamsters and the casinos, we can get everything we need there.'

'And then what will you do?'

He ran a forefinger around one of her nipples.

'Trust me. I have a plan. Once we really have the goods on them, there's no problem.'

'You may not find the evidence you need. If the community in Dallas is like it is here, we will learn nothing there. And if Mrs Odio will not see you, or me, or someone we trust—'

'If we learn nothing in Dallas, then we're up against the same ultimatum. They're going to want me to talk. Their way.'

She threw one leg over him and sat up on her knees, straddling his hips. She moved her body against him.

'And if you say what they want you to, I will be forced to kill you.'

He answered her by grabbing her shoulders and pulling her down to him. He rolled them over so that he was on top of her. But even as he plunged himself into her, he could feel the depth of his disgust and his anger and his fear.

Angelo picked him up in the limousine the next day.

'I've got something for you. From somebody we know in Washington.'

'Washington?' Jensen was intrigued.

'Yeah. We got connections there, too. So happens, it was the FBI where this came from.'

'The FBI? Really?'

'Never mind that. Just listen. There was a guy in Tampa, a Cuban guy in his twenties. He was a member of the Fair Play for Cuba Committee. And he went to a big meeting last

252

November. Some kind of slide show about Cuba. And all the time during the meeting he kept saying he was going to go back to Cuba, but there was something he had to do first. He was hanging around this house where they had the meeting, waiting for a phone call from Cuba to give him the go-ahead. Next thing you know he gets a Mexican tourist card in Tampa on the twentieth of November and goes to Texas. Then on the twenty-third, the day after Kennedy's shot, he goes down to Mexico and hangs around a couple of days and hops on a plane for Cuba. That mean anything to you?'

Jensen shrugged, but his mind was racing: If the Cuban-American had been waiting for a go-ahead from Cuba and then had gone to Texas on or after the twentieth to do something that would get him admitted to Cuba . . . And the date, the twentieth, narrowed down the number of names to check out on the lists Narvaez had got him from the consulate.

He said, 'It might mean something. It fits with some other things I'm checking into. It certainly sounds like the kind of thing we need. Providing we can connect it more directly with the assassination.'

'Yeah. Well, that's your job. And you don't have much more time to do it in.'

Jensen got to Narvaez's garage during the Cuban's morning break. He was sitting on a stool, with his feet up on the workbench, leafing through a battered copy of *Playboy*.

'What do you want?' he asked when he saw Jensen.

'Do you remember the man whose name I was looking for on the Mexican tourist-visa list?'

'*Si* . . .'

'He was pro-Castro. I still don't know his name, but I can tell you this. He was a member of the Fair Play for Cuba

Committee. He attended a meeting here in November. There were photographs, slides of Cuba shown that night.'

Narvaez swung his feet off the bench and faced Jensen.

'*Qué?*'

'He was a member of the FPCC.'

'*Sí. Sí.* The meeting. You say he went to a meeting.'

'In mid-November or late November.'

'With slides?'

'That's what I heard.'

'There is more?'

'Yes. He was waiting for a phone call from Cuba. He said it would be the go-ahead signal for him to leave the country.'

Narvaez seemed to be debating whether to speak or remain silent.

'Wait,' he said, and left the garage through a back door.

Jensen waited. He had no idea what to expect.

When Narvaez returned, he handed Jensen a white business-size envelope. It was smudged with dark, greasy fingermarks, and it had been opened with a dull knife.

Or a screwdriver, Jensen thought.

On the front of the envelope was the single word 'Horacio,' typed in capital letters. Inside was a sheet of paper, its edges smudged. The note was short:

TO: Horacio
FROM: Ricardo
SUBJECT: The Cuban-American we discussed

The fellow who took that intriguing solo flight got his Mexican entry permit in Tampa on November 20th. More interesting: My informant tells me our young man was 'involved in the assassination.' So far, no more details than that, but the informant is reasonably reliable. When you've read this, destroy it.

Hasta luego, amigo.

PS: Just heard we had a bug in the Cuban embassy here that picked up Oswald's September visit. How's them apples? No definite word on the contents, but the rumor is that he was asking them for a transit visa so he could go to Russia. Raises more questions than it answers, especially combined with his visit to the Soviet embassy. I'll poke around and see what I turn up.

Jensen stared at the page after he had finished reading it. Touhy had turned up more than he had bargained for.

But he had also given Jensen the missing pieces he needed. Now the Cuban-American was linked both to Castro and to the assassination. It was only hearsay, and not even firsthand hearsay, but he did not think Angelo and his friends would mind. Elena, on the other hand, would be very unhappy.

He looked up from the letter. Narvaez was glaring at him belligerently.

'You opened this?' Jensen asked him mildly.

'*Sí.*' Narvaez put hands on his hips.

'Why didn't you tell me about it before?'

'I do not know about this man in the letter. If he is not a Fidelista, people will think some Cubans here in the United States have killed Kennedy. Many say so now. It is bad.'

'You didn't trust Ricardo? Trust him not to make trouble for his friends?'

Narvaez shrugged. 'I trust no one.'

'But you gave me the letter now.'

'You say the man is in FPCC. I know of their meeting, with slides of Cuba. And I was told of a man there, waiting for a call. From Cuba. So I think now this letter cannot hurt us, and I show it to you.'

'Is there anything else?'

'No. *Nada*.'

'Can you find out more about the man? Now that you know whose side he's on. And whose side I'm on.'

'*Sí*. I will try.'

'*Gracias*. I'm going out of town, but I'll be back to talk to you.'

Jensen took a cab back to his hotel and told Elena and Angelo he was ready to leave for Dallas.

Chapter Sixteen

Edward Love pointed the day sailer closer into the wind and hauled in on the mainsheet until the mainsail was smooth and taut. He leaned back on the bench that ran along the side of the cockpit and looked at Jensen appraisingly.

'You sure were right about not coming to the office,' he said, and laughed his big, hearty bray. 'Holy shit, Harry. With that beard, you'd've never got by the front desk, and I'd've been a week explaining where I got any kind of friend looking like that. You know, you're liable to get yourself shot for a freedom rider, you run around Dallas with a beard like that and those clothes.'

Jensen smiled. 'I'd be better off pretending to be a Texan, the way you do.'

Another laugh, longer and louder. 'Hell, yes. You bet your sweet ass.'

Jensen twisted around and faced his friend. 'Now that you're a name partner in the firm, do they make you an honorary Texan? Or have you fooled them into thinking you're the real thing?'

'Well ... shucks, pardner. You know, Love is a grand old family in these here parts. You might have noticed, you flew into Love Field. They just hear the name, they figure I'm related.'

'Very handy.'

'Shit, yes. About time the dumb name did me some good.'

They were running out of lake. Love brought the sailboat about and set it up on a broad reach going back the way they had come. Jensen had to scramble to stay clear of him; he took up a lot of cockpit when he moved. Edward Love was one of the few people Jensen had ever met who made him feel small. When they had walked down the corridors of the law school together, the other students had frequently stopped and stared at them. Their combined height was a good thirteen feet.

'What brings you down here looking so disreputable?'

Jensen took a breath. 'The assassination.'

'I might've known. You still with that same outfit at the White House?'

'Nope.'

Love's eyebrows went up, but he didn't pursue the issue.

'You know,' he said, 'it's not the best time to be poking around Dallas about the assassination. The Warren people are in town, and folks are kind of fed up. Dallas got a hell of a black eye on account of that shooting, and people'd just as soon forget the whole damn business. They especially don't want to be reminded of it by some damn Yankee.'

'I'm not surprised.'

'Besides that, half the goddamned town probably thinks it was a good thing Kennedy got shot anyway, all things considered. I know plenty of folks, myself, who wish it was them as pulled the trigger.'

'That bad?'

'Shit, yes. Worse. What you saw about it in the national press wasn't the half of it. That man was hated down here. I mean hated.'

'What about the assassination?'

'What about it?'

'Can you tell me anything about it – about Oswald, say, or Ruby? About the way the police handled it? That seemed very peculiar, what I caught of it. Is that how they always do things here?'

Again Love laughed. 'Hell, boy, you never saw a sorrier bunch of law enforcers in all your born days. Can't even tell a German rifle from an Italian one, to start with.' He paused to make a small correction to the set of the sails. 'I guess I can tell you some stories. Maybe they're what you want, maybe not.'

'Why don't you try some, and we'll see.'

'Sure thing.' He stretched out a long arm and snagged a beer from a cooler under the bench across the cockpit from him. There was an opener chained to the tiller – he punched a couple of triangular holes in the top of the can. Beer foamed up and flowed down over his hand.

'I sure hope that Warren Commission has a sharp staff, because they're going to have a hell of a lot to straighten out, judging by the rumors I've picked up.'

'Is there a lot of talk around?'

'Not anymore. Like I said before, the big thing around here is to be relieved the bastard's dead. I even got invited to a party to celebrate. Didn't go. Don't talk much to the people who threw it, either. These days, with a local boy in the White House, folks are more concerned about the new cotton subsidies and how far old Lyndon is likely to go on this civil rights thing of his. There's still a couple of committees to improve Dallas's image, but that's about it. That, and wishing Earl Warren'd get his commie ass the hell out of town and take all those nosy young lawyers back to Washington with him.'

'But you've heard rumors?'

'In the early days, mostly. And I got interested, so I still ask questions when I'm talking to folks I know real well. Most everybody I talk to has a pet assassination story.'

'Like what?'

'Like there's a fellow name of Bogard, used-car dealer, had a visit from a fellow named Lee Oswald, wanted to buy a used car. They took a test ride out on the Stemmons Freeway. This Lee Oswald, he drove so fast, he like to turn old Bogard's hair white. And then they get back to the lot, and he says he doesn't have enough money. But he was going to come into some soon, and he could make a down payment. Wanted credit for the rest. When they gave him grief about it, he said he was going back to Russia, because they had respect for the working man over there.'

'He said he was coming into money soon? And that he'd go *back* to Russia?'

'That's the way I heard it. But that's not the whole point of the story. What I also heard is that Lee Harvey Oswald didn't know how to drive.'

Jensen whistled. 'What the hell do you make of that?'

Love shook his head. 'Beats me, boy.' He glanced at Mountain Creek Lake's approaching shore. 'It's about time we came about. Try your hand?'

'Sure.' Jensen switched places with Love and took the tiller. He snapped the mainsheet out of its jam cleat and held it ready. 'You handle the jib for me?'

'Aye, aye.'

'Okay. Coming about.' Jensen pushed the tiller hard over and ducked as the boom swung across the small cockpit. For a dozen seconds he had his hands full working the tiller and adjusting the mainsail.

'Not bad,' Love said when the maneuver was over.

'Tell me more about Oswald.'

'I don't know much else, except what you've already seen in the papers. There are other stories about his doing things he couldn't have or being in two places at once. You know how that is – a guy gets notorious and everybody and his brother turns out to have been ass-to-elbow with the bastard in the last two weeks. I heard some things about Ruby, though. And Officer J. D. Tippit.'

Jensen took a beer and occupied himself opening it.

'You probably know already Ruby was connected up with the Syndicate. Mafia. Whatever you want to call it. But I'll bet you didn't know he worked for Al Capone.'

'Come on.'

'That's what they say. When he was a kid. And over the years he got to be a big man in the dope business. He was the guy who put in the fix with the cops for the Syndicate in Dallas. Whatever you wanted to do in Dallas – dope or numbers or whores – you went to see Jack so he could clear it for you. He had big friends. Like, Frank Nitti.'

'*The* Frank Nitti? The one who took over for Capone?'

'Yep. And he's just the man at the top of the list. You wouldn't recognize most of the names. But being an assistant US attorney, even in LA, gave me a broad education. Not like you fancy-pants types who went clerking instead of doing the real work.'

'You always were jealous,' Jensen kidded.

'You bet your ass I was. But the US attorney's office turned out to be the road to riches, so I'm not complaining.'

'So Jack Ruby was more than just a strip-club owner.'

'A lot more, if what I hear is right. And I also hear he knew Oswald. And Tippit. They were both seen in the Carousel Club, and Jack talked to them both like he knew them pretty well. He even kicked Oswald out once. That's in line with how he treated his friends, too – he was a violent little bastard. And Tippit. I hear whispers from time to time that Tippit had his hand in drugs, some way.'

'How much of all that do you believe?'

'Depends on the day. That's why I'm so interested to see what these hotshots from Washington do with it all. Oswald the commie. Ruby the mobster and police go-between. And Tippit, who was maybe more than just another cop. Crazy, man.'

'Yeah,' Jensen concurred. 'Crazy.'

Standing next to the bed in their motel room, Elena pulled a red and black silk dress over her head and turned her back so that Jensen could zip it up for her. He leaned toward the mirror over the dresser and tied his tie.

'Where do you want to go for dinner?'

She was putting on lipstick. 'I don't care.'

He went to the closet and took out a sport jacket with a western-style yoke of fancy piping across the chest. 'There's supposed to be a good place for steak off the turnpike. And maybe they'll have enough experience with tourists not to mind the beard.'

'Or the fact that I'm not white.'

When they left their motel room, he closed the door and made sure it was locked, and then he knocked on the door of the unit next to theirs. After a moment, it opened.

'Yeah?' Angelo said.

'We're going out to dinner. We'll be back in a couple of hours.'

'Where you going?'

'Down the road a piece. The Longhorn, I think it's called.'

'Longhorn. Okay. Maybe I'll drop in.'

'Whatever you want.'

He and Elena got into their rented car, and he turned on the radio. He didn't think the car was bugged, but he was not interested in taking foolish chances. Elena sat close to him and whispered in his ear.

'I do not know if I can reach Mrs Odio. Three of the people I spoke to about it said they thought it would be impossible. One man said he would try. He will let me know tomorrow. If necessary, we can find a way to reach her directly without asking permission.'

'No. Not as long as Angelo is around. He's got to keep believing we're on his side.'

'There must be a reason you could give him for wanting to talk to her.'

'Maybe there is. But I can't think of any.'

The next day he went to Dealy Plaza, where John Kennedy had been shot. He stopped first at the tailor shop he had gone to the day before. He was pleased to find that his new suit was ready, as promised, and that it fit well enough for his purposes. He changed clothes in the tailor's dressing room and put his work shirt and fatigues into a briefcase.

He left the tailor shop, resplendent in a white suit, white shirt, black tie, and broad-brimmed white hat. His boots and his briefcase were black, and a pair of sunglasses completed the outfit. It was the same basic disguise he had used in Mexico City, and he had trimmed his beard so that it reinforced the Latin American image he was trying to project.

He suspected that Love's comments about his beard were only slightly exaggerated. It might hide his scar and make it harder for old friends and new enemies to recognize him, but here in Dallas a beard made him the object of attention and more than a little hostility. As a prosperous Latino, he would not gain anyone's respect or affection, but he could hope to take on some of the invisibility that went with being firmly lodged in a stereotype that threatened no one.

He spent hours in and around Dealy Plaza, walking the motorcade route, examining lines of sight, standing on the railroad overpass looking out along the curve of Elm Street toward the school-book depository, trying to visualize what had happened there less than five months before.

He went over the route several times and studied the seven-story facade of the depository and the white picket fence and the grassy knoll where so many people had heard shots being fired. He could not walk away from the site of the assassination. It was as if by staying there long enough, he could solve the problems that still plagued him.

There were other people, he saw, who were in Dealy Plaza because of what had happened there. That did not surprise him. What was amazing to him was that so many people passed through in the course of their everyday business, walking the streets as if they were not saturated with blood and grief and history.

He began to worry that staying longer would make him the object of too much attention. He decided to take one more look around and then leave.

He was walking east along Elm Street past the Stemmons Freeway sign when he saw Jill standing in front of the school-book depository. She was with two men in dark suits, Stetsons, string ties, and cowboy boots. They were pointing out the sights to her.

She craned her neck to look up at the sixth-floor window where Oswald had supposedly knelt to fire the fatal shots. Her blonde hair fell gracefully around her shoulders, spreading over her bright red dress.

Jensen couldn't breathe. He was paralyzed by a combination of shock and fear.

One of her companions was saying something. He pointed along Elm Street, toward Jensen.

As she turned in his direction, Jensen willed himself to move.

Jill and the two men walked toward him. Her attention was still on what one of the men was saying. Then she looked at the sign and – Jensen kept walking, hoping he looked natural but feeling as though he were slogging through waist-high cobwebs – her eyes moved toward the grassy knoll, pausing the briefest of instants as they met his and then sweeping on.

They passed each other. She had given no sign that she had recognized him.

At the book depository he turned to see where she had gone. She was standing with the two men, looking at the grassy knoll and the white picket fence, then at the overpass and at the street in front of the knoll; they were engrossed in conversation.

Jensen's mind was racing frantically and yet it was totally empty. Before he knew what he was doing, he was taking long strides toward the trio. As he approached, they turned away from the grassy knoll. One of the men almost ran into him.

'*Perdóname,*' he said. 'Can you tell me, is this the place of shooting *el presidente* Kennedy?'

One of the men said curtly, 'Over there,' and pointed down Elm Street. The other man started to move away.

Jill had recoiled at his first approach, putting both of the men between herself and Jensen. Now she lingered, studying him.

'*Muchas gracias,*' he said. His eyes met hers. '*Y mis flores para su belleza.*'

She stared at him.

He nodded slightly. Touched his hat with what he hoped looked like Latin American gallantry.

'*Buenas dias.*'

'Come on, Jill,' one of the men said. 'Don't encourage him. He's been raping you in his mind the whole time.'

'Frank. That's no way to talk.'

He took her arm.

'All right, Frank.' She turned, still talking, her voice raised. 'I'm tired. Can you drop me back at the Continental so I can get some rest before dinner?'

'Sure, honey.'

Jensen watched them, unaware that he had not moved, until one of the men turned around and saw him there. Quickly he started walking the other way.

He gave her twenty minutes before he called. He had planned to wait half an hour, but it was more than he could stand.

They met at a lounge near Nieman-Marcus. It was, as Jensen had hoped, full of people burdened with purchases, relaxing after a day's shopping. He had a package of his own; he had made it to the store barely in time to buy something before they closed. His Nieman-Marcus package and the brown bag that concealed a half pint of gin combined to make him one of the crowd, even if he did look like a Mexican. He did not take his sunglasses off.

Jill was five minutes late, breathless when she arrived.

'I didn't believe it was you,' she said as she sat down.

'I didn't believe it was you either.' It came out as anger. He was still very frightened about her being in Dallas. 'What are you doing here?'

'Now, wait a minute . . .'

He leaned toward her. 'Keep your voice down. I'm sorry. I didn't mean to yell at you. But, damn it, this isn't a kid's game.'

'And I'm not a kid, Har—' she caught herself. 'I'm not a kid.'

'All right. All right. Look, let's get our drinks and start again. I have some gin.'

'Good. A gimlet, I guess.'

Jensen signaled to a waitress. 'Lime juice,' he said when she came over. 'And two on-the-rocks.'

'For gimlets?'

'Please.'

They waited in silence until the waitress had brought them their setups. Jensen poured stiff drinks for them. They lifted their glasses to each other before they drank.

Jensen took his sunglasses off.

'Now. What brings you here?'

'Business. I told you we had a client in Texas.'

'An oilman.'

'Yes. He's based in Houston, but he has business here, too, and he insisted that I come out to see him. It's a big account. I couldn't refuse. I didn't know you'd be here, so I thought it was all right.'

'Did he offer you a trip to Dealy Plaza?'

'Damn it, Harry, I can't hide in my apartment. This is no different from the way it used to be for us. You keep trying to protect me from life.'

'You really think this is something like fighting for a promotion, or twisting some arms on Capitol Hill? People are being killed.'

She started to protest, stopped. She looked at him closely in the subdued light. Reached across the table and touched his left cheek.

'Is that . . . is that your scar?'

'Yes.'

She pushed his beard aside gently and ran her finger the length of the scar.

'My God.'

'That's why I want you to go back where you belong. It looks gruesome on me. It would look a lot worse on you.'

She tried to smile. 'As long as it's not because of another woman,' she joked.

He could not keep a picture of Elena, in bed, from flashing into his mind.

'No,' he said. 'It's not another woman.' He took a drink.

She sat looking at him.

'You're sure?'

He returned her gaze. 'What do you mean?'

'There was something about the way you said that. The look on your face.'

'Oh, come on.'

'Okay. But . . . Look, just tell me again. Is there another woman?'

He closed his eyes. Took a breath. Opened them.

'This is ridiculous.'

'Maybe it is. But I listen to you about Ralph. So humor me and answer the question.'

There it was: He had to lie outright or risk the truth. Neither seemed safe.

'There is, isn't there?'

'No . . . not the way you think.'

'Not the way I think! How many ways are there?'

'Jill, please . . .'

'That's great. No wonder you want me out of town.'

'It's not like that. There is someone here with me, but it's all tied up with this . . . investigation. I can't do anything about it.'

'I'll bet you can't.'

He was suddenly furious. 'I don't get it. I really don't get it. You come to me with a story about your great love for Jack' – he stopped and looked around self-consciously, afraid that he had already said too much. No one seemed to be paying attention.

'Your great love,' he resumed. 'And then you get me together with your latest lover, and that's all supposed to be okay with me. But now you hear I've got a woman with me and you get on your high horse. What kind of shit is that? What kind of sense does it make?'

'I'll tell you what kind of shit it is: All those things you said about me just now, those are all things that happened before we got back together. Before we had such a wonderful time. I haven't been near anybody else since then. I just sat there in Washington worrying about you, and not hearing a word. So I played Penelope, while you were off at war. But you don't seem to have any such scruples. That's what makes me so mad. I don't care what you did before. I don't care if you screwed the whole world. But not after what happened between us. What I thought happened between us.'

'Penelope? Is that what it was when I called and Ralph was there? You were fighting him off, I suppose.'

'Harry, don't be more shitty than you have to. I just told you—'

'All I know is, every time I turn around, there's Ralph

Norris. Holding your hand. Giving you advice. Sending you to Texas. Is that why you're here? To find out something for Ralph?'

She closed her eyes. 'This is ridiculous, Harry. You're the one who's got a lover here, not me.'

He poured more gin into his glass, rattled the ice in it, and took a drink.

He spoke slowly and calmly: 'The woman I'm with is a Cuban; she's all tied up with what I'm doing. I can't talk about it here; I'm afraid to say some of these things out loud, even whispering. But I'll tell you this much. I have to keep her with me. As long as we're together, there's a whole group that won't think about killing me. It makes life a lot simpler. And she's been helpful, too. She helped me pick up some information, and she's the one who nursed me back to health in New Orleans.'

'Damn it, I don't want to hear about it! What do you want me to do, give her the Florence Nightingale Award, or something?'

They sat in angry silence.

She looked at her watch. 'I've got to go soon, and I've got more important things to talk about than who's jealous of whom.' She touched her glass. 'Give me some more gin.'

He added gin to the ice water in her glass.

She sipped at it, then said, 'I was at a party last night, and there was a man there from the Dallas police. An assistant commissioner or some such thing. A perfectly horrible man. But he didn't think I was perfectly horrible. He didn't let me alone all night. He kept getting drunker, but he didn't seem to realize it. And he wanted so badly to impress me. If he hadn't been so obnoxious, it would have been touching. As it was, it was educational instead.'

'What did you learn?'

She drank some more gin. When she resumed talking, it was in a voice so low he had to strain to hear her.

'The Dallas police have an affidavit from a woman who says she saw a man at the wheel of a truck parked in Dealy Plaza not long before the shooting. She says there was a second man taking a gun case out of the truck. He carried the gun case up the grassy knoll. She says there were three policemen standing talking near a motorcycle just up from where the truck was illegally parked and not far from where the man carried the gun case up the knoll. She gave the affidavit on November twenty-second, after the shooting. Now here comes what I really don't understand. My boastful policeman says that an FBI man told him, on the QT, that this woman picked out a picture of Jack Ruby as the man driving that truck.'

'That puts him at the scene of the assassination on the morning it happened. And if there were shots from the grassy knoll—'

'Yes. It makes it seem like Ruby was part of a conspiracy. And that goes with the idea that Ruby shot Oswald to shut him up.'

'And the FBI has some evidence of it. At least this one woman's testimony. Which did not appear anywhere in the FBI report on the assassination. Damn.'

Jill sipped again at her drink. 'It's very strange. But that's not the thing I don't understand.'

'What is?'

'The FBI questioned her on the twenty-third of November. Ruby shot Oswald on the twenty-fourth. What was the FBI doing with a picture of Jack Ruby on November twenty-third?'

'Holy shit.'

271

'That was how I felt after I thought about the story. And my policeman told me one more interesting story before it dawned on him he was talking too much. It seems that on the twenty-fourth there was a meeting at Ruby's apartment. It was so soon after Ruby shot Oswald that the cops hadn't even got to the apartment yet. Ruby's roommate was there – George Senator – and two lawyers and two reporters. One of the reporters was named Bill Hunter and he was from California. And right after my policeman told me that, he looked at me sort of strangely and said something about getting another drink, and then wandered away and didn't come back.'

'He didn't say anything else?'

'No.'

'Nothing about what the meeting was for, or who the lawyers were?'

'Not a word.'

Jensen finished his gin. 'Jack Ruby keeps popping up lately. I went for a boat ride with Ned Love yesterday. You remember Ned, from law school?'

'Oh, sure. What's he doing here? Wasn't he in Los Angeles? An assistant US attorney or something?'

'He's a Texas lawyer now. Hobnobs with the state attorney general. Knows everybody. He had some interesting stories to tell, most of them about Jack Ruby and his connections with organized crime and the Dallas police force.'

'Like what Ralph said about him?'

'Yes. Only in much greater detail. Ruby is a lot more complicated, and he was a lot more involved in big-time doings than I would ever have guessed. And now these two stories of yours. Damn. I'd love to know why those particular four men met with George Senator so soon after Ruby killed

Oswald. There hasn't even been a whisper about that meeting anywhere. More stones in the wall of silence around the assassination. I wonder what they talked about.'

'So do I.'

He frowned. 'I'm glad to have the information, but not at the expense of your talking to people about the assassination. There's something you ought to know. Ned told me that since the assassination – less than five months, right? – four people associated with what happened that day have died. A fifth was shot in the head, but it looks like he's going to pull through. Two of the five were supposed to know something about a connection between Oswald and Ruby. One of them had a heart attack, the other had his throat cut. The other three all knew something about the Tippit killing, and every one of them died violently. This whole thing keeps getting scarier, the closer to it we get. I'm beginning to think I've been lucky to get off with some broken bones and a bad scar. Dallas is a damn dangerous place these days for people with any connection to that assassination. You've got to get out of here.'

'All right. I'll do what you say.' She put her hand on his. 'And you take care of yourself, too, okay? Be careful. I'll worry about you.'

He stood up and put some money on the table. 'The Nieman-Marcus box is for you. A present.'

He walked away before she could thank him.

Chapter Seventeen

Jensen had taken it for granted that Angelo's people were following him in Dallas. Until the meeting with Jill he had done nothing to avoid them. They were protecting him while keeping tabs on him, and he did not want to make their job any harder than it had to be. Besides, if they thought he was easy to keep track of, they would relax, so that when the time came for him to make his break he could catch them off balance.

He had made a game of trying to identify the men who were following him. A few were so clumsy or careless that they were easy to spot. But for long stretches of time he was sure he was being followed and yet he could not find out by whom.

Before going to meet Jill, he had shaken off one of the clumsy ones: a cadaverous, olive-skinned man whose clothes seemed two sizes too large for him. Jensen assumed that Angelo had had time since then to cover the airport and the other simple ways he could leave town. Still, leaving town was what he had to do. He had to track down the connection between Ruby and Oswald, and the meeting at Ruby's apartment might be the key. He had to find Bill Hunter. And he had to get out of town before the Mafia picked him up again. If not, he would have to answer questions about where he had been when they lost him. And Angelo might well try to restrict his movements or intensify the surveillance. Then, there was no saying how much longer it might be before he got another chance to make a break. He had been supremely lucky today. He could not count on its happening again.

He pushed through the revolving door into the lobby of the Sheraton Hotel, his eyes scanning for a sign to the telephones. When he found it, he walked quickly across the lobby, slid into a booth, and closed the door. He called Love Field. He could get a plane to Houston in half an hour.

He took a chance and called the motel.

'Mrs Jones,' he said. 'Room Four-o-five.'

There was a pause, and then the switchboard girl said, 'I'm sorry. Mrs Jones checked out.'

'What?'

'She checked out.'

'When?'

'I don't know.' Annoyed: 'I'll give you the desk.'

He hung up and walked quickly back through the lobby and outside to a cabstand. If Elena had checked out, he had no way to reach her. It could be Angelo's doing, or she could have bolted on her own. Either way, he didn't like it.

On the way to the airport he ran through the plans he had made for his break. It was only as he was paying the cab fare at the terminal that he realized he might not be in the clear, even now.

What if the man in the baggy clothes had been intentionally clumsy, just so that Jensen would feel confident of being able to shake him? Then if there was a backup man, they could keep after him when he thought he was alone.

In an instant the notion became a certainty: Jensen was sure

276

they had fooled him that way. And that meant they knew he had met with Jill. It meant that someone in one of the cabs pulling up now might be following him.

Jensen took his change and hurried into the crowded terminal. He took off his white hat and held it in front of him as he worked his way into the densest part of the Houston-bound throng.

At the last moment he broke out of the ticket line and joined a line of passengers entering the terminal from a plane that had just arrived from Houston. He worked his way up in the group so that he was one of the first through the doors to the cabstand.

He told the cabby to take him to Carter Field. He could go a lot farther from Carter Field, the Fort Worth International Airport, than he could from Love Field.

He could, but he didn't. He settled into a seat in a four-prop Constellation bound for Phoenix and steeled himself against looking around the cabin to see which of his fellow passengers might be following him. His only chance of getting away later lay in seeming to be unconcerned now. He took a newspaper from the stewardess and stared blankly at its pages, pretending to read.

His vision clouded. He shook his head and tried to focus, but the words blurred, and his head dropped. The paper started to slip from his fingers. He folded it and tucked it into the seatback pouch in front of him, closed his eyes, and let sleep overcome him. He did not awaken until the man sitting next to him pushed by to get off the plane in Phoenix.

He bought a ticket for San Francisco, where he could begin his search for the reporter named Hunter. He spent his waiting time moving from one airport shop to another. He wanted to be surrounded by people, and he wanted to keep moving.

A half-dozen times in two hours he spotted men he was sure were following him. None of them reappeared. He told himself he was imagining things, but it did not help him relax.

He slept again on the flight to San Francisco and awoke feeling drugged. Before the plane landed, he locked himself into its cramped toilet, took off his jacket and shirt, and put on a red, western-style shirt he had bought at the Phoenix airport. Buttoning the shirt, he was painfully aware of how much thinner his money belt had become. He put his white shirt back on over the red one and retied his tie. Then he put on his jacket and went back to his seat.

Leaving the plane in San Francisco, he put his hat on immediately. He was carrying the shopping bag from Phoenix that had been his only luggage. As he walked, he loosened his tie.

He ducked into the first men's room he saw, closed himself in a stall, and whipped off his jacket and shirt. He left them behind, stuffed into the shopping bag with his hat, and he got out as fast as he could.

He took a bus to San Francisco and from there another bus to Berkeley. He wandered around for a while, trying to determine if anyone had followed him this far. He felt no tingling between his shoulder blades, no sensation of eyes boring into his back. And he saw no one who looked like he might be following him.

He found an Army-Navy store on Telegraph Avenue not far from the campus and bought the things he needed and a duffel bag to put them in. At a coffeehouse on Telegraph, he had a cappucino and watched the motley procession of students that streamed by. He used the coffeehouse bathroom to change from his Phoenix shirt and his Texas trousers to some of the clothes he had bought at the Army-Navy store. When he paid for his cappucino, he got five dollars worth of change.

He found a pay phone and a San Francisco phone book. He called the *Examiner* first. The person he spoke to there had never heard of Bill Hunter. He dropped in some more coins and dialed the *Chronicle*.

'Bill Hunter?' asked the assistant city editor. 'Bill Hunter. I know that name. Damn it. He won some kind of prize or something. Hang on a minute.'

'Sure.'

Jensen heard him yell: 'Any of you guys know a Bill Hunter? He's with some paper either in LA or maybe Sacramento. Won a prize once, I think.'

There was the sound of the phone being dropped on a desk and then a shouted conversation. Jensen couldn't make out the words; they were lost in the general hubbub of the *Chronicle*'s newsroom.

It was almost ten minutes before anyone came back on the phone. While he waited, Jensen fed more coins into the box. Then the receiver was picked up, and a new voice came on the line.

'Hello?'

'Hello. I'm trying to find a reporter named Bill Hunter. All I know is that he works for a California paper.'

'Why do you want him?'

'I have a follow-up for him on a story he was doing.'

'Oh. All right. There's a Bill Hunter in Long Beach, on the *Independent Press-Telegram*.'

'Thanks a lot. I appreciate it.'

'Don't mention it. Tell him Al Newton says hello.'

'Sure. And thanks again.'

Jensen shouldered his duffel bag and went to find out where he could get a bus that would take him back to the airport.

It was dark when he got to Los Angeles. The first thing he did was stop at an airport phone booth and call the *Press-Telegram*. Hunter was there.

'Yeah,' he said. 'This is Bill Hunter. What can I do for you?'

'You were out of town on a story last fall. I want to talk to you about it.'

'Last fall?'

'Yeah. Look, I don't want to talk much about this on the phone. But I've got some information I think you're going to be very interested in, and it's about that assignment. It's something that can't wait very long, either.'

'You're talking about . . . Thanksgiving.'

'That's right. And I don't want to say any more. I want to see you as soon as I can.'

'Where are you?'

'Not far.'

'In LA?'

'I'm on my way.'

'The airport?'

Jensen said nothing.

'All right. I was just trying to see how soon you could get here. Look, I'm booked up tonight, but I can see you tomorrow night, after I get done here. Why don't you come by the paper about seven? If I'm not here, there'll be a message for you.'

'Fine.'

Jensen left the phone booth and found a men's room. Ducking in and out of men's rooms to change clothes was beginning to be routine for him.

He took a stall and sat down on the toilet seat, his army-surplus trousers pooled around his feet. From his duffel bag, he took out a Navy life jacket he had bought and his folding hunting knife. He slit open the life jacket and removed some of the padding around the shoulders and along the back. He tried it on twice while he sat there, making adjustments until he was satisfied with how it fit. He stuffed the waste padding into the duffel bag.

He stood up, undressed quickly, put on the life jacket and strapped it into place, and then got into the oversize trousers and shirt he had bought at the Army-Navy store.

He looked down at himself. From what he could see, he gave a convincing appearance of a man fifty pounds heavier than the one who had walked into the stall. He pulled a sailor's watch cap down over his hair, picked up the duffel bag, and went out to rent a car.

He stopped at a motel on Sunset Boulevard. In his room, he examined himself in the mirror. He looked decidedly portly, and his beard disguised the thinness of his face. He undressed and lay down on one of the beds. He had a night and a day to kill and a lot of sleep to catch up on.

He got to Long Beach early. He drove out to Seal Beach to watch the sun set and then he drove slowly back to town. It was a little after seven when he got to the *Press-Telegram*. Bill Hunter wasn't there, and there was no message. Someone told him that Hunter wasn't likely to check in again until at least nine.

Jensen found a bar and nursed a beer and tried to be patient. At nine o'clock he left the bar and drove around looking for a phone booth he could use in private. He found one on Long Beach Boulevard and made his call.

'I'm supposed to be meeting Bill Hunter later on. Has he come in or left a message for me?'

'Nope. And he's not going to.'

'What do you mean?'

'Some motherfucking cop shot him in the head.'

'What!'

'That's it, buster. He's dead.'

'Hey! Wait a minute. How did it happen?'

'What's it to you?'

'I had business with him. I have the key to a story he was working on.'

'What story?'

'How did he get shot?'

'He was sitting in the police station reading a mystery novel. Waiting for an interesting call to come in, I guess. Or maybe he was waiting to see somebody. And a couple of cops came by where he was sitting, and one of them shot him in the head.'

'Just like that?'

'Just like that. They say it was an accident. The cop dropped the gun, and it went off. And if that doesn't wash, they'll probably say he was cleaning it or he was showing it to his partner, or maybe he was practicing his fast draw.'

Jensen hung up and left the phone booth. As he walked toward his rented Ford, he could just make out in the darkness two figures leaning against the car's right front fender. He turned immediately and walked in the other direction. After a block he looked back. The two men were following him.

He was walking south down Long Beach Boulevard. Except

for the automobile traffic, it was almost deserted. He did not remember how far it was to Ocean Boulevard, but it seemed to him there was an entertainment pier there: people, light, activity. He walked faster.

The two men behind him drew closer. He could hear their footfalls mingled with the sounds of his own feet on the pavement. He began to jog. The life jacket under his shirt made it awkward; he became hot and sweaty. No one in the passing cars seemed to notice. Ahead of him, against the night sky, he could see what looked like the glow from the pier he was hoping to reach. He increased his pace, stretching his stride, running. He twisted his head to look behind him. The two men were gaining on him. And now the street was as deserted as the sidewalk.

As he ran, Jensen groped in his pocket for his knife. He was not going to make it to the pier.

He looked for a place to make a stand. A half block ahead there was a length of brick wall with a dogleg in it, the facade of a store of some kind. It made a solid corner: If he stood there, his two pursuers would both have to come at him from the front. It would reduce their advantage slightly.

He sprinted there and whirled, panting, pulling the knife from his pocket and opening it.

The two men stopped just out of his reach.

'How about that?' one of them said. 'He's got a knife.'

'Tough guy,' the other one said.

They were both tall and wiry, but neither of them was as tall as Jensen.

They were holding knives of their own, longer and sharper and more deadly than his own clumsy sportsman's tool.

Without pause or warning, one of the men lunged at him.

He sidestepped, but his reaction was late. His assailant's

knife slipped neatly past his defense and slashed through his shirt, opening a gash two inches deep and six inches long in his life jacket.

Jensen struck with his own knife. The other man danced lightly back out of reach.

The two stood watching him, obviously waiting for him to react to his wound.

He clutched his belly and groaned. It did not seem to satisfy them. Even in the dark he could tell they were confused. They looked at him and then at each other.

They seemed about to make up their minds to strike again, but the wail of a siren, urgent in the still night, growing quickly louder and clearer, gave them something new to consider.

To spur them on, Jensen groaned again and slumped back against the wall.

The siren was closer.

The one who had attacked said, 'Let's go.'

The other hesitated. 'Let me finish him.'

'You crazy? He's finished.' He turned and ran. His companion followed him into the darkness.

A squad car slammed to a halt in front of Jensen, and two patrolmen jumped out, their guns drawn.

Jensen remembered the reporter's voice on the phone saying, 'Some motherfucking cop shot him in the head.' He froze with fear, watching the patrolmen approach.

'You all right?' one of them asked.

Mouth dry, Jensen nodded.

'You okay?' the patrolman persisted.

'Yes.' His voice was a croak. 'I'm . . . fine.'

'What happened?'

'A couple of guys . . . came for me with knives.'

'They get you?'

'Just cut my shirt.'

'You sure?' The cop moved forward as if to check.

'I'm sure.'

'Did you get a look at them?'

'To identify them? No.'

'Shit. You have a car around here?'

Jensen pointed. 'Up the block.'

'Okay.' The patrolman motioned to the squad car. 'Get in. We'll give you a lift.'

Jensen hesitated, then moved toward the squad car. 'Sure. Thanks.'

'You shouldn't be walking around at night, anyway. Just get into your car again and go wherever you're going.'

Jensen got in the squad car's back seat, and the patrolman closed the door. There were no handles on the inside. Jensen looked through the steel mesh at the back of the patrolmen's heads.

The driver made a U-turn.

'Which car?'

'A red Ford. On the left, maybe three blocks up.'

They stopped next to his car, and one of them got out and opened the door for him.

'You all right to drive?'

'Yeah. Sure.'

'Okay. Good. Take it easy, now.'

'Yeah. You, too. And thanks again.'

He made his way over the freeways to Beverly Hills. His fear made everything vivid; he kept the rented Ford slipping in and out of gaps in the traffic until he reached Wilshire Boulevard. He found a parking space and, in front of the Beverly Wilshire Hotel, a cab to take him to the airport.

He called Jill from a pay phone in the terminal. It was almost three in the morning in Washington, but Jill did not answer. He let the phone ring fifteen times and then tried again. No answer.

A sleepy desk clerk at the Continental Hotel in Dallas told him Miss Lazar had checked out the previous morning. More than thirty-six hours before.

He just had time to catch a late plane for New York. It was a direct flight, not a nonstop. He had an aisle seat in the first row of the first-class compartment, purchased on L. O. Jones's credit.

He settled himself in the seat and watched the rest of his fellow passengers file in past him. He missed no one, and no one looked familiar to him. If there was someone on the plane following him, it was someone new.

He had three aspirins and as many martinis after the plane was airborne. He did not know whether to try to sleep or not. His internal clock was so out of whack that he had no sense of what time of day it was. The plane trip was an agony for him; he slept fitfully and tried to read, but time dragged by impossibly slowly. Neither the aspirin nor the martinis helped his racing pulse or the pounding headache he had developed. The first-class food looked appetizing enough, and it did not taste bad, but after the first forkful he stopped eating.

His mind kept returning to the two men who had attacked him and to Bill Hunter lying dead in a Long Beach police station. The two murders – one thwarted, the other disguised – were clearly connected. Whatever Bill Hunter had known, it warranted not only his death but also the death of anyone who claimed to have related information. Or else, Jensen thought, whoever was behind Hunter's death had known it was Harry Jensen who was looking for the reporter, and why. Hunter's phone had to be bugged, that much was sure. And Jensen could not know which of his enemies had been responsible. The Mafia or the CIA, if Hunter could have tied them to the assassination. Or Castro's people, if it went the other way. Elena? he wondered. If she had made it out of the motel before Angelo got to her. Or it could have been the Southeast Asia branch of the CIA, the ones who had killed Touhy. Or the Vietnamese.

He could not afford to stay involved any longer. This was no search for the truth; it was a massive, dangerous power struggle, and he was in the middle of it. He had been fooling himself, going to LA to talk to Bill Hunter in the hope that he could find the one piece of information that would put him on top. That was all an illusion. The only thing that made any sense at all was for him to get out of the whole thing, and to get Jill out with him.

As they approached Chicago, where the plane would lay over for half an hour, the Chicago-bound passengers began to gather themselves for their arrival. One of the the stewardesses announced that she had been glad to serve them and asked them all to come again.

Jensen reached for the pillow and blanket he had put on the empty seat next to him and curled up for a rest.

Some time after the plane touched down, he actually fell asleep. He awoke to find the Chicago passengers filing on to the plane. He almost sat bolt upright with the shock, but he made himself readjust his pillow and blanket, moving with the groggy precision of a man jarred out of the depths of sleep.

The last of the passengers walked by him, and then there was a lull in the traffic; the two stewardesses at the plane's forward door checked their passenger lists to be sure everyone had boarded.

Jensen watched them through slitted eyes. They nodded to each other; they seemed satisfied. One of them walked back toward him, heading for the microphone clipped to the bulkhead just forward of his seat. The other knocked on the half-open cockpit door and leaned in to say something to the flight crew.

Jensen pushed off his blanket, stood up, and walked purposefully toward the forward door. As he reached the stewardess nearest him, she moved to block him from passing.

'Sir? We're about to take off.'

He took her shoulders and moved her out of his way; he hoped they weren't attracting too much attention.

'I've got to get off.'

'But . . .'

He kept moving. The stewardess by the cockpit door looked at him, then, questioningly, beyond him to the girl he had just passed. She nodded to her colleague, shrugged, and – clearly puzzled – watched Jensen leave the plane.

He hurried down the boarding stairs. The ground crew was already in place, waiting to roll the stairs away from the plane. They looked at him in disbelief.

'It's okay,' he said. 'Everything's fine. They're taking off on schedule.'

He turned and watched the plane's door close. The ground crew rolled the stairway clear. The plane's engines roared louder. The plane began to move. Jensen turned and walked into the terminal.

He wanted a plane to Philadelphia, but there was none leaving for more than two hours, so he settled for Pittsburgh.

From Pittsburgh, he flew to Richmond. He bought himself some clothes and threw out the baggy, knife-slashed shirt he had been wearing since California. He rented a car to drive to

Washington, and as he pulled out of the rental garage he debated throwing away his Lawrence O. Jones identification. From now on, he was afraid it would be as much a snare as an asset, an easy way for Angelo to trace his movements. But he kept the credit card in his wallet. There was still Washington to be dealt with, and he did not know what would happen there.

He fortified himself with coffee twice on the hundred-mile drive. It was almost two in the morning when he parked the car just north of the Library of Congress and began to walk.

His mind was cold and empty. The caffeine was keeping him superficially alert, but he was deeply weary. He had no more hopes or illusions, only a leaden awareness of the things he had to do.

Two blocks from his townhouse apartment, he stopped walking. Among the people who wanted to use him or to silence him, someone had to be watching for him to return home. He turned and went a block out of his way, then another. Then he walked quickly and quietly to the townhouse that shared back-to-back gardens with the one he lived in.

The wrought-iron gate was locked. He grabbed the crossrail that ran just below the points of the iron pickets and pulled himself up. His experience driving the Jaguar had reminded him to favor his left hand. Now he didn't see how he could avoid putting his full weight on it. He jammed his feet between the fence's iron uprights, but they gave him no real purchase. Still holding the crossrail, he heaved himself upward; quickly, he moved his right hand, then his left, to the pickets. The sudden pain in his left hand radiated through the whole arm. He gasped; his grip loosened. He pulled with his right hand and let his momentum carry him over the fence, turning his hands as he cleared the top. One of the pickets gouged his left thigh, and he almost lost his balance and plunged to the ground, but he managed to hold on until he was secure enough to finish turning around and take the six-foot drop quietly.

He hugged the side of the house as he moved past it. At the corner he crouched low, then flattened himself to the ground.

He crawled on elbows and knees, keeping his belly close to the ground and his butt down, the way they had taught him in the Marines. He stopped as soon as he had a good view of the back of his townhouse. He lay there watching for a long time, but he saw nothing. There was a foggy sliver of moon in the sky; only a few stars shone through gaps in the wispy overcast.

He was about to give up when he saw a flicker of motion. He stopped where he was and scanned the back of the house, keeping his eyes moving, trying to refresh his vision. He saw the motion again but restrained himself from focusing on it. The third time, he let his eyes narrow their search pattern to the vicinity of the motion. He saw it again, and this time he followed it and made out clearly the dark outline of a man against the lighter bulk of the townhouse.

He watched the man for several minutes. There could be no doubt why he was there: He was waiting for Harry Jensen.

He scuttled back into the shelter of his neighbor's house. It took him three tries to get over the fence again, and when he reached the street, he had a bruised knee and a scraped right palm to add to the gouge in his left thigh. His left hand throbbed with every beat of his heart.

He stopped at the end of his own block and watched the front of his house from the cover of a massive oak tree on the corner. He saw no one distinctly, but he was sure he caught signs of movement in the deep darkness where the base of the stoop met the wall of the house.

That was enough for him. He turned away from his home and started back down the hill to the car he had rented under a false name.

He drove to Virginia and parked in the lot of a roadside diner. He slept in the car until the sun woke him.

He was stiff when he got up, and famished. He got out of the car and stretched. In the diner he ordered coffee and a breakfast of eggs and potatoes and sausage. While the food was cooking, he went into the men's room to wash up and survey the damage of the night before. It was not as bad as he had feared.

He felt better after he ate. He called Jill at home but got no answer.

He drove to a sporting goods store he knew and sat in the car until nine o'clock, when it opened.

For the first time in a long while he used his own identification. Harry Jensen, a resident of Washington, DC, filled out a short and essentially meaningless form in connection with the purchase of a Smith and Wesson .38 caliber revolver. He also bought an AR-7 collapsible rifle, patterned after the Air Force's floating survival rifle, and ammunition for both weapons. He asked the clerk where he could find a rifle-and-pistol range that opened early, and the clerk told him there was one he could use in the basement. He bought more ammunition and put in a half hour of target practice. He was pleasantly surprised by how well he did.

At ten fifteen he called Jill's office.

'Hello, Ruthie. This is you-know-who again.'

'Oh. Yes.'

'Is the boss lady in?'

'No, I'm sorry, she's not. Can I take a message?'

'That's awfully formal for an old friend.'

'Well, she isn't here.'

'When did you see her last?'

No response.

'This is important, Ruthie.'

'Well . . . she was going to come back from Texas, but then she called in to say she was taking some time off first.'

'You haven't seen her since she left for Texas?'

'No. But I talked to her on the phone.'

'Just that once?'

'Yes.'

'And she didn't say where she was going?'

'No.'

'All right. If she calls, try to find out where she is.'

He tried to convince himself that Jill might really be taking a few days off, but he knew better. He had to find out what had happened to her. Until he knew, he had to take himself out of circulation.

He found a room with a separate entrance in a Victorian house in Charlottesville; its former tenant had left unexpectedly after flunking out of the university, and Jensen convinced the landlady to let him rent it by the week. Not far from the campus there was a place that rented typewriters. He chose a cheap one; it was old and the action was stiff, but it was adequate for his purposes.

The following day he spent hours at the typewriter, interrupting himself to stretch and to pace, deciding how to make a point or in what order to put things down.

At five o'clock he went out and called Jill's office from a pay phone. He talked to Ruthie only long enough to learn that Jill had not returned. He hung up, more worried about Jill than ever. And he could not keep calling indiscriminately; he would have to ration his contact with Jill's office. He had to assume that each time he called Washington, he increased his danger of being discovered.

In spite of his worries, he slept well that night, and in the morning he did some roadwork.

He spent the rest of the morning typing. When he was finished, he had fifteen single-spaced pages, with two carbon copies. He typed three covering letters, and then he took all of his typing and went out and bought three manila envelopes and three business-letter envelopes. He didn't address any of them until he had bought the necessary stamps at the post office. Once they were addressed and stamped, he dropped them immediately into the proper letter slots.

He had a late lunch and then he called Washington.

'Oh, hello, Mr Jensen,' Ruthie said. 'I have a message for you.'

His heart leaped. 'You heard from her.'

'She called this morning. I told her you were trying to get her, and she gave me a number for you to call.'

'Did she say where she was?'

'No, but it's a Florida number. It must be a new one – it's all numbers. You know, that direct dialing they have.'

'Did she say when she'd be back?'

'No. Just the phone number.'

'All right. Go ahead.'

He wrote down the number, thanked her, and hung up.

He dialed the ten-digit number slowly and carefully, with a trembling forefinger.

The phone rang three times. A man answered.

'Yes?' In the single word Jensen could hear a Spanish accent.

He hesitated, concerned, then plunged ahead. 'Is Jill Lazar there?'

'Who is this?'

'Harry Jensen.'

'What is the name of your mother?'

'What?'

'I ask you the name of your mother.'

'For God's sake, what's this about?'

'You say you are Harry Jensen. What is the name of your mother?'

Identification, Jensen thought, *like in a bank*. He said: 'Carolyn.'

'What is the name of your father?'

'Robert.'

'Where did you have your marriage?'

'New York.'

'At what church?'

'No church.'

'Where?'

'At my wife's mother's home.'

'On what street?'

'Central Park West.'

'Jill Lazar is well and safe. You will do what I tell you, or we will kill her. Go to New York. Go to the Plaza Hotel. There is a reservation for Arnold West. You will be Arnold West, tomorrow. There is a message at the hotel for you.'

'Who are you?'

'Go to New York tomorrow, or the woman will be killed.'

Back at his room he settled with his landlady, giving her an extra week's rent to hold the room for him, in case he needed a bolt-hole. His money belt was getting thin; it would not be long before he would have to go to the bank for money, and he was not sure how he could do that safely. He spent the evening sketching out an emergency plan.

It only took him a few minutes to pack his belongings. The only things he cared about were the rifle and the revolver, which he wrapped in his spare shirt and pants and tucked into a flight bag he had picked up in Richmond.

Chapter Eighteen

As promised, they were holding a room for Arnold West at the Plaza. He checked in and was shown immediately to his room. He insisted on carrying his bag himself, but a bellboy came with him to unlock the door.

When the bellboy left, Jensen sat on the edge of the bed and opened the letter the desk clerk had given him, addressed simply to 'Mr West, Plaza Hotel.' The letter was one page, typewritten on Plaza stationery. It said:

Dear Mr West,

We would love to meet you at the World's Fair. Come tomorrow at about ten, and we can play a game together. At 10:23, get in line at the Vatican Pavilion. Stay there for 16 minutes. Then go to the Johnson's Wax Exhibit and get in line for the movie at 10:52. Try to stay there for 19 minutes. Next, go to the General Motors Futurama and get in line at 11:30 sharp and wait for 25 minutes. Last of all, go back to the Vatican Pavilion and go all the way through and look at the *Pietà*. It's very beautiful. When you come out, we'll join you. You'll know us right away.

Please don't miss the fun. Play the game exactly by the rules. Some of us will be very hurt if you don't.

Your mystery admirer

He reread the letter several times and then went back out into the city and bought a guidebook to the Fair, an inexpensive lightweight jacket with large pockets, and a Timex watch. He was left with more then twenty hours of waiting time. To get through some of it he went to see *Dr Strangelove* at a movie theater near the hotel. It seemed very mild to him, almost realistic.

After the movie he went back to his room to go through the guidebook and plan his day. He had room service send him a steak and a good bottle of Burgundy. He didn't expect to be paying the hotel bill.

At ten in the morning the World's Fair was not yet crowded, but Jensen guessed from the rate at which people were arriving that it would be soon. The day was clear and bright; the striking shapes of the Fair buildings stood out among the trees and the acres of blacktop with unnatural clarity.

He made a quick tour of the route that connected the three buildings that were on his official itinerary, translating into reality the map he had studied the night before. At ten twenty he was back in sight of the Vatican Pavilion, scanning the crowd around it and the serpentine queue of people waiting to see the *Pietà*. He was not surprised that he could not find a familiar face. When his watch read ten twenty-three, he joined the line. People crowded in behind him at once.

He stood tensely in line, craning his head this way and that for a glimpse of someone he recognized. He took the guidebook from his windbreaker pocket and tried to lose himself in its pictures and descriptions, but he could not work up any interest in a giant model dinosaur or a lifelike talking model of Abraham Lincoln.

298

He looked around him at the other people in line, trying to see them as fairgoers, not potential enemies: boys in blue jeans and girls in toreador pants; serious families of tourists intent on seeing the wonders that would be here only for two brief summers; lovers who didn't really care where they were; wisecracking, horseplaying teenagers.

For this one moment he felt a desire for kinship with them. If he could have been the harried father of four who was standing about a dozen people ahead of him, instead of Harry Jensen, he would have been content.

He put the fantasy out of his mind and tried again to interest himself in the guidebook. Again he failed.

He looked at his watch. Ten forty-one, almost time to leave the line and go over to Johnson's Wax.

On the way, he saw a crowd around a low building with half-open sides like long, glassless windows. Moving closer, he collided with a trio of teenagers whose attention was absorbed in eating what seemed to be foot-square, two-inch-thick waffles covered with immense strawberries and powdered sugar. A sign told Jensen that they were, indeed, waffles: The building was a Belgian waffle stand.

The line for the Johnson's Wax movie, *To Be Alive*, was even longer than the line at the Vatican Pavilion, and it was more varied. Movable metal partitions defined narrow lanes that kept the line folding back on itself repeatedly. Unlike the Vatican line, which had a continual glacial movement, this line was stationary. Signs posted along the route of the line gave the approximate waiting time; where Jensen was standing, it was an hour and a half.

There was a large family in front of him. The father was a tall, angular man with hair so blond it was almost white; the mother was a redhead; and the children's curly hair came in varying shades of strawberry blond. Jensen tried to count the children, but even in the congested space between the partitions they moved too fast for him to keep track of them. There were at least seven, and he thought there might be eight or nine. A few slowed down long enough for him to hear them arguing about the movie they were waiting to see. They didn't seem to know whether it was three different movies or one movie on three screens or a three-dimensional movie, but two of them, and their father, agreed that it was three something. A boy of about eight held out for its being a movie that was shown all around the audience in a circle, but one of his brothers – ten or eleven – scoffed at the idea.

When it was time, Jensen moved on. Now, as noon approached, the crowds were much denser. The flow of people reminded him of the New Orleans streets during Mardi Gras, only here it was the buildings that were in costume.

A college-age girl in line next to him at the General Motors Futurama reached into a green plastic insulated bag, took out something wrapped in aluminum foil, and gave it to the Ivy League-ish young man standing with her. He pulled off the foil, revealing a fried chicken leg; he handed it back to her and asked for a breast. She giggled, looked at him meaningfully, and took a bite of the drumstick before rummaging in the bag with her free hand for another piece of chicken.

The line shifted forward. Jensen moved with it; the gun in his windbreaker pocket bumped against his hipbone. Abruptly his fascination with the fair disappeared. The byplay between the girl and the boy next to him became an annoyance; their slyly sexual laughter set off a flash of anger.

The line moved again. He looked at his watch. Eleven

thirty-seven: eighteen minutes left in this line.

Someone at his side said, 'Hello, I almost didn't recognize you.' The voice was soft and melodious, a voice he knew.

He turned. Elena stood next to him; she was wearing a simple pair of straight-legged pants and a matching salmon-colored jacket over a white silk blouse – she looked elegant and up-to-the-minute, without being out of place among the other fairgoers. And she looked beautiful, he thought, as always. For an instant, in spite of the circumstances, she took his breath away.

Then his jaw tightened and his fists clenched: There could be only one reason why she was here.

'Hello, Elena,' he said coldly.

'Are you surprised to see me?'

'I was, at first, but I suppose it makes sense that it's you.'

'I had no choice.'

He turned away from her.

She moved around a barrier and came to stand with him.

A belligerent voice said, 'Hey, where do you think you're going, lady?'

Jensen looked behind him: The challenge had come from a man whose Hawaiian-print shirt stretched over an ample beer belly.

'We got a line here,' the man went on. 'We ain't standing here like this for our health.'

'She's with me,' Jensen said, his teeth clamped tight.

'So then the both of you go to the end.'

Elena touched his arm. 'Ignore him, Harry.'

He looked down at her, and anger and frustration surged in him. He wanted to smash her, to feel her bones break. He took deep, fast breaths and opened and closed his hands.

It was a long wait. He stood next to her in silence. He had

301

nothing to say to her, and she offered nothing.

Inside the building, in semidarkness, they were given seats in a kind of soft and luxurious, low-speed roller coaster. The train of small, open cars rose up a gradual incline surrounded by music and special lighting effects and narration that could have been a voice from heaven.

They passed through a portal into a brighter, more open area. Below them and on both sides was a vast and busily working model of a human community on the surface of the moon. The celestial voice of the narrator described the activities of the vehicles and machines scurrying about among the model craters.

Jensen felt Elena's warmth as she moved closer to him; her breath was on his neck. He recoiled, but there was nowhere to go.

'The time for action has come, Harry,' she said in his ear. 'If you wish to see your precious Jill Lazar again, you will do exactly as I tell you.'

He turned to her. 'Why Jill?'

'That is a stupid question for such an intelligent man. I know that she is more to you than merely your ex-wife.'

'Who told you that?'

'You told me, yourself. In New Orleans, we talked of your being in love. I thought it would be useful to learn your lover's identity. It was not difficult.'

'What do you want?'

'I want exactly what the Mafia wants. I want you to expose what you have learned. The people of this country have a right to know about Mr Oswald and Mr Ruby and their connections with each other and with the CIA and the Mafia and especially with the Cuban exiles. Don't you agree?'

'It's not so easy to get that information out. I tried going to the press once. They want something solid.'

'You don't have to worry about that. I can arrange for the necessary news coverage. Our gangster friends were right about one thing: It is essential to have someone of stature to bear witness. You were in the White House, and you worked with the CIA and the Cubans: It will not be easy to disparage your opinion. And, of course, I will help you with evidence, as well.'

Jensen let his eyes wander over the exhibit. The moving seats were passing through an underwater community. He lost himself for a moment in the unreality of it.

He turned back to her. 'All right. I think we can work something out that will satisfy you. But first I want to see Jill.'

'No. First you will do as I tell you.'

'You say you have her. You say she's well. Why should I believe you?'

'You can speak with her on the phone.'

'No. I want to see her.'

Elena was silent.

'There's no other way, Elena. You need me, and those are my terms. I have to see her. If you want, we can use the meeting as a planning session, too, so it won't cost you any time.'

'All right,' she said after a long silence. 'If I can arrange it . . . Later today or tomorrow. But it will be our only planning session. We will discuss in detail exactly what you will say and to whom. As soon as we are finished, you will begin to comply.'

'I'll want some safeguards for Jill, once I begin.'

'We shall see.'

His footsteps echoed back at him from the walls of the

deserted pier. Somewhere on the upper level a loose loading-bay door banged sharply against its concrete frame, swung by a harsh wind off the river.

He tried to judge the size of the pier, but in the dim light that filtered in through small, grimy windows and a single missing door it was hard to make an accurate estimate. He thought it was at least two hundred feet from where he was to the riverward end of the pier. He was walking alongside a ramp that sloped down from the upper level; the wall at his shoulder dropped lower until for the first time he could see all the way across the pier. It was bigger than he had expected – more than fifty feet wide – and that meant it was at least three hundred feet long.

Over his head empty light-bulb sockets dangled from the concrete ceiling on old, dust-covered lengths of wire. He passed a three-foot-square, metal-sided box that had once held electrical connections; it hung askew on the wall, supported uncertainly at one corner.

Three quarters of the way down the pier was a structure that looked like a concrete blockhouse. It was protected on the shoreward side by a low cinder-block wall.

He kept walking, listening to his own footsteps and the wind and the intermittent banging of the loose door. He was intensely aware of his body – stiffness in his left hand, a tight feeling along the scar on his cheek, the hardness of the gun against the small of his back.

The blockhouse was closer now. He could see the empty frame of what had once been a large picture window; he visualized the man who had once sat behind it, supervising the loading and unloading operations going on simultaneously in a dozen separate bays.

He passed the bay with the missing door and looked out.

The surface of the river was dimpled with rain, and large drops spattered on the narrow concrete walkway that ran around the outside of the pier.

There was a noise from the end of the pier. Jensen looked that way.

Elena stepped out of a side door of the blockhouse and stood behind the cinder-block wall; it came to just above her waist. She was joined by a man who, in contrast to her, looked massive and square. More interesting to Jensen than his size was the fact that he held an automatic rifle with a long banana magazine. Jensen did not recognize the rifle, but he was sure it wasn't American.

A second man emerged from the other side of the blockhouse. He was smaller than the first; he, too, held one of the foreign rifles.

Jensen stopped walking.

Elena peered at him.

'Come closer.'

He walked to within fifteen feet of the low wall and stopped.

He said: 'Where is she?'

Elena took a moment to respond.

'She's here.'

'Where?'

'Inside.' She motioned to the squat structure behind her. From this distance Jensen could see that it was whitewashed cinder block, not concrete.

'Let me see her.'

'We have some matters to discuss.'

'Until I see Jill, we don't have anything to discuss.'

A pause. 'As you wish.'

She said something to one of the men. Jensen could not

make it out; it barely sounded like Spanish to him.

The man went quickly back into the blockhouse. He came out with Jill; another man followed her, training his rifle on her back. Behind him was a fourth man, also carrying one of the automatic rifles.

Jill moved slowly and without spirit, her head down. Her dress – the red one she had been wearing in Dallas – hung on her loosely.

'All right,' Elena said. 'There she is.'

'Not good enough.'

'Please, Harry, don't push me too hard. Bear in mind the disposition of forces.' She looked at her gunmen, and at Jill.

'You're very convincing.'

'Shall we get down to business?'

'You want me to go public with what I know, is that right?'

'Precisely.'

'All of it? Including the stuff that points to Castro?'

'If you wish. The parts that seem . . . contrary to my point of view . . . can easily be dismissed as a false version of the assassination invented to throw suspicion on the wrong parties – a frame-up. But we must know what you are going to say, and to whom, and when, so that we can observe your performance and coordinate with it properly. And there are still things I do not know about how much information you have and how solid it is.'

'What do you want to know?'

'Is there enough evidence in what you know to make a strong case against the counterrevolutionaries?'

'There might be. To begin with, there's Sylvia Odio, if only somebody could get to her, and then you can probably use Oswald's New Orleans shenanigans with the FPCC as a clumsy attempt to make himself look like a Fidelista in order to divert suspicion. If you combine the things you were telling me about Oswald's being in Russia for the CIA – though I still think Naval Intelligence is more likely – with the CIA's connection to the Cuban exiles, you have a pretty neat package. What's likely to put it over the top for you is Jack Ruby and the Mafia. It all fits together. Basically, you've got a three-way deal – the Mafia, the Cubans, and a faction in the CIA. They all have a long history of working together; they all had good reasons for getting back to Cuba. But Kennedy was in their way, and they all hated him for what he'd done to them in the past. Ruby is definitely connected to them, and Oswald may be, too. And all the evidence that points at Castro could easily be part of their plan. A frame-up, as you said. By throwing suspicion on Castro, they get the United States to invade Cuba, which is really their primary goal. I think, with the right support, you could sell it that way.'

'Good. That is what I hoped. I have many recordings from my clubroom that will be useful to us. But now we have to talk about the specific arrangements we will make.'

'No. You told me Jill was well. I want to see her up close. I want to talk to her. Then we can discuss details.'

He unzipped his windbreaker and held it out from his body.

'Nothing up my sleeves. No tricks.'

'All right.' Elena turned and said something to the men with her.

One of the men prodded Jill with his rifle. She moved forward, stumbled, then moved slowly ahead of him out from behind the cinder-block wall. A second gunman came around the other side of the wall and walked abreast of Jill, about twenty feet from her, his rifle held at waist level and aimed at Jensen.

'Jill? Are you all right?'

She walked faster as she approached him. He studied her: Her skin was gray, and there were dark circles under her eyes; her hair was dirty and matted. There was an uncertainty in the way she walked. Closer, he could see smudges on her dress and discolored circles under her arms.

She stopped. Swayed. She was about to collapse.

He hurried to her and wrapped his arms around her and pulled her to him. She leaned on his chest, limp, and began to sob.

He held her like that, gently stroking her head and her back. Shudders passed through her body. He held her tighter.

Gradually Jill's sobbing subsided. She put her arms around him and hugged him weakly. His hands moved again on her back, massaging her tense muscles. She sighed.

'Are you all right?'

'Now that you're here.'

Elena said: 'Very touching, Harry. Now let's get back to work, shall we?'

He took Jill's arms and carefully disengaged himself from her. So far, she had not touched the gun tucked under his belt at the small of his back; he was afraid that if she did, her reaction would give him away.

He held both her hands.

'I was worried about you.'

Elena said, 'That's enough. She can come back here now.'

One of the guards exhaled sharply, a forced grunt. Jensen looked up in time to see him stumble and fall.

Elena and the two men behind the wall with her were momentarily confused. Jill's second guard was searching wildly for the source of the attack. Before he found it, he pitched over backward; his rifle flew out of his hands and clattered to the concrete floor.

Jensen dove for Jill, bringing her down to the floor with him. There was a burst of automatic-rifle fire from behind the cinder-block wall, but it was not directed at them. Jensen inched forward and crawled over Jill so that his body shielded hers. He raised his head only far enough to catch a glimpse of a pair of black-clad figures scurrying through the doorless loading bay, firing their submachine guns as they moved.

One of them was caught by return fire from behind the wall. His body twisted and rose into the air, elevated by the repeated impact of high-momentum bullets; then he crumpled to the ground.

The noise of gunfire was constant and deafening, echoing and re-echoing from the concrete walls and floor and ceiling.

Then, as abruptly as it had begun, it stopped. Jensen's ears rang.

Cautiously, he lifted his head; he saw a loose grouping of men in black; they were looking down at something behind the wall. He pushed himself back off Jill and surveyed the pier: Elena and her two defenders were nowhere to be seen. The two men who had guarded him and Jill seemed to be dead. As Jensen watched, three of the black-clad men approached one of the inert figures, prodded him, and rolled him over.

Jensen turned his attention to Jill. She was sitting up, shaking.

'What happened?'

'The cavalry arrived.'

'Who are they?'

'I'm not exactly sure, but I don't think they're what you'd call the good guys. Are you okay?'

Her face started to crumple. She squeezed her eyes tightly

closed and rubbed a hand over her face.

'Harry, I can't take much more.'

'I know, baby. I know. It's going to be all right.' But he had no confidence that it would.

He stood up and helped her to her feet.

'Jensen!'

The voice came from near the cinder-block wall. It was Angelo.

'Get over here, Jensen. Quick. The lady wants to talk to you.'

Elena was behind the wall, lying on the concrete floor, her head pillowed on the arm of one of her dead comrades. Her white blouse was stained a dark, rich ruby, and streaks of deep red ran over her jacket and her pants. Her face was untouched, framed by a pool of jet-black hair.

He thought, as he kneeled beside her, that he had never seen her so serene; in this moment of peace she was her most beautiful.

He cradled her in his arms, oblivious to the blood he was getting on his hands and his jacket.

She smiled. Her eyes held his.

'Harry, listen . . .' Her voice was so soft he could barely hear her. He bent his head closer.

'I have to tell you—' Perplexity marred the calmness of her face. She turned her head from side to side. 'Harry! I can't see!'

He kissed her forehead softly. For a moment her eyes seemed to focus on him. He listened to her labored breathing.

'You'll . . . never . . . know . . . who it was . . . Never.' She breathed heavily, gathering strength. 'Poor . . . poor Harr . . .'

Her mouth froze around the last word and her body stiffened. Her breathing became noisier. Caught.

He felt her body relax. After a moment he lowered her to the concrete and stood up.

'Jensen!'

Angelo was standing with Jill and a half dozen of the men in black. Jensen went to join them.

'What'd she say?' Angelo wanted to know.

Jensen shook his head. 'Nothing much.'

'Her dying words, Jensen . . . Nothing much?'

'Regrets . . . And: "You'll never get away with it." That kind of thing.'

'Shit. For that, she hangs on to talk to you?'

'Victory in the midst of defeat. Maybe she wanted the last word.'

Angelo spat. 'That was some pretty story you were telling her, before we interrupted.'

'She was about to kill us. What did you want me to say?'

'You didn't sound like a guy saving his life. You sounded like you believed it.'

'I'm very convincing when my life is at stake.'

'Enough jokes, Jensen. This isn't funny. You know, I can't figure you. That first night, you sounded all convinced it was Castro who killed Kennedy. And we bought it. We thought we had an alliance. We followed you all over the fucking place, and you damn well made it as hard for us as you could. That was dumb. I got to say it, Harry, that part was dumb. You could've got yourself killed that way, you know? Sure you do. Damn near happened a couple of times, didn't it?'

'Yes. But I'm still alive.'

'Listen to him. "Still alive." You'd be as dead as the rest of these Cuban communist shits, here, if it wasn't for us.'

'What do you mean?'

'You think those Long Beach cops just happened to be

there to save your ass by some happy coincidence?'

'That was you?'

'It was the cops. Real ones. But we made sure they kept close to you in Long Beach, and we got them going when we saw you were in trouble.'

'My apologies. And my thanks.'

'That's not the only time, either. There was a guy in Dallas we had to take out. And two of our guys got in a fight in Tampa on account of you. One got a busted arm.'

'I guess I owe you more thanks than I thought.'

'Thanks isn't the point. The point is: After all that, we don't expect to find you running around with this communist chick trying to pin things on us.'

'I was in a very tough position, Angelo. If I did the wrong thing, Elena would have killed me on the spot. You were out there, and I was trying to get more evidence for you without having her put a bullet in my head. And I did all right. I told you what I heard about the man in Tampa who waited for a go-ahead from Cuba and then passed through Texas on the twenty-second and flew from there to Havana. And that he was connected with the assassination.'

'Yeah . . . so what? What does that buy us? The fact is, we can't trust you. You say one thing, you do another. What about this chicky-baby here? You're one hell of a lady-killer, aren't you? One communist Cuban who looks Chinese, leading you around by the nose, and now here's another one, another looker, and she runs around Texas working for oilmen. We told you about oilmen, didn't we? You know what you are, Jensen? You're a *strunz*. Like, a big, fat Sicilian turd. And you know what else? We could have used you. It could have been good for all of us. A big plus. But we can live without you. We've taken enough of your shit. More than enough. And you know what that means. It means, "Bye-bye, Jensen," is what it means. And "Byebye, pretty blonde girlfriend," too.'

'Now, wait a minute, Angelo. You're making a mistake.'

'That's what they all say.'

'But this time you *are* making a mistake. I'm as much use to you now as I was before. More, in fact. Think about what I said to Elena – the evidence against Castro could have been planted by the people who want him out. A frame-up.'

'Yeah. That's why we don't need you hanging around any more, ideas like that.'

'But it could work the other way around, too, couldn't it?'

'What d'you mean, the other way around?'

'All that evidence against the Cuban exiles, or against you, or the CIA – all of *that* could be a frame-up, instead.'

'Yeah. Sure. Sure it could.'

'All we do is take the same evidence and the same stories, only we turn them around. We say Castro did it, and he had his agents in the Cuban communities in Dallas and New Orleans try to make it look like it was a right-wing, anti-Castro, CIA plot. The thing you have to keep in mind is that the evidence points in both directions. The only way it makes sense is if one side did it and is framing the other. It's all a question of how you look at it.'

'Okay. But how do we know which way *you're* going to look at it? And talk about it?'

'If I look at it or talk about it wrong, you're going to kill me, the way I understand it.'

'Yeah. That's right.'

'I find that very persuasive.'

'Funny. Very funny.' Angelo thought for a moment and came to a decision. 'Okay. Then we're ready to go ahead. I'll get my associates to set something up with some reporters.'

'No.'

'No? What's this "no"?'

'I don't like the balance. Right now, it looks too much like you and your associates did it. There are more things that point to you than to Castro.'

'So leave some of them out.'

'I could do that, but your enemies won't. Once this gets into the public eye, they're going to have to come up with a counterattack. Think of the damage those former associates of yours who are working the dope trade in Southeast Asia could do if they let out some stories about your helping the CIA with the attempts on Castro.'

'They're working with the CIA, too. They wouldn't dare.'

'No. I think it works the other way. It's *your* CIA friends who are at a disadvantage. I'll bet that by now the Cuba people in the Agency don't have a fraction of the power of the Vietnam people. Cuba was yesterday. Vietnam is tomorrow. They may not abandon Cuba entirely, but it's going to take a backseat.'

'That's the whole damn trouble. That's what we want to prevent. We don't have time to go looking for a whole lot of new evidence.'

'What I have in mind won't take long, and it might make the difference.'

'If it's so smart and so easy, why didn't you think of it before?'

'To tell you the truth, I'm not sure. I don't know why *you* didn't think of it, either. It's pretty obvious. It only came to me earlier today, when Elena was talking to me about how important it was to have a credible spokesman.'

'All right. What is it?'

'Who's the most credible possible spokesman on this question?'

'I don't want to play guessing games. Just tell me.'

'The Kennedy family.'

'Yeah. So?'

'Two things. First, we don't know what information they have that may fit in with what we have and improve our case. Second, I think we can assume we know things they don't. I can't believe they'd willingly go along with covering up the truth about the assassination. And if they support our version, that's the best help we could get anywhere.'

'Just like that, you're going to go talk to them?'

'I've known them a long time. I was a freshman at Harvard when Bob was a senior, and Ted came along before I graduated. That means with Bob I go back to '48, although I only really got to know them during the presidential campaign. I wouldn't say I was their best friend, but I know them, and – what's more important – they know me.'

Angelo said nothing.

Jensen said, 'Jill knows the family, too, I guess.'

'Yes,' she acknowledged.

'Can we use that somehow?'

'I'm not sure,' she said. 'They knew about me and Jack . . . anyway, I'm sure Bobby knew. But I don't know how they'll feel now.'

'We may not have to go that route,' Jensen said. 'I can probably set up a meeting myself.'

'You two done babbling?' Angelo interjected.

'We're trying to work out the best way to get to the Kennedys.'

'Yeah. Well, if you two have trouble with that, maybe we can help. We know some friends of theirs.'

'Good. We can get right on it, then.'

'Not so fast. This, I've got to clear first.'

'All right. And in the meantime my friend needs some food and fresh clothes and a soft bed.'

'Yeah. All right. Let's go. You come with me. Both of you.'

Jensen wiped his palms on his jacket and took Jill's hand. Together, they followed Angelo shoreward. Jensen was surprised to see that while they had been talking, Angelo's soldiers had taken the dead bodies off the pier. It looked no different now from the way it had when he had arrived.

Chapter Nineteen

The rain had stopped. They got into a black limousine and were driven uptown and over to the East Side. Jensen expected to be taken to a hotel. Instead, they went to a large apartment house on Park Avenue. The doorman greeted Angelo pleasantly and pretended not to notice that his guests were a dirty, disheveled woman and a tall man with a frightening scar and some odd, dark stains on his clothes. The elevator man was similarly discreet.

The apartment was large and well furnished, in a neutral, impersonal way. Angelo showed Jensen the living-room bar and went into the foyer to make a phone call.

When he came back, he said, 'It's all arranged. In a few minutes, there'll be four people here. One to watch the front door, one for the back, and a maid and butler. They'll buy clothes for you, food, booze, whatever you need. They'll be here all the time. Even get you take-out food from the best places in town if you want. You've got the master bedroom and bathroom, the dining room, kitchen, library, and living room. Do anything you want in those rooms, nobody'll bother you. But you can't go out. You understand? And no phone. That's the first thing the butler's going to do – take out all the phones. So take it easy. Relax. You've had a hard day.

Tomorrow, when you've had some rest, we'll talk about what we're going to do next.'

Jill spent an hour in the tub, soaking away the grime of her week in captivity. Jensen brought her things from the kitchen – cheese and crackers, a pear, and then, at her request, a peanut butter sandwich and a glass of milk.

'You know how I am when I'm anxious,' she said. 'I starve, or I eat everything. This time I starved.' She handed him the empty glass. 'Delicious. Is there more?'

'Sure. You want another sandwich, too?'

'No, but I'll have some more of that cheese. And another pear, or an apple or something.'

When she had soaked long enough, she let the water out of the tub and rinsed off in the shower.

Jensen pushed the shower curtain aside and stepped in with her.

'Hey!' she said.

'Hello there.'

'Hello, yourself. Want a wash?'

She lathered him with great care and then rinsed him off. He did the same for her.

They toweled themselves quickly. Still damp, they raced each other into the bedroom, laughing, and dove on to the bed.

They joined immediately, still laughing – not with amusement but with joy.

Later, after they had slept, she lay next to him and ran a forefinger over his scar.

'Can it be fixed?'

318

'The doctor who sewed it up said a good plastic surgeon could make it almost invisible. He was really apologetic about not having done a better job closing the cut in the first place, but he didn't have the right equipment.'

She put her head on his chest.

'Harry . . .'

'Yes?'

'What's going to happen?'

'Well, Angelo'll be back tomorrow, probably with some of the people he calls his "associates," and we'll all talk for a while, and then we'll agree I should go and see the Kennedys. If I hadn't convinced Angelo that they could help, or at least that it was worth trying, he'd have killed us on the spot.'

She shuddered. 'That's not what I meant, really. I meant after. To us.'

He kissed the top of her head. 'Let's get this resolved before we worry about that.'

The following Monday Jensen made the eight-block trip from Angelo's apartment to the Hotel Carlyle by limousine. Two of Angelo's men accompanied him upstairs in the elevator and waited for him in the corridor.

He was wearing a brown tweed suit, which Angelo's butler had bought for him at Brooks Brothers; a tailor had come to the apartment and made the necessary alterations, doing all the sewing by hand. For luck, Jensen had worn his Texas cowboy boots. As far as he knew, his gun was still tucked under the seat cushion of an easy chair in the master bedroom. He had never even thought of using it on the pier once the shooting started; he certainly did not expect to need it here.

The door to the suite was opened by an earnest-looking, crew-cut young man in a business suit. He was about an inch

319

shorter than Jensen, with the bulk and carriage of a football player.

'Mr Jensen,' he said. 'If you'll bear with me a second, I have to be sure you're not carrying any weapons or any recording devices or cameras.'

'I'm not.'

'Of course. But I do have to check.'

'Go ahead.'

He did it slowly and thoroughly. 'Thank you,' he said. 'I'm sorry to have had to inconvenience you.' He went to stand next to the door.

Jensen glanced around the suite's sitting room, and for the first time he noticed the man on the couch.

The man nodded to Jensen, but he did not say anything and he did not get up. He was about sixty, Jensen judged, with a deep suntan and wavy silver hair. His suit looked like silk, and he wore a gold watch with a heavy gold band on his left wrist, a gold identification bracelet on his right wrist, and four massive gold rings, one with a small diamond set into it.

Jensen went to stand by the window. They were in the hotel's tower, and he could see across Madison Avenue and Fifth to Central Park. The reservoir sparkled with afternoon sun. The trees were still dusted with the pastel greens of spring, like the trees in Washington had been an eternity ago.

He heard a door open behind him; the door to the bedroom, he guessed. He turned away from the window.

Robert Kennedy walked quickly across the room and shook his hand.

'It's good to see you, Harry. I'm pleased you could come. I'm afraid I won't be able to stay, and I'm sorry about that, but this gentleman is Mr Dimitriou. He's a good friend of the family, and anything you wanted to say to me, you can say to him. As a matter of fact, he's been handling the entire matter for us.' He smiled. 'Thanks again, Harry. We appreciate your interest.' He started for the door. 'I hope I'll see you again soon.'

For several moments after Kennedy had gone, Jensen did not move. Then he walked toward the couch.

'I'm Harry Jensen.'

Dimitriou stood up and put out his hand, smiling.

'I am Stavros Dimitriou. It is a pleasure to meet you.'

They shook hands. Dimitriou was short, about five four; he had immense charm and presence.

'Please, sit down. Would you care for a drink?'

'I don't think so . . . Yes, thank you. A martini.'

'George, would you make us a pitcher of martinis, please? Mr Jensen and I are going to have a nice, friendly conversation. When you are done with the drinks, call down and have them send us an assortment of hors d'oeuvres. Is that all right with you, Mr Jensen?'

'That's fine. Thank you.'

'Now,' Dimitriou said when their drinks were in front of them, 'I understand you have some information for us about the tragic death of the late President Kennedy.'

'Yes, I do, but I had understood I would be speaking to the Attorney General or to Senator Kennedy.' Jensen kept to the polite form Dimitriou had established, but anger and tension leaked into his tone of voice: His life, and Jill's, could depend on the outcome of this meeting.

'Certainly, certainly,' Dimitriou said soothingly. His smile was warm, almost fatherly. 'But you must understand that both of those gentlemen are extremely busy. Of necessity, they must delegate certain tasks. This matter, especially, is unpleasant for them. Please do not think that you are not being taken seriously. Quite the contrary. What the Attorney General said is true – by talking to me on this subject, you are in effect talking to him.'

'All right. I'll accept that.'

Dimitriou leaned back. 'Good. Then, perhaps, when you are comfortable, you will tell me your story.'

Jensen did not see what choice he had. He started with his own experiences in Mexico City and Katzenbach's letters to Bill Moyers and the Warren Commission, building a case that important facts and theories, especially those relating to Cuba, were being ignored or stifled.

He talked about George Hammond and the CIA assassination attempts and Castro's threat of retaliation, emphasizing that the CIA's would-be assassin was almost certainly a double agent for Castro. And he described some of the anomalies involving Lee Harvey Oswald and the Fair Play for Cuba Committee and the right-wing Cuban exiles, and the bizarre circle that connected Jack Ruby and the Mafia and Cuba.

Dimitriou listened, asking few questions, but focusing his attention on Jensen with remarkable intensity. Their hors d'oeuvres arrived shortly after Jensen began talking; they stood on the table, untouched.

When Jensen was done, there was a long silence. The bodyguard brought a fresh pitcher of martinis and two clean glasses. Dimitriou poured drinks for both of them. He sipped at his own in reflective silence and nibbled an hors d'oeuvre.

Jensen, suddenly hungry, ate several and quickly finished his drink. The bodyguard poured him another.

'That's a very interesting story,' Dimitriou said. 'You tell it well. You have obviously put a good deal of effort into this matter.'

'Not all of it was voluntary.'

'So I gather.' Dimitriou put his drink carefully on the cocktail table. 'I want to give you my assurance that what you have told me will be of great assistance to us. I thank you very much for coming.' He smiled warmly and stood up.

'I'm dismissed, then?' Jensen asked, furious. 'Just like that? Pat me on the head and send me home. That wasn't the idea, you know. I risked my life over this. I'm still risking my life. I expect something more than a perfunctory thank you.'

'Oh? And precisely what did you expect?'

'To talk about this information, not just to hand it to you on a platter. Maybe to fill in some of the holes. You must know some things I don't. I'm sure I told you things you didn't know.'

Dimitriou hesitated before saying yes.

'Then a little reciprocity seems in order, don't you think?'

'No, Mr Jensen, I'm afraid I don't. I can sympathize with how you feel, but I cannot help you.'

'That stinks, Dimitriou. Is that what Bobby wants you to do? Pump his friends dry and kick them out?'

'I did not pump you, Mr Jensen. You came here on your own initiative, and what information you gave me, you volunteered.' He sighed. 'Forgive me. I am too familiar with people who make demands. I am trying to understand you. Let me ask you to try to understand us, as well.' He sat down again next to Jensen. 'This matter is far more complicated than you know, even given the complications you yourself have seen. Your information will make a difference. But I must ask you – indeed implore you – not to carry your inquiries any further. There are pressures being applied here beyond anything you can imagine. Pressures that make it necessary for us to consider everything we do with the utmost care. You can rest assured that we are doing everything that can be done, within the bounds of prudence.'

Jensen held Dimitriou's eyes with his own. It seemed to him that Dimitriou was telling the truth.

'All right. I'll buy it. But tell me one thing, Mr Dimitriou.'

'If I can.'

'Who are you?'

Dimitriou smiled and stood up. This time Jensen stood up with him. They walked together to the door of the suite.

'I am Stavros Dimitriou. I am an attorney, and I have some experience in conducting judicial investigations, although my work no longer involves such things. But that is not what you want to know. I have also, for many years, been a friend and business associate of a man who is a dear and close friend of Mrs Kennedy. That is why I am here today, and that is all I can tell you.'

He stopped at the door and held out his hand. 'It has truly been a pleasure talking to you, Mr Jensen. Thank you again for coming. And good luck.'

The trip back to the Park Avenue apartment was too short for Jensen. He would have preferred more time to straighten out his thoughts.

Jill opened the door. He kissed her cheek and walked past her into the living room.

Angelo was waiting for him, and so were three other men. Jensen had met them all and heard vague references to their prominence at the conference they had held to discuss and approve his visit to the Kennedys. Like the bodyguards they employed, they were fundamentally the same man. Jensen thought of them as the short one, the fat one, and the one with the high voice.

'What do you have to tell us?' the one with the high voice asked.

Jensen sat down. He was slightly drunk. 'Not much, I'm afraid.'

'What does that mean?'

'I'll tell you. I did what I could. I gave it the old college try.'

'But you didn't succeed,' the short one challenged.

'I wouldn't put it that way.'

'How, then?'

'It's like this: The Kennedys are going at this their own way. I'm not sure exactly what they're doing, but they've got it very well organized. They made one thing clear to me – they want the field to themselves. They won't help us, and they don't want our help, either. They don't want anybody interfering in this at all. The way I understand it, there's a whole other level to it, one that we don't know about. They were very serious about that, and I believe them. They impressed me, and they scared me. I'm willing to let them handle it their own way. And I think you should, too.'

'Do you?' the fat one asked. 'Why do you say that?'

'First of all, for the reasons I've already given you. Your case isn't strong enough or unambiguous enough as it stands. You'd be as likely to do yourself harm as good. And we're not going to find the key to it in a hurry, not without the Kennedys' help.' He paused and looked at each one of the four men.

'I'll tell you what I really think. Either this is the world's most incredible set of coincidences, or else somebody set it all up very cleverly. There are so many contradictions in the evidence and so many guilty people covering their tracks that it would take a whole squad of people a long time to begin to make head or tail of it.' He had a sudden painful vision of Elena, a froth of blood on her lips, spending her last breath to taunt him with the impossibility of ever *knowing*.

'I gather you don't think that's going to happen,' said the one with the high voice. 'Not in time to get at the truth.'

'Frankly, I don't think there's a chance. Unless the Kennedys do it. I think they're closer than we are.'

Assuming, he thought, *that this isn't just an elaborate charade and you didn't do it yourselves*.

'There's something else,' he said. 'I think it may be too late for your point of view to have the effect you want it to, anyway. Things are cooling down with Cuba. A couple of weeks ago Fulbright made that speech saying we should accept Castro as a reality, and then Khrushchev said Cuba could trigger a world war if we weren't careful there. You notice he hasn't said that about Vietnam. I think the handwriting is on the wall. If we have any military adventures in the near future, they're going to be in the Far East, not the Caribbean.'

'I'm afraid I agree with you, Mr Jensen,' the fat one said. 'In fact, we all do. We hoped you would accomplish something at this meeting today, but we didn't expect very much. Frankly, we've already begun talks with our associates who are operating in Asia, in the hope that we could come to some mutually profitable accommodation.' He cleared his throat. 'I'm afraid, though, that we're now back where we were when you and Angelo were on the pier together. You understand, I hope, that there's nothing personal in this. We all like you, and we like Miss Lazar. But I'm afraid we're going to have to ... terminate your services.'

'Why?' Jensen challenged immediately. 'Why bother? We're no threat to you.'

'You know too much,' the short one said.

'A lot of people know too much. There's a lot to know, and

you don't rub out everybody who knows some of it. What about all the people who know about your connection with the CIA and their assassination plots? You don't kill all of those people. You have to draw the line somewhere. I've played pretty square with you, and I'm certainly not going to go shooting my mouth off now. All I want, and all Jill wants, is out. As far away from all of this as we can get. I told you, I'm willing to let the Kennedys handle it. I mean it. And when you're making your decision, think of this, too: I wrote down everything that happened. The whole gruesome mess. And I sent out three copies of it and three covering letters, with the usual instructions about opening them in case I die but not before. And there's no way in the world you can get at all three of them. That means if you kill me – or Jill – to keep what we know from coming out, you'll get just the opposite result, instead. In fact, it would be a good idea for you to keep protecting us for a while, to prevent our mutual enemies from causing us all a lot of unnecessary trouble.'

The one with the high voice laughed, birdlike. 'Very good, Mr Jensen. I'm impressed. I don't know about my friends, but you've convinced me.'

The others nodded their agreement.

'But there's something for you to remember, Mr Jensen. We'll be watching you. We'll always be watching you. And if you step out of line, even a little, you're a dead man. And the same goes for the lady.'

She woke him in the middle of the night.

'I can't sleep.'

He put his arms around her.

'Is it really over?'

He kissed her. 'I think so. As long as it's clear to everybody that we're no threat. That's how you want it, isn't it?'

'Oh, God, yes.' She held him to her tightly. Then, 'Can we get up?'

'Sure.'

Naked, they padded into the living room and looked out the window. Park Avenue was dark and silent. A lone car sped uptown.

'I'm hungry,' she said.

They went into the kitchen. They were alone in the apartment: Angelo had told them it was theirs for as long as they needed it.

She opened the refrigerator and stared into it. She took out a plate of cold cuts and a jar of pickles and a bottle of imported French mustard. She put it all on the kitchen table and then took out a cold six-pack of Dutch beer.

'What are we going to do?' she asked as she put plates and knives and forks next to the food. She added a loaf of bread.

'You and me?' he responded.

She started to make a sandwich.

'Well . . .' he said, 'I guess we're going to get married.'

'Do you think it's smart?' she asked, spreading mustard on a slice of bread.

'I don't know if it's smart. I just think it's inevitable.'

She put ham and salami and sliced provolone cheese on her bread. 'You say the nicest things.'

'Jill, it's very simple – I love you.'

'But we've said that to each other before.'

'We were different people then.'

'Were we?'

'When we split up? I think we were. We were so damn intent on our careers, we competed with each other all the time. It was terrible.'

'I didn't think you cared about me,' she reflected. 'And I was sure I didn't have the time or energy to meet your needs. Not to mention your demands.'

'Did I make demands?'

'Harry.'

'Yeah. You know, it's funny, but I felt just the same way. I thought you didn't understand me, or my needs, and I knew I didn't understand you. God, all that constant conflict.'

'We both needed space. We'd helped each other grow up, and once we were grown up, we didn't know what to do.'

He considered that. 'You're right. But do you think we know any better now? I mean, I know how I feel about you, but that's emotion. And emotion isn't enough. We have to be able to *live* together. Suppose this is just sex, or the fact that we were sharing an adventure and we were liable to get killed at any moment—'

'Don't knock sex.'

'Hell, I'm not knocking sex. The last thing in the world I'd knock is sex. Especially with you. But I can remember a time when we fought all day and still made very good love at night. Enjoyable as those nights could be, I wouldn't want to sign up for a lifetime like that.'

'No, you're right. Neither would I.' She reached across the table and took his hand. 'But I don't think it'd be that way now.'

'No. I don't, either. I really do love you, Jill. I want us to be married again. Not the way we were. A better way. And I think we can do it.'

She smiled. 'We can. I know we can.' She drew his hand toward her, then suddenly let it go. 'My God, will you look at this. I must have been really nervous. All that food . . .'

'Come on,' he said. 'Let's throw it all into the icebox and go back to bed.'

'You've got yourself a deal,' she said, laughing.

The next day, they talked about where they might live. The joy of the night before was tempered by the grim certainty that there were people who still saw them as a threat, or who might still want to use them.

'We've got to take ourselves out of the game,' Jensen said, 'make it clear we're turning our backs on it all. The Mafia will protect us, up to a point, but that's not enough. I think we've got to leave the country.'

'For good?'

'For a while, until things cool off. Most of the danger we present is political, and it's hard to play politics from overseas. If we just lay low for a while, it should be okay. Once the war really gets going in Vietnam, we won't be so important. Especially if Warren comes out with a good, solid verdict and people stop asking questions.'

She looked at him, thinking about it. 'You know, I could get to like that idea. Living for a year or two in . . . Paris?'

'Well . . . I don't know about Paris. It's a little too dense with Vietnamese for my taste.'

'Ouch. I hadn't thought of that.'

'What about London?' he suggested. 'Doesn't your outfit have an office there?'

'Yes. But no women.'

'You can convince them.'

'I guess I could, if I worked at it. But what about you?'

'No problem. With my background, if I offered myself as a consultant on relations with the American government, I'd have to fight people off. How many members of the National

Security Advisory Staff are looking for work with private companies in England?'

'Not many, I guess. I suppose I wasn't asking whether you could get a job. It was your political ambitions I was worried about. Weren't you going to be secretary of defense? Or was it secretary of state?'

'At least. If not President. But that's all dead now. I guess it was killed when Jack Kennedy was.'

By mid-June they were established in London. They were both working, and they had sublet a duplex flat in a house on Russell Square.

Their first weekend in residence they got all the Sunday papers and asked their housekeeper to serve them a typical English breakfast: juice, porridge, eggs, kippers, toast, marmalade, coffee.

'I can't get over it,' Jensen said, looking up from the international *Herald-Tribune*. 'It looks like the whole world is going to swallow the lone-assassin theory. Ever since *The Times* reported that the Warren Commission was going to say Oswald acted alone, there hasn't been a peep out of anybody. I keep thinking maybe it wouldn't have mattered even if I got to Warren. They must have put some kind of pressure on him, too.'

He put his paper down and took a piece of toast. 'I wonder what the Kennedys turned up. And if they'll go ahead on their own, now that they know what Warren is going to say.'

'Maybe they don't have any choice.'

'What do you mean?'

'You told me Mr Dimitriou said there were pressures on the Kennedys. Pressures that no one else knew about. Well, maybe those pressures will make the Kennedys go ahead on their own, no matter what the Commission says. Or maybe they'll make them stop. Though I don't know how you could make them just drop it if they didn't want to.'

'Ah, the hell with it. It's screwed up our lives enough. We ought to forget about it.'

'I don't really think we're likely to forget it in a hurry.'

He was buttering his toast. 'Nope. Not a chance. Besides, it brought us back together. Maybe we should be grateful.'

'Maybe we should, at that.'

They went back to their breakfast and newspapers. The housekeeper cleared the dishes from the table and brought them a fresh pot of coffee. They switched papers. She took the *Tribune*, and he started to read the *Sunday Times*.

'Harry,' she said suddenly. 'Did you see this?'

'What?'

She read: '"Senator Edward Kennedy, Democrat of Massachusetts, narrowly escaped death today when a light plane in which he was flying crashed outside of South-hampton, Massachusetts."'

'I wonder,' she mused. 'I wonder.'

Afterword

Though it has been thirty years now since John Fitzgerald Kennedy was gunned down on a street in Dallas, Texas, that shocking event still has the power to fascinate. There are now, as there have been almost from the beginning, many theories about who was responsible for it, and who actually did the shooting.

Because so much information was covered up, distorted or explained away in the assassination's immediate aftermath, new details continue to come to light. As time passes it becomes harder and harder to know which newly uncovered 'facts' to believe.

One thing of which we can be certain, even at this distance in time, is that successful efforts were made in late 1963 and 1964 – as the result of not one but several independent and differently motivated high-level conspiracies – to put across as quickly as possible a politically sanitized and apparently benign version of the assassination: that it was the work of a lone, crazed gunman. And we can be sure, too, that this version, true or not, does not account for many things of a suspicious nature that were going on prior to and immediately after the shooting.

Unfortunately, that knowledge does not help us decide which of the many theories is true. It is, perhaps, easiest to consider the cases *against* some of the more popular guesses: for instance, the principal argument against an assassination plotted by communist governments – Cuba, or the then Soviet Union – is the danger of war. Nobody in power in Havana or Moscow, it is argued, would have been so stupid as to risk nuclear retaliation. The assassination of a head of state is, after all, one of the clearest of acts of war. (The original working title of this book was *Act of War*.)

Interestingly, it is also true that one of the reasons Lyndon Johnson gave to Chief Justice Earl Warren to talk him into heading the investigating commission (a job he emphatically did not want) was this: Johnson said he feared that if the populace became inflamed by the idea that Cuba had been responsible for the assassination, a nuclear war might be inevitable.

But Moscow and Havana could not have known in advance that Johnson would get cold feet. After all, hadn't John Kennedy faced down Khrushchev over the Cuban missile, explicitly at the risk of war? So, the argument goes, for Cuba or Moscow to have been involved in the assassination would have been suicidal.

As for the equivalent argument against an assassination plotted by people on the right – well, actually, there is no similar argument that I know of against a right-wing conspiracy. Individual conspirators would, of course, have been liable for extreme criminal penalties, perhaps even execution, but that risk is a given in any such plot. Beyond that, what would Cuban exiles (for instance) have had to lose? They already believed that they had lost the support of the United States, and there were too many factions to punish them all, as groups. Similarly, nobody was going to wage a real war against the Mob, or corrupt trade unions, or even rogue agents of the US intelligence community. Nuclear deterrence only work against nations.

It is a shame, I think, that a recent motion picture has given worldwide prominence to a flamboyant mishmash of self-promotion, homophobia and paranoia partly based on the questionable work of a late District Attorney of New Orleans. New Orleans was certainly a focus of activity for both Oswald and the Cubans, but some of the prosecutorial antics there in the years that followed may have done more to obscure the truth than to reveal it. If a significant movie was to be made about the assassination it could have had better source material, both more compelling dramatically and more convincing.

The most fascinating infrequently-cited theory, for my money, is the idea that the murder of President Kennedy was an act of revenge – not by Cubans, but in retaliation for the assassination of Vietnam's President Ngo Din Diem not three weeks earlier. This theory is quite convoluted and requires the Vietnamese conspirators to have acted very quickly. It is unlikely actually to have happened, but it makes for undeniably interesting speculation. And I do believe, as is discussed in the preceding pages, that the selection of Vietnam as the military enemy of choice played a significant part in the decision to obscure the possibility of a Cuban role in the assassination.

My own opinion about the killing itself, one I am confident of, is that we shall never know the truth. Nobody in the Kennedy-assassination industry (not even the author of a major thirtieth-anniversary critique of the conspiracy theories) has proven immune to a tendency to understate and distort the cases made by the people he or she disagrees with. To be sure, some conspiracy theorists are nut cases, but they are not all, by any means. Much that happened remains unexplained.

Believing one story or another depends heavily on believing or disbelieving specific witnesses and forensic experts. Too many of the people who might have known the truth are dead: some deceased under odd circumstances, some in the natural course of things. As time passes, fewer survive.

There will always be, as there has been from the beginning, the camp that says the assassination of John Fitzgerald Kennedy was the work of a lone gunman, Lee Harvey Oswald, acting independently of any conspiracy. I remain unconvinced of that. Not just because of the anomalies in the evidence, but because it is profoundly disturbing to think that something with such great and lasting effects could have been the result of a meaningless, impulsive act.